Escape from Babylon

Babylon

Chris Woolgrove

Published in Germany by Berge Publishing, February 2013,
Schlossberge 3, 06526 Sangerhausen, Germany.

ISBN 978-3-00-041658-3

www.Escape-from-Babylon.com

For Siegrun

ACKNOWLEDGMENTS

So many people have helped and inspired me in the writing of Escape from Babylon that I would hate to place them in any particular order or try to name them all, but there were some specials:

Thanks to my original inspiration, Karl Schirok, a lovely man.

To my sister, Diane Clifford, for her reading and constructive comments.

My two dear Gillingham School heartthrobs Pip Brown and Olivia Bastable. Their input inspired me.

To Sarah Challis for making me believe that I could write.

To Steffen Siebenhüner and Nikolay Demydov for their work on the web-site.

To all my students, particularly those at HALFEN and THIMMSCHERTLER who frequently gave me feedback and encouragement as part of their English lessons.

To all the many other friends who in one way or another helped, listened to and motivated me.

To Antonio Salieri and Kevin Costner, who made me dream and to W.A. Mozart, Peter Gabriel and U2 who kept me calm.

However, one is above all and that is Siegrun. She has done all that everyone else has and more. Putting up with thousands of hours of me being in a different world, making endless cups of tea, not minding when I skipped the hoovering, and for being there.

Prologue

November 1962.
Schwandorf, East Germany.

Thirty-six year old Franz Schmidt lay in bed listening to the rain pattering on the window. It had been raining heavily for about sixteen hours onto bone-dry land. Most of the rain had run off into the river, which had risen by two metres. He was calm as he concentrated on the task ahead. If he did not perform tonight, he may die.

He played with his fingers, swallowed saliva and brushed his hands through his hair. His breathing was faster, he licked and bit his lips, flexed his fingers and made a fist, circled his feet, spread his toes and breathed deeply. *Believe, Franz, believe.* All the time, he concentrated on the window and listened to his heartbeat. Until he heard the church bell strike three o'clock. Time to go.

He carefully got off the bed and crept over to the wardrobe. There, on its top, he had hidden the football bladder and pump underneath some boxes. Franz could not take any personal articles so everything belonging to his old life would have to be left here. Everything that is, except the only two pictures he possessed of his parents. He kissed the pictures before wrapping them up in a small plastic bag, which he sealed with the glue from his puncture outfit. Then he opened the small zipped pouch on the hip of his swimming trunks and placed the bag in the pouch.

Franz had decided to dress in his room for his escape, which would save valuable time on the riverbank. On with his swimming trunks. On with his tight black T-shirt and insert the bladder underneath the back of it so that the end of the pipe stuck out just in front of his mouth. Now, the weighted belt. On with his tracksuit and his training shoes, pick up the flippers, the pump and put the air tap into his tracksuit pocket.

He carefully removed a tin of shoe polish from a drawer and blacked his face before he wrapped the tin in a handkerchief so it would not rattle against the air tap, put it in his pocket and secured the zip. On with the helmet and one last check. Over to the window, and slowly open it.

Franz was happy that the wind had dropped and so there was no sudden rush of air as he opened the window that might wake up his wife, Brunhilde, in the next room. One last look around his room and the icons of his life. He sighed and uttered a hushed "Goodbye and good luck," to himself, and he was out.

He did not have too far to drop as his room was on the ground floor, enabling him to close the window behind him. Franz quickly made his way down the lane at the back of his house to the corner of the hayfield. Suddenly, one of those cursed dogs belonging to the Henning family must have heard him and barked, which in turn set off two other dogs elsewhere in the village. No stopping, he must push on.

The dogs were not a problem, everyone, including the security patrols, was used to them barking the whole night. He jumped over a stone wall and as he ran along the other side of it away from Henning's, the dog relented. Satisfied with its work, it huffed one last time and returned to the comfort of its kennel.

Franz had to restrain himself from running too fast as he trotted lightly on his toes. His adrenaline, his fitness and his natural athleticism gave him boundless energy; so much that he wanted to run the three hundred metres to the stone bridge as fast as possible. He could not afford to do that, he might be seen, heard or expend too much energy. No, now he must walk. He must have control.

Stop, look, move silently to the next cover. In three minutes, he was at the bridge.

The rain had virtually stopped and a half moon occasionally poked its head through some gaps that had appeared in the cloud deck. Maybe good, maybe bad, he would soon find out.

Franz had first heard the river when he was fifty metres from the bridge. Now as he crouched on its waterlogged bank, the water rushed noisily by, and in the dim light looked so forbidding as it bubbled and lapped under the bridge. The black maelstrom was barely ten centimetres from bursting over the top. He bit his lip as he questioned his judgement. Just for one moment. *Come on, no time to look at it now,* he thought, *no time for the faint-hearted, move yourself!*

Keeping a low profile, he moved the fifty metres or so along the riverbank to the trees. One last look behind him towards the lights of the village. No. No one was following, and he vanished into the trees.

The church clock struck three-fifteen as, keeping near to the river, he crept his way through the wood. A stick broke under his foot. He uttered a silent curse as he dropped down and listened. Nothing.

Onward. Franz could now see the border lights twinkling through the trees, he must be getting near the edge of the wood. It was difficult to see the river but he could hear the lapping of water, he must be close. *Christ!* His heart almost stopped as a crash of branches above his head made him look up into a tannenbaum where he could see the eerie black silhouette of an owl as it left its perch. It swooped down towards the river before levelling out and moving off in search of pastures new to a slow, steady, slap of its wings.

Then nature called, his bowels were moving. Franz only removed his swimming trunks just in time and was empty in a second. "Oh well, less weight to carry," he whispered.

During his brief squat, he had seen the outline of the river as it left the wood ten metres further on, he decided to make his final preparations and inflate his artificial 'lung' where he was.

Franz removed his tracksuit top, connected the pump to the rubber pipe, the many blind rehearsals in his bedroom over the last two days now paid dividends. He counted the strokes as he pumped...

He knew he needed fifty strokes to inflate it, which was enough to give him two lung-fulls of air. Franz's T-shirt tightened around him as the bladder inflated. *God, what if it bursts? Every VoPo and NVA for two kilometres will be here in two minutes.*

He kept pumping, the T-shirt tightened. *Forty-seven, careful, Franz. Forty-eight, please don't burst, forty-nine, fifty, that's it.* Pinching the end of the tube, he removed the pump and inserted the tap before attaching a cir-clip over the joint. He listened for the tell-tale hiss that would signify his next problem, but no, the air was locked in the bladder. Would it stay there under the added pressure of three metres of water?

Franz had been unable to test this, but had tested the bladder and tap to a pressure of sixty strokes of his pump; he had not dared to push his luck any further. He hoped it would be enough.

OK, off with his tracksuit trousers and tighten his T-shirt around his waist with a safety pin on either side. "Yes. Got it. That will fix the bladder in place." He allowed himself a small chuckle, he must look like the Hunchback of Notre Dame. What would Charles Laughton have thought of him? Lastly, he blackened his legs and arms, picked up his flippers and he was ready. The church clock struck three-thirty.

Breathing deeply, he moved to the riverbank and then along it until he was behind the last tree. The field stretched before him, he could clearly see the border and its brightly illuminated but sinister fence five hundred metres distant. All clear.

Off with his trainers and on with his flippers; his mouth was completely dry, he could not even swallow. Four last big breaths. His head started to feel light, a good sign.

Sitting on the side of the muddy bank at the point where the river finished its last bend before the long straight run to the wire, the dark figure immersed his feet into the swirling water.

Entering the water on the outside of the curve, and therefore directly into the main current, the water almost ripped his flippers off as soon as they were knee deep. He jerked backwards. *Stop! No. Go back. You're going to die....*

Shut up. You'll die if you stay. No turning back. One last giant breath and he eased himself up on his hands and slipped into the turbulent depths. It was cold, icy cold. Struggling to get control and body position on the surface, he started to count, *one, two, three, four.* Maybe he didn't have to dive; he couldn't see anyone. *Don't be a fool, because you can't see them, doesn't mean they can't see you. Don't change your plan. Dive!*

1.
5 June 1944
Le Hamel, Normandy, France

The back flap of the lorry clattered open and twelve German soldiers spilled out. Eighteen-year-old Franz Schmidt stretched and groaned as he straightened himself up. He, nine other young private soldiers, two corporals and a sergeant of the 352nd division had begun their journey from their training unit in Germany in a crowded troop train before switching to a lorry in Rouen. Their sadistic sergeant, who had sat comfortably in the front seat, had allowed them only one short stop during the six bladder-breaking hours on hard wooden seats as it groaned, rumbled and bumped its way over the French cobblestones and potholes. Nervously smiling as their senses slowly returned to their limbs, they looked young, very young. So this was Normandy.

They stared at the shabby, grey houses of the shabby grey French coastal hamlet of Le Hamel. Only a small place, just a few houses seemingly in need of renovation scattered along a main street with one or two tracks off to the side. It looked like a village keeping its head down, no bright colours, and no bright people. A young mother with dark hair walked past on the other side of the road.

Despite towing her small son along the uneven pavement at a speed that was sure to dislocate his shoulder, she looked attractive as she stooped under her headscarf to hide from the rain and the expected comments from the soldiers.

Although it was June, she had dressed the boy in a faded-brown winter coat in an effort to keep dry; well groomed, he wore a pair of apparently new shiny black shoes. *Looks like a visit to Grandma,* Franz thought. The soldiers, whose heads had followed the mother in unison like a crowd watching a slow motion tennis match, stared in silence as she passed.

The small boy was the first to comment as he looked back over his shoulder and barked, "Boche!" His mother yanked him two feet off the ground as she cuffed his head with her other hand before dumping him down and dragging the boy away at an even greater rate of knots. Neither looked back.

Franz and his mates had been happy when they first heard about their Normandy posting. This would be like a holiday camp. "The Allies won't land here, too far across the sea."

They had always feared a posting to the Eastern Front, from where progressively fewer had returned. Paradoxically, Dr Göbbels often proclaimed that they had inflicted multiple defeats on the hated communists. To speak about his contradiction in public would certainly lead to your execution. The official line to be quoted was that there was no contradiction at all, it was all part of the Führer's master-plan, especially when you were so grateful to the Führer for sending you to quiet, sunny France. OK. Rainy Normandy.

Only driving rain and an aggressive Sergeant Nolte welcomed them. This man had been the bane of their lives for the two weeks since he had joined their unit. One of the few who had returned from Russia in one piece, he had also returned as a decorated hero. Single-handed, he had wiped out two Russian machine gun positions in a house after he gained entry through the basement and fought his way up.

Nolte was indeed a classic, his bent teeth and squashed purple-veined nose looked as if it had been a receptive target for every drunken fist in Russia. The French rain gave his unshaven, pockmarked face a sweaty appearance and made him squint, which accentuated Franz's opinion that the sergeant's pale blue eyes looked too close together. Nolte had an obnoxious personality and like most sergeants believed that sarcasm and drill were the answers to everything. True to form, he lined the platoon up for inspection.

Strutting slowly down the line, Nolte exaggeratedly eyed each soldier up and down before stopping in front of Franz. At that moment it came to Franz that Nolte looked like a gargoyle. He must be the original sculptor's delight. He imagined that face, lips pursed and with cheeks puffed out as it spewed rainwater over all below. In spite of the stench filling his nostrils,

Franz had difficulty controlling his mirth and started to twitch; his eyes gave it all away.

"What is your problem? Do you find something funny, boy?"

"No sergeant." A pause, with much eyeballing from a pair of narrow set eyes.

"Why are you twitching? Do you suffer from St Vitas Dance?"

"No sergeant."

"Do you want a shit?"

"No sergeant."

"Do you want to fart?"

"No sergeant."

As if it wasn't raining enough, Nolte leaned towards Franz and sprayed, "I can arrange a transfer to the Eastern Front you know." Franz flinched under the dousing. Self-preservation took over from humour and an intense stare signified the end of the episode.

Their interrogation and inspection complete; the men stood easy for five minutes until, "Achtung," bellowed Nolte. A shining motorcycle combination pulled up in front of them and out of the sidecar sprang Lieutenant Albert Hess.

Classically blond haired and blue eyed, Lieutenant Hess prowled up and down the line of attentive soldiers, pausing in front of each man and looking into his eyes as if asking an unspoken question. No laughs this time. Once this silent inquisition had finished, Hess stood to attention. He clicked his heels, paused, pushed his shoulders back and cocked his head a further five degrees back, as if he already savoured victory.

"Welcome to Le Hamel. You are here to defend the Reich from those that seek to destroy everything that the Führer and all of us have fought for many years to create. Forget not who you are and what you have. You are the inheritors of a Europe that has learned to respect and admire Germany. We have cleansed Europe of the Jewish lice.

"But there are those that want to sweep this all away. The Americans and the British want to be the masters; they want to turn the clock back fifteen years. They want to put you under the heel of their boot.

"If they were to succeed in this stupid plan do not think that they will go about it as gentlemen. Oh no! I am sure that many of you have girlfriends, sisters, and mothers. Think of them now. Picture them in your mind." Hess paused and knowingly, nodded his head as he looked up and down the line. "What do you think that Tommie and Yankee will do to them?" He paused again. "They will rape them.

"Think about it. Imagine the scene. Imagine them drunkenly awaiting their turn, and their perversion? Never forget that vision that you have in your head at this moment of your woman as she suffers that appalling, filthy, diseased fate. Because that's what is going to happen if they come!

"They may indeed come. If they do, you will play your glorious part as you throw them back into the sea to lick their wounds as they skulk at the bottom with the eels and the flatfish. You will fight with distinction shoulder to shoulder with your brother German soldier.

"You gentlemen are different. You are Aryan, the Master Race. You will not retreat. You will defend the Fatherland and our great leader, Adolf Hitler with your lives!" His arm shot up into the Nazi salute, his heels clicked and screamed "Heil Hitler."

For a moment Franz's chest puffed out with pride, not because he agreed with the Nazis, but because he took pride in being German and what he saw that it meant to the world. The Nazis had brought an order and pride back to a German people who were in the depths of despair in the aftermath of the First World War and the Great Recession.

He could easily remember how his father changed from a fat to a thin man as a result of forgoing evening meals so that Franz could eat. He could never quite work out why his family were so short of food when his father carried pocket loads of money. Surely, they must be rich? He remembered the day when his father took him out to buy new shoes and took a whole suitcase full of money with him, only to return without any shoes, because there were none.

When Hess had told him to think of his loved one, Franz had only wished that he had been able to do just that. He had never had a girlfriend. Oh. What he would give to have one! Whenever he found himself alone with a girl she soon warmed to him, only to go cold again when they were in company. What did he do wrong?

Franz liked Freja Arndt and was sure she liked him. He liked to walk some of the way home with her after school. They would walk slowly and she would look up at him with those wonderful blue eyes and wiggle her body whilst she held her schoolbooks across her voluptuous chest. Horst Alm usually shadowed them. Horst was a good mate but he never gave over; every time Franz talked to a girl, especially Freja, it seemed Horst would be there to poke fun at him. "Oooh Franz, what are you up to there?" Why did people laugh at him so much? Why didn't they just keep quiet and get on with their own lives?

He was desperate to kiss Freja and become her boyfriend. But, what if she said no? She would be sure to run off and tell all her friends that Franz Schmidt had tried to kiss her and they would all laugh at him too. Yeah, big confident Franz, best school footballer in the region, afraid of what people might say.

However, Franz would certainly fight the Americans to keep her pure. He didn't want anyone violating her.

Hess then got down to business. He told them that they would man two new heavy machine gun emplacements on a slight hill overlooking the beach on the western side of Le Hamel towards Arromanches. They would be able to direct a withering field of fire both out to sea and across the beach from these new mini castles which were gas proof and well-nigh impregnable. Sergeant Nolte would work out a watch rota, and they would live there twenty-four hours a day until they were relieved. They would find rations and beds in a dormitory at the back of the emplacement. No female visitors of any kind and by that he meant voluntary or professional. That was all, but they would do well to remember his words. The officer gave the ensemble one last glance, clicked his heels, gave the Nazi salute, sprang into his sidecar and sped away into the mist.

"Now you know who you are and what you're fighting for; let's go," bellowed Sergeant Nolte and off they goose-stepped to their new home. They had trained for this; their big moment. Trainees no more they were now soldiers on active service, out of the village then up and around the back of the hill. They had never marched so well. At this moment it didn't matter who they were fighting for, they were together and they were proud.

As he marched, Franz pondered the sergeant's words. Would he be fighting for Germany, for his family, for Freja or for the Nazi's? He had never thought about it before. War was just what you did. What you had to do.

As their new concrete gun emplacements came into view, so did the beach. The ebb tide had exposed a mass of steel defences. Barbed wire by the kilometre looking like a mass of curly hair as it had been strung out, woven and criss-crossed to form a forbidding barrier to a would-be invader. Franz had seen pictures of the trench wire of World War One but even that was no comparison to this. *No one could possibly penetrate that. How much pain would a man endure if he were ensnared in such a barbarous trap?*

The infinity of the answer made him shiver. Although physically hard, his training had often been a laugh and there were no serious injuries. He had always felt secure. Yes, he had heard the bombers overhead. But they had never dropped bombs on him and he had never seen anyone killed or seriously injured in front of his eyes. That side of the war had seemed a remote, almost clinically clean experience. It was fun to watch films of the Luftwaffe shooting yet another "Terror Flieger" out of the sky. It was great to see the remains of a Russian tank split open like a melon. Never any pain, it was all just like Hollywood when the hero gets shot in the shoulder but gets up to win the fight without a thought that the bullet would probably have irreparably smashed many of his shoulder bones to pieces. The referee had suddenly blown time on that game the moment

Franz had seen this horrific heap of wire. He momentarily lost step with the other men.

And not only the wire. The low tide had exposed the 'Hedgehog' tank traps; three sections of steel girder each two to three metres long, welded together in the middle at right–angles to each other. These forbidding obstacles were also set out in long lines across the beach and into the sea. The line furthest out to sea was only just visible, only the jagged tops of these killers poked out of the water like hungry three-eyed crocodiles lying in wait for their next, unsuspecting meal.

And mines, over to his right he could see a team of engineers. Two men furiously digging at the sand whilst nearby, two others were on their hands and knees around a newly dug hole. A fifth soldier stood next to them holding the terrible disk shaped explosive as he waited for his chance to conceal the vicious device that would blow an unlucky invader into a red mist.

Franz looked out to sea; he had never seen the sea before. It was supposed to be tranquil and blue, but this wasn't; the grey-brown colour was just as it looked in the photographs he had seen in his schoolbooks. In the distance... where was the distance? There was no distance. Somewhere out there, the endless grey sea and the endless dense and featureless grey sky became one.

The powerful sea prowled, heaved and roared its exclamation of power as it became tumultuous surf crashing, gushing and frothing over the tank traps and on into the wire. The young soldier's perception changed from a scene of defensive strength from the land to one of a threat from the sea. "Astounding!" *It's like being besieged by a huge hungry wolf salivating over its endless lines of tank trap teeth, biding its time before it pounces and rips its meal to bits.* He gasped at this exhibition of foreboding power.

Reality came when he arrived outside his gun emplacement. Heavy, impregnable and double decked, like a huge green and brown elephant's turd, it looked as though some vast elephant had squatted and splodged the top story down on top of the lower one. They entered through the back into the mess room, which contained six metal bunk beds, a bare wooden table, some chairs and a stove. The ubiquitous picture of Adolf Hitler hung over the food cupboard and was the only decoration. The low concrete ceiling and the lack of windows gave a feeling of entombment beneath thousands of tonnes of concrete just waiting to thud down on those inside.

Naturally Nolte pulled rank and chose his bunk first. This done, the men rushed to bag the bunks furthest away from the smelly sergeant. The unlucky loser in this race was Josef Franke, who found himself with the bunk directly over Nolte's; the others gloated as they wrinkled their noses at him. Josef didn't see the joke. However he immediately cheered up when Nolte barked, "Schmidt and Franke. You will be our operational spotters and will have the honour of the first guard."

Franz and Josef grabbed a quick bite to eat and then took up their post in the two-man observation area at the top of the emplacement. This was directly above the position's principal armament, the MG 42 Panzerlauf heavy machine gun. When fired through the slit in the armoured steel shield at the front of the gunroom, this fearsome tripod-mounted weapon was capable of firing 1,200 rounds per minute of its 7.92 millimetre ammunition, although the maximum burst allowed was 250 due to excessive heat causing barrel wear. Barrel changing on this gun was very quick, about 10 seconds, meaning an almost unbroken period of fire was possible. Its effective range of over a kilometre meant that from their position, they could cover the entire beach or inbound landing-craft long before they landed and disgorged their contents of fighting men or tanks.

A disadvantage of this weapon was that because of its massive firing rate, it frequently ran out of ammunition. No such worries here, the gun room was stacked to the ceiling with ammunition boxes and they had plenty of replacement barrels. Surely their position was impregnable!

The light faded rapidly as night closed in. The rain had stopped, but the wind still crashed the sea onto the beach below them. Franz studied the blank, cold, concrete walls surrounding them and thought, *Maybe this is what prison must feel like?* When it became dark, they could no longer see the coldness of the concrete or the sea. Never-the-less they did their duty and peered through their new Zeiss binoculars, but to no avail. Like coconuts at a fair, only their heads protruded over the battlement, they were sheltered from the wind and felt quite cosy. With no Nolte around, they folded their arms on top of the parapet, rested their chins on their hands, and talked.

They discussed Hess's speech and Jews. "I knew a Jewish family in Oberfeld." Franz sighed before continuing, "Mr and Mrs Rabinowitz. They were always friendly. They took part in all the village activities and made good shoes in the family business. Mr Rabinowitz was a "Schuhmachermeister" and respected by everyone. Nobody thought of him as a subversive element. Then the Nazi bullyboys arrived. About ten of them, arrived on..." Franz halted abruptly and looked questioningly at Josef, who was studying him intently. *Oh my God! Have I opened my mouth and rattled? That's dangerous talk, and I've done all the talking.*

Although he had felt Josef was a kindred spirit from the moment they first met, he had not known him for that long and he wasn't sure of his views on Jews. A short tense silence followed until, much to Franz's relief, after a careful look around, Josef agreed with him.

"What happened to them?"

"Same that happened to all of them. One day about three months later they just disappeared. There one day, gone the next. I don't know where and I didn't ask."

They each lit a cigarette and peered into the gloom. Josef bit his lip as he looked for demons. "What do you think will happen if they land here tonight?" he asked.

"They won't come here, Josef. If you were a General wouldn't you take the shortest route?" Franz didn't wait for an answer as he continued, "they'll go to Calais. Anyway, look at this shit weather. No one would come in this!" They heard a church bell chime midnight and wondered if they would see any ghosts? Not yet.

2.

A hot June day in a village in Cambridgeshire and Gerald Clarke lay daydreaming on his bed. He gazed outside into the cloudless blue sky and marvelled at aerial dexterity of the swifts as they darted, wheeled and floated ever higher in the thermal currents. Gerald's eyes glazed.

How nice it would be to have a girl alongside him. He cuddled her, kissed her, admired and explored her. Then tutted. *Yeah. Yeah, Gerald. Dream on. It's always only bloody dreams with you. Seventeen and a half years old and you've never had a girlfriend.* He flicked out at a fly that had dared to land on his stomach. His head crashed back on the pillow. *I'm so bloody frustrated.* Then he smirked, maybe his luck was about to change.

His eyes glazed again as he replayed his latest chatting-up of Sue Moore in the baker's shop, and how he had dallied a little longer with each visit. Yes, she had begun to flirt with him too. Definitely warming to him; and didn't her arse look good in her new skirt. His fantasy developed these meetings to erotic climaxes until the screaming swifts diving past his window jolted him into reality.

Gerald's gaze moved to the pictures of the Glenn Miller Band on his bedroom wall. He stretched and yawned. *Oh, to be like Glenn,* he thought. *He doesn't have to take orders from anyone. He can have every woman, as and when he wants. What a life.* He sighed and scratched his head. *Maybe Sue will be at the Drakesford dance tonight.* He clicked his fingers. *Time to make your play for her, Gerald.*

Finding just enough energy to roll off his bed and put 'In the Mood' back on his new gramophone for the twenty-sixth, or maybe the thirty-sixth time that day, Gerald remembered the rest of East Binningham. They must all think this music is wonderful and would want to hear it a little bit better. Maybe they would also be jealous of his new toy.

Gerald skipped back to the gramophone and turned up the volume to a distorted maximum. Jigging and spinning to the music, he imagined the girl fans going wild. The screams in his ears got louder until suddenly he could hear no music, only screams.

There in the doorway, arms folded and gramophone record in hand, looking like an aggressive starling with small dark eyes and pinpoint pupils, stood his mother. Her grey-blond hair frizzed as if she had generated six megawatts from her five-foot-three frame.

Gerald's shock turned to anger. He leapt towards her and towered over her small scraggy figure. His eyes bulged, as with the aggression of a Rottweiler he barked, "How dare you? Put my record down."

Innes, of whom it was said that when she got angry, you could make toast on her breath, stood firm. Her eyes narrowed and in her best toasting voice she started, "You lazy, good-for-nothing waster. Do you know who has just complained to me at our front door? Do you? Do you?"

"The man in the bloody moon," he sneered. "How am I supposed to know?"

"PC Shilling, that's who. He threatened me with god-knows-what if you don't turn that terrible row off. Mrs James and Mrs Leadon have both complained to him about that rubbish you play on that hellbox of yours," she stamped her foot, "and don't you swear at me."

Gerald's face was now scarlet. "It's not a hellbox, it's a gramophone, and you are so out of touch, you don't recognise art when you hear it. It's only rubbish to miserable old fogies like you. Give me my record back."

Innes nonchalantly tossed the record onto his bed. Her glare intensified. "The only life I have at the moment is to work so you can sit on your arse. You do nothing in this house, except blast us out with that rubbish," she stamped her foot again, "yes, damned rubbish! You lie there like a cuckoo. Don't you know there's a war on?

"The only time you move is to go and play stupid soldier games with those Dad's Army fools. Come next year you'll have to join up." She whirled her arms heavenwards and implored,

"God help us all then. Hitler will have a bloody field day. You get off your arse this minute, get into the garden and pick cherries. I want to make jam this evening."

Gerald's eyes bulged. "I am not going to pick cherries now. I'm off to the dance at Drakesford."

"Get out in the garden and pick those cherries. Do as I say."

Gerald drummed his hips with his fists. "I don't give a damn about your cherries. I'm late for the bus."

"You will not go anywhere on any bus without my permission. And you don't get that until you have picked the cherries." Innes stood feet astride in the doorway, eyes locked on to his. Her mouth twitching as they glared at each other. After some seconds, Gerald slowly shifted his gaze and crabbed sideways through the door.

Ignoring each other, they stalked out into the garden and worked in stony silence for the next two hours. As the sun remorselessly beat down, the only sounds that penetrated Gerald's anger were the chugging of the bus as it left for Drakesford, and the swifts calling him to freedom. Eventually, the basket full, it was time for another bus to Drakesford. "There," he barked as he thrust the basket on a stool in front of his mother, "is that enough to make jam?"

She folded her arms and gave the basket half a glance. "Seems enough to me."

"Good, then let me make your jam for you." He clenched his teeth, plunged his fists into the basket and red arms pumping like pistons, pummelled the cherries into a pulp.

Innes gazed in shock as the pulp oozed out through the wickerwork and dripped onto the earth. Aghast, she raised her eyes to meet his. Gerald thrust his head forward and glared at her.

Gaining no retort, he exultantly threw his head back and stomped away to the bus stop, slamming the gate as he went.

Innes limply flapped her hands against her sides and stared at the gate. "Why is it that a mother should hate her son? Sometimes.

"Why is it that a son should want to be so bad to his mother? He wasn't always like this."

She sagged against the tree, stared downward at the growing pool of cherry pulp and began to sob. "I have failed with him. Is there anyone out there who can tame him?"

She would have never believed who it would be.

3.

The weather up in the observation point improved. The sky had started to clear, although down below them Franz and Josef could still hear the rhythmic crashing of the waves breaking over the beach. They had not seen or heard anything suspicious and now, as fatigue set in, they took periods of rest as one sat down whilst the other kept watch for invaders or the dreaded sergeant They saw little difference. Around two a.m, what sounded like a swarm of bumblebees came from the direction of the sea and lumbered overhead. Josef nudged the slumbering Franz who instantly became alert at the urgency in his friend's voice, "Bombers?"

Franz listened intently to the sound of motors in the night sky. "This is a new sound to me, Josef. I've heard Lancasters before but these sound different, and not so high." It sounded as though there were a lot of them as the noise continued for a few minutes. They could also hear some more over to their left further along the coast where the anti-aircraft defences started up and gave a show just like a New Year fireworks party. Franz shook his head, "I haven't a clue what sort they were but they seem to have gone now. Maybe one of them has come down. I can see the glow of a fire in the distance."

The sound of the sea once more became the dominant factor in their night. They discussed where the bombers could be heading, which poor sods would be underneath that lot in an hour or two and whether or not they would hear them on their return flight? Maybe they would see a little bit of action if one of them crashed nearby?

All seemed to be clear. They heard no alarm and so resumed their seaward observation, oblivious to the happenings a few kilometres inland as the first allied parachutists regrouped and swiftly moved to secure their first objectives. Operation Overlord had begun.

Twenty minutes later all hell broke loose. The alarm bells rang and the other soldiers spilled out of their bunks and scrabbled for their boots. The telephone rang almost immediately. A confused Sergeant Nolte answered it, and after a short moment barked, "Jawohl" to his caller and slammed down the phone. "Achtung, Achtung, move your arses while you still have them. The fucking bastards are coming. Parachutists have landed."

Although unsure of which way to look, everyone took to their positions in seconds. The gun position covered the seaward and beach directions so only those in the observation point, Franz, Josef and the hurriedly arrived Nolte, had an all round view of the area. They could clearly see two or three large fire fights some kilometres to their left and anti-aircraft tracers in the direction of Caen to their right. Then above them came the sound of more aircraft, and more, and more.

In the battery they waited, seeing movement in every shadow, wanting to go to the toilet, shaking, waiting for the bang, gripping their rifles, sweating, mouths so dry that their tongues stuck to their teeth. They looked in every direction for the paratroopers. None came. Not yet. "Maybe they are only a few metres from us. They must be creeping up," whispered Josef.

"Keep your eyes peeled, your mouths shut and your guns ready," growled Nolte as he turned to go below to the gunroom. "I'll send Schneider up to help you. Report anything you see or hear but don't shoot unless you're sure it's the enemy. Our own messengers may be running up and down this track behind us, so be careful." At this moment, in spite of all that they had said about Nolte, they were glad to have him around. Suddenly he was a solid father figure. Nolte scurried below cursing as he went.

Ten seconds later the sound of hurried footsteps echoed up the stair well. A stumbling sound and some cursing before a determined looking Corporal Schneider appeared alongside them.

The tension in the observation bay was unbearable. Silently, the three men gazed all around, twitching as they tried to focus on possible movements in the gloom.

The night moved on with no action in their immediate vicinity other than their need to continually relieve themselves. They watched the flashes and heard the explosions with trepidation. On the one hand, was this just a diversionary raid that would not involve them? Half of the time they hoped that it was, but on the other hand, this was their moment. When would they get their chance? That time came at just about dawn.

A series of flashes out to sea rippled along the horizon like a line of very active thunderstorms, followed a few seconds later by the loud bumping rumble of heavy navy gunfire and the explosive roar of the landing shells; fortunately not on them. The gunfire continued non-stop for two hours as the shells landed on the beach below and around the heavy coastal batteries nearby that were returning fire. As it got lighter and they could make out the profiles of individual ships, they began to grasp the full size of the armada. "Scheisse!" They stared dry-mouthed in disbelief.

Ships of all shapes and sizes covered the horizon. There were so many, and were so tightly packed that from the shore it looked as though they had formed up into a huge grey wall. Most of the bigger ships were firing; flash after orange flash randomly prickling along the line like flash bulbs at a Hollywood premiere. Many of the smaller ships had lots of even smaller ones fussing around them, like ducklings around their mother. It then became apparent that the 'ducklings' had turned and were moving as one in the direction of the beach below. The beach henceforth forever known as 'Gold' beach.

At about seven twenty-five, as the first line of landing craft approached the beach, the naval barrage around the beach lifted and concentrated more inland on the German heavy gun positions. At precisely seven thirty, the first wave of allied soldiers hit the beach and Nolte gave the order for the machine gun to open fire.

It was like a turkey-shoot for the first minute or so. The sea went red as the young men spilled out of the landing craft and died before they had lived. But they kept coming. "Look!"

squeaked Franz to anyone who could hear as he pointed to some fast moving, ever growing black shapes that had appeared in the sky. Twelve Typhoons were heading straight for them, coming in very low and very fast.

Rolls-Royce Griffon engines whining, the Typhoons directed their acidic cannon fire against some defensive positions nearer the village. Franz winced as three seconds later they unleashed their fearsome payload of one thousand pound bombs on the same position. The Typhoons banked right towards them. Throbbing and hissing, they whizzed overhead at no more than fifty feet. "Not us this time. But they'll be back," growled Schneider to anyone who was prepared or able to listen. On the beach they just kept coming.

More and more they came, screaming, shouting, and running for cover behind anything they could find. Yard by yard inching their way up the beach, setting off mines, dying, shooting, screaming, running, more coming, swimming, bleeding, dying, losing feet, losing brothers, further up the beach, nearly to the last wire, shooting, resting, counting, praying and dying.

The Germans could see men falling; they wanted to see men falling. This was no time for morals or questions, it was dog eat dog. Unbelievable noise, without any let up. The full fury of the allied war machine was hitting the Germans from land, sea and the air as more and more aircraft made strafing runs at the defensive positions.

Franz no longer had time to be afraid; full of concentration, firing his gun again and again, the stench of burning gun oil made him gasp. On the beach, men prayed that it was not their turn to die. In the gun emplacement men prayed that it was.

It seemed that they had managed to halt the British advance at the wire until suddenly, a series of explosions flung wire and sand into the air with such an effect it was as though someone was tossing spaghetti. Specialist troops had employed their deadly wire busting Bangalore Torpedoes, and like the Red Sea parting for Moses, so the wire parted for the British and like the Israelites, they flooded through to escape the hell of the beach and drive on. Still they came.

Another landing craft with every wave, bringing more and more young men who leapt into the sea, rifles held high over their heads and who were bursting their lungs to yell their loudest banshee screams as they ran to join the fray. What was this now? Bigger landing craft? Plumes of black diesel fumes pummelled skywards as the craft's doors swung open. Franz yelled, "Oh my God. Tanks!"

Through the gap in the wire closest to Franz the men of B Company of the Hampshire regiment charged, exactly in his direction. "Here we go!" Nolte appeared in the observation point alongside the three furiously firing men who were now swearing oaths of defiance for the benefit of their own courage.

Nolte raised his gun over the parapet, and was taking aim, when his head exploded like a rotten tomato all over the other horrified occupants of the position. They stopped firing and looked at each other until Schneider coolly said, "Thank God that wasn't me," then turned and resumed his firing. His two comrades automatically followed suit.

By about eight thirty, the full force of the Hampshire regiment now turned on the German position. Bullets 'cracked' as they flew overhead, pinged and whined in all directions as they hit the concrete.

Franz could not put his head over the wall to see where he was aiming, he just held his gun over the top and fired in the general direction of where he thought the British were. Afraid to look, he didn't know that the British were now underneath them.

The heavy machine gun paused to change a barrel. Ten seconds later a loud thud beneath them drove a shock wave up through their boots. Followed by nothing. Franz checked his gun.

The grey green object, about the size of a knobbly goose's egg lazily floated through the air, turning slowly end over end as it went. Franz stared at the grenade, hypnotised by its horror. For a split second, his world seemed to be in a helpless slow motion. The grenade looped towards the concrete wall at the back of their position in a direction to the left of Hartmut Schneider. In one movement, like a cross between an international goalkeeper and a ballet dancer, Schneider arched through the air towards the deadly egg. At full stretch, he caught it one handed with his right hand, scraping his knuckles in a red stripe on the fresh concrete as he fell, and rolled on top of it. And that was it.

Franz could not have seen the shock-wave that, like a large slab of supersonic oak, hit him on the head and chest simultaneously.

Had he been conscious, Franz would have seen Schneider's body arch up into the air like a bucking bronco at a rodeo before he fragmented into many pieces, large, small and atomised. He would never have seen the hot jagged chunk of metal spinning towards him that subsequently entered his bent knee, shattering his kneecap before it took a chunk of bone from his femur and passed out through his lower thigh.

Did Schneider do it out of self-preservation intending to throw it back from where it had come? Did he do it in a miscalculated attempt to be a hero and gain a Knights Cross, forgetting to calculate that he would certainly die? Did he in an instant realise he was done for and gave his life to save others? Was it pure, unthinking reflex? No one will ever know. Even Schneider would probably have never known.

Numbness... Then a slight tingling... High pitched whistling in his ears... A hand in his pockets, roughly searching and pulling... Can't speak... No air... "Leave me alone, don't touch me..."

A small gulp, then a big gasp of air, shouting and pain. Pain growing by the millisecond, throbbing, searing. Surely, someone had put a large flat screwdriver in his knee and was now twisting and levering it?

Pressure, pressure and more excruciating pressure in the knee. "Can't see properly." *A coloured fog, fizzing, prickling with colour.* "Let me see." More bangs, more everything. "Stop. Oh stop, let me die in peace. Oh my God, help me! I don't want to die. I can hardly scream for the pain."

"Shut him up! Shoot him or get him a medic, but shut him up," barked an aggressive English voice.

Franz was frantic with the pain. "Don't move me, don't touch me. Help me. My knee, Jeesus my knee." He saw the needle, he hated needles but this one was never more welcome.

"You'll be OK, Lad. Lie still while we get you on the stretcher." The medic wiped his fingers across Franz's fragmented knee and, in order to signify to future carers that he had been given Morphium, with his now bloodied finger daubed an 'M' on Franz's forehead. Franz screamed as they heaved him onto the stretcher; although it was a scream only heard by him as another high explosive shell exploded nearby, and another, again and again. Such unbelievable noise.

Luckily, the Morphium took over very quickly. *I'm dying. This is it. I'm going,* he thought as consciousness left him; mercifully he had only fainted. The medics heaved and pushed Franz into position on the stretcher, quickly strapped him down, and with a mighty grunt, lifted him vertically over the sidewall of the bunker.

He regained semi-consciousness to the grunts and the curses of his two sweaty, dirty, very frightened and very brave stretcher-bearers as they bumped, slid and pushed him over the sand towards the sea. It seemed like a song to him as he floated on a sea of Morphium. His head felt a little tight at the temples but he was calm.

The sand slid past with a whoosh and a hiss. The crack of a passing bullet caused him no alarm. Things were happening around him. He could see it all. A tank churned past, its tracks squealed in protest as they threw two plumes of sand high into the air behind it. He saw every detail of that and of the soldiers as they ran in a crouched, stumbling manner behind it. "They've got different hats to me," he said to the two donkey-like characters that were sweating even more as they laboured to get him to the shoreline. "That's interesting. Oh look!" One of them had red sweat running down his face. No pain, he had forgotten about that. Once he remembered about the pain and for an instant he felt something before he drifted off into his floating world again.

This is.. nice... I'm.... going.... into...... a boat....... I like........ boats.

Finally, the Morphium took him into its painless, cotton wool, nightgown.

4.

Before the war, young people in the Drakesford region had no social events to look forward to, except the annual flower show ball. Admiral Sonpat R.N (retd.) ran this highlight of the year like a military operation and disapprovingly waggled his bushy eyebrows at any of the young ladies and gentlemen who danced closer than the regulation arm's length. When the war began, young airmen came to fly Hampdens to the Ruhr from the nearby RAF Imton. Those that returned looked for some way to celebrate today, forget tomorrow and live a little. They needed a dance, and the community gratefully provided one. The brave men arrived on bicycles and motorbikes, in overloaded cars and on busses. The girls loved them all.

Three years later the Americans came, with their nylons, cigarettes and a new dance called the Jitterbug. Local farm youths stood little chance against the glamorous airmen, but it did not stop them from trying.

The dancers at the weekly Saturday night dance at Drakesford village hall were especially jubilant thanks to the unbelievably good news from Normandy. The sixth dance finished and Angela Green gazed up into Gerald Clarke's pale blue eyes. About five feet four inches tall, Angela's blue eyes and long eyelashes complemented the locks of curly blond hair tumbling down to the middle of her slim back. *He looks after himself,* she thought. *Nice, well groomed hair. Never really liked boys with ginger hair before. But this one... Nice smooth skin and interesting blue eyes. Hmmm...* She smiled at him sensuously.

Gerald gazed back, his eyes asking an unspoken question. He had become besotted with this dream of a girl, and he knew how to lure her. He had often practised this situation in front of the mirror or whilst lying on his bed, and in a voice as close as he could get to Clark Gable asked, "Where have you been hiding all my life?"

"Maybe you're the one who's been hiding?" His eyes widened; the first of many things that would not go as he had planned that night.

However, it encouraged him to keep a tight hold of his new dream in defence to the advances of several Americans. The air in the hall grew hot and smoky. Drunken airmen frequently collided and spilt beer over everyone. Angela clung to Gerald and flicked nervous glances in all directions. After several heavy bumps from a New York-accented flyer who would not take a 'no' from Angela for an answer, Gerald suggested they go outside for some fresh air.

Like a refreshing shower on their skin, the cool air elevated their senses; they embraced. Gerald's eyes flashed; he had always thought that you kissed with your lips closed. Angela's were open.

"Hey, Honey. How about trying a real man?" They separated sheepishly and turned to see who had disturbed them.

"Oh, God." Gerald mumbled. The drunk New Yorker had followed them outside, and with a great deal of effort he let out an ear-splitting wolf-whistle, following which, he stumbled and smashed into a bush before landing boots moonward. Gerald squeezed Angela and whispered, "Let's go somewhere quieter."

"Yes, let's," Angela said as she looked anxiously over her shoulder. "We can go to the barn on my farm. It's only half a mile away." Gerald did not believe his luck. He had been through this situation a thousand times in his dreams, but now the reality made his heart pound so much his head began to spin. Dizziness was not in the plan. Neither was the individual following them.

Every turn, every doorway presented a kissing haven. Learning was fun and Gerald became increasingly excited, to the extent that he had an erection so stiff it was painful. He felt himself blushing and each time they kissed, tried to hold his hips away from her. No good, it would not go down, and anyway, Angela pushed her hips towards him as much as he pulled his away.

After a few such kisses, he gave up and pushed back as hard as possible. Then they heard a cough.

"Shit. It's the Yank," Gerald muttered. "Come on, let's run and make a few quick turns. He's pissed. I'm sure we'll soon lose him."

The barn door rattled and creaked on its hinges as Gerald pulled it open. One last look behind. "All clear," whispered Angela as she squeezed Gerald's hand and they nervously tiptoed into the barn, which felt warm and smelled of musty dried grass. Pausing by the door, their eyes adjusted to the soft moonlight gently streaming in through the upper level windows; it slowly illuminated quite a large area of hay. **Bang!** The barn door clattered shut behind them. Silence....

"What's that?" Angela hissed as she grabbed her boyfriend's arm. "Something moved in the hay." Her pulse raced. "Who's there?"

"Show yourself!" Gerald roared. Angela shuffled closer to him. "If you don't come out, I'm coming to get you." He manoeuvred Angela safely behind him and whispered to her, "Open the door." He saw further movement. Then he could hear it, louder, growing by the second. Fists clenched, he began to sweat. Angela held her breath. Gerald flexed his legs, ready to spring. "C'mon, Yank. I'm ready for you."

With a dull thud, something hit the floor. Gerald held his breath. Angela gasped before collapsing into a crouch. She reached towards the sound and bleated, "Fred!"

Like a neurotic meerkat, Gerald's eyes and body twitched in all directions. Then he heard Fred meow, and deflated like a balloon.

Fred's family were also in attendance and had taken up residence in the hay as an intertwined pile of warm, furry slumber, but when Gerald, cursing with embarrassment, unceremoniously removed them, the cats stood and disapprovingly flicked their tails before turning away in disdain. Angela, choking with laughter, opened the door and out trooped the cats.

Embarrassment and mirth soon gave way to passion as Gerald guided Angela down onto the warm patch where the cats had been and they kissed again. As he slipped his hand under her blouse and cupped one of her breasts, she broke off the kiss, shook her head and lightly gripped his wrist. "No, Gerald," she said unconvincingly, "I should go." Her fingers ran through his hair, belying her words, and she kissed him again.

Gerald opened her blouse, uncovered a breast and sucked the nipple while pushing his erection against her. Angela shook her head and Gerald heard her faintly groan, before he felt her slowly reach down and stroke him.

Gerald no longer followed his fantasised plans; instinct and excitement took over. As they kissed again, he moved his hand to her knee and without pause, moved upwards. They petted each other for some time, never breaking off the kiss until Angela made one last insincere plea, "Not on our first night, Gerald," which went unheard and unwanted as they undressed each other. "Gerald! It's not right."

Too late, he entered her. As they both lost their virginity, they no longer cared about the consequences. Although it was quickly over, and even though Angela had not reached an orgasm, the moment had been wonderful for both of them. They lay in silence, floating, looking at the smiling moon, listening to each other breathing and feeling their hearts pounding in unison.

Angela stiffened, her eyes flashed open and she pushed him off. "I hope I'm not going to be pregnant. You didn't use one of those rubber things. Oh God, we should not have done it. It was wrong. Terribly wrong."

Gerald stared at her in horror. "Now slow down. Stay calm. You're probably not pregnant. But if you are…" he shook his head, "there are ways to get rid of it you know."

"What? How?"

"I'm not sure. I heard Bill James talking about something at the Home Guard last Tuesday. I'll ask him."

"Don't you dare. One word to him and the whole community will know in two minutes. We'll have to hope, pray and wait and see." They dressed quickly. "Quick, Gerald. I have to be home by eleven. Dad will go crazy." Grabbing his hand, she lunged for the barn door.

"OK," pleaded Gerald, "we have time. Now stay calm. Don't worry; it'll be all right, I'll always be there for you."

This night, having beaten the curfew by six minutes, Angela took a deep breath and smacked her thigh before positively opening the farmhouse front door. Yawning as she passed through the farmhouse lounge, she casually bid her father goodnight. His eyes scanned her and seemingly satisfied that nothing was amiss, he grunted a goodnight.

Dave Green looked every inch the classic farmer with a ruddy complexion, windblown brown hair, grey streaked temples and a purple nose. Regarding himself as a symbol of the outdoor life, he claimed to live by the rules of the country; most of which he drafted in his own parliament. Others, including Angela, broke them at their peril.

Angela sighed with relief as her oak bedroom door clunked shut behind her. Having successfully run the gauntlet, she began to undress. Still warm, wet, and alive between her legs, she closed her eyes and could feel Gerald in her. She looked in the mirror, smiled wistfully and swayed her hips. *I did it.* She twirled her soft hair around her hand. *At last, I'm a woman. I never thought it would feel this good. Not a silly little girl anymore.* She pirouetted and flopped onto the bed, where she opened and closed her legs in ecstasy, reliving the moment and thinking of **her** Gerald, until...

Pregnant! She sprang up and began to undress, slamming each successive garment ever harder onto the floor. Naked and with her head in her hands she rolled back onto her bed and curled up.

What am I going to do? You're a bad girl... a slight smile, *woman..., Angela. What a fool, no protection. You're supposed to be intelligent, why'd you do it?*

You knew it was wrong. The emotional maelstrom gathered pace. *Don't want a baby, not yet. Ways of getting rid of it? I **do not** want that. Maybe I'd bleed to death. Don't want adoption.*

No, I must keep it. Oh, shit, shit, shit. The church bell struck two and still no sleep. Bathed in sweat and for the twentieth time, Angela imagined the scene with her father; the shouts, his bulging eyes and maybe even the violence. *Mum?* Angela shook her head. *She'll be more worried about the neighbours. Always, always, 'What will the neighbours say?' Yeh, and what'll Dad do to Gerald? God. He might even castrate him!*

She recalled how Sammy Johnson, her first boyfriend, had been unwise enough to ignore the curfew by ten minutes. Dave chased Sammy some five hundred yards back towards the village shaking his fist and threatening the terrified lad with castration. Angela shuddered as she thought of how lustily Dave castrated the calves, and how he would throw the detached testes high in the air for the dog to catch before they landed. As a farm girl, it was normal to see castration but she questioned her father's morals. His cronies at the King Edward pub had christened him 'Bollockov,' of which he was proud.

Angela bit her tear-soaked pillow. *Oh, Bloody Hell. Why'd I do a thing I knew was so wrong? Poor me. Yes, I wanted Gerald. I still want him, so much. What if Dad forces us to get married?* A flash thought of Gerald and her standing at the altar calmed her... *Hmmm... I wish Gerald were with me now...* Something moved on the landing.

Her head jerked up; she stared at the door. *Gerald?* The floorboards creaked; a shadow under the door.

Dave's smoker's cough dumped Angela back to reality as he tottered along the landing. *Dad. Shit!* Her head flopped back onto the pillow. Her fretting continued unabated in illogical, sweat-bathed circles until dawn.

She needed Helen.

5.

Franz awoke to farm like noises. A doctor and two nurses were examining him. Pain throbbed back into his knee. "It's not bleeding now. He'll keep until we get back to Blighty. Give him fifty milligrams of Morphium and make him comfortable." The throbbing in Franz's leg increased in intensity, men were moaning. His bed slowly rocked; activity all around. The walls and the floor were metal and there were pipes everywhere. Some of these pipes were used as sling hitches suspending various medical appliances and rows of gently swinging bare light bulbs, which only gave out a dim light. *It must be a ship. A ship? What am I doing on a ship?* He frantically looked to his right and asked the same question to a legless man, who stared at Franz for a moment before turning his head away. Franz noticed a sign on the wall. The words were not German.

An orderly with a shiny bucket and a long mop was as busy as a hamster, continually cleaning up the various spillages of vomit, blood and other liquids. It struck him that the scene before his eyes was a cross between a market, a hospital and a butcher's shop. There were men with no legs, no arms, no feet. His pain became excruciating. A soldier in the bed to his left was the subject of intense aid from a doctor and two nurses. The doctor had both his hands on the soldier's chest and was pumping as hard as he could. Franz remembered what had happened to Sergeant Nolte and felt lucky to be alive.

A nurse came to give him his injection, he looked into her brown eyes; they were warm. She had a beautiful soft looking skin, mousy brown hair and was quite tall. She looked into his blue eyes and saw not a look of steel, which was what she had been led to expect from a German, but a look of fright. She held his hand for a moment. Yes, she did have soft skin and a warm smile to go with it. "You'll be OK," she said softly. "You will be safe now. You are going to a hospital in England." Franz only understood the word "England."

She prepared the injection. "This will take the pain away and make you more comfortable." Her words were just a sound in his ears, but nevertheless a soft, calm sound among the background noises of pain and despair. He managed an apprehensive smile that abruptly stopped as the needle went in.

Franz slipped into his chemical coma for the entire channel crossing and only stirred when the ship uncomfortably thumped the quay whilst docking.

Half an hour's frenzied activity from the nurses preceded the arrival of four or five pairs of stretcher-bearers. He looked to his left and even through his drugged mist, sighed when he saw the soldier who had been 'pumped' by the doctor was now only a corpse covered with a white sheet. After a bumpy disembarkation from the ship, which due to the morphine he hardly noticed, a large jolt and a 'clack' from his stretcher brought him back into the world.

Franz gazed at a flaky wooden roof and some postage-stamp sized windows. He strained his head around to see that it was some sort of a wagon where both sides of the interior were racked to take stretchers leaving a gangway in the middle, above which swung a row of several bare light bulbs. The wagon soon gained a full complement of casualties with the same assorted wounds that he had seen on the ship, although all seemed conscious.

A tall, elderly doctor with bloodshot eyes, a furrowed brow, handlebar moustache and bushy eyebrows that spiked up liked devils horns came to examine him. Franz's eyes widened at the doctor's fearsome appearance. Surprise turned into dislike as the doctor quickly and roughly examined his wounded leg, mumbled something to a nurse by his side and brusquely moved on to his next patient. This nurse was not like the nurse on the ship. Her face showed little compassion; she never smiled, she just got on with her job as the train rattled and jerked on its way.

Franz was in one of the back wagons of the train. Each time it stopped he could hear a steadily louder metallic crashing noise rippling towards him as each truck concertinaed into the one in front. Anticipation of the halt made the actuality of the painful jolt all the more traumatic. He knew that worse was to come when the train started again. A shrill whistle from the engine, then the clanking ripple of sound moving towards him as the train's new momentum took up the slack between the trucks. "Brace, brace, brace," he told himself. "Here it comes..."

A forward lurch of the truck, thud, wince, and a quiet scream as his feet slammed into the upright at the end of his bed. This painful process repeated itself countless times over the next few hours of the journey. *Arghh. Not out loud. Don't let the others know you're German.*

Franz noticed that he received less attention from his nurse than the other wounded combatants. *What pain must she have suffered in her life? Probably during this cursed war. Yes, cursed war.* He sneered. *Fuck the 'Great Patriotic Adventure.' Maybe she has lost family or maybe she's seen too much death and pain and is now anaesthetised into a zombie-like world? Curse war! Look what it does to people.*

He tried to eavesdrop on conversations between the nurse and the other patients. Each time he shook his head and closed his eyes. *I'm in a bubble. I can see mouths move and hear noise but nothing else. I can't understand anything and no one understands or wants to understand me.* The nurse spoke at him. Franz nodded and smiled back before closing his eyes and clenching his fists. *Fucking idiot. You don't know what you just agreed to. She was probably saying, "You're a stupid alien arse licker aren't you," or something else bad and you simply nod your head and agree. Is this what's it going to be like?*

Locked in his bubble Franz lay back and smacked his fists on to the bed. *Why did I have to get hurt? Why didn't our boys help me instead of being captured by this bunch? You're a total alien here; away from everyone at home for God knows how long, maybe forever. A prisoner with an indefinite sentence. I'll never see Freja again. Look what they did to Nolte,* he glanced at the patient opposite and sighed, *yeh, and look what we did to them. This whole shit thing!* He tried, unsuccessfully, not to cry

The brakes squealed and his head slammed into the upright for the umpteenth time. He waited with clenched teeth for the train to start again but then jumped as the door slid open and stretcher-bearers clumped in and gently removed him.

Steam, people waiting, people rushing, ambulances, slamming doors, shouting, whistles, cursing, hooters, and laughter. *This place is like a circus not a railway station.* He looked at a station identification sign which had been painted out, but not enough to hide the letter-relief; he was able to make out the word Lancaster. *Where on Earth is Lancaster?*

6.

Gerald did not go straight home after the barn. His stroll back to the dance hall from Angela's became a fast walk, then, as he got to the last hundred yards, a run. With clenched fists raised to the moon, he threw his head back and laughed, "I did it. I've actually done it." The moon smiled benignly back; it had heard the same sentence a hundred million times before. "Give me more, Moon." However, whilst he had been dancing with Angela, another pair of eyes had locked on to him. Not only eyes, he had winced as a small hand with sharp fingernails gripped his bottom. He had kept calm, not allowing his eyes to stray from Angela's, but who was it?

He had manoeuvred Angela around so he could view his amorous assailant, but the hand let go as they turned. Another quarter turn, a quick glance and, a small hand with long fingernails rippled its fingertips at him over the shoulder of a tall American. Who was it?

Three complete turns later, and only a fleeting glance, but long enough to finally identify his assailant.

Now, at the dance hall bar, he heard a soft female voice behind him, "Don't get drunk, big boy." He turned around from the bar to see a familiar set of fingernails rippling in front of the face of their owner. "Just because she's had to go home to Daddy? Ah, shame."

Gerald licked his lips. "Where's your Yank, Sue?"

"Fallen down, like his bombs. Except I don't think bombs get pissed." She waggled her head slightly and pursed her lips before all in one breath, she rapidly added, "Don't like pissed men they fall asleep and are no use to woman or beast and you've got a nice arse, Gerald."

"Not as nice as yours."

"Really, you like big ones, do you?"

Gerald waggled his head and smiled. She moved closer. Close enough for her breasts to touch the back of his hand as he held his pint.

They gazed at each other and said nothing whilst he slowly brushed the back of his hand up and down. "I've only seen your arse through your skirt and wondered."

"Wondered what?"

He gulped. "Wondered what it looked like; what it felt like." He blinked rapidly. *Gerald. That was bold.* His lecherous smirk dropped a fraction.

"Ooh Gerald," she cooed. "Well, I never thought it. But we can't have you going through life wondering if only." Her lips slightly apart, she moved her tongue back and forth, just enough to tantalise him, before demurely tilting her head to one side, looking at his lips and fluttering her eyelashes.

Gerald leant towards her, gave her a small peck on her neck and whispered in her ear, "I know a place. Let's go."

Sue's eyes widened a fraction. "I'll bet you do. Come on then."

Gerald pumped his fist. *I can't believe this.* **Two** *in one night. Wow!*

Angela had needed leading. Sue ripped off his clothes with the ferocity of a starving cannibal.

On his way home, Gerald repeatedly shook his head and muttered, "Two in one night! My whole life with nothing, then two in one night. Even the hay in Angela's barn was still warm." He beamed skywards. "Don't stop now, Moon."

7.

Lancaster Infirmary was an imposing place. Franz passed through a doorway guarded by two elderly soldiers who made a big effort to glare at him as he arrived in what was to be his ward. A high, creamy coloured ceiling with two rows of bright lights that hurt the eyes gave way to bare cream painted brick walls whose only relief was that the bottom six feet or so was painted brown. It looked austere and disciplined.

Two lines of about fifteen beds, mostly occupied, were arranged against the walls down the length of the room. A large, no-nonsense nurse, whose head-dress made her look like a grotesque flying Swan, gave him what he assumed to be a grudging greeting, took his pulse and stuffed a thermometer into his mouth.

He had not been in the ward for an hour before he was taken to the operating theatre where the surgeons did their best to put his splintered bone back together. It took him about a week of drowsiness, vomiting, hallucination and nightmares of Normandy before he returned to reality and became fully aware of his new surroundings.

To his relief, he found out that he was in a German only ward. At last he could talk! Just as soon as he realised that he also realised that for him, the war was not over. Nobody wore uniforms but rank and unit were quickly established and it seemed that Franz was at the bottom of the pecking order. He, a private in an infantry division of the Wehrmacht, had landed in a ward full of Waffen SS.

The SS believed they were in every way superior to the Wehrmacht and looked down their noses at anyone who was not of their breed. Franz could not believe it; they were all incapacitated in one way or another, prisoners in a foreign land and, or so he had thought, defeated. Not a bit of it.

Captivity was only temporary, plans were already being made to escape once full bodily capability had been restored and of course, Hitler was still God. They also decided that if they couldn't get home to Germany, then it was their duty to make a big nuisance of themselves here. When their chance came, whatever or whenever that may be, they would take it. They spent hours and hours discussing the possibilities.

Not only escape. What had happened in Normandy was also a big discussion topic. They quizzed every new arrival for information about the progress of the battle; the news became more and more depressing. Of course, the international divisions, composed mostly of Eastern Europeans, had let them down, and the Wehrmacht! They had no guts these people. Where were the Panzers? Why didn't they arrive sooner? If there had been another twenty divisions of SS, the allies would never have got off the beach!

Franz kept quiet throughout these frequent phases and sank down into his bed in the hope that nobody would notice him. It was all bravado and venom. He wanted to escape and get home too, but he didn't want to know any of their crazy ideas.

The bravado also shone through via bawdy toilet-humour directed towards nurses, particularly the fat one. She could not understand a word of what was being said, only the tone and amid many guffaws, this nurse stoically carried out her duties. However, revenge is sweet and with troublesome patients the administration of injections allowed her to take it.

The theatre of loading the syringe in full view of the increasingly timid troublemaker. The excess fluid being expelled with a lust equal to that of a Trafalgar Square fountain. The slight pause as, with the primed needle pointed in the direction of its target, she looked into the eyes of the condemned. The simultaneous raising of the left eyebrow and wicked smile. The eyes widened and the rapier plunged in; often with a satisfying gasp from its victim. True discipline had been restored.

Franz observed these retribution episodes with gleeful satisfaction and he often nodded his approval to the triumphant nurse as she marched past him. He felt sympathy for her as well as a certain amount of admiration for the way she coped in the face of such torment. She was never aggressive with him and although business like with her treatment, she did manage one or two smiles and words, which of course he couldn't understand. He resolved to end this communication problem.

After two false starts, he finally plucked up courage one afternoon when she came to change his dressings. She undid the first safety pin and he winced rather theatrically. The nurse bit her lip and shook her head. "That didn't hurt, you big baby." Franz had no idea what she had said, but he recognised the tone. He pushed out his bottom lip and whimpered, but then gave her a knowing look and a shy smile. His eyes looked up at the ceiling and half closed before they opened again and playfully returned to hers.

She smiled. "You're OK. You're not going in your box yet." Her face dropped and she sighed.

That could have meant anything to him but he took encouragement from her smile. In fact, when she smiled he thought she looked really attractive. Her eyes were a soft brown and her nose in perfect proportion to her face, and she had nice teeth too... *To business, Franz.* He pointed to his chest and said, "Franz."

She pointed to herself. "Josie."

"Josie," he repeated with a big smile. He enthusiastically nodded his head, whilst desperately trying to think of what to say or do next. She smiled, looked into his hopeful eyes and patiently waited for the next round. Franz put his hand to his mouth and blew her a kiss. "Josie, mmmmm." In the same instant he thought, *Oh my God. That was bold. You've never done that to a girl you've just met. Hang on, Franz. You've never done that to any girl!* He felt himself blushing.

She slowly enquired, "How old are you?"

Franz enthusiastically nodded his head and agreed with her. *Oh dear. What is she saying? Keep smiling, Franz. Keep it going.*

"Think again," Josie muttered. "A new tack." She pointed to herself and said, "Josie." Then held up her hands and flashed them open twice, followed by two fingers, to show twenty-two.

Ah yes, Franz understood. He flashed both his hands open three times and, accompanied by an angelic smile, "Franz, dreissig."

She flashed her left hand three times and pointed at him. "Oh no, no, no. Franz, fifteen." There followed furious shaking of the head from the pillow, countered by equally furious nodding of the head from the chair. A long stare, much pursing of lips and twenty-six fingers came from the pillow, with a self-satisfied smile. A sceptical smile, plus sixteen fingers returned from Josie. Mutual chuckling as the auction continued until they agreed on the number twenty-one. *Liar, liar,* thought a victorious Franz as he held out a shaky hand towards his nurse.

Every time she passed he tried his sign and single word technique with her. To his delight he got a positive response and quickly learned some basic English vocabulary.

None of the SS spoke any English. It was clear that not only Josie but the other nurses too, had no time for them and were only interested in talking to Franz, which gave him more opportunity to learn. After three weeks he could put small sentences together and hold basic conversations with the nurses and even the doctors. The whole idea snowballed and learning English now became his passion. Josie brought in some children's books for him and they had a lot of fun with sign language translations.

He had found another bubble. One in which he became a sponge, absorbing knowledge like never before as he shut out the constant rhetoric going on all around him. In this time of little hope and great pain he had found a purpose. No time to think about anything else, not even Freja, he could almost have described himself as being happy. However, once a day everyone in his ward became quiet. The nurses became decidedly uneasy. Like being in the eye of a hurricane. When would the storm hit?

The doors whooshed open, and in would strut Matron attended by two snooty looking satellite nurses and a secretary all sticking as close to their chief as suckerfish stick to the belly of a shark. She swirled around the ward in about two minutes clucking instructions to her secretary who scribbled every word on her note pad. Words that underwent metamorphosis to emerge as razor sharp memos destined to appear with a flourish on the desk of every apprehensive ward sister. Nurses were reduced to shaking wrecks as they stood by their patient's beds. This rat-like matron exuded authority; a point not lost on the SS who recognised authority when they saw it.

If it had been possible for them to stand to attention whilst lying down, they would have done. They visibly stiffened at her entry. It had been noticed that Matron had blue eyes and that although her hair was visibly grey, one or two blond hairs were definitely still in existence. She must be Aryan! Of course! Wasn't it wonderful to see the racial theory proved once more? Such command, such authority; the personification of respect.

Franz disbelievingly shook his head. *Like stupid brainwashed chickens. Look at them stretching their necks to attention. Look at them! The appearance of rank and order is like switching on a light; they love it. They're back on the parade grounds of Nürnburg.* Their eyes sparkled as she marched between the two rows of beds.

They must surely be imagining that she is the Fuhrer strutting like a peacock down the avenue between the massed ranks of storm troopers. Yeah, look. Göbbles and Himmler are in close attendance. Don't know where the one with the notebook came from. "Yes, ma'am. No, ma'am. Three bags full, ma'am and please may I have permission to breathe, ma'am?"

Franz would often slightly shake his head and chuckle at the whole pompous scene, one time too loudly. She saw him and stopped at the end of his bed, drilled him with her ice blue eyes, glanced at his record card, drilled him once more and then crackled, "Are you the one learning English?"

"Yes, matron."

"Then I suggest that you also learn how to present yourself properly or do you have wind?"

"No wind, matron. I am just pleased to see such order." Was that a slight smile that cracked the porcelain of her face?

"Very good. Carry on," she commanded as without another flicker she turned on her heel and whirled off towards her next storm phase in another ward.

"What did you say to her?" the panzer sergeant in the next bed asked.

"I complemented her on the turn-out of her ward."

He looked flabbergasted. "You? You complemented her? You are only a wehrmacht private and she is a general."

"I took it upon myself, as the communicator of the ward, to complement her as if we, collectively, were the inspecting officers of her parade." He looked around to see twenty-nine other faces staring aghast at him before adding, "she accepted my congratulation." He raised his nose and nonchalantly returned to his books.

Such bravado and arrogant cheek was definitely one back for the Reich.

8.

Angela waited until her father had gone outside before she made a stomach knotting entrance for breakfast. *Stay calm, Angela. Stay, calm.* She stood next to her mother and tried not to shake as she poured herself a cup of tea. "Did you have fun last night, dear?" her mother trilled.

"Yes thanks, Mum. I'm going over to see Helen this morning, is that OK?"

"Yes of course," Ethel said. "Don't be late for dinner. Twelve o'clock sharp."

Angela and her best friend Helen sat down on the floor next to Helen's wardrobe, cramped into the space under the sloping roof, as they had always done every time they had shared a secret since they were tiny. "Come on then, Angela. Spill the beans...

"You didn't! Oooo... Where did you do it? Did it feel good? Did it hurt?

"Ooh, Angela, I hope it's that good for me when I do it. Jill Thomas said that when she did it, 'it was over as quick as opening a bottle of pop,' and doesn't see why people go on about it.

"You didn't bleed!

"Angela. There's something else, what? Tell me...

"You didn't protect yourselves! Oh no. Oh my God." She slapped her thighs and looked to the heavens. "Keep calm. Go to the doctor if you miss this month.

"Haven't you heard? He uses rabbits to tell if you are pregnant; you don't have to wait for the bump. No idea how it works. I heard it costs five pounds.

"Yes, it is an awful lot, but better to find out sooner.

"Jill's parents persuaded her to have it adopted. What'll you do?

"No. Me too. It's part of you, you can't just give it away like a sweet.

"No, Angela, you mustn't be worried about your father.

"Yes, I know that's easy to say, but I have known him nearly as long as you. I've heard him blow his top and then ten minutes later, he's fine. Remember when I broke that window, and we both hid under the hay in the barn? Cor. He went crazy; then cuddled us an hour later.

"I know this is different, but...

"Yes, quite a few local girls have had to get married, it's wartime. But don't tell anyone else. It may never happen. But if it does, your mum and I will still love you."

Angela's normal period day came... Nothing happened. Helen said to wait for two more weeks. Angela dreamt of Gerald; but only dreamt, he was always busy.

Two weeks after that... Still nothing. "You have to go." Helen said.

Doctor Hastings shook his head and tutted when he heard that intercourse had taken place halfway through Angela's menstrual cycle. She paid her five pounds and he took a sample. "Come back in four days and you will find out then."

Angela went white and thought she would faint when, four stomach-knotting days later, Doctor Hastings confirmed the pregnancy and gave her an unsympathetic lecture about responsibility; which she did not hear. She stumbled as she got up to leave but steadied herself before opening the door to the waiting room.

It opened, and she stared straight into the eyes of her mother.

9.

Franz had been in Lancaster for eleven weeks and two operations before being declared fit for discharge. Hobbling out to a waiting lorry on a crutch and clutching an envelope containing his medical notes, he felt that his student days were over and that he was about to become a prisoner again. Along with two of the SS, both of whom had big scars on their faces which made them look more aggressive than normal, he was taken to Preston North End football stadium. Here he stood in a cage on the football pitch with several hundred other prisoners.

The men were a dishevelled bunch, decidedly smelly and looking hungry. No toilets, just a stinky bog engulfing what had once been one of the corner areas of the football pitch. As he tiptoed through the mire to find a firm place to relieve himself, the positive thought that at least the groundsman must be happy that he will never have to fertilise this part again, helped take his mind off the mess on his boots.

This motley gaggle of humanity had formed itself into a queue that wound its way towards a tent. General speculation agreed that it all had something to do with interrogation. After several hours Franz reached the front and could see what was happening. Men were being questioned for two or three minutes before being given a label and a coloured patch of cloth from one of three piles, white, grey or black. Which would he get?

The two SS men were four places in front of him. Franz watched as they presented themselves before a corporal seated behind a wooden trestle table. He had seen the corporal salute each prisoner as they came to him. Some didn't return the salute; some saluted with a normal army salute and some, including the two former SS patients, saluted Nazi style. After each reaction the corporal made a note on his official record card. Some questions, followed by more writing of notes, then the prisoner was given his card and patch and sent on his way down the tunnel over which was emblazoned "PLAYERS."

Franz observed that the Nazi's were given black patches, the non-saluters grey and the Army saluters white. Well, he wasn't a Nazi so he didn't want a black patch and he didn't want to give that salute anyway, so that method was out. Army salute, or no salute? What should he do?

He decided that grey meant that maybe the corporal thought that the prisoner might be a Nazi and white meant that you definitely weren't. Right or wrong he decided to salute. His turn, he entered the tent.

Franz stood before a corporal and saluted. The corporal made a cross on a record card next to a white square. "Name, rank, number, unit," the corporal crisply asked in very English accented German? He answered all four although he wasn't sure if he should have answered the fourth.

He handed the corporal his medical records containing all his details. The corporal questioned Franz about his involvement with the SS and did not seem too convinced by his denial but he did seem interested in Franz's English capability. After several questions in English, the corporal studied a list for a few moments before he gave Franz a further cold stare, wrote something on the form and then on a green label. "Take this patch and this label. Give them to the staff sergeant at the end of the tunnel. Next."

Franz walked down the tunnel and stared at his white patch, still unsure of its exact meaning. The staff sergeant, upon reading the label turned his head towards a row of Army trucks waiting in a line under the main grandstand and shouted, "Camp 229." Whereupon Franz was escorted to a truck into which he awkwardly climbed and flopped onto the hard wooden bench. After a deep breath he looked up at the other occupants and felt an electric shock through his system as he stared straight into the eyes of the two SS scarfaces.

They looked at each other, nodded their heads and returned their gaze to Franz. They gloated as if they had won some great prize. "So little English speaking soldier boy, you are coming with us. You will be useful!"

10.

"Angela! What are you doing here?"

"Oh. I just had to see the doctor. Have to go now." Ethel stood aghast as her tearful daughter swept out of the waiting room.

Angela's hands shook uncontrollably as she made herself a cup of tea. "The day of reckoning. Why did it have to happen to me? Why me?" She sat at the kitchen table, cried and waited.

A bicycle skidded on the gravel outside. Angela shivered. Biting her bottom lip and brushing a strand of hair from her forehead. She focussed on her teacup and steeled herself. Ethel strutted into the kitchen and stood stiff legged in front of her daughter. In a voice twice as loud and one octave higher than normal she proclaimed, "Something's wrong. Doctor Hastings wouldn't tell me. Now you tell me; what's the matter? Why were you at the doctor's? Tell your mother."

Angela buried her face in her hands, and sobbed. "I can't."

"Why can't you?"

Angela shook her head, "I just can't, bring myself to..." She paused. *You'll have to. Go on, get it over with...* She shook her head and spattered tears all over the table top. "I'm pregnant."

Ethel clasped her face and flopped down on the chair opposite her daughter, eyes stunned in disbelief. She gulped and leant slowly towards her snivelling child. "We'll start at the beginning," she demanded. "Who was the boy? A Yank? Sammy Johnson?"

"Sammy Johnson!" The explosion did not come from her mother, but from a source of far greater volcanic proportions. Having heard everything from outside, Dave burst in through the kitchen door and with eyes bulging, nostrils flared, and arms akimbo, stood in front of the now howling Angela. "Was it that Johnson boy?"

"No."

"Take your hands away from your face when you address me," he yelled as he jerked them away. Angela trembled as she peered at him through the grille of wet hair that had stuck across her puffy eyes. "I'll find out sooner or later, Angela. So you'd better tell me now."

"I don't want you to hurt him."

"Who?"

"Gerald Clarke."

"Oh, the shame of it!" Exactly on cue, Ethel clasped her face and launched into her drama. In a routine good enough for a professional mediterranean mourner, she wailed, bobbed and twisted. "In our family. A child out of wedlock. **What** will the neighbours think?"

"They 'ain't going to think anything." Dave gnashed his teeth. "I shall have a little word with Mister Gerald 'Lover-boy' Clarke." He strode to the fireplace, and with a flourish removed his shotgun from above the mantelpiece.

"No!" Angela screamed, "don't hurt him. Don't touch him."

"I'm not going to hurt him; so long as he's sensible."

Dave stalked out into the farmyard, pursued by a terrified Angela and a finger wagging Ethel, who continued to pour out, "We shall all be thrashed through the village. We shall have to give the farm to the workhouse," and other unintelligible forebodings.

Dave mounted his bicycle but the two women blocked his way. Ignoring his wife, he addressed his daughter in an exaggeratedly calm manner, "I told you. Nothing is going to happen. Provided he acts like a gentleman, which he certainly has not done to date."

"What do you mean?" questioned a wide-eyed Angela.

"I will not have any bastards born into my family. You, my dear, are going to have a husband!" He pushed the two women away and rode forth on his crusade.

Ethel nodded, pursed her lips, folded her arms tightly under her breasts and jacked them back up to where they had been twenty years before. "You be careful, David," signified her approval. Angela's stomach heaved.

Dave propped his bike against the barn wall at Marsh Farm and shotgun in hand, kept low as he tiptoed alongside a wall seeking signs of his quarry. *What's that? Could it be..?* He froze and listened. *Yes. Broom on stone.* Creeping ten yards to the end, Dave carefully peered around the gate pillar, his eyes narrowed.

Gerald was quietly whistling as he swept the yard. The first he heard of Dave's approach was the double click as Dave cocked the twelve-bore's firing hammers. Gerald spun round and came face to face with the shotgun's muzzle, which Dave pushed under the youth's chin, jerking his head backwards.

"Hope you understood what it meant to have your way with my daughter. Did you?" He prodded Gerald's throat with the gun. "I'll tell you what. You're going to be a father, you little arsehole." He jerked Gerald's head back again. Gerald tried to back away, but Dave was too quick and with an even greater shove of the gun, pushed Gerald against the wall. "It means you've got three choices, my lad." Dave paused for a moment before he cocked his head slightly to the right and squinted.

"One!" Dave's eyes widened, "I blow your head off.

"Two!" Dave reached down and slowly undid the fly buttons of the now chalk-white Gerald. Dave's fiery eyes turned chillingly cold as he reached into his waistcoat pocket and slowly pulled out his favourite castration knife. The blade glinted in the morning sun as Dave pressed it to his captive's cheek. Gerald's face twitched. The knife descended and entered the front of his trousers. Gerald winced in terror as the cold blade touched his penis before coming to rest at the back of his scrotum. Dave growled, "They don't call me 'Bollockov' for nothing." Dave's eyes bulged again as sweat ran down his, and Gerald's, temples.

"Three!" He glowered as he slowly moved his face closer to his hostage, his sweaty bristles scratching Gerald's soft cheek as he and hissed in the boy's ear, "You marry my daughter forthwith!"

Gerald gasped and gulped before he squeaked, "We're too young."

"You weren't too young a few weeks ago. You're both over sixteen, that's old enough. I will not allow tongues to wag. My daughter will get married in white. And that's an end to it. Or?"

The gun jolted Gerald's head further back and he felt a sharp nick in his skin as the grip around his genitals tightened.

"OK. OK. I'll marry her," mumbled a defeated Gerald. The gun lowered, the knife withdrew, the bristled face pulled back, and half-smiled.

"Don't think I won't make you very, very sorry if you try to get out of it, Mister Gerald Clarke. I will not have my daughter dishonoured." Without taking his gaze from Gerald's slightly relieved looking eyes, he moved back a yard, pushed his shoulders back and puffed out his barrel chest. "Now. It's time we paid a visit to your parents to give them the joyful news."

Innes Clarke stood at the sink preparing lunch. The peeling knife flashed and swiped as she slaughtered the potatoes, reducing their original size by at least fifty percent. With little to choose between the severity of the knife or her tongue, John, her husband, did his best to stay out of the way; adding to Innes' view that, 'This terrible world has forsaken me.' The only person who seemed to listen to her was Granny Ciss, her virtually deaf octogenarian mother.

The back-door latch clacked, Innes looked up. The door opened and half a ginger head peered around it, momentarily pausing when it knew it had registered on Innes' radar. Then, with a small lurch as if he had been pushed from behind, Gerald sheepishly entered, escorted by a determined Dave. Innes stopped her work and as if frozen in a block of ice, coldly stared at the pair for a moment before acidly remarking, "Visitors normally enter this house through the front door."

Dave realised he had little time to waste before Innes went ballistic, and so came straight to the point. "Sorry, Mrs Clarke, but we must talk. This boy of yours has been up to no good; with my daughter!"

Innes dropped the peeling knife into the sink, her jaw dropped and her face flushed as she glared at her son. John cleared his throat and shuffled from one foot to another. "I think we had better sit down."

Dave fidgeted on the wooden chair, smoothed back his hair and began. "Your boy and my daughter were together last month. And they, well they... they were intimate together."

Innes turned to face her son. Coldly, with a slight growl she asked, "Is this true?"

The ashen Gerald croaked, "Yes."

"That is not all, Mrs Clarke." Dave looked sternly at Innes. "I have to report that the doctor confirmed my daughter Angela's pregnancy this morning."

"What makes you think it was Gerald?"

Dave uncompromisingly leaned forward. "Because my daughter says so! There was no other boy. Angela was not out of the house at any other time, except when she was with your son."

Innes placed her hands together on her lap and closed her eyes. She remained motionless for five seconds, which seemed like five minutes to the assembled company, before she slowly opened her eyes and stared down at her feet. None dared interrupt her. All awaited the explosion.

She took a deep breath, and turned towards Dave. For the first time in her life, she spoke quietly and imperturbably, "I, and I am sure, you, do not want the scandal that this will bring should the matter remain unsanctified." She closed her eyes before continuing.

"I am sorry, but I have to use this disgusting word, but now that we know she is," Innes swallowed and composed herself, "***pregnant.*** We must make plans for the wedding, you can't leave these things too long."

Innes turned to her son once more. "You'll have to marry her if she is with child. You know this, don't you?"

Gerald's mouth was so dry that his tongue felt twice its size as he nervously glanced at Dave. "Yes, Mother."

The kettle hissed on the hob and Granny Ciss gently snored. The tabby cat on her lap showed his mistrust of the situation by keeping one slit eye open on the proceedings. Innes glared daggers at her only son, her eyes indicating pre-eruptional earth tremors. "Well," she said in her more normal tone, "It must be a white wedding. If we are quick, they could get married at St Stephen's. We might get away with it; it is wartime. We can say it's because Gerald's call-up is imminent." She nodded and stared at her white knuckled fists. "It might work."

"My thoughts too, Mrs Clarke. I'll talk to my wife and she will contact you."

"Of course. Now if you'll excuse us, Mr Green, I wish to talk to Gerald, alone."

Dave bid his goodbye and left by the back door, accompanied by the uneasy cat. He had not gone more than ten paces when he heard a loud metallic crash come from the kitchen. Followed by a screech and more crashes. He quickly mounted his bike and hot-biked it home.

Dave informed Ethel and Angela about the proceedings and that in his opinion a wedding should take place within the month. "The 'happy couple' can live here. I could do with the help on the farm. We shall all go to the evening service at St Stephen's on Sunday, we need to get on the right side of the vicar. Until then, Angela, you will remain in your room and reflect upon your sins."

Following a lot of crying, sighing and a pious attendance at St Stephen's, 'Mrs Gerald Clarke' gradually became the dominant echo in Angela's head, and she became calmer. She thought of the dance, the barn, his eyes, his skin, a wedding, a baby, happy families, and, Mrs Gerald Clarke.

Gerald and Angela had no further contact until the following Thursday, when they met by chance in the village as she was riding her bike.

She dismounted and appealingly gazed at him, reached out and touched his hand. He uncomfortably glanced left and right. Angela hugged him, rested her head on his chest and let out a satisfied sigh. Gerald shuffled his feet and checked the horizon again.

They were kissing when Gerald broke it off, and in his most sincere voice said, "Don't you think we are too young to marry? After all, there's a war on, I might get killed and you would be a widow." Angela's eyes widened. He rested his hands on her shoulders and sighed before continuing, "This might be a big mistake, because even if I do survive, we may go off each other."

Angela hung her head before returning her eyes to his. "We cannot think about what might be, Gerald. Many couples marry precisely because it is wartime and they want to show their love. Just as importantly, we have the baby to think of. It must have married parents and after all, you have already promised my father you will marry me."

Gerald pulled her to him and as she rested her head on his chest, pondered his future. *The first time I do it, and I get caught. I hope Sue is OK. Must be, she would've told me by now. Maybe it takes longer from woman to woman, don't know. That would really complicate things.* **Fuck!**

He just about stopped himself stamping his foot.

I'll have to face up to my responsibilities. I'll never get another girlfriend if I don't. **OR.** *I could lie about my age and join the army early. No, might get shot. Huh. By the Jerries or her old man, what's the difference.* He gently squeezed her and said, "I love you."

Angela burst out crying, "I love you too. Everything will be wonderful, you'll see," she snivelled. After a long tender kiss, Gerald gazed over Angela's head into the distance towards 'their barn.'

He fondly remembered his first love with her. What had happened in that same barn with Sue Moore. And what had happened with Sue down by the bridge only thirty minutes before meeting Angela today.

11.

Glen Kannock in peacetime and on a sunny day, would have looked beautiful surrounded by its wild heather covered hills. Long-horned highland lurked in the glens, where they could feast on the lush green grass. They could find shelter from the elements behind short, windblown trees that grew near the crystal clear streams.

Glen Kannock in autumn 1944 was a different proposition; cold, wet and windy. The wild heather covered hills would soon become snow-capped and were as forbidding as the blot on the landscape that was Prison Camp 229.

Surrounded by a double wire fence and overlooked by watchtowers, the German compound contained about eighty huts laid out in a 'U' shape around a sloping parade ground facing the adjoining British compound. Also surrounded by barbed wire, it boasted three large gun emplacements positioned to threaten the main gate of the prisoners compound. "Welcome to Scotland," Franz cursed to himself as he surveyed the dismal view. "Welcome to Hell."

The new arrivals stood in line on the parade ground and waited to be addressed by the camp commandant. As they did so, some groups of inmates gathered and formed a gallery a few yards further back. A rough looking crew, these spectators scowled at the proceedings as they slouched around with their hands in pockets. They resembled a pack of hyenas biding their time for the lion to finish eating before they ravaged the carcass themselves.

"The Lion," as he had become known amongst the Germans, was a somewhat euphemistic description of Colonel James Bushel, Commandant of Camp 229, Glen Kannock, Perthshire. A man who, due to his connections and his own indifference to his fellow officers, had managed to miss out on a lot of the wartime action but had found a niche as a jailer. Consequently, someone in the war office had decided that Scotland would be the best place for him. Bushel however, whilst happy being a POW commandant, did not like being 'miles from anywhere in bloody Scotland.' He often gave the impression of a frustrated and bored man who found amusement at other people's, notably the prisoner's, expense.

A guard sergeant called the parade to attention. A command largely ignored by the Germans. "The Lion" cleared his throat to speak. No sooner had he done so than a loud chorus of exaggerated coughs answered him from the direction of the ever-growing crowd of raucous spectators. The colonel ignored this and began his discourse, all of which meant nothing to those lined up before him, as they could not understand any English. After a few sentences he paused and a captain attempted to translate the colonel's words into German.

The captain was a rather puny product of the English public school system. His poor German combined with his accentuated upper class accent, produced an incomprehensible translation to the ensemble. As soon as he opened his mouth a chorus of loud guffaws rang out from the POW's. Men doubled up, even cried with laughter. Without knowing it, the captain mispronounced so many words that many of them took on completely different connotations and meanings. This led to loud, exaggerated jokes and simulated pronouncements from the hyenas.

The more the Germans laughed the more the colonel sneered, as if to pre-empt some explosion of retribution. All he could muster as soon as the captain had finished was "Carry on, sergeant," whereupon the two British officers turned on their heels and with cheeks puffed out in exasperation, stiffly marched off to the Officers Mess for an even stiffer single malt whisky.

The sergeant scrutinised a clipboard before he bawled, "Private Schmidt. F." Franz was a little surprised to hear his name and took some seconds before he answered. The sergeant strutted over and came to a halt in front of him.

As if in possession of X-ray eyes, he scanned the young German up and down twice before accentuating his lip movement to the extent that he looked like a circus clown and said, "You – can – speak – Eng – lish – can – you?"

"A little bit, yes."

"We have a job for you. You will be the new liaison assistant between the authorities and the prisoners. You will work as assistant to the senior German officer, Rear Admiral Schwanz. Do you understand? Every communication will come through you. Do you understand?"

"Yes."

"Yes what?"

"Yes, sergeant." The sergeant seemed satisfied and dismissed the parade.

"Are you the English speaker?" snapped a commanding voice with Hanoverian clarity. Franz turned to see an erect looking naval officer standing to address him. "I am Konteradmiral Schwanz."

Franz snapped to attention and gave an army salute to the officer, at which another officer standing next to the admiral barked, "Heil Hitler!" as his arm shot up into the Nazi salute. Franz automatically followed suit.

"At ease, private," Schwanz interjected, "you will be my spokesman when I deal with the British. You will translate everything I tell you to say and everything that they say accurately, without bias."

"Yes, sir."

In March 1940 Konteradmiral Erich Schwanz had decided to observe the systems and crew performance on a U-boat proving voyage off the Scottish coast when the U-boat hit a mine and sank in shallow water in the Firth of Forth. Schwanz and the crew were rescued without loss. He had always been the Senior German Officer in every camp he had ever been in and as such imposed a Nazi discipline on every other inmate. This had been well received in the early days of the war when hope was still high among the POW's of a swift German victory.

However by 1944 discipline problems had arisen, particularly amongst inmates from the regular army who had had enough of the Nazi doctrine and wanted a quiet life for the duration. When such subversive episodes arose, Schwanz always relied on the tried and trusted Nazi intimidation and punishment methods meted out by his henchmen.

The British often turned a blind eye to such "internal altercations," but when the camp hospital population swelled they had to take notice. 'Moles' identified Schwanz as an ideological troublemaker and so he was often moved.

Schwanz was not unique. The British identified many agitators and troublemakers and resolved to put them all out of harm's way into special camps. These camps also contained those prisoners of whom it was thought were at the very least Nazi sympathisers if not devotees, notably SS, Paratroops and U-Boat crews. Most went to Canada and America; Schwanz went to Glen Kannock.

Nearly all of the POW's in Glen Kannock wore a black patch on their clothes; some wore grey. Franz bore the only white patch.

12.

"It's time to break the ice, Gerald. You must come to the farm and at least talk to my mother."

Ethel saw them walking up the drive holding hands and having decided that now was the time to have her say, strode out to intercept them at the gate. In a doom-laden tone like Neville Chamberlain declaring war, Ethel began her long-prepared speech.

"Well, Gerald Clarke, my daughter is with child. Now you will have to live up to your responsibilities as a man, although you are hardly that, and as a husband. What has happened has happened and that is that." She addressed them both as she added, "You are both very stupid and immoral children. I never thought such disgrace and scandal would ever land on my doorstep. How can I ever look my neighbours in the face again?" Her bottom lip started to quiver. "Heaven only knows what will become of you but one thing is sure, you will both make the best of this for everyone's, especially your child's, sake. Nothing less will do!" Tears in her eyes, she stalked off.

Angela hugged Gerald who rested his head on hers. "This pregnancy is not what we wanted to happen, at least not yet, but I know I love you and you love me. I know you will make a wonderful husband. I will do my best to make you a good wife. I am sure Dad will be OK, he has been coming to terms with this since his explosion that day. Perhaps it's better if we let Mum cool down a bit, although we mustn't leave it too long. Come to the farm again tomorrow after work."

Although they now allowed him to visit, Dave and Ethel were at best only tolerant of Gerald, at worst frosty. At visiting times, Gerald always checked the horizon as he tiptoed to the farmhouse door and rapped the doorknocker at arm's length. Angela would grab her coat and tow him away from the house as quickly as possible.

Angela and Gerald stopped to cuddle under the river bridge. It was a little cold and Angela opened Gerald's jacket so that she could wrap her arms around him to keep warm and feel loved. Then she noticed a red smudge on his white shirt just above his breast. "Oh." Angela lifted her head and scrutinised the patch. "What's this red smudge?"

Gerald stiffened. "Red smudge?" He looked down and examined his shirt.

"I thought it was blood," Angela said, "no, maybe paint?" She rubbed it with her fingers. "No, it's not stiff. It's slightly greasy." Angela gave Gerald a puzzled look. "Lipstick? Gerald, are you OK? Your face is a similar colour. Why are you blushing?"

"I'm not blushing, it's the cold wind on my face. Maybe it is lipstick on my shirt." Angela's eyes opened wide. "My mother said she had lost her lipstick in the bathroom this morning. My shirt was also in there. Her lipstick must have fallen down and smudged my shirt on the way."

"You said your mother was an old fashioned stick-in-the-mud. She wears lipstick?"

"She's just started. 'Wants to modernise for the wedding."

Angela sighed. "Oh good. For a moment, I thought that you had another girlfriend."

Gerald burst into exaggerated, almost relieved, laughter, "No, no, no. I love you, Angela. No girlfriends."

Angela smiled weakly, turned her head away from the smudge and resumed her cuddle. *I do hope it's his mother's lipstick. Yes, must be. He's not a two-timer, he loves me.* She hugged him.

Gerald's blushes receded. He stamped his foot. "Getting colder now. Let's go."

They had now decided that as she was already pregnant, and because they were going to get married, then it no longer made any difference what they did, or how often. He would move slowly whilst they gently kissed. She gave him gentle vaginal squeezes whilst she stroked his soft-skinned back.

Sometimes, when he was inside her, she visualised Gerald placing the ring on her finger at their wedding. *Mrs Gerald Clarke. Good morning, Mrs Clarke, Mrs Gerald Clarke, How do you do, Mrs Clarke.* Her orgasm would pulsate for ages. A week before the wedding as they lay in the hay, Angela asked, "What shall we call the baby?"

Gerald opened his eyes. *Why does she want to talk about that now?* "I don't know. Let's wait until we see if it's a boy or a girl."

Angela blinked several times and humphed, "We'll have to think about it before then. No, go on, you must have thought about it. You must have an idea."

"Sue, or John, then."

Angela lifted herself up on one elbow and gave him a questioning look. "That isn't very original," she said. "You couldn't have thought about that for long." Her luscious breasts now hung in front of his face and ignoring her comment, he lifted his head to indulge himself. She moved away. "Don't you care what we call the poor little thing?"

"John is my father's name. It's a good name."

"And Sue is ordinary." Angela fastened her blouse and sat up.

"Sue is my aunt's name," Gerald said. Angela lay down again. Silence reigned. *Why did I say Sue?* Gerald thought.

Angela sat up. "What do you think about Anne? Or Winston if it's boy?"

"I can think of nothing more stupid than calling our son after Mister Churchill."

"What's wrong with the Prime Minister? He's a fine man, we owe him a lot."

"Common people call their children after public figures. No. If it's a boy, we'll call him John."

"Common! Who do you think you are Mister La-Di-Dah Gerald Clarke? What do you mean, 'we'll call him John?' You've decided, have you?"

"Yes."

Angela burst into tears. "I wanted to be fair, and ask you what you think. But no, *you* must decide. Well, *I* will not have it. I do *not* want John. I want a name that we've discussed and agreed. If ever I heard a common name, it's John. No chance!"

Gerald pushed Angela away and sat bolt upright. He clenched his teeth and shook before pounding the hay with his fist. "We'll call it John, and that's final!" He raised his eyes to meet Angela's, daring her to question him, which she did.

"Not with me it's not. If that's the way you want it to be, you can get lost!" She bit her lip, then questioned her intelligence.

"OK, I will," Gerald said as he pulled himself to his feet, dressed and strode towards the door. Angela sat wide-eyed in the hay with the sleeve of her blouse clenched between her teeth. On his way, Gerald swooped down and grabbed an old bucket from the floor. He wheeled the bucket around his head and, with an aggressive grunt, smashed it back onto the ground sending a cloud of dust into the air and rusty bits of bucket spinning all over the floor. Gerald huffed as he elbowed past the barn door before slamming it shut behind him.

Dust filled the air and Angela sobbed. "I was right to say that. I love him very much, but I don't want him to trample me. Oh God. I hope that was just a one-off." She flopped back in the hay and stared at the dusty wooden beams above. "Sue is also the name of that fat girl in the bakers shop. I've heard she's a right trollop. No. Definitely not 'Sue' for a daughter of mine."

It was twilight by the time Gerald looked over the privet hedge at the glowing light in her ground-floor bedroom. *Luck.* Yes, he could see her combing her hair. Remembering the squeaky gate, he vaulted over the top before creeping round the corner of the stone-built cottage and ducking under the protruding thatch. Another two steps and he reached her low-level window. She was sitting on her bed. Gerald tapped the glass.

Sue Moore spun around and jumped back in shock when she saw a face at the window, but fear turned to joy when she recognised Gerald. She skipped over to the window and opened it carefully. "Oooo, this is exciting," she cooed as she put her index finger to her lips and whispered, "would you like to come in?" He muscled his way in. She flicked her head in the direction of her parents' room. "You must be quiet, they're having a nap."

She looked him over and playfully sneered. "Couldn't get it today, eh?"

"Actually, yes. I did have it about an hour ago. You always tell me you're better than her, so I thought I would give you the chance to help me compare." He lay on the bed, put his hands behind his head and smiled cheesily.

"I'm not a whore, you know," she said as she undid her blouse. "You can't simply use me when you want." She dropped her skirt. "I've been bought up to have principles." She slipped her thumbs inside the elastic of her knickers and slowly pulled them down over her ample thighs. Gerald devoured every movement and was fully aroused by the time she knelt astride him and unbuttoned his trousers.

Six minutes and forty-three seconds later, as he buttoned up his trousers, Gerald turned and gave Sue a long, affectionate kiss. "Yes. Top marks. You're very good. See you, kid." He climbed out of the window and strolled off.

Sue covered herself up, closed the window and drew the curtains before shuffling over to her dressing table. On her way, she hooked her knickers up from the floor with her foot and caught them with one hand. Naked, she flopped down on her chair, put her elbows on the table, rested her head on the white flowery knickers and looked in the mirror. The knickers became wet from her tears. Sue had never cried over Gerald before.

He had used her. She had been happy to be used. She had wanted to be used. She liked a man to be a man. "But I don't want to be used in *that* way," she cried out.

Sue sobbed for a short time until she had enough control to whimper, "I wish he would stay a bit longer. Well, OK, he had to go. But, maybe once, just once, he could take me to the pictures or something." She screwed up her face and beat her dressing table with her fist. "Why did he have to give me that wonderful kiss?" She flopped on to her bed, hid her face in the pillow and silently cried herself to sleep.

Gerald jigged back to his house like a macebearer at the head of an Irish marching band. *No point in going back to Angela*, he thought, *she'll only talk weddings.*

A slight, but chilly, east wind accompanied the first Saturday in November 1944. From the cloudless sky, the low sun cast long shadows, but little heat, over the crunchy leaves covering the gravel path to the church door. The Church of St Stephen was cold. It was always cold in there, even in summer.

Angela was demurely dressed in a long white wedding gown that trailed a yard behind her. Beaming, she slowly walked up the aisle on her father's elbow. She wore a crown of woven autumn chrysanthemums and carried a bouquet of the same.

Gerald looked uncomfortable as he waited at the altar. His new suit was a little on the tight side, or so he said, which was the reason he gave for his red face and look of pain.

He had celebrated his stag night at the Queens Head the previous night. His mates had shackled a ball and chain to his ankle for the whole of the drunken evening and he had woken up with it still attached that morning. He wondered if he was about to gain the metaphoric version. However, the moment he looked into Angela's eyes, he melted. "You are the most beautiful woman I have ever seen."

Many of the ladies in the congregation unfolded their handkerchiefs and smiled as they dabbed away their tears of happiness.

Hidden high above in the gallery, to where she had crept unseen an hour before, Sue Moore wept for another reason.

At the reception, Innes managed to be civil to Angela, and made a point of praising her dress. Angela noted that her mother-in-law was not wearing lipstick.

13.

The only private possession of a prisoner in Glen Kannock was their wooden bunk and each of the Nissen huts that made up the Prisoners Camp had eighty such bunks. Franz was shown to his. The bunk gave out a loud squeak as it took his weight and a louder groan from the post joint when he lay down, followed by even louder abuse from the occupant of the bunk above who warned Franz not to be so energetic or otherwise he would suffer one hundred kilos of retribution when the upper bunk collapsed. He lay on top of an itchy wool blanket, which was at least clean. *I'll need this* he thought as a cold draft from the nearby window tickled his face.

Franz looked around and assessed his new home. Apart from the bunks, the only furniture in the hut consisted of two tables, four benches and a stove, which provided the only heating. As the ring of men jostling around this small fire in the middle of the hut endlessly discussed the greater glory of the Reich or the Jewish part in its inevitable demise, they absorbed any heat that might have radiated to the rest of the hut. Schwanz had the only single room in the camp at the end of Franz's hut, as was due to the Senior German Officer.

The bleak Scottish winter of 1944 would be one of the coldest winters on record and as winter set in it did its best to freeze everyone to death inside the hut, let alone outside. There were no showers and no running water, everything was frozen solid. Franz spent hours on his bunk wrapped in his blankets trying to keep warm.

Throughout the day, very bored men mostly squatted on the edge of a bunk or lay in it; the same faces, the same faces at every turn, every blink, in every view at every moment. Whilst doing his best to occupy his time by reading, it was impossible for Franz to find a single moment of real peace surrounded by games of cards, stories, discussions, disputes and other noises.

Franz's daily translation work as the official camp 'mouthpiece' with the British added a certain amount of variety and interest to his day. It also gave him the chance to ask for some educational books, which duly appeared.

The twice-daily roll-call parades were a real hazard. The parade ground sloped, and with so much ice underfoot, it was very difficult for the Germans to stand upright. Under their outer clothes the men often wrapped their bed blankets around their bodies as extra insulation. A practice that made them look a little portly. Looking like a rookery of Emperor Penguins, they would jig from foot to foot whilst flapping their arms to keep warm and avoid being completely covered by the frequent white dustings of snow. Conditions were just as unpleasant for the British, who did their best to complete formalities as soon as possible before returning to the warmth of their own huts.

Away from everyone he knew and loved, in with a group of arrogant Nazi's whom he hated and no end in sight, Franz's daydreams as he lay in his bubble on his bunk were varied. He thought of Freja and Josie, of home and his family. Did they know that he was still alive? Were they still alive?

Now the first German professor to head the English department of the most prestigious college, whichever that may be, at Cambridge University, he arranged scholarships for many outstanding young students from his homeland. He became a celebrity back home in Germany and won the Nobel Prize for literature. This of course required an acceptance speech in which he expressed how grateful he was to win such a prize and how he hoped that his success would inspire others who came from humble beginnings. The assembled scholars were impressed by his decision to use his prize money to found the Franz Schmidt foundation....

Then something would happen in the hut that snapped him back to reality and the good times came frustratingly to an end. He was sometimes able to take up his daydream where he left off, in fact he became quite good at it.

He scored the winning goal for Germany in the World Cup final. Yes, he was a success, he won medals, scored goals, saved them, became a hero, all of that and much, much, more. He was so versatile; he was good at everything. Soaring through creative infinity he often came to rest in his childhood.

Childhood had been a mixture of fun and fear for him. He relived the happy times fishing, playing fantasy games and playing football with Willi, Bernd, Dummer and Jan Ingit. The thoughts of these times never lasted very long, something in the hut always broke the spell, but he came back to reality with a smile. He dearly hoped that his friends had survived this terrible war. However, sometimes he came back to reality with clenched teeth and fists.

Bullying had been the fearful side of his childhood. His mother had always told him to "turn the other cheek" if anyone ever hit him. Being a good lad, he had always done this at the cost of many bruises. Why had he been so stupid?

Older boys picked on him without mercy and were it not for the fact that he was the best footballer in the school, and therefore accepted and respected by his own peer group, he hated to think how far this bullying would have gone. It stopped when he had enough and flattened one of them. Why hadn't he done it sooner? He never told his mother.

Those thoughts were for the day. In the comparative calm and anonymity of the night his mind became even more active. Only then did he have the time and the privacy to become a lover even greater than Rudolf Valentino. He dreamt of girls from home and he dreamt of Josie.

They would meet in a café and have a wonderful conversation during which, she laughed at all his jokes and tempted him with some come-on looks before they left to visit a cinema. Here they kissed and cuddled before he started to fondle her breasts and then as she opened her legs, slide his hand up her skirt until he reached the moist delights concealed in her hairy bush.

Later they made love under the stars on a riverbank, he did it again and again six, seven times and she loved it. Not only Josie.

Franz would also have the girl who looked down upon the frustrated inmates of his hut from the poster on the wall near the stove. He didn't know that the majority of the other men in his hut were simultaneously sharing her. They were all in their private night-time dream world that nobody mentioned, but everybody couldn't wait to enter. The necessary solo physical relief that habitually accompanied such dreams had to be accomplished with as little movement as possible under the blanket. Discovery would be just too much to bear. Just about the only private pleasure possible was usually followed by sleep.

The German prisoners received the same rations as the serving British soldiers who guarded them, which at that time turned out to be more than the civilian population received. However the cooking left a little to be desired so Franz often ate with his eyes closed, using his powers of imagination to their full limit. He imagined Schnitzel, Bockwurst, Saurkraut and Eisbein, Schweinebraten and Onions....

Role-call meant Franz stood next to the rear admiral in case Schwanz wished to speak to Colonel Bushel, as he frequently did. Schwanz was a natural 'nit-picker', always wanting to score points by complaining about something he perceived highlighted the inefficiency of the British.

Whenever this happened, Franz had noticed that some minor sanction occurred such as the lights going off fifteen minutes early or the next parade lasting fifteen minutes longer. Bushel also loved to irritate Schwanz by referring to him as his Royal Navy equivalent rank of Rear Admiral as opposed to his Kriegsmarine rank of Konteradmiral. Franz did his best to keep the peace between them. Dangerous, but he often left the parade ground with a smile, knowing that either side never really knew what he had said to the other.

Franz's responsibility and its consequent closeness with Schwanz, gave him a privileged position among the captives, belying his lowly rank and Wehrmacht unit. Some treated him quite warily, suspicious that one word could lead to a visit from Schwanz's enforcers.

After a few weeks Schwanz became friendlier towards Franz. He even offered his young communicator a cup of coffee and a piece of cake. Franz accepted out of politeness but continued to feel very awkward in the presence of the officer. Schwanz's normally cold blue eyes seemed a little warmer as he asked Franz a little about his family and any girlfriends.

Franz, as ever, answered truthfully that he didn't have a girlfriend and when pressed upon the subject, that he had never had one.

"Oh, a virgin soldier?" enthusiastically piped up an astonished rear admiral. He leaned forward and gently tapped Franz's hand and whispered, "Don't worry lad, it's our little secret."

14.

Christmas was a very lonely time for all the prisoners at Glen Kannock, although they did their best to make the atmosphere more bearable and to jolly-up the huts. Men made decorations from whatever they could, toilet paper, ration boxes, even corned beef tins and strung them from their bedposts, the rafters, everywhere. On Christmas Eve they all sang carols before they got very drunk on some homemade potato schnapps.

Schwanz, who had become progressively friendlier to Franz, even gave him a model U-boat he had carved, which was given with the usual warm smile and pat on the back. *It cannot be right that a konteradmiral gives a present to a private. I'll have to accept it. I have to stay on the right side of this bastard. One word and...* "Thank you, sir."

Any headaches that may have lingered from the schnapps were dispelled some days later as news filtered through about the Ardennes offensive, or 'Battle of the Bulge' as it became known. All the Germans were lifted by this, the Führer was coming to free them. This galvanised Schwanz into action as he had also heard about a planned uprising of all POW's if the 'Bulge' offensive was a success.

At this time over three hundred thousand German prisoners of war were in Britain, considerably more combat manpower than the British, whose troops were mostly overseas. If a mass breakout and seizure of weapons from the numerous weapons storage facilities happened, it might be possible that the 'Trojan Horse' could work once more.

Schwanz held many planning meetings in his room; if this plan was to succeed they must be prepared. The camp was to be formed into four companies that were each given a command structure and specific objectives as far as could be ascertained from geographical knowledge gained from the escape committee. Preparations were at fever pitch, men began to smile.

This euphoria disappeared with a mighty thump when it was learnt that both the offensive and uprising had failed, the former for military reasons the latter through treason. Someone had informed and the SS wanted vengeance.

In the middle of January a new intake of prisoners arrived; mostly 'Blacks,' ten 'Greys' and this time, two more 'Whites.' A great deal of suspicion surrounded these two 'White' arrivals. They had been transferred from the camp near Devizes that had been at the centre of the planned rebellion.

Among the 'Blacks' were two men who were also from Devizes and who took no time at all in pointing the finger at the two 'Whites.' The British had moved them as far away from Devizes as possible for their own safety, but some corporal somewhere, had blundered; he had sent them straight out of the frying pan into the hottest of all fires. Schwanz heard the news and called a court-martial of the two 'traitors' for that evening in his hut. "We will find the truth and deal with the liars."

Later that day a tired and depressed Schwanz called Franz into his room. "Shut the door lad. Come and sit down over here." Schwanz motioned Franz to join him as he sat on the only sofa in the camp.

"No thank you, sir. I prefer to stand."

"Sit down when a senior officer tells you to." Franz sat down on the edge at the opposite end of the sofa. The rear admiral's eyes fluctuated between warmth and desperation. The older man looked at the younger man for a few seconds, before he moved closer and placed his hand on Franz's thigh.

He leant towards Franz and whispered through lips that had thinned, "Don't be nervous. You know I like you. Everyone has to have a first time sometime." A globule of saliva appeared in the corner of Schwanz's mouth. He moved closer until his body touched the now sweating private soldier.

Schwanz leant further forward and began to kiss Franz on the cheek and as he did so his hand moved up Franz's thigh and fumbled with his crotch.

Breathing heavily, Schwanz turned to come even closer and put his arm around his victim's head. The sleeve of his jacket brushed the face of the lad. It was a rough jacket, like sand paper, a horrible feeling which although so short in duration, was to remain with Franz for the rest of his life.

Franz squirmed free. "Don't touch me. I don't want it."

"Stay calm. Don't be nervous. I'll be gentle"

"Be gentle with someone else, sir, not me."

"You will do as I tell you," fizzed the rear admiral. His expression hardened as he gripped Franz's shoulders. "Now undo your belt."

Franz hardened his expression and ignoring all rank, went on the offensive. "The Führer has said that all homosexuals are depraved and should be wiped out from society. Do you want everybody out there to know that you have contravened one of the proclamations of our great and beloved leader? Do you want everyone, and I might say *everyone*, to know?

"Everyone includes Colonel Stannesmann, who as both you and I know wants to be senior officer and would love to find a reason to remove you from your position. Unless you let me go at this very moment, I shall tell him." Franz's look of strength and determination burned into the startled officer like gamma rays from a super-nova.

Schwanz drew breath to reply, but before he could do so, the young private gripped the rear admiral around the throat and continued, "I can get out of here and get to him before you can call for help because I'm bigger and stronger than you. Even if you do call for help and get me killed, mud sticks! The suspicion of you will remain, and your days will be numbered."

The two men glared at each other, the only sound was the choking noise coming from Schwanz. "I am going to take my hand away now and we are not going to say any more about this are we." Franz released his grip and Schwanz slumped back on the sofa. They both shook.

"Get out," hissed Schwanz through clenched teeth.

Franz did not stop by his bunk; he went straight outside into the cold evening air. His emotions ran away with him. He was proud that he had been so brave as to stand up for himself in such a situation. He shook, but who would believe him? *Only a private against a konteradmiral, whom I have physically assaulted. That look in Schwanz's eyes, his lips, the feel of his hand moving up my leg, and the kisses. Oh my God the kisses!* He stood still and placed his hand on his stomach as he became queasy. *The jacket. That feeling of roughness. The hand probing and fumbling between my legs. Ugh.* Franz threw up and as he did so, the wind blew his vomit back over his boots and trousers.

He didn't feel the cold, he didn't see the snow and he didn't see the wire. He just ran until he fell over the trip-wire that was laced around the compound perimeter, a few feet in front of the main wire. He rubbed the snow into the part of his face that the rough jacket had touched. He opened his trousers and stuffed snow into his underpants. *I can still smell him in my nostrils. That jacket, brushing my face. Ughhh.* He retched again.

He sat, raised his hands to his face and burst into tears. "You had to do something, but that? Schwanz'll get you. You'll have an 'accident'. You're a dead man, you won't see home again." He clenched his fists and flopped, face down, into the snow.

"Get up. You have gone over the trip wire without permission. You're on a charge, my son, unless you get back quickly," barked a highland accented voice. Franz turned to look up the barrel of a '303' rifle and into the face of a moustachioed guard who glared at him through a pair of large, bloodshot eyes.

"I want to speak to the colonel. I am Private Schmidt, Konteradmiral Schwanz's English Liaison."

"Oh is that so? Well why didn't you come to the main gate as usual?"

No answer. The guard humpfed and lowered his rifle. "Anyway, come with me." Franz brushed himself off and walked in front of the guard to the main gate, which he passed through as normal just as he did two or three times a day as part of his liaison duties. However since the weather had got very cold, Schwanz rarely came with him, so it was also normal for him to see the colonel alone. Franz was now perspiring. *This whole situation is just running away with you. You are lurching from one disaster to another. Get a grip on yourself!*

Franz drew a deep breath as he approached the commandant's office. He clenched his fists and whispered to himself, "Stay cool, you've got to stay cool and see this through. If you don't, you will die. This is your only chance. Stay cool. Think!"

The colonel was seated as usual behind his large oak desk. The room was warm, it had a good paraffin heater, a picture of the King and Queen on the wall but very little else in the way of furniture. The colonel looked up as the young German stood to attention and gave a military salute.

"What can I do for you now, Schmidt? It's a bit late in the day to come to see me isn't it?" The colonel scanned the dishevelled private up and down. "Your jacket is soaking wet. Take it off and hang it by the fire." Franz removed the jacket and hung it over the back of a chair facing the heater.

Returning to the colonel, he said, "I have a question for you, sir."

"Go ahead."

"I am going to be killed, sir. Can you get me transferred to another camp?"

"What the blazes do you mean, man? Tell me what's happened."

After he heard Franz's explanation, the colonel wore a pained expression.

He puffed out his cheeks, shook his head. "Don't come here wasting my time with your 'lovers tiffs'. This sort of thing used to happen all the time when I was away at school. It was part of being a fag to a prefect. We learnt to take it like a man and certainly didn't go blubbing to a teacher! Go back and make up with him. Don't waste my time again." The colonel looked back down at his papers spread out on his desk and resumed his work. The interview was over.

Franz returned to the camp the way he had come and hoped that any Germans who saw him would assume that he was on camp business and ignore him. *What am I going to do now? I must keep this episode quiet. You are so dumb, acting without thinking. How stupid, how very stupid! This situation's getting worse by the second. Now you're even more alone.* "God! Every time the wrong option," he muttered, "and you've forgotten your jacket." He hesitated by the door to his hut, *Will I be met by the hangman?*

Stannesmann! He's your only chance. Franz could hear a lot of noise coming from the hut. *The court-martial, will they go for a full house and make it three whites? Franz, you acted quickly and coolly when Schwanz attacked you, trust yourself. You always rise above it when the chips are down. Trust yourself.* He took a deep breath and cautiously opened the door.

Many other men had arrived to witness the proceedings. A table had been placed in front of the stove. It had been coloured red with a black Swastika drawn in the middle. Behind the desk was seated a gaunt Rear Admiral Schwanz, who was flanked by a resolute Colonel Stannesmann and the black unformed Colonel Bormann. Seated and facing the table, were the two accused, both shaking. Schwanz looked through Franz as if he wasn't there, no flicker of emotion. The room was soon full, two hundred men were in attendance and every hut was represented. Schwanz cleared his throat and ordered all cigarettes extinguished.

The two "Black" accusers were hailed as heroes by the ensemble as they described their part in the uprising plan. They described all that they had done and planned to do, often to muted cheers and gasps from the transfixed throng.

They told how the British arrived as if by magic and how they and the other ringleaders were taken away to be questioned. "It was clear," they said, "we must have been informed upon." They mooted how it all seemed to fit together that the two accused "Whites" were both employed as cleaners in the British Officers Mess, that they were friendly with all the British and were both of Hungarian origin. Heads all around the hut nodded their agreement to every detail of the evidence. The

"Whites", who were ordered to be quiet each time they had dared to interrupt, stared at the floor.

Then it was their turn. They protested their innocence as they remonstrated with the tribunal that the evidence was all circumstantial and that it was just bad luck that the British had walked in on a meeting as part of their normal patrols. Various hands, belonging to faces that looked as if they had a smell under their nose, were waved dismissively in the 'Whites' direction. Their evidence was not allowed to take long and they were not allowed to cross-examine the "Blacks". The evidence over, the tribunal retired to consider its verdict.

In the confines of the rear admiral's room, the verdict was never in doubt; nor the punishment. What was in doubt was how to do it and make it look like an accident or suicide. There came a knock at the door, which opened without waiting for an answer. "British!"

The three senior officers returned to the main room to see men milling around in all directions; some bed blankets had been spread over the swastika and some books placed on it. Within five seconds it looked as though a lecture was taking place, just as the door opened and the British duty sergeant entered.

He was taken aback at the number of Germans in the hut. He saw Franz and walked over to him. The sergeant held a German jacket in his outstretched hand. "You left your jacket in the colonels office. Here it is."

A very pensive Franz stepped forward and retrieved his jacket. The sergeant looked around once more, turned on his heel and went into the night without saying another word. Franz stood alone in the silence holding his jacket. He was the focus of attention of two hundred pairs of very suspicious eyes. "When were you visiting the colonel?" rasped Schwanz.

"About a half an hour ago. It was all a mistake."

"What do you mean, a mistake?"

Franz snapped to attention, took a deep breath and looked the rear admiral in the eye as he replied calmly and with a smile,

"I didn't feel well after our last meeting, so I went for a walk and some fresh air."

Colonel Stannesmann gave Schwanz a short sideways look. He had had his suspicions about the konteradmiral's sexual orientation for some time. The private should be expressionless and look straight ahead when addressing an officer. *This must not be! And, the konteradmiral has **not** admonished him.* Could this be the evidence that he needed to put one over on the Kriegsmarine and remove his adversary once and for all?

Schwanz noticed the colonel's bewildered look out of the corner of his eye, but chose to ignore it. Franz continued, "I was walking near the fence and fell over the trip wire in the snow. The guard took me to the colonel."

"Why the colonel and not the duty sergeant?" interjected Stannesmann who was glared at by Schwanz for presuming to steal his question.

"I don't know, sir."

"And are you in the habit of taking off your jacket when you are visiting your *friend* the British colonel, *alone*?" Without waiting for the answer, Stannesmann looked at the kontoradmiral.

"I shall ask the questions, Colonel Stannesmann," Schwanz said.

"Answer the question, Schmidt."

"No, sir. It was just that my jacket was wet and for some reason the colonel told me to take it off and put it near a heater whilst I explained myself."

"And what did you explain? Did you explain about tonight's court-martial? Is that why the sergeant came in just then?"

"No, sir. I just told him that I fell over the wire, sir. I didn't know that the sergeant would come in then. That was just coincidence."

"It seems that soldiers who wear white patches have a lot of coincidences."

As it was not a question, Franz did not answer but decided to continue to look at the kontoradmiral. This uncorrected insubordinate look had brought Stannesmann to boiling point, as it seemed to him that the private was talking with his eyes. Something was definitely amiss here. Should he risk interrupting again? Yes. He drew breath when...

"British!"

"I will question you about this later, Schmidt, now move away," Schwanz said out of the side of his mouth as the door burst open. In came the British security officer accompanied by the duty sergeant and a platoon of determined looking guards. It was the well-bred captain.

"What is happening here, rear admiral?"

"We are learning, captain." Schwanz answered in English.

"What are you studying?"

Schwanz did not understand the question and so the captain turned and looked at Franz to translate. But rather than translate Franz blurted out, "English."

This prompted a fierce glare from Schwanz. "What's going on, Schmidt? Translate immediately."

Franz did not answer as he watched the captain who had noticed the two frightened and ashen white patch prisoners, whose expressions implored the officer to help.

Without comment, the captain walked over to the table. "Rather unusual to have blankets draped over a table for an English lesson," he commented. "No books, no paper." He dislodged one of the blankets to expose a patch of red coloured wood, a further sweep of his hand exposed the Swastika.

"Why do you have this illegal flag, rear admiral? What is going on here?" Without waiting for the translation or the answer he turned back to look at the two cowering 'whites.' He now recalled who they were and why they had been transferred. He further recalled that he had advised Colonel Bushel that it was a mistake to receive these men at Glen Kannock and that they represented a security risk but that the colonel, as ever, showed little concern for the problem. In fact Bushel had even sniggered to himself in a macabre way. The captain turned around and surveyed the scene. It was a veritable who's who of the prisoner community, every hut was represented, all the hard liners. "This is a kangaroo court."

Franz stared at him, he didn't understand 'Kangaroo Court.' "I don't know what you mean?" questioned Franz.

"Oh you don't do you. "Swastika," he pointed at the table. "Accused," he gestured in their direction. "Everyone here," he gestured to the back of the room. "This is no English lesson, this is a kangaroo court."

"No. I don't understand the meaning of kangaroo court," interjected Franz.

All this talk between the captain and Franz without a word of translation was too much for Colonel Stannesmann who knew a rat when he smelt it. "What are you telling your English friends, Schmidt? Tell us what you are saying."

Franz explained to the sceptical Stannesmann that it was a translation problem but before he had finished the captain butted in. "What is the captain saying, Schmidt? What is going on here?"

Remembering his conversation with Colonel Bushel earlier on that evening and his rebuffed request, Franz saw his chance to illustrate his point that he was in danger, so he translated Stannesmann's question word for word.

The captain surveyed the hyena pack once more and was now clearly sweating. "Get back to your huts. All of you." The sergeant raised his gun, "Move!" After the hut emptied, he requested that Schwanz and his translator accompany him to see Colonel Bushel.

They walked in silence for a few yards. Franz realised that he was now a 'dead man walking,' or at least in very serious danger of physical injury from both Stannesmann and Schwanz, all be it for different reasons. *Got to go for broke.*

Looking at the glowering Schwanz he whispered, "I want to get out of here and you don't want Stannesmann to know that you are a homosexual." A shocked looking Schwanz tilted his head to one side. Franz continued, "Colonel Bushel enjoys making you uncomfortable. If I tell him what you are, he will certainly enjoy letting Stannesmann know.

"After we have denied what was really going on back there, you can use the excuse that the other officers are suspicious of my translations to the British and that it is now a dangerous environment for me and that maybe I should be transferred elsewhere for my safety. Do that. Get me transferred, and you are safe." Schwanz clenched his teeth, looked ahead and said nothing.

15.

The New Year came, and so did Angela's bump. Gerald was affectionate to her, when they did not argue about one of his ideas or the baby's name. However, he went out every Friday evening, alone. *Why alone? He never gives me a straight answer. Spends a long time in the bathroom. All that, for his mates? I wonder if any of them wear red lipstick? Don't be so stupid, Angela, it can't be...,*

She decided to see if Helen had any answers.

"I heard Gerald was seen talking to that Sue Moore last Friday. And I've seen him in the baker's with a big smile on his face and her looking bashful.

"I'm not saying anything's happening, Angela.

"Don't get so defensive. You asked me what I knew. If you didn't want to hear it, you shouldn't have asked. Watch out for her, Angela, that's all. She's been putting herself about a bit with the U.S Air Force from what I've heard.

"Yes, she does wear red lipstick. Must get it from the Yanks, for services rendered.

"Make sure you keep giving Gerald a nice time. Don't let him, or yourself, go."

On the last Friday in January, Angela looked in the mirror and prodded the three recently erupted facial spots. "I look so ugly. No wonder he goes out alone." Her head dropped and she started to cry. Deep, passionate sobs. *Snap out of this, Angela! If you always look and act miserably, he definitely won't want you.* She wiped her tears away and slapped her thighs. "I'll try my best when he comes home, it'll be dark then."

Gerald returned home at one o'clock in the morning. He crept in, undressed and slid into bed. Angela put her head under the blankets and moved down, but stopped, sniffed and slowly returned to her original position.

Gerald began to sweat, his mouth went dry. *Oh shit!*

16.

The two Germans walked to the Commandant's office in silence. Both looked confused. They mounted the steps from the footpath to the colonel's office and exchanged one quick glance before entry. Schwanz took a deep breath as his cold blue eyes drilled Franz. Franz pushed his shoulders back and looked ahead. Was this to be the end?

They entered to see the colonel looking at some signals on his desk. He always liked to appear to be at work and always took time before he looked up at his visitors. This time it seemed he was genuinely deep in thought as he stroked his chin and blinked rapidly whilst reading the message. They waited. Franz's full bladder forced him to squeeze his legs together.

Colonel Bushel looked up flicked his eyes from Schwanz to Franz and back again several times before he turned to his security officer and asked the captain for a report. The captain said that he thought that there had been a kangaroo court in progress and that he suspected that the two new 'whites' were the defendants. He added that also Franz seemed to be in some way implicated. The colonel, through Franz as translator, asked Schwanz what was going on.

"There was no court in progress, Colonel Bushel."

"Then what was the meeting about, Rear Admiral Schwanz? Why was the table coloured with a Swastika? Why the acid comments aimed at your translator here?"

"I repeat, there was no court, it was just a social evening and somebody must have amused themselves with the table." He paused, drew breath and his eyes drilled the colonel. "However, questions were raised against Private Schmidt. These questions centred on his visit to your office earlier today, why he was here and even more so, why he had removed his jacket?

"People are suspicious about the reasons for his solo visits and even though I have given assurances that they are official communication visits, sanctioned by me, others are not so sure. Colonel, my official sanction does not extend to the visit in question and I too am suspicious of why he was here earlier on his own initiative, and returned without his jacket."

The captain's expression changed. He looked shocked and even affronted at this revelation. He turned his head and glanced questioningly at the colonel. Bushel also looked shocked at the implication and even blushed a little whilst he returned an imploring look to the captain. The captain appeared to pout for a moment before he returned to the business in hand. He would have a few private questions of his own for the colonel later.

Bushel resumed commandant mode. "Whilst I respect your rank, rear admiral, I remind you that you are a prisoner here and that it is not for you to be impertinent to me! I should think that *you* would be the one who knows why this private was here earlier."

"I have no idea, colonel," replied Schwanz in a flat voice.

The colonel leaned back in his chair and looked down his nose at Schwanz, "Could this kangaroo court have had more to do with you in particular, rear admiral?" He paused. No answer came from the puzzled looking German. Bushel suddenly leant forward on his elbows, narrowed his eyes and looked into Schwanz's eyes. He paused again as he inwardly savoured every second of the rear admiral's growing discomfort before continuing.

"Could it have anything to do with any impropriety on your behalf that your fellow prisoners have heard?" He made a slight gesture with his finger in the direction of Franz, "Or would like to hear about? Is it true to say that such things between men are a matter for extreme disapproval in your society? Eh?"

Schwanz' lips had lost some of their colour, his scalp itched, his stomach turned. He glanced at Franz whose bowels felt as though they were about to empty but who held his nerve and returned the look with one of steely determination.

"Colonel Bushel," began Schwanz, "There was no, as you call it, "Kangaroo court" going on. It was just a social evening." The colonel drew breath in disbelief prior to a stern rebuff of such a denial.

Before he could deliver it Schwanz continued, his voice resumed authority, "But I feel that you should be aware of a potentially difficult situation that has arisen, which may be difficult to completely control bearing in mind that many of my men have been cooped up for so long.

"It has come to our notice that an offensive was planned in some other camps in England, but that this offensive did not take place due to treachery on the part of some prisoners bearing white patches. As you know, today some new 'white category' prisoners arrived and naturally, in the course of our social evening, some men had asked these men if they could shed any more light on the matter of the offensive. After some conversation on this subject, some of my men were suspicious towards these new arrivals.

"This in turn led to fingers being pointed at Private Schmidt because of course he is the only 'white' here and he does have direct contact with you. A fact highlighted by his jacketless return from your office." Schwanz now flowed with all the arrogance within him as he glanced in the direction of the captain before he offered, "Personally, after the jacket incident, I must say that I am not entirely sure what sort of contact that could be. But...," he shrugged his shoulders and turned once more to the colonel, "it is true to say that in the present situation sentiments amongst my men towards 'whites' are running high. It may be, although I will do my best to control things, that it becomes a little difficult to control any 'renegade' action. That could get messy, and I am sure that the colonel would not want such problems in his camp, would the colonel?"

"What are you suggesting?" Bushel asked.

"I am suggesting that because I am sure that you want no unpleasantness in your camp, that you transfer these new 'whites' a long way away from here immediately," as if in afterthought, he gestured towards Franz, "and this private too. Then we can all start with a clean slate." He half smiled and glanced at the captain.

The colonel sat back in his chair, stroked his chin and looked again at the signal from headquarters before he returned his look to the rear admiral. "If I agree to this request, can you guarantee that there will be no repetitions of today's kangaroo court?"

"I can guarantee that there will be no unfortunate incidents of any kind that will shake the equilibrium, Colonel Bushel."

"OK," replied the thoughtful colonel, much to the surprise of his security officer, who saw no reason to do a deal with Schwanz. Bushel turned to address the captain and added, "Captain, you can act as translator from now on." Schwanz made a slight grimace as Colonel Bushel looked back at him and said, "You can go back to the camp, Rear Admiral Schwanz. Captain, take Private Schmidt to the punishment block, he can stay there until he is transferred, and then get those other two 'whites' and put them in with him. Good night, Rear Admiral Schwanz."

After Schwanz had left but before the captain had taken a highly relieved Franz away, Colonel Bushel passed his captain the signal that he had been reading. The signal said that all commandants should be vigilant with new arrivals after an incident at nearby Cromrie camp. Here a newly arrived 'white' called Feldwebel Wolfgang Rosterberg, who was believed to have been involved as an informant on the planned uprising, was found hanged in the latrine after he had been severely beaten.

It further said that if commandants felt that they had any new arrivals that could be considered 'at risk', then they should be segregated, prior to immediate transfer.

17.

"I can smell what you've been doing, Gerald. You could have at least washed before you came to bed. Why? Why, Gerald? We've not long been married. I'm pregnant with your baby. Why? Why her? It is her, Moore, isn't it?"

"What do you mean, Sue Moore?" Gerald hissed indignantly.

"Oh! So you know her first name then. You know who I'm talking about. I heard that you've developed a liking for fresh bread. And what's more, your mother doesn't wear lipstick. Come on, Gerald, tell me the truth."

Gerald sighed, "Angela, it's quite normal to have a wife and a girlfriend, It's..."

"What's normal about carrying on when you've only been married for ten weeks, and you tell your wife that you love her?"

He banged his fist down on top of the blankets. "I do love you, you know that. It's only for the sex. A man has to show he is strong and that he has drive. Since your pregnancy has become obvious to everyone, most people must think we don't do it anymore, and they would expect that I must satisfy my needs. So it's quite normal."

Angela sat bolt upright and turned on the light; she clenched her fists and glared at him. "What do you mean most, people, would, expect? Who do you tell that needs to know? Do you boast about it up the pub? Do people laugh behind my back?" She turned away from him and clasped her head.

"Angela, it's simply a perfectly normal man thing. Actually, she's not very good, so it helps me appreciate you. Don't you see?"

Angela's little sobs were the only sounds in the room for some minutes until Gerald heavily sighed, pulled her around, rolled on top of her, and took her. She tried to push him off, but he persisted, and once inside, was gentle.

He repeated how much he loved her, how good she was in bed, and how proud he was that she would mother his baby son.

Angela tried to remind herself how angry she was, but became compliant. Much to her surprise, she had an orgasm. *An orgasm? After all that? How? Why?*

Moonlight had now illuminated the room and Gerald's tranquil post-coital face. Angela's discontented feeling returned, to the point that her stomach retched. She quietly went to the bathroom and washed, several times.

Returning to her bed, she lay on her back and placed her hand over her womb. For the first time she thought of it as her baby, not theirs. Her silent tears flowed again. She looked at the moon; it calmed her. She glanced at the lightly snoring Gerald. *An orgasm, I must still love him. How could he hurt me like this? Am I right to assume that he really loves me?* Her feeling of pain and insecurity returned, and was relentless.

Next morning, Gerald acted as if nothing had happened; he seemed particularly cheerful, falsely cheerful. Angela looked like a zombie. Ethel tried her best to find out what had happened but all to no avail. "Whatever's happened, you'll have to work it out. Your father and I have had our troubles too, but remember, Angela, till death us do part."

Gerald's manner changed as the week wore on; *Stupid woman. She doesn't understand me. Or men for that matter. How many times must I explain? She knows I still love her. I'm not leaving. We have fun together, well, mostly. What more does she want? I'll buy her some flowers tomorrow. That'll make her happy. They all like flowers.*

Friday came and Angela was beside herself. Would he go out? Gerald had avoided her gaze most of the day and had worked alone in the fields down by the river. He said little at dinner, but looked at the clock several times before going upstairs. A sallow Angela helped her mother clear up, and then followed him.

Hardly able to climb the stairs, her nausea welled up inside her. She paused and sighed as her hand rested on the door latch. "Please, no. Not this time," she whispered before gingerly opening the bedroom door.

There he stood, resplendent in his 'Friday Night' outfit of black trousers, checked shirt and waistcoat. He smiled at her lovingly. She fainted. When she came round, she lay on the bed and Gerald was mopping her brow with a damp cloth. He held her hand. "You've done a bit too much this week, my dear. Take it easy this evening, I won't be too late. Can I get you anything?" A blank stare answered him. "No? I'll be off then." He donned his jacket, blew Angela a kiss and went.

The intense pain started as Angela got up to go to the toilet. It was difficult to walk, and by the time she closed the toilet door, she knew something awful was happening inside her. The maelstrom gathered pace as the cramps in her stomach rose in intensity. Sitting on the toilet she grasped the washbasin. Her head spun and she started to bleed. *Can't call my mother. She'll fuss, fuss, fuss.* "Oh my God. Going to pass out. Mother! Help. Mum. Help."

Ethel immediately dispatched Dave on the tractor to get the doctor. Doctor Hastings arrived about fifteen minutes later, but too late to save the baby.

Gerald arrived back at the farm at about midnight, the empty faces of Dave and Ethel greeting him. Gerald showed no emotion when he heard the grave news. He merely hung up his coat, bade the Greens goodnight and went upstairs.

Angela looked sallow. The tranquilliser had relaxed her to the point where, in the gently flickering candlelight, her angelic appearance epitomised her name. Gerald sat gently on the bed, stroked her limp fingers and sighed deeply before noticing that she was looking at him appealingly.

A tear trickled down his cheek. "That's terrible luck, my love. I wanted it as much as you did, but if it wasn't to be, then it wasn't to be.

"The main thing is that you're OK. We'll have another chance, we'll have a big family one day." He stroked her cheek. "But you'll have to take it easier next time. As I said, you must have been doing too much work on the farm this week." Angela's eyes glazed, until, without a word, she closed them.

For the next few days, Gerald tried to be normal; he often cuddled and kissed Angela. She could not look at him. She concluded..., well, what conclusion was she coming to?

Getting married was all a mistake. Too rushed. But I still love him. I want to make this work. 'Till death us do part.' I suppose it's a woman's place to accept these things; a part of married life. She glanced at her parents. *I wonder if they've ever been through anything like this? If they had, they would never talk about it. Never.* She studied her father as he stared into the evening log fire. *I wonder if he has ever had a girlfriend. God! Such a thought has never occurred to me. Just what is normal for a man?*

Gerald continued to heap affection on his young wife, which included telling her that he could not wait to make love to her again.

A few days later it was Gerald's eighteenth birthday, and some of his friends came to the house for a party. They all drank cider and had a merry time, apart from Angela. She put on a brave face and physically joined in the laughter, but often shook her head as she watched Gerald in his element as the centre of attention.

She excused herself to go to bed at about nine o'clock, where she lay sobbing until her drunken husband came to bed two hours later. When he came to her, she hugged him so tightly that she shook. *Don't do this, Angela. Don't. But I **need** him....*

A week of turmoil preceded the arrival of the postman. Gerald's conscription orders had arrived and after basic training, Gerald Clarke left for Crete on 7 April 1945.

Exactly the same day as a nineteen year old German Prisoner of War, Franz Schmidt, arrived as his work replacement at Green Farm.

18.

This green island! Only repatriation could have made Franz happier. Compared to anywhere he had seen, in any book, in any film, England was the greenest place on earth. The fresh spring air invigorated him. He laughed at the springy legged lambs, sniffed the early spring flowers and whistled along with the birds. Cambridgeshire had woken up from hibernation, and so had he.

Shifting from foot to foot as he stood before Franz, Dave tightly clasped his hands in front of his chest. Loudly and exaggeratedly mouthing like a horse chomping a carrot, he asked, "DO-YOU-UN-DER-STAND-AN-Y-EN-GL-ISH?" As he awaited results, he studied Franz as if he was studying the intricate workings of a time bomb.

Franz composed himself and remembered that first impressions counted most of all. He remembered how he had once heard an English captain in his new camp at Drakesford introduce himself to another captain and how he had often practised the same words, in the same accent. Franz cleared his throat and stood to attention. He offered Dave his hand, and in a perfect Oxford accent said, "Certainly, old chap. My name is Schmidt, Franz Schmidt. How do you do?"

Dave looked like he had seen a ghost. "Cor blimey! A posh Jerry. Are you a V3?"

Franz looked puzzled. Dave recovered his composure and stood to attention. "Green, David Green. How do you do?" They shook hands. "Come with me, I'll show you what to do." Dave motioned Franz to come into the barn. As they walked, he flicked a suspicious look at the new arrival out of the corner of his eye, maybe this V3 was aristocracy?

The day passed quickly for Franz as he attacked every task with great gusto. Dave was impressed as was Ethel, although she kept her distance 'just in case.'

Franz found it a little difficult to adjust to Dave's accent and dialect, such as when they entered the tractor shed and Dave mumbled, "The chaos in here, 'don't know why 'tis."

Franz heard it as, "The Kaa - rs in 'ere, 'don't know wei 'tis" Franz looked around before giving Dave a blank look and half-heartedly pointing to the green tractor on his left. "Here it is. In Germany, we call it a traktor."

When the lorry from Camp 918, Drakesford, arrived at five o'clock, an exhausted Franz heaved himself up into the back and flopped down on the wooden bench with a huge smile. He looked at the lump of farmhouse cheese Ethel had given him and smiled at how carefully she had wrapped it in a white handkerchief. He inhaled its strong scent and took a little nibble; this was true heaven, a real luxury. Nevertheless, he shared it with his friend, Otto, back at camp. For the first time in a long time, he slept soundly. Prison camp? What prison camp?

Hedges. Everywhere. Hedges that divided the land up into a patchwork quilt made up of small fields and gates. This needed a lot of head scratching. Each field seemed to have its own colour or pattern, and its own shape, no two were alike. *There has to be a system. Everything must have order. It is simply a matter of finding it. It is easy in Germany, all the fields are regular squares and rectangles. OK, some fences for animals, but no hedges. We have order. Maybe they are trying to confuse the Luftwaffe! What is this English system?*

At lunch time on his third day, Franz had just come to the table when suddenly it sounded as though a heard of horses was descending the stairs. An even bigger surprise awaited him when the door swung open and in marched Angela. Franz's eyes widened. Their introduction was formal but friendly, a shake of the hand, a smile and an exchange of names before they sat down at the wooden kitchen table for lunch. Angela said little, except that she would go to the post office after lunch, to post her daily letter to Gerald. Ethel cleared her throat, this was the time to explain to Franz that her daughter was married to a young soldier. "Oh really, where is he based?" Franz enquired.

"Can't tell you that," Ethel snapped, "It's secret." Dave and Angela tutted in unison.

Franz gulped. *Secret? He might be a special agent. After all, look at his wife; she is beautiful, and don't the top soldiers always get the best women? Imagine that, I work for a spy family!* His imagination fuelled his fantasy as he managed a glance or two at Angela. Franz admired her beauty, but resolved to keep his distance. She was married, and he did not want any trouble from the professional killer that was her husband.

As his English improved, Franz even engineered situations like the 'car and tractor' for fun. Dave always rose to the bait. However, although he found mirth in most things Franz was occasionally serious; especially when he looked up into the bright spring sky and watched the Lancasters wheeling around above him like a shoal of brown and green fish.

Dave noticed his young helper's concerned expression. "It's nearly over now, Franz. You should thank God you're alive. Many are not. You're lucky, one day you'll go home."

"Go home to what? I see thousands of bombers take off and head east. God knows what I will find when I get there. I haven't heard from my family since Normandy. Some of the other boys get post, but I've had nothing."

"Where do you live?"

"Near Leipzig." Dave looked puzzled. "It's on the East side of Germany. My village is about twenty-five kilometres east of the Elbe."

"Then probably your village has been occupied by the Russians. I heard the Russians joined up with the Americans on the banks of the river Elbe yesterday." Dave seemed a little surprised when Franz turned a little pale. "What's the matter with that? Your Nazi friends will soon be out of power and then you can all go home."

Franz frowned. "They are not my 'Nazi friends.' I was never a Nazi. They were just a bunch of bullyboys who forced everyone to do what they wanted. We had no choice. They have ruined my country and killed many people on both sides, I hate them." He stabbed the ground with a stick.

"Voted for them though, didn't you? Democratically elected Hitler was." Dave nodded in self-agreement, his jaw set. Franz looked puzzled, he did not understand 'vote' and 'elected,' but before he could ask for clarification Dave asked, "How old are you?"

"Nineteen."

Dave studied the youth. "I suppose you were too young. Come on, let's get on."

That evening and for the first time that year, the Green family ate their meal in the garden. As the big red sun dropped lower over the apple blossom towards the horizon, the sunset was spectacular.

Dave lit his favourite pipe and ignoring the looks of disapproval from the two ladies in his life, eased himself back in his chair and continued to marvel at the changing sunset. As the natural clouds cleared, a multitude of white vapour stripes replaced them, all headed east.

The sun went down and the stripes turned red, their passing accompanied by the familiar throb of the bombers engines. Dave thought it was quite prophetic, "It signifies blood and fire." He sighed and shook his head as he watched, "I wonder how many of them won't come back tonight. I hope to God it's over soon, everyone has had enough."

Nobody answered him. The family gazed at the scene that would stay in their memory for the rest of their lives. Tens of thousands of similar onlookers shared the same thought as they stared from their gardens, looked out through taped-up windows, stood on guard and said prayers for husbands, brothers and sons, alive, dead or missing in action.

The Greens thoughts stopped when Ethel began to scratch her arms as the gnats fed on their human blood banks. "Nice lad Franz. There doesn't seem to be any harm in him. I don't think he is a Nazi. Do you, Dave?"

"No, Ethel. I spoke to him about it today, not much, but I think he hates them. He's simply an ordinary young lad caught up in it all a long way from home. He's no different to us. I like him." Angela listened but said nothing. Her thoughts lay with another young lad now serving King and Country on an island in the Mediterranean.

Back in Camp 918, men looked up at the aerial lightshow from their barbed wire cage, thought of home and said prayers for their families. Such demonstrations of the power and inevitability of the Allied victory spread great depression over them. One or two shook their fists but many shivered and could not bear to look, some vomited. The bombers went and the men returned to their huts in silence where they flopped on their bunks, stared at their pictures or carvings and wondered if memories would be all they had left.

As the darkness grew and threw its melancholy blanket over the men, more than one or two silent tears rolled down some screwed up faces. Sometimes, when the wind was in the right direction, men counted how many Lancasters took off from RAF Imton, and how many returned the next morning. The departure figure was always greater than the return figure. This one night, 25 April 1945, every Lancaster returned.

A few days later, Franz and Dave were working to repair the tractor when they heard the bells. Dave dementedly jumped up and down and whirled his arms like a windmill. "The church bells! It must be all over."

Ethel rushed out of the house with arms open wide, she was crying. "It's over. It's over. We've won! They just said it on the radio. They've surrendered!" Dave and Ethel embraced. Suddenly, the sky erupted with a loud bang.

Dave punched his fist in the air, "Ha. Ha! That'll be Andy Spencer's rocket," he shouted in triumph. "He's kept that rocket dry since 'thirty-nine. He always said that he would only let it off once we'd won." Dave and Ethel embraced in the most passionate kiss they had shared for six years.

Their observer turned around and got on with his work. Like the cup final where the winners forget all the pain, all the sweat and all the tears and are so jubilant that they could go on forever. The empty losers aimlessly prod the ground, tired, sad and thinking of what might have been. They want to slink away, be alone, and go home.

Angela swooped through the farm gate on her bicycle and just managed to brake before she crashed into her parents. She jumped off the bike and flung herself into the midst of the celebrating duo with such gusto she destabilised the scrum and they all fell over. As they rolled on the ground, she caught sight of Franz, who was aimlessly tightening something on the tractor. She jumped up and skipped over to him.

He heard her approach, but did not turn around until, "Franz. Cheer up. You'll be going home." His eyes widened and he gasped as she stood before him. She had never directly addressed him before; his first chance to look deeply into her eyes where he saw warmth and concern. "No more work today, Franz. We're all going to party," she sang before turning to her mother. "Mum, let's have a celebration feast. Can we roast a chicken?"

A large chicken was promptly despatched to its maker and was in the oven before Dave could open his second bottle of cider. It was the first time Franz had ever tasted the drink and he quickly began to smile. As the radio played cheerful music between frequent news broadcasts, the moment was becoming too much for Ethel. "The formal surrender is going to be signed tomorrow and Mr Churchill wants to speak to us at three p.m."

Dave was startled. "Is he coming here? Why us?"

"No, on the radio, you silly drunken Arse. He wants to address the nation on the radio. How many ciders have you had?"

"Not enough, My Love!"

Franz thought the roast lunch tasted wonderful; heavenly even. For over a year, these tastes had only been dreams. Dreams now come true, and all complemented by the golden elixir.

The cider worked its magic, and Franz became mellow. He felt privileged to have been included in what was a family celebration. His hosts showed him no malice, only friendship and relief. *Maybe this will be the start of a new order.*

In spite of his newly acquired alcoholic haze, Franz realised that he was continually staring at Angela. Each time he noticed this, his eyes flicked away to some other object or person, but like a magnet seeking north, they always returned to her. She did not appear to notice. Was he happy about that or not?

After his return to the camp that night, Franz and all the other prisoners learnt that because the British had declared a public holiday, there would be no work the following day. At that news, the Germans, in anticipation of early repatriation, decided to party too. Long concealed and hoarded stocks of distilled potato and carrot alcohol miraculously appeared. The camp guards, who were also drunk, completely ignored it.

This clandestine schnapps had four distinct effects: first, happiness and fun: second, moroseness and homesickness: third, deep sleep: fourth, the mother of all hangovers. Everyone drank as much as they could get, and with great bravado proclaimed that for them, it would only be the first and third effects this time; the fourth effect was definitely only for beginners. No one ever mentioned the second effect.

8 May 1945, 'VE day,' gave rise to many fourth effects in the camp and many strange sights out of it. The guards' military discipline seemed to have disappeared as many wore paper hats and flowers in their buttonholes. Many handed out cigarettes to any grateful inmates capable of standing.

However, the elation of VE day slowly gave way to the reality of no repatriation. Far from that, new prisoners arrived at the camp daily.

They told how the Allies had taken the majority into captivity in the form that they had surrendered, that is, as complete army units. Of course, men also arrived at Drakesford individually. Many had taken off their uniforms and tried to drift back home, but were stopped and taken into custody. POWs 'must pay for peace; in hard work.'

Dave asked Angela if she would help Franz get the cows in. What started as a brisk walk soon slowed to an amble as they began to talk. Angela asked questions about Germany and seemed interested to hear about Halle and the Christmas market in the city square. "Your English is excellent, Franz. You must have studied a lot in school."

"No. I started to learn in hospital. I was lucky. I had a helpful nurse. When I arrived I couldn't understand anything, but we helped each other."

"What do you mean? How?"

"I was put in a ward full of SS soldiers. This nurse, Josie, became the butt of their humour, simply because she was a little, a little … Oh, I don't know the word. What is it, Angela, when someone is not pretty and looks boring?"

"Plain." Angela answered.

"No. Not flying." He spread his arms and made flying noises. Angela chuckled.

"This." He stretched his face into a dole expression.

Angela chuckled again. "Yes, plain. We call that plain."

Franz looked mystified. "Not a Spitfire?"

"No. A Spitfire is a plane, but we also use 'plain' to describe someone who is not pretty and looks boring. Two words sounding the same, just spelt differently."

Franz nodded sagely, "Well, I don't know about a Spitfire. Josie was more like a Lancaster." Angela clasped her hands and shook with laughter. "The SS called her "The Knockwurst." That type like to pick on someone who is not of their breed, that's why they're SS.

"Sometimes she cried. I felt sorry for her and because I wanted to learn English, I used that as an excuse to talk to her. From what I later found out, I think the fact that she looked plain might have been due to the stress of her losses in that damned war. She had given up. We used sign language and drawing to learn the first few words, it was a laugh. Then it just took off from there. And you know what?"

"What?" Angela said.

"She started combing her hair and smiling. She had a lovely smile and lovely eyes when she smiled. I thought she looked quite attractive."

Angela stopped walking and leaned back a little in mock examination of Franz. "Fancied her, did you?" Franz immediately blushed.

"No. No. Well, not exactly fancied. Well, she was nice, and laughed a lot too."

"Hmm," Angela said rather loudly as she folded her hands behind her back and strode on ahead.

Spring gave way to summer on Green Farm and their conversations became more frequent, particularly when Angela helped at milking time. Haymaking at the end of June was a busy time and Dave needed all the help he could get, which included many casual workers from the village.

Franz continued to be amazed at how these people accepted him without any animosity and indeed, with friendship. He waited for the first aggressive comment, one unfriendly remark, the push or the shove that would slam him back into remorseful isolation, which never came.

Children played hide and seek under the hay. Dogs sniffed interesting sniffs in the hedges and chased butterflies. Everyone laughed a lot as they built hayricks. Many times people fell into unseen crevasses in the rick amid much laughter. Jovial rescuers often retrieved the unfortunates by the most ungainly methods. A rather unladylike whistle from Angela heralded lunchtime.

She and her mother waddled out to the hayricks, each struggling under the weight of two large food baskets. A simple lunch of bread, cheese, pickled onions and a glass of cider or milk; followed by a cup of tea. The hungry workers made themselves nests in the hay in which to sit, eat, drink, chat and admire the beauty of the countryside. Heaven. This day, Franz had the luck to find a place next to Angela.

"Dad says you're not a Nazi. I get confused about this, German, Nazi? What's it all about, Franz?"

Franz scratched his head and looked slightly bemused before he took a deep breath and began. "To be German is like you are English, or British, or whatever you are. To be Nazi is to be so arrogant that you think you are superior to everyone else, and that it is therefore your right to dominate everyone who is not of your blood. Anyone else has no value, or is, at best, only valuable as a servant to the Reich."

"What's a Reich?"

"Empire. Nazis are bullies. Like that SS crew in the hospital. Their whole manner and methods attract bullies. They spread their fear to the masses by bullying minorities, like Jews. I have no problem with Jews." He gazed into the distance. "I knew a Jewish family in Oberfeld. The Rabinowitz family. They were always friendly, jovial people and made good shoes in the family business. Mr Rabinowitz was a respected 'Master Shoemaker.' Nobody thought of him as a bad man. That is until the summer of 1937, when the Nazi bullyboys arrived.

"About ten of them, arrived on, some of them even hanging off the side of, an army lorry. All laughing and shouting as it pulled up with a jerk outside the shoe shop. Their expressions changed as they jostled inside and smashed the place apart.

"Shoes and tools crashed and spun out into the street followed by Mr and Mrs Rabinowitz. The Nazis pushed them to the ground and used them as footballs. The 'game' continued for some time. They laughed each time a kick landed on Mr Rabinowitz's bald head or Mrs Rabinowitz's breasts.

"Before they left, they painted the shop with a huge Star of David and from that day on, two thugs always guarded the door and turned customers away."

Franz looked sad as he stared at his piece of cheese, which he had squashed so hard in his fist that it oozed out between his fingers. Angela shook her head and stared at Franz in a mixture of shock and concern. The cheese dropped like tears to the hay as Franz continued. "Everyone saw that one of these guards was Tomas Baumann.

"He was nineteen. He was actually from Oberfeld and had played in the same football team as David Rabinowitz. Their son. He had always been David's friend. Baumann now wore a new shirt of brown that put fear into everyone. How strange, Angela, that this thin weed, who was afraid of spiders, now bawled orders and barked insults at passers-by. Through the possession of, being part of, unchallengeable Nazi terror, he had satisfied his weaknesses and become strong. That's what a Nazi is, Angela." She nodded and studied him intensely.

"I suppose you had to go and fight, did you? Like everyone here."

"Of course. It was what you did. What you had to do." He looked at Angela a little sheepishly. "I actually wanted to fight. Much as I hate Nazis, I was proud to be German. That's all we ever heard, all we ever saw in the cinema. There's a word for it. What's the word, Angela?"

"Propaganda."

"Ah, yes, thanks. Propaganda." Franz nodded. "It caught you up in the great patriotic adventure. There was no pain. I'd never seen anyone killed. No bombs fell on Oberfeld." He looked at Angela, his eyes pleading. Then he averted his gaze. "I'm not so sure I'm proud to be German anymore."

He shook his head again and slowly rubbed the cheese from his fingers. "It's easy to say all these things now we've lost, but we Germans must all accept responsibility. Look what we have done to the world."

Angela shuffled her feet and smiled at him. Franz noticed tenderness in her eyes as she rolled her shoulders and clasped her hands tightly. It seemed to him that she wanted something. Was she blushing?

Then Angela sat up and her expression changed to one of enthusiasm. "We used to have a flower show in the village every August, the social event of the year, the last one was in nineteen thirty-nine. I loved it." She clapped her hands like a five-year-old.

"We'd be up all night preparing our exhibits. Exhibits is the name for things that we wanted to show like vegetables, flowers, cakes, wine." Franz nodded. "Mum would bake the cakes. We would both clean the vegetables and arrange the flowers, and Dad would taste the wine. Every bottle!" They hooted with laughter.

Franz squashed his nose and said, "Ha-ha, that's where he gets it from then."

"Oh, yes. He says he is a connoisseur."

"Connoisseur of sweet dreams, more like."

"Don't let him here you say that, Franz. He likes you." Her wondering smile returned as her eyes flicked back and fore between his. They only became aware of how much they had been talking when the others started back to work and they realised they had only eaten half of their rations. A point not lost on Ethel as she strolled back to the farmhouse with her daughter.

"What were you two so deep in conversation about then?"

"Everything, he's so easy to talk to. So interesting. So likable."

"Is that so?"

Angela became a regular helper at milking time. She and Franz always seized the chance to chat as they sat and milked their cows, accompanied by the rhythmic spraying sound of the milk as it squirted into the pale. Dave, who usually milked a third cow, rarely spoke. Occasionally, a chance for something else occurred.

Dave had taken a cow out to the yard. "Hey, open your mouth." Angela turned and without thought, did just that. A hot stream of fresh milk spurted the five-foot distance from Franz's cow to leave Angela sitting aghast on her stool with milk dripping off her hair and down her face.

"Pig!" She immediately retaliated in kind from her cow, also a direct hit. Both dripped with milk, but as Angela attempted to duck the next salvo, she slipped from her stool and rocked with laughter as she sat in an ungainly position on the wet stone floor with her upturned stool between her legs. Pleasure turned to horror as Franz picked up his bucket of milk and held it over her head. "Don't you dare. Franz! No please. No, no..."

Dave's boots clumping on the stones outside brought them to their senses and Angela was only just able to regain her position on her stool and turn her back to the arrival of her father, who appeared to notice nothing at all. As Dave took his position next to his cow, there were fingers wagged, silent laughs and even a badly aimed feminine kick.

"Heard from Gerald today, Angela?"

"No, Dad."

19.

Heraklion in December 1945 was warm and sunny. Gerald had seen no action during the last couple of days of the war and his first months on the island had been notable for the boredom of post-war Army life. His entire existence consisted of an endless round of bull and guard duty, and with no prospect of any return to Britain, even his officers referred to them all as the "Forgotten Army."

However, the highlight of any week was a patrol in his Bren Gun Carrier, or BGC. Every patrol always managed to include a stop by a secluded beach or a pause for refreshment in a country taverna. Gerald used these excursions to meet the local women, but whilst he developed an excellent technique of eye contact and smiles, his lack of ultimate success frustrated him. However, in early December, luck presented him with an interesting situation.

He had demolished a stone wall after misjudging a bend in the road when driving the BGC. The lady-owner of the house heard the crash and bustled out of her house brandishing her fist in rage at the surprised soldiers. Their officer promised that Gerald would return later that day, and personally repair the damage.

Gerald mounted a bicycle and trundled off down the potholed Greek road for his afternoon's work in the sun. His twenty-minute journey took him along a road parallel to the azure Mediterranean. A gentle on-shore wind blew up the occasional flurry of dust in his path, but otherwise only served to rustle the leaves of the olive trees that formed a silver and green canopy over his route.

The sound of the Mediterranean and the rhythmic, rubbing noise of the cicadas filled his ears. He loved this hypnotic sound. It always started around breakfast time and would continue into the heat of the day. Crete in December still had many flowers, and their scent, mixed with that of the olives, was like a perfumed drug.

In the space of fifty yards, he passed rocks of deep red ochre, salmon pink, orange, sand or white; a complete natural spectrum in stone. He chortled as his clattering bike scattered a small flock of happy sparrows enjoying a dust bath on the road ahead of him. How lucky he was to be alive, here, on an island in the sun.

The hated Germans had gone and it was a time to be thankful. Gerald knew that in 1941, when the Nazi paratroopers had invaded, the British, and particularly the Commonwealth soldiers, had valiantly fought and died against a better-organised enemy to keep Crete free. The islanders were grateful to the British and where possible, always showed it.

This thought was in Gerald's mind as he drew up next to the crumbled wall. He hoped the black-clad lady of the house had cooled down and would now be friendly to him, because after all, he was British.

The house and its yard sat on a raised piece of land, surrounded by olive groves and overlooking the sea. A large mournea tree dominated the backyard. Its crooked and entangled branches supported hosts of large leaves, which gave shade to many small camomile plants whose little yellow flowers added a tiny amount of contrast to the reddish brown dust of the yard.

Gerald leant on his bike and ran his eyes along a vine-draped pergola that ran the whole length of the back wall of the two-story house, partially obscuring the flaky salmon-pink plaster. In its shade, a rectangular wooden table and a few rickety wooden chairs stood on the dry earth, along with a faded blue sofa and some terracotta flowerpots cascading with bright red geraniums.

Wooden shutters covered the windows, giving the house a sleepy appearance. The original 'Tranquillity Base,' just like the rest of Crete on a sunny afternoon.

Gerald's mellow expression changed when he surveyed the damaged wall. The impact of his BGC had scattered stones up to three metres away from what was now a hole some two metres wide. The damage, whilst it looked severe, would probably not take too long to repair, normally a couple of hours. *In this heat, maybe three?* He stripped to the waist and began work.

From the dark room, she watched through the shutters. She liked the look of his youthful body and gazed at the bulge in his army fatigues that sometimes appeared when he dragged one of the heavier stones up his thighs to stomach height. It had been three and a half years since the Nazis pulled her husband from the street, shot him and another nineteen randomly chosen Greek men, as a reprisal for partisan activity. Her shock and sense of loss had been unimaginable; she had hardly spoken for six months. Every day since, she had worn her black widow's outfit like a uniform. At first, she had worn it with pride and she was still proud of what it stood for and in whose memory it was, but she so longed to live again.

Gerald's shining sinewy body glistened in the sun, her suppressed emotions and needs screamed at her. She spun away from the window, clenched her fists, looked at the ground, stamped one foot hard enough to hurt her heel and cursed herself for her disrespectful thoughts. How could she? She raised her head to glare at the ceiling, or maybe to seek divine guidance.

Why not? She spun around and again spied through the shutters. Now very hot, dusty and sweaty, Gerald paused from his work and wiped his brow. He turned towards the house and hoped there might be a chance of a drink. She answered his prayers when she came out of the door with a glass of lemonade. "Hot day," she said in surprisingly clear English, "especially for December."

"Hard work," he nonchalantly responded. He took the glass and without averting his gaze from her eyes, downed its contents in almost one gulp.

She motioned him over to the pergola. "Would you like to sit for a moment?"

"Must get on," he said.

She tutted and rather flatly said, "Make sure you do a good job," as she turned and ambled back to the house.

Gerald watched her. Her black clothes did her no favours, and did not hide her ample posterior, which was exactly where his eyes came to rest. He smirked.

She did not retreat into the house, but sat on the old sofa in the shade and stroked her cat. A short meeting of eyes later, Gerald returned to his task.

It got hotter and although the work progressed well, the sun took its toll on Gerald's skin and he began to turn the lobster colour that so distinguishes the British from everyone else. He briefly glanced at her. *What is that?* She had undone the top button of her black blouse. He was sure this newly exposed part of her chest had not seen the sun for some time. *It must be hot, very hot, under those vines.*

"Come and cool down. I'll get you another drink." She got up and went into the house. Gerald slowly walked over to the pergola and sat down at the table.

She returned and placed two glasses of lemonade on the table, sat down opposite him and motioned him to drink. She placed her hands under her chin, rested her elbows on the table and watched him drinking the lemonade she had made from fresh lemons only an hour before. And he watched her.

He drank, slowly this time, slow enough to notice two undone buttons. The fresh tang of the lemonade served to raise his senses and cool his head. She had some small beads of sweat at the base of her throat.

She moved slightly, the beads flowed into one, and slowly ran down the top of her chest before disappearing behind the third button of her black blouse.

Gerald wondered what delights were concealed where the perspiration drop had now reached. *She doesn't look that big; but you can never tell under black, can you?* She still watched him.

She saw where he looked, and noticed the twinkle in his eye. She shifted her gaze to study his shoulders, now sunburnt and lightly covered with dust and even though not heavily muscled, they looked masculine and in every sense of the word, raw. His chest was slightly hairy, broad and had potential for future development. It might need a little massage.

The rhythm of the cicadas matched Gerald's heartbeat. He continued to look into her eyes and smiled nervously. She smiled confidently back. They studied each other's faces. Her wide mouth made a 'Mona Lisa' type of knowing smile. Her full, rosé lips looked warm and were moist in the corners. His were dry and slightly cracked.

He has interesting light blue eyes. She smiled at the freckles across his nose. *He is different to a Greek. Interesting, very interesting.* She sat still. He shuffled on his chair as he put his glass down. She fixed him with her gaze as she picked up her glass and slightly rolled it along her lips before she took a gentle sip of the cool elixir. She placed the glass softly back on the table, slid her thumb and forefinger slowly down its side until she reached its bottom then slightly quicker back up to the top, before slowly down again. And once more, his eyes followed the motion. "My name is Krista. What's yours?"

"Gerald. You have a nice place here. Do you live alone?"

Her eyes glazed. "Yes," She answered a little sombrely. "My husband was murdered by the SS nearly four years ago. Both my parents are dead and sadly, I have no children." She paused, looked down at the table and then back at Gerald. The fire had returned to her eyes, her voice quickened, "I have one goat, fourteen chickens and a cat, how old are you?" A tiny drop of saliva reappeared in the corner of her mouth.

"Eighteen."

"How do you like Crete?"

"It's lovely. Everyone seems so friendly, but it's very hot. It's lovely. Yes, very nice. Very...." He bit his bottom lip and remembered he was supposed to be in control of this situation. "Very nice indeed." He leaned back on his chair, only to jump slightly forward when his seared skin touched the wood.

Gerald's controller smiled knowingly at him. "I can help your sunburn. Would you like to stay where you are for a moment whilst I mix up an olive oil, yoghurt and camomile mixture that will do the trick just nicely?" Without waiting for an answer or taking her eyes off his, she slowly arose from the table. Krista's voice assumed an authorative tone and her eyes flashed as she ordered, "Don't move," before floating away into the darkness of her kitchen.

He watched her bottom sway through the kitchen door, the rhythmic throbbing of the cicadas seemed to have quickened, but all else was quiet, even the birds silently hid from the hot sun. Gerald heard the clink of a bottle from the kitchen. *She is indeed a fine woman. How can I handle her? She seems so different to other women. Well of course, she is. She's much older. God, maybe even old enough to be my mother. What will my mates think?*

Krista returned with a small jug and a serene smile. She had rolled up her sleeves; her arms looked strong. There was more. Gerald noticed two more undone buttons, exposing a hot looking cleavage. She looked at him grandly. "You must lie face down on the table, Gerald." He tried not to jump onto it too enthusiastically. She hoped he would retain such agility.

The relief as the cool balm touched Gerald's hot skin was a kiss from the gods. Her gentle hands slowly massaged his shoulders; her touch, light as a feather. His chin rested on his hands and he inhaled the scent of the camomile. His skin no longer screamed with pain as he relaxed with every second.

Her hands slid along every muscle. They probed their way along the line of his shoulders, up his neck, slowly down his spine, back up to his shoulder blades, round to his armpits, back under his shoulder blades, down to his waist, back up the length of his spine to his neck, out to his shoulders, down to his elbows and back to his neck. Again and again. Gerald imagined gentle waves lapping on the seashore.

Still the music of the cicadas, the smell of the camomile, the tenderness and sensuality of the touch.

"Do you have a sweetheart at home?"

"No."

"Why not? I don't think you have told me the truth, have you?"

"Yes I have."

"Have you ever had a girlfriend?"

"Yes, one or two, nothing serious though. My skin feels much better. That stuff you put on works miracles."

"Yes, it's good for the muscles." She lowered her voice. "Good for everything."

Her hands... No, now only her fingertips, moved around his sides and along the small of his back. "Your muscles are tight from your work. That cramped tank of yours is so bad for you. Turn over, I'll massage your chest."

He lifted himself up and turned around to lie on his back, but winced as his back touched the table. She shook her head. "This is no good. Come inside you can lie on my sofa." He sat up and studied her as he got off the table. She had a serious, enquiring look in her eyes.

He followed her through the dark kitchen into another dark, sparsely furnished room. The shutters had kept out the heat of the sun and it was blissfully cool. A simply furnished room, a radio and a posy of flowers stood on a small, plain table against the far wall. A small footstool, covered in embroidered flowers, stood in front of a pale blue sofa.

The sofa was clean and draped with a white cloth and was long enough for Gerald to lie on when motioned to do so.

She smiled reassuringly as she covered her hands with balm. Gerald's heart was pounding. Krista used her foot to hook the stool into a position close to Gerald, and with a great amount of poise, knelt down on it. She knelt level with his hips and when she was sure she was comfortable, placed her hands on his chest.

Around and around, her hands massaged with the same dexterity as she used on his back. This meant sometimes she had to lean forward reach his shoulders. Gerald only looked at one place; noted with great satisfaction by his masseuse.

He could see further down her cleavage with every push forward, pushes that grew to become a little exaggerated. *Look at the size of her tits! She's massive!*

She theatrically wiped her brow. "This is hot work." She sat back and started to undo the next fastened button, then stopped. He had not taken his eyes off her cleavage. "You're not nervous, are you?"

He shook his head in fast little shakes, and swallowed before he croaked, "No. It's true, it is a little warm in here." Some beads of sweat appeared on his brow as she deftly undid her blouse and exposed two ample breasts. They were bigger than Angela's and Sue's combined. "My God, it's actually going to happen to me," Gerald whispered.

"Oh yes, my boy, it is indeed. Would you like to massage me?" Krista cupped her breasts and presented them to him as if offering a sacrifice to the gods.

Seconds turned into minutes, turned into head-spinning hours in the Black Widow's Web. Beneath that black, she was a magnificent woman. She had had to do all the physical work in the house and garden since her husband died, which had kept her in good shape. True, she did have a rather large bottom, but Gerald liked that and showed his appreciation and strong grip as he entered her repeatedly from behind.

She buried her face in the sofa and muffled her moans of ecstasy. It had been so, so long.

20.

Gerald had been due to come home for three weeks in spring 1946, but a security problem in Palestine caused his leave's cancellation. His consolation had been nine days with his mates in Cairo, which had depressed Angela immensely. Eventually, when she was alone with Franz in the barn she confided in him about her loneliness. Franz listened before moving closer and for the first time, holding her hand.

"Angela, I know how you feel. I am lonely too, but I get through this loneliness by understanding that these years, even though they seem unending, will soon fade once things get back to normal. They will be only a small percentage of my life. What's two years out of seventy or eighty?" *God, she's got lovely eyes.*

Angela smiled and sighed. That was good logic. *He always has a way to make me calm. What is it about him…? Come on, shake a leg, do something else to take your mind off everything. It's the warmest day of the year so far, I think I'll go riding.*

She returned with her complexion a little rosy and moist and her long blond hair looking attractively windblown, *I should not have worn this tight shirt. It would have been nice to feel the wind blowing about my body.*

As she led her horse into the barn she saw Franz standing alone at the other end. Angela clearly saw him look her up and down before slightly smiling and getting on with his work. She turned and saw to her horse, all the time being aware or at least thinking that she was aware that he must be watching her every move.

Bridle in hand, she turned and began to carry it to the tack rack. She had two options of passing Franz, who was fixing a bracket onto the wall. Two feet behind him was the tractor, the other side of the tractor was a clear path. She wore a seductive smile as she chose to push slowly past Franz. He smiled, but said nothing and carried on with his work as she slowly hung the bridle up and left by the back door.

Franz could feel where she had touched his body. *Did she mean to do it?* He recalled the look in her eye. That was no accident. He replayed the incident in his mind for the rest of the day, to the extent that he often lost track of what job he was supposed to be doing. This out-of-world feeling continued back at camp. He went to sleep with a smile on his face. As did Angela.

But the storm clouds were gathering, usually at lunchtimes, when Ethel would sometimes take the opportunity to lecture no one in particular about family morals. There was one day when she spoke of some family no one had heard of that had broken up because one or other of the couple had "gone off with" someone else. "People should remember their marriage vows. This war hasn't only killed people, its killed families too." Angela was noticeably caustic to her mother as they cleared the table.

Later, on their way to fetch the cows Franz sighed and turned to Angela, "My mother drives me crazy too." Angela studied him. "She has a cliché for every situation; robbing Peter to pay Paul, a bird in the hand is worth two in the bush," and so on. She proclaims these as a rhyme without a thought as to their consequences. 'People' or 'They' say this or that, so it must be right."

"I know exactly what you mean. It must be a 'Mother's disease." She playfully pushed him and they both chuckled.

Then Franz seemed a little more serious. "No. Really. Looking back at it now, I can see how my parents controlled my behaviour and indeed, my life with this blanket of sayings."

"What do you mean?"

"Father and Mother are always right," was their answer to any of my awkward questions or objections. Bloody stupid. Why did I ever accept it?"

"You're not alone there, Franz. I lived, probably still do live, under the iron rule of my father." She told him about the Sammy Johnson incident.

Franz bit his lip and blinked several times, crossed his legs as if he needed the toilet and grimaced. "Nasty." He returned to his parents. "One of my mother's rules especially irked me. She always told me that if someone hit me, I must turn the other cheek and not retaliate." He looked up to the heavens and shook his head. I kept to this due to my blind faith in my parents." Angela managed a small stumble on a small stone and unconvincingly apologised as she brushed against him.

"Do you know, Angela, I sometimes used to come home covered in bruises because a group of older boys often picked on me, probably because they knew I wouldn't retaliate. If my mother saw the bruises, I was always stupid enough to tell her it had only been a hard game of football. I didn't dare say what had actually happened.

"Then one day I had enough of being a punch bag. I was fourteen and I separated two boys picking on a younger one. But then the older boys' friends picked on me. The usual crew. This time, I decided that as I was going to get hurt again anyway, what did I have to lose? To my surprise, I flattened two of them and the others backed off. No one ever bullied me again. I felt great."

"Oh, a boxing champ as well as a footballer," Angela cooed.

"No, no, no. But this is me, Angela. I don't like trouble. I always need pushing many times before I push back. It's so annoying because whenever the chips are down, I always seem to win, or at least do well. I am sure I could have done so much more and had more fun, if it were not for Mother and her stupid clichés." Angela clasped her hands behind her back and happily swayed her body as they walked on.

The 'accidental' touches between Franz and Angela became more frequent, but the instigator always regretted it. The voice of conscience had started to echo in the background to chide the guilty. These thoughts boomed away like a migraine. They never mentioned it and the more it continued, the more they could not speak about it.

There was one thing Franz did speak about that was unintentional.

Again, they were walking out to get the cows when Angela casually asked, "Dad says, you were in another camp before Drakesford. In Scotland. Why did they transfer you down here?"

After some generalities, the word Schwanz slipped out, Franz paused, before deciding to carry on. As the story continued she looked progressively more intensely at him. "Why did you grab him around the throat? I know this is a crazy question, Franz, but if your life was at risk, why didn't you simply give in?"

Franz did not immediately answer. They walked another twenty metres while he looked intensely at the ground, his hands became sweaty, until, "When I was eight years old, I remember going to Halle with my parents. It was a hot day and to cool down a bit we went into the Marienkirche, it's a big church in the city centre." He took a deep breath. "I needed the toilet and this church had one. My father said I could go, alone.

There was a man washing his hands when I went in. He smiled at me. I stood and went to the toilet and when I had finished I turned around and he was still there. I became nervous and went to leave but he stopped me and told me to wash my hands. I had been brought up to do what adults told me and so I stopped and washed my hands. It was then that he picked me up and started kissing me."

Franz noticed he was shivering, he continued, "I tried to grab the tap, to stop him lifting me up, but he was too strong. He hadn't shaved, I remember that. His cheek was rough on mine, like sandpaper as was the sleeve of his jacket; an orangey-red jacket. Then he put his hand up my trousers and started fiddling. He had a red face and beads of spit in the corners of his mouth. Then he stopped and put me down. I ran away.

"I went back to my parents. For a few seconds I didn't say anything. Then I told my father a man had kissed me in the toilets. I didn't tell him about the other bit.

"He asked me what the man looked like and then went off to find him, unsuccessfully. I actually hoped he wouldn't find him. I didn't want a scene. I didn't want a conflict. I can see that man now, a rough jacket and an even rougher face. I will never, ever, forget it."

Angela looked at him caringly, she wanted to put her arm around him. She thought that was all. But it wasn't.

"A year later, I went fishing with my mate, Dummer. We went to the lake in the village as we did almost every day in the summer. It was safe. We fished all day but Dummer caught nothing, he was a good laugh but not much good at anything really, hence 'Dummer.' Franz laughed nervously.

"So Dummer went home leaving me and a man called Eduard Ingen, he's dead now, as the only anglers persisting. Ingen came and sat next to me, made some general conversation, and asked if I would like to play a game? I don't want to go into too much detail any more, Angela." He glanced at her tearful eyes. "However, the game was I'll show you mine, you show me yours; except his version involved touching me.

"Once again I didn't tell my father. Frightened? Ashamed? I'm not really sure why. Nevertheless, as I got older I swore to myself that I would never allow this again. When Schwanz looked at me as he did I wondered what to do. I knew that if I refused, I would be in danger. But when he touched me, and I felt the roughness of his jacket, the decision was taken away from me. I reacted. Thereafter, everything was a chain reaction."

Franz shook and tears ran down Angela's cheek. He gently wiped them away. Her expression changed again. The incredulous look returned. "How on earth did you keep the advantage? How did you think of it all?"

"Motivation. Life or death. I know from my football that if you believe you can win, you usually do. If you believe you can win, you play with confidence, if you have confidence, your opponent feels it and often backs off... just enough for you to win." He paused for a moment and scratched his head, Angela looked at him in awe. "Unless he is well prepared and knows he is much better. If he isn't and is caught by surprise, then you've got him, at least for a short while.

"I knew that I had the advantage of surprise and that I had to show confidence, even if I was shitting myself. I did also get lucky later when the officer came in.

"In a long fight with them, there would only be one outcome. That was my motivation and my concentration. When the chips are down, it seems I always think of something, I wasn't going to be Schwanz's sex toy. Once I refused him I was dead, so I went for it." He looked directly at Angela and smiled. "Here I am, looking at someone very nice, so it must have worked."

"Wow! Wow, wow, wow. That'd make a good film."

They looked into each others eyes for a long time, until he stopped shaking and said, "You're the only person in the world, other than me, who knows all that." He squeezed her shoulders and smiled. They collected the cows and walked them back for milking. Angela stared ahead and wondered.

As time went on they shared many opinions and stories, but the truth got a little distorted when they spoke about other relationships. Franz heard all about the lost baby, but not about Gerald's indiscretions. "He is such an intelligent and devoted husband. I could not wish for better." Franz noted that whenever she spoke of Gerald, it was always a bit too much, too good, and she always avoided eye contact.

Franz spoke at great length about his 'great love' Freja, "We kissed every day before school and during break. At lunch time, we did it so much that we didn't have much time to eat and we kissed all the way home, when I carried her books."

Angela looked a little puzzled, "Every day?"

"Yes, the same every day. We couldn't get enough of each other."

Angela nodded and recalled the similarity to a girl's romance novel she had lent him. She smiled like a mother. *Imagine that. Twenty years old, and I'm sure he's never had a girlfriend. How could that have happened to a man as handsome as him? Change the subject, Angela.*

Whilst he worked at Green Farm, Franz earned the princely sum of one pound per week. This was little more than pocket money because the Green family provided him with food and clothing and of course he slept at the camp, so he had spent almost none of this money by the time of Angela's birthday. *Shall I buy her a present? Yes. Or would that be too familiar?*

121

Two days before Angela's birthday, Ethel asked Franz to go to the post office and for the first time in his life, he saw nylons. Perfect. He had often heard Angela eulogising over them to her mother. *Yes, Angela would look great in them. Familiar? Yeh, good.*

At lunch, two days later, Franz sat very formally, exactly as he would have done in Germany. Three times he cleared his throat and opened his mouth to give his congratulations, three times Ethel butted in. *Fourth time lucky, Franz.* He reached over the table to shake Angela's hand. She looked at his outstretched hand and then at him.

Franz smiled and waggled his hand. She got the message and reached out to shake hands. Ethel and Dave stopped eating and looked at each other.

Franz cleared his throat again and began to vigorously shake Angela's hand. "Angela. I wish you everything good. I wish you many good health. I wish you many money. I wish you many happiness. I wish you fun. I wish you many children and I wish that you stay as you are." Angela began to smile. Dave decided that this called for a clarifying slurp of cider.

Ethel scrutinised Franz. "Not sure about the last bit, but in England we say 'Happy Birthday,'" Ethel said. The Greens laughed and Franz, whilst not letting up on the hand shaking, looked sheepishly around the table before reaching into his jacket pocket and producing the present, which he handed to Angela before finally giving her hand a rest.

Angela's face lit up, but fell immediately at her mother's shocked expression. Angela's blue eyes flickered demurely at Franz. "Thank you, Franz. You should not have, they are too expensive to waste your hard-earned money on."

Franz, acting the dumb foreigner, countered, "In Germany, it is quite normal for workers to buy their employers personal gifts and I am happy to do so here." He nodded in certainty. "Well, there it is." Ethel looked thwarted.

Familiar or not, Angela insisted on wearing the nylons whilst celebrating her birthday tea on the lawn. Just as her parents were clearing up, Angela rather provocatively lifted her skirt above her knees and gave Franz a twirl. Her skirt flared out as she spun, to the extent that Franz actually caught sight of her stocking tops. She winked at him and walked off with a satisfied smile on her face.

Franz gasped for breath and shook his head. *She could **not** have realised how high she had lifted her skirt.* He had only ever seen such things in the pictures on the camp hut wall. *Maybe she did. What did Jan Rijke say? A woman always shows you what she wants you to see. Corrr!*

The frequent brushing past became even more frequent, as did occasional water throwing and, just for a moment, as they looked at something in the distance, sometimes even a hand on a shoulder. Angela always stood close to Franz, often so that they touched, which he pretended to ignore. He had to ignore.

September 1946 was unusually warm. Dave said it was an Indian summer, which took a while to explain to Franz until, "Ah! An 'Alte Weiber Sommer.' That's an Old Female's summer in German." Nevertheless, it was unseasonably hot; hot enough for the village children to continue swimming in the river down by the Ace Bridge.

"Go on then, Ed. Your turn." Eleven-year-old Donald Evans said. As the loudest mouth, he had decided that everyone should try to see who could dive and retrieve the biggest stone from the riverbed. Ed was not sure about this. Then he remembered he had once thrown in a big one by the tree a few yards downstream. Maybe he could climb out on the submerged branch to where the stone was.

His sister, Jenny, bit her lip, "You're not a good swimmer, Ed." Egged-on by Donald, Ed nervously climbed out, took a big breath and dived in. That was a minute ago. Now there was panic.

Franz had been working nearby and had been delighted that Angela had ridden up on her horse to 'check how he was getting on' and to 'see if he needed anything' when they heard the commotion from the river and saw the children agitatedly pointing at the water.

A girl screamed. They could hear crying. As Franz ran the fifty yards to the tree, a young girl turned towards him and pleaded with him to run faster. "My brother. My brother. Help him!" Franz arrived to see two boys gingerly climbing out along the submerged branch.

"What's happening?" Franz shouted.

"Ed hasn't come up. He was out by that branch." Franz kicked off his shoes and told the boys on the branch to go back. Angela clasped her face as he dived in.

Franz swam down. *Where is he? Muddy water. Ahja!* Franz felt a sharp pain down his side as a broken branch dug into his ribs. *Might be trapped under this tree. Keep swimming. Check to the end.* He pulled himself to the end of the big branch. *Nothing.* He pushed out into the main stream. Left. Right. *Turn back. Circle. Nothing. Tree again.* He breathed out a little, he wanted to breathe in. *Keep looking. Kick harder. Need air.*

Franz broke the surface sounding like a huge whale as he exhaled before sucking in a huge breath of fresh air. He scanned the surface. A smaller branch coming off the main one; he would check that. *Down.* Once more at the bottom, he saw it, *a foot. Not moving.*

Got it. A pull and it came free, but... *He's not coming. Other leg's caught.* He saw Ed's right leg bent around a cleft in the branch the foot pinned behind a large stone. The child's lifeless body wafted in the gentle stream.

Franz held on to the tree and placed his feet on the riverbed. *Get the ankle. Got it. Lift the tree, PULL...* The pressure of his effort was pushing his feet into the mud of the river bed He wrenched the boy's ankle free and tried to strike for the surface.

Feet stuck! Push the kid up. With all his might he threw Ed upwards and let go. *Get the branch. Stay calm. That's it...* He pulled on the branch and wiggled his feet from the mire, struck for the surface and came up underneath Ed.

Angela helped him lift Ed onto the grass where they laid him face down. The girls in the group were clutching their faces and sobbing. The boys simply stared in horror. Donald sat on the grass biting his fist and shaking. Franz checked his pulse. *Yes, His heart is still beating. 'Got to make him breathe.* Franz pushed hard down on the boy's back, so hard that water gushed out of Ed's mouth. Franz pushed again. Only a little bit of water this time. Franz pulled the boy's arms hard behind his head then relaxed and pushed his back again.

A few more times and then Ed coughed. His head moved. He coughed again and started to move his arm before he retched, coughed and cried. Franz sighed deeply and looked at Angela. "He's OK." As Ed regained full consciousness, the other children crouched down beside him and comforted him. Franz stood up, turned to Angela and smiled. "That was close," he said.

Angela shook her head and gazed at her hero before putting her arms around him and giving him a squeeze. "You were so brave, Franz."

"Nothing brave about it. I didn't have time to think. Didn't have time to be afraid. You OK, lad?"

"Yes, sir. Thank you, sir."

"Let's get you out of those clothes," Angela said. Franz's eyes widened. "You can wear something of Gerald's. Franz's face fell. Angela helped her hero onto her horse so that he sat behind her. As they rode back to the farm, Franz had the luxury of wrapping his arms around her and the ecstasy of her breasts occasionally bouncing down to touch his forearm. His closed eyes kept him oblivious to Angela's broad smile.

Ethel and Dave were full of admiration for Franz. The two women fussed around him as he drank a cup of tea. *Never been a hero before. I could get used to this.*

Over the following days, Angela seemed on a different planet. She became aware of staring at Franz whenever he was near, which would lead to her either clenching her fist, clenching her teeth, slapping her thighs or looking heavenwards and closing her eyes.

"What's the matter, Angela?" Ethel said one time when they were alone. "Are you in pain, dear? Or is there something troubling you? You seem rather strange to me."

"I don't know what you're talking about. Nothing's the matter with me. Don't be so stupid, Mother. I'm just a bit tired that's all. Don't keep bothering me. What do you mean, strange?"

"You keep screwing your face up and things; like you're hiding something or something is bothering you. Is there anything you want to tell me?"

"I'm not hiding anything. OK! If I want your help, I'll ask for it. Now, leave me alone."

"Phew, sorry I asked. I'll be asking for permission to breathe next." Ethel turned to get on with her housework. "Never mind, Angela. Gerald will be home soon."

"I know."

21.

It was now early evening, and Crete had woken up for the second part of its day. Krista leant on the kitchen door arms folded and watched the young soldier climb back through the unfinished wall repairs. She sighed. "I could do it again, even now."

Without looking back, he tenderly mounted his bicycle, adjusting his position several times in an attempt to ease the pain in his joints. He chuckled as he pedalled back to base.

Every night, Gerald dutifully kissed Angela's picture and the almost daily letters he received from her. The weekly letters he sent back about the 'nice, but boring,' island never dampened his lust for Krista one jot and over the following weeks, the pain in his hips rarely had time to go away. However, after about three months, Krista forbade him to call at her house any more. The wall had taken longer to repair than any wall in history, and people on Crete did not miss a trick. Someone would be sure to notice and she did not want tongues to wag about her. They arranged to meet in a secluded spot in the hills overlooking the sea.

Krista looked younger now. Her face was relaxed and she smiled all the time. Gerald noticed that she swayed her hips more as she walked. She would often pick a wild flower, close her eyes and inhale a long, long breath of its scent before slowly lifting her face to the sapphire sky. As she did this, he loved to watch her long black hair tumble even further down her back. Without a doubt, she was a magnificent woman. He explored regions of sexual complexity and lust he never thought existed.

Although they had not kissed much initially, as time went on, she increasingly kissed him and searched deep in his eyes for signs of lurking girlfriends. "Am I just fun for you, Gerald, or do you really like me?"

"You know I like you, Krista. Very much. You have taught me so much."

"I am not simply a sex teacher, Gerald. I make love to you because I want you." Gerald's eyes widened a little. "What do you mean, 'want me'?" He blinked rapidly. "Do you want to keep me here or something?

"No, no. I would never force you to stay here. You are a free man and can go as and when you want. But now you come to mention it, it would be nice if you stayed." He stopped blinking and scratched his head. "After all, you don't have any girlfriends to go back for. Do you?"

"No. No I don't. But there's no work for me here, and I am British, so I should go home." He looked thoughtful, calculating. "Although *it is* lovely here," Krista looked interested, "I'll have to wait and see. Now then, I haven't kissed your tits today." He leant towards her and started to unbutton her blouse. Just as he started to kiss her, she stopped him with, "I have an aunt living in London, in a town called Camden."

Shiiiiitt. He slowly came up for air and stared intently at her. "You live here on this lovely island in the sun. You must know about the English weather, fog, smog, rain, wind, snow, freezing temperatures, everything. We have a good thing going here, and as I said, maybe, just maybe, if you don't push me, I might stay. Now, your left one needs some more attention and if it tastes good, maybe somewhere else will too."

Her questions could wait, she never liked to spoil a good opportunity.

22.

Christmas was approaching and as the family ate its evening meal, Ethel fidgeted in her chair. She waited until Dave and Angela had finished eating, folded her hands and cleared her throat. "I want to speak about Franz. It seems such a shame to me that he will be behind the wire, in that camp, at Christmas time." She tapped the table with her index finger. "People, families, should be together at Christmas, but he can't be with his family." Ethel looked around imploringly. "For the last three or four weeks, we all must have noticed he goes quiet and looks a little sad whenever Christmas is mentioned. Well, he's almost one of us, and so I wondered if it would be possible to invite him here for Christmas." She paused, and purposefully added, "With us."

Dave cleared his throat and placed both hands on the table and leaned forward as if he was about to get up, but he turned to his wife. "Haven't you forgotten a small detail, Ethel? He is a prisoner and has to go back to his jail every night."

Ethel vigorously shook her head. "Dave, the war is long over. You often see POWs walking around the village by themselves. Well, *we* even send Franz to the village by himself." She nodded in emphasis, "I have read of a travelling German POW choir that has been on tour in Lancashire, where they stayed, unguarded, overnight in people's homes. So it must be possible."

Dave leant back in his chair and puffed at his unlit pipe. Ethel stared at him intensely. "My point is this. Do we think it's a good idea and do we want him to come to us for Christmas?"

Angela matter-of-factly piped up, "On the face of it, it seems a reasonable idea. It's true; he is almost one of the family, and the commandant can only say no." She sat back, folded her arms and wanted to hug her mother.

Both ladies stared at Dave. This time he used an extra match to light his pipe. He savoured the smoke, and his power. The women looked on whilst he appeared to have an argument with himself before he benignly smiled. "Why not?"

Ethel bubbled with triumph. "I have two chickens in mind, which I have been fattening up to roast, and we've had a good year in the vegetable garden. There'll easily be enough food to go round." The nodding heads and smiling faces of her husband and daughter said it all. Ethel tapped the table twice with her index finger. "There it is then!"

The next morning Ethel walked down to the post office to phone the camp commandant and was pleasantly surprised when without hesitation he answered, "Yes, I don't have a problem with that. But you must guarantee to return him at the normal time on the twenty-sixth." Ethel was bursting to tell someone, so she told the postmistress, who had been listening in anyway.

Drakesford had never needed a local newspaper. Why, when they had Mrs Morris? Anything said to, or heard by her was sure to be around the village in half a day. Confidential information would be common knowledge within the hour. Mrs Morris excelled this time. Most Drakesford residents thought this was a particularly friendly idea and many wanted to do likewise. Family meetings were held, decisions taken and an amazed commandant besieged by telephone requests for a Christmas guest. Forty-five of them in fact, all granted.

Ethel jigged around the kitchen as she prepared lunch for the men. Before they had taken three steps into the kitchen, she blurted it all out. Franz beamed with delight and asked many questions about what would happen. *An English Christmas. I never dreamt this would actually happen.* He was like a dog with two tails as he worked at hurricane speed for the rest of the afternoon and exchanged warm smiles with Angela at every opportunity. Franz now only had two things on his mind, Christmas and Angela.

Angela only had one thing on hers. *Why am I so especially happy that Franz will be with us? Don't kid yourself, Angela, you* **know** *why. Calm down. He's just a nice chap, anyone would like him. Everyone does like him. Yes of course, that's what it is. I wonder what Gerald is doing now?*

I haven't had a letter for nine days; that's a long time. I'll bet Franz... Gerald, has a good suntan now. I'll bet his body looks good. I wonder if it looks as muscular as Franz's? **Get on with your work, Angela!** *Think of Crete.., or something.*

Franz arrived for work on Christmas Eve with a parcel of clothes under his arm, and red eyes. "I'm sorry if I look a bit washed out. I didn't sleep much last night." Dave suggested that after morning milking, they should all go to the copse and choose a Christmas tree. Angela flapped her hands against her sides and squeaked her five-year-old child squeak.

The selection of the Christmas tree was a chance for Franz to show that what Germans did not know about christmas trees was not worth knowing. He explained the differences between Tanne and Fichte and which would last longer in the warmth of the lounge.

Dave and Ethel were impressed. "They're all Christmas trees to me," Dave muttered to his wife. Angela squeezed her hands together and smiled.

The ladies erected the tree in the lounge. This was not without its problems as the tree had proved to be about two feet too tall, exactly as Ethel had predicted. However, after a lot of sawing, and the occasional un-ladylike curse muttered through clenched teeth, the tree finally found a vertical position.

Everyone helped to decorate it, Angela had cut out shapes from paper and silver foil. "What's this shiny stuff?" Franz said.

"Window," Dave answered, "this is aluminium foil. The RAF cut the foil into strips and dropped it over Germany so it would reflect the German RADAR beams and confuse the night fighters. The RAF no longer has any use for it and is happy to give it away to anyone who wants it. Great for Christmas tree decorations."

The aroma of good cooking filled the house, teasing Franz's senses. He sat on the rug in front of the log fire and looked over at the tree, and some presents that had mysteriously appeared under it.

Ethel bustled in from the kitchen proudly bearing the source of the heavenly aroma, Mince Pies, with pastry so fine it melted in Franz's mouth. Dave handed him a glass of beer then turned on the radio. Franz gazed into the fire as the sound of Christmas carols completed his feeling of belonging.

"It's Christmas Eve and not Christmas Day that is the big day in Germany," Franz remarked. "If I were in Oberfeld now, I would be sitting with my family just as I am sitting with you. We would all be dressed in our best clothes. The family, well, that's only Dad, Mum, Uncle Fritz and Aunty Ariane, and me, would have got together in the middle of the afternoon to drink coffee and eat freshly baked plätzchen. Afternoon coffee is a big tradition in Germany, just like teatime here in England. An absolute must." He chuckled and rubbed his hands together.

"Plätzchen?" Angela said.

"A type of decorated biscuit made in countless different shapes. Very tasty. They are perfect with coffee." Everyone nodded their understanding and waited for Franz to continue as the soft fire-light supplemented the flickering candlelight to cast gentle shadows over the walls. "After coffee we would have put on our coats and walked through the snow to the church. The snow seems to have a special sound on '*Heilige Abend*.'" Franz paused and stared into the fire. For the first time that day, he looked sad.

Angela nodded and leant towards him. "What's '*Heilige Abend*,' Franz?"

He snapped out of it with a forced smile towards no one in particular. "Today. Now. Christmas Eve. Translated, it means holy evening. Like I said, it's our big day." His expression changed when he looked at Angela and he returned her sincere look with one of slight surprise. *Of course, she wouldn't know, would she?* Now he was smiling naturally, Angela nodded and maintained her encouraging expression.

"On our way to the church we would have held hands as we followed the sound of the Oberfeld brass band. Every *Heilige Abend,* the band stands in the belfry and plays Christmas carols. The sound carries, so you can hear them the moment you leave your house. It gives such an atmosphere." Passion oozed out of him as he scanned his attentive congregation. "Pure magic."

Then he chuckled. "Of course, the band members have usually been celebrating. Sometimes too much. I remember the time when, just as the pastor had finished a prayer, one of the band members knocked over his beer bottle. The whole congregation heard it roll along the wooden ceiling above the knave together with the muffled chuckling of the band. Not only that. The spilled beer began to drip through the cracks in the wood. Directly above the pastor. Everyone looked up, except for him.

"Wet marks appeared on the floor all around him. The pastor, who must have heard the bottle and the drips the same as everyone else, ignored them. He tried to look natural whilst shuffling about in the hope that he wouldn't get a direct hit. Naturally, 'God looked after his own,' and the pastor remained dry. You see? On the holiest of days, miracles do indeed happen."

Everyone chuckled. "After the service we would have returned home and feasted on a fat carp, before handing out our presents." Franz's face glowed with warmth and his voice softened, "You see. That's what I mean. It is different in Germany. It all happens on Christmas Eve, *Heilige Abend*."

Everyone gazed into the fire and tears came to more than one pair of eyes.

Then the carol singing changed. The ladies sprang to their feet and ran to the window. When Franz and Dave arrived at their side, Franz quietly gasped as he saw a group of about fifteen people huddled around two candlelit lanterns. *I know that tune. It's Stille Nacht!*

As he listened to the English words of the traditional German carol, "Silent Night," Franz's silent tears returned. He had never seen a group of carol singers before and he shook his head as he looked at the scene in wonder.

Mince pies for the hungry singers and a contribution for St Stephen's church later, the Greens and their guest retired to the fireside. Angela folded her arms and sat back on the sofa. *It's been so long. Twenty-one months. We'd only been married for five months. Seems like a dream. If it were it not for his pictures and letters, I would've begun to wonder if he really existed.*

She flicked a glance at Franz. Franz is real. He's here. I know him so much better. Twenty-one months now, three times longer than I have known Gerald. She gazed into the fire. *Of course, this is different. Isn't it? You must stop this. Think of a reason not to want. No. Not want...* She clenched her fist... *Like him. Yes, Franz is more like a brother to me.* She relaxed for a millisecond. *If that's so, why do I find him attractive?* She shook her head as if removing an insect before her eyes met with her mother's, who seemed to be studying Angela with some concern. "More beer, Dad?"

Wonderful smells of good home cooking filled the warm kitchen when Dave and Franz returned from milking the cows on Christmas morning. Plates of bacon, eggs, porridge, slices of freshly cut steaming hot bread, butter, cheese, jam and honey all adorned the holly and snowdrop decorated breakfast table. Everyone laughed, joked and ate heartily before it was time to open the presents.

Franz's lack of sleep during his last night at the camp had been due to finishing some woodcarvings he had been making as presents. He had decided to make these gifts for the Greens even before he knew about spending Christmas with them, and now was his chance to show his gratitude.

With a wide smile of anticipation and his hands clasped behind his back, Franz rocked up and down on his toes as his hosts unwrapped their gifts.

He beamed with joy as Ethel opened the paper that concealed the pair of cooking spoons, which had taken him a week to carve. Dave was impressed with the model of Rosie, his prize cow, and congratulated Franz on its accuracy.

Ethel studied Franz's clear expression of joy at Dave's pleasure and as her smile grew, she said, "You just love to make people happy, don't you?" She sighed and slightly shook her head.

Angela gasped as she opened her present. Franz had carved a dove in flight and had managed to find some paint to paint it white. Dave suggested that he could carve another one next year, and then Angela would have two Turtle Doves for Christmas. Angela and Ethel smiled. Franz did not get it, but smiled anyway. Five seconds later, Angela spontaneously put her arm around his shoulder and kissed him on his cheek. Dave ignored it. Ethel looked down at her spoons and pretended selective blindness.

Angela released Franz, put her hand up to her mouth and sniggered. Franz blushed as he looked sheepishly down at his feet and back to Angela's beaming face.

Ethel broke the moment by stooping under the tree and emerging with her presents. She had knitted a long scarf and a pair of gloves for Franz. He thanked her profusely. Dave gave him a bottle of elderberry wine and Angela gave him a double thickness woolly hat, which he immediately placed on his head. Franz and Angela shook hands this time; much more German.

The chickens had just gone into the oven when Dave, speaking to no one in particular, suggested, "I know it's early, nevertheless, it is only two hours to Christmas dinner. You know, I always find elderberry wine gives a man a good appetite." He rocked on his heels and pretended to whistle to himself. The hint taken, Franz offered to open his bottle of wine and miraculously, a corkscrew appeared in Dave's hand. Angela glared at her father, who chuckled. Franz occasionally stroked his newly kissed cheek as he drank and tried not to look at Angela, who seemed to be fluctuating between warmth and distain. Ethel bit her lip.

When she got up to finish preparations for lunch, Ethel walked to the kitchen sink and gripped it until her knuckles went white. She looked up to heaven and silently cursed.

All I can do is to chaperone them whenever possible and trust in Angela's morals. OK, she made a mistake once before, but she's a nice girl. Trouble is, Franz is such a nice guy, and thanks to stupid me, he's here. Please, God. Don't let Gerald fade.

Ethel summoned the ensemble to the table. Franz eyed the strange coloured pieces of paper next to each place setting. Angela saw his uncertainty and demonstrated the English tradition of wearing paper hats at Christmas dinner. Looking like a cockerel that had fallen into a paint pot, Angela shook with laughter as she donned a large floppy orange hat that had some feathers sticking out of the rear end. Franz found the idea of wearing paper hats rather strange, but when in England...

His hat was green and had multi-coloured stars painted on it. He carefully tried to place it on his head but to his embarrassment found his head was too big, or was it that the hat was too small?

Dave and Ethel mounted their multi-coloured frivolity on their heads as if it was a perfectly normal matter of course. The required formalities completed, the English were now prepared for Christmas dinner. Franz tried to take in the scene in front of him. "This island race," he muttered in German.

The meal began with a vegetable broth, Ethel's speciality. The main course astounded Franz, he had never seen so much food on a table at one time. The two golden roasted chickens, five different types of vegetable, including roast parsnips, and lots of crispy roast potatoes. "So much!" he exclaimed.

Ethel nonchalantly reached over to Franz's glass and poured him some Elderberry wine. "The idea is that you don't go hungry on such a day." She nodded as she cleared her throat and smiled, "that you should be able to have as much as you want, of what you want. I know things are tight, what with rationing and all that, but there are advantages to being a farmer you know."

All of this, plus the flamed Christmas pudding and mince pies to finish, flabbergasted Franz. He became so full, he could hardly move, although he took comfort from the fact that his hosts were also in the same state. Again he shook his head, such hospitality, and such friendliness to someone who had been in the midst of adversity and deprivation for such a long time, but even more unbelievably, to someone who had so recently been their enemy.

The last lunchtime formality was to listen to the King's Christmas message on the radio. Franz did not pay much attention to the speech, instead, he smiled as he watched his hosts give every word their full attention whilst frequently revering their portrait of the King and Queen over the mantelpiece.

Although milking time was fast approaching, Dave had now started on the cider and smirked in agreement when Franz suggested he stay in front of the fire; he and Angela would see to the cows. Ethel shuffled in her seat, and coughed loudly as they left.

Franz was unusually quiet as they worked in the cowshed. Like mirror images, they simultaneously finished milking their cow, stood up and turned to face each other. After a longing gaze, Angela inched toward the receptive Franz. Their lips were almost touching when, as she looked into his eyes, she suddenly jerked her head away, turned and silently led her cow out. Franz let out a heavy sigh, which Angela must have heard but chose to ignore.

Outside, she tightly folded her arms and stamped the ground. *If only Gerald was here. I wouldn't even have looked at Franz. He would have been just another worker, but now I can't get him out of my mind. I know it's forbidden, but I know what I feel.* She slammed the gate shut.

Ethel flicked her eyes over the pair upon their silent return to the house and satisfied their body language did not communicate union, beckoned them to the table.

Another gastronomic volcano awaited in the form of a Christmas cake. Although still in pain from lunch, Franz was too polite to say no. Ethel piled it on, and Franz kept eating.

Eventually, eating and conversation ceased as they all settled down and gazed into the fire. Dave put on some more logs, one of which was a little wet. As the surrounding logs burst into fire, the wet one hissed as it blew out two thin plumes of steam, one of which spiralled eight or nine times upward before vanishing into the dark of the chimney. The fire flickered and glowed, its warmth gave the final touches of luxury and comfort to the four souls staring glassy-eyed into its depths.

Franz kept glancing at Angela, who looked sad as she dreamt of Gerald. Or was she? He would have given the world to know what was going on in her mind.

So would Angela.

23.

Ethel had fallen asleep and with each breath, her knitting slowly slipped down by her side. She had been a good wife and mother and fed her 'family' and if they were all happy, so was she. Franz sighed with envy as he thought of such contentment. She looked ten years younger. Dave smoked his corncob pipe. He was especially proud of this pipe, as he had made it himself a few weeks before. It suited his image and certainly impressed everyone at the pub. Lusty as ever, he seemed intent on melting steel as he blasted away in front of the warm fire. His already red cheeks glowed even brighter as they soaked up the heat. As the crucible faded, the cider and fire took over and his grey-streaked hair flopped down over his forehead and over one eye, he began to doze. Ethel and Dave began lightly snoring in unison. For all their daytime bluster, Franz smiled at their peace, and looked over at Angela.

Lounging peacefully on the sofa with her legs curled up, she had kicked off her shoes to expose her dainty feet. Franz had never noticed her feet before. Their elegance amazed him; everything seemed in balance. Her ankles were in perfect proportion and her skin was like velvet. Franz watched her well-manicured toes move gently as she soaked up the warmth of the fire. They reminded him of the gentle flowing movement of long, fine birch branches, elegantly swishing to and fro in a summer breeze.

Angela's skirt had slid up one of her legs, just enough to expose one knee. He had only ever seen her legs once, that quick glance on her birthday. Now, even though he could only see half of one, he had the time to appreciate its lines. His eyes moved upwards and marvelled; she had slightly twisted her body, so accentuating the form of her outstandingly firm breasts.

Her head rested on her arms, which she had folded over the arm of the sofa in a position mirroring his as he lounged on his sofa. Only an arm's length separated them.

Angela looked into his warm brown eyes, saying nothing. Slowly, she changed her position to rest her chin on her hands.

Although her lips gave away no secrets, he could detect a faint enquiring smile in her eyes. The reflection of the fire flickered softly across her face, making her look tanned. He started to feel strange; light, floating. It was as if he was standing outside of himself. He could see Angela's eyes through his own and at the same time, he could see the scene of the two of them together until his out-of-body observer became his commander, "Go on then."

It was a strange power that did not allow either of them to notice that they were not consciously thinking, merely looking at each other, communicating subliminally. Franz slowly lifted his hand, gently reached out towards Angela, stretching out his index finger as he did so.

His fingertip moved slowly towards her. She did not flinch, did not avert her eyes from his. Very, very gently, Franz touched the tip of Angela's nose. His touch was so light, words would have been superfluous. A warm smile crept over his sad face before he slowly withdrew his hand. Angela smiled, and the moment was over. Their eyes slowly returned to the fire.

Angela's perplexity returned. *What **did** I just allow him to do? Why is my heart beating faster?* Her breathing quickened. *He electrified me. Not even on my first night with Gerald...*

Franz only had one thought; *I just want to be happy. I want love too. **Do** something about it!*

They engaged each other's eyes again with desire and a yearning to touch once more; eyes asking questions now, searching for unfound answers. Then Angela seemed to become agitated and nodded towards her sleeping parents. Returning to Franz, she drew breath but sighed and looked sad once more.

She held up her left hand, and unconvincingly gazed at her wedding ring and stroked it with her thumb. She looked at Franz, bit her lip and slowly shook her head. He sighed.

It was bedtime. Franz turned to his hosts. "I will remember today for the rest of my life. People are the same all over the world. We just want to live in peace." Then he addressed

Angela, "I can honestly say that I've enjoyed *every* single moment of today."

"Me too," Angela responded. She nervously flicked a look at her parents and encouragingly nodded her head at them as if to say, "And you?"

Ethel, who was looking uncomfortably at her daughter, changed her expression as she responded. "It was wonderful, Franz, and made all the more special with you being here. We are so glad that you could come."

"Yes. Well, I had a gap in my social calendar and I only live around the corner." They all chuckled.

"You're becoming excellent at English now," Dave said. "We'll have to watch our tongues in future. Anyway, the war screwed up many things for lots of people, but we hope it made you feel a little bit better about being so far away from your home at Christmas. I want you to know that you're our friend, and I hope always will be."

Franz's eyes started to fill. "Your kindness will always be with me, wherever I am. My English Christmas." Franz politely shook everyone's hand and retired to his room.

He gently lowered the door latch, leant against the closed door and whispered, "So, that was Christmas."

Not quite.

He undressed and went to his washbasin. He thought of the Greens and their kindness. He had shared their food and their presents, but the best present of all still eluded him. His hands grasped the edge of the washbasin, he leant forward and raised his head to see what he perceived was his pathetic image in the mirror. "Why can't you just be a bastard like every other man in this world? Just go for her.

"No, you won't will you. You'll respect what she said, won't you? You might have tried, but you *cannot* get her out of your mind. *Why* won't you do it?" The mirror did not answer.

He heard the top step of the stairs creak. Dave and Ethel were downstairs, it had to be her.

Angela had excused herself to go to bed. As she climbed the stairs, she focused on Franz's door, and paused. *He is just behind there. Only one inch of wood separates us. Thank God, we're separate...come on Franz. Come to the door. No, please don't make me choose.*

One step higher. *Is he waiting? Maybe I've read this wrong. No. Oh my God. Do not come to that door... Yes come... That touch, it did something to me. Come!*

Top stair. *I can almost feel him, touch him, smell him, and sense him. No need to talk, those eyes do it for him.* The stair creaked. *Don't be a fool. GO, TO, BED!* She tiptoed past his door.

Their bedroom doors were immediately adjacent, only the thickness of the doorpost and the dividing wall separated them. She lifted the latch; it made a light 'clack' as it lifted. Her eyes flicked to his door. It was opening.

One, then two brown eyes looked at her. She froze, but only bodily. The brown eyes were welcoming, wanting, asking. He opened the door a little further. She could see his face and the right side of his body. Franz smiled gently. His right hand, gently opening the door with his fingertips as his muscles flicked and twitched like a finely trained racehorse. His shoulders, like an ox. Even in the dim light of the landing, she could see his pulse pounding in his broad neck. Then, it was only a twitch, but a twitch in his direction. Then another, her eyes did not leave his. Then a bigger twitch, a small move and...

"Do you need a towel, Angela?" Ethel trumpeted from the lounge.

"No, Mum," she abruptly hissed as her eyes flicked down the stairs and back to Franz's. The briefly interrupted moment returned. She moved forward to kiss him, Angela was out of control. They came closer. Franz looked down at her opening lips...

"What was that you said, dear?" trilled up from below.

Angela thought such timing only belonged to Joe Louis. "I do **not** need a towel, Mother," Angela growled through clenched teeth towards her mother's approaching shadow at the bottom of the stairs.

Ethel peered round the corner of the stair door and in a whisper loud enough to wake the vicar she said, "OK. Don't make too much noise, you'll wake Franz."

Franz no longer stood in his doorway longing for Angela. He was now slumped against the dividing wall with his hands over his mouth. His eyes were brimming with tears as he convulsed with silent laughter. Angela looked to the heavens then rested her head against her hand on the doorpost and let out a huge sigh. "Mother!"

Angela watched Franz try to control himself, her pained expression changed to one of serenity. She reached out and gently tapped his nose with her fingertip. "Goodnight, Franz." Without waiting for an answer, Angela turned, floated into her room and closed the door.

24.

The headboard of Franz's bed rested against the dividing wall. He lay there and thought that if her bed were in the same position in her bedroom, then perhaps their heads were, at the most, one foot apart. *Damn this wall.* He constantly strained his ears for any sound of movement and thought his heart would jump out of his body every time her bed creaked. *Maybe she's coming to me?*

He waited, but nothing. *Should I go to her? No, think of all the problems if that went wrong. I'm free, she isn't. She must make the first move.* He tried to clear his mind and think of something else. His mind flicked over all that had happened that day. It had been wonderful, such a demonstration of kindness, he knew the Green family would always have a place in his heart, which brought him back to Angela.

He had spent many sleepless nights thinking about Freja or Josie, but this was different. They were pure fantasy, nothing had ever happened between them. Angela had at least strongly returned his affection, if only in innuendo. *No, the cowshed, and that moment on the stairs. What damned luck. Angela is everything I have ever wanted. But...*

Angela also lay listening and wondered if he would come to her. She had been just as excited when she first met Gerald, but this was different. Franz had grown on her, she had known him first. She loved his basic charm and calm personality, he seemed intelligent and she seemed to laugh more with him than with Gerald.

It was also true that she found him physically attractive; *tall, soft brown eyes, and those shoulders.* She liked his smile. Her thoughts swung back and forth between the excitement of the feelings generated at milking time, in front of the fire, at the top of the stairs, and the guilt of Gerald.

Poor Gerald, only other soldiers for company, stuck on an arid island in the middle of nowhere doing his bit for the country. There's no future with Franz, he'll return to Germany, and married ladies do not fancy other men. Or do they?

Footsteps on the landing, her heart leapt. A cough, *Oooh, it's Dad!* Her heart sank.

Franz's heart leapt at the noise too, he had even started to get out of bed, but flopped back at the smoker's cough.

Breakfast, smelt and tasted wonderful but there was little conversation. Franz and Angela avoided each other's gaze. Dave appeared to have a headache. Ethel talked to the ginger cat, alias 'The Feline Dustbin', to which she fed the bacon rinds. Although today was Boxing Day, life on the farm had to go on. Dave arose from the breakfast table and shuffled towards his boots, which were waiting by the kitchen door. "No holidays for farmers, what's a holiday?" he proclaimed. Franz took the hint, gulped down the last of his tea, stood up and thanked Ethel for her fine breakfast. He glanced at Angela intending to say he would see her later, but paused as their eyes met. In that instant, they both knew it was still there.

Ethel had seen the glance too and humphed loudly as she smacked her knife and fork down on the plate. After the men had gone, a short silence was broken as Ethel arose and turned to take the dishes to the sink, but paused with her back to Angela. In a low, clear voice she said, "You wouldn't happen to be going soft on that young man? What with you being a respectable married lady. Would you?"

"**How** could you possibly say such a thing, Mother? How could you even **think** it? Franz is a nice friendly person, but **that's all**. OK?"

Ethel turned around and her eyes speared her daughter. "OK, Angela, just keep it that way. Remember your husband, out there serving King and Country. I don't want any more scandal under my roof." Angela stomped up to her room and sat on her bed. Gerald smirked at her from his picture. She turned the other way, lay back on the bed and thought of brown eyes and muscular shoulders.

Franz and Dave spent the morning at work in the fields erecting a new wooden fence. Normally this was hot, hard work. However, on a crisp and clear winter's day, the work was still hard but not so hot.

Stunning beauty in the form of Angela and rural England surrounded Franz, but he did not smile. He had been away for over two and a half years. However nice these people were and even if, in their stupendous kindness, they had made him one of them, they were not his family. They were his captors. He could not have Angela, and he was not home. Home was home and he wanted to see it again.

Were his friends having a drink of Glühwein at the Sportplatz? If they were, they would be laughing, bragging, swapping jokes and telling stories. Or would they? How many of them were dead? How many had returned? Had any returned? Willi Junker, Bernd Wolf, Dummer, Jan Ingit. Was the Sportplatz empty? Was it still there at all?

"You got a hangover? You don't look too good, my lad. I told you the wine was strong." Dave's rustic voice chortled. It was a little difficult to tell the difference between the sound of Dave and the guttural splutter of the tractor engine; both seemed to choke for air. Dave spun to face Franz, passion radiated from his face as his arms gesticulated like an Italian goal-scorer. "Take some deep lugs of fresh air. Look at the country. God's country. Nowhere better to make you feel better."

Franz looked around and breathed deeply. *True,* Franz thought, *life could be a lot worse, or...*

Ethel had prepared a hot farmhouse lunch and the men were hungry. Angela announced that she would help with the hay in the barn after lunch, prompting another glare joust between her and her mother, who loudly cleared her throat. Franz stayed quiet and looked anywhere but at Angela. His expression scarcely concealed his delight.

Almost as soon as Dave had gone to re-fuel the tractor, Franz and Angela stopped working, looked at each other for two or three seconds, moved together and embraced.

The kiss did not rip with passion. They did not tumble to the floor and grip each other so tightly that they could not breathe. No. This was a kiss so tender and gentle, so sensuous it made both of their skins tingle. They floated. This was no prelude to raw sex; it was the exchange of pure feeling.

No one had ever kissed her like this before. He knew no other way.

After a short time, they were, of course, disturbed. Dave never had been light on his feet, and his footsteps forced them to finish their union, but not before they gazed at each other, squeezed hands and smiled. There would be another time.

The work in the barn took about an hour but nobody spoke much. Each time Dave faced the other way, Angela and Franz exchanged longing looks and embarrassed smiles. "I'm going to move the tractor." Dave said as he clumped off into the yard.

Two pairs of eyes watched him go and waited, they stared at the empty doorway. The tractor chugged into life. Like the start of a race, they simultaneously spun round and lunged at each other with arms outstretched. They squeezed and writhed in their passion until the tractor stopped when, with a longing look and swollen lips, they parted and returned to work.

Milking time came and Franz went to get the cows in. This entailed a walk of about half a mile to their field. He walked, walked and occasionally spoke her name and walked some more. It might have been twenty degrees below freezing or two degrees above boiling point, the heavens could have opened and thrown down hailstones as big as eggs, lightning could have struck him twice. Oblivious to everything, he would never have noticed. Conscious of only what was in his head and his heart, he finally realised he was running. He chuckled.

Only when he reached the stream did he realise he had run past the cow's field by almost half a mile. "Idiot." He jogged back to the brown and white Ayrshire cows who saw him open the gate, heard his whistle and ambled in his direction, but he took little notice. *Wow. Imagine someone as beautiful as Angela actually liking **me**!* "How did I get so lucky?"

The cows plodded past him. He skipped, smiled and playfully swished his stick at pieces of grass as he followed them back to the farm. It was wonderful to feel like this, all his years of frustration and doubt had left him, all in two kisses, and he could not wait for the next one.

Franz looked forward to holding her, walking with her, picnicking in the field, swimming with her, and being with her. Mostly, simply being with her. He had always looked so longingly at other couples, envious of them doing things together. Envious of what it must feel like to have someone who wants you as much as you want them. No one laughing at you. No need to feel embarrassed, only proud and happy.

Angela lay on her bed, which seemed more comfortable and warm than normal. She could still feel that tender kiss on her lips. She closed her eyes, and hugged her pillow as she relived the moment. However, she could also feel the nag of guilt returning. She opened her eyes. Her guilt looked down at her from his picture on the wall. Angela whined her repost, "No. Not you, Gerald. Not at this moment. Allow me this moment." She burst into tears. "Why me? Why, oh why can't I have a normal happy romance, just like everyone else out there? Why should I be the one to have these problems?" Gerald's smirk made him look as though he knew everything.

She closed her eyes and turned away, which calmed her, and for a few minutes, she curled up and relived her moment with Franz.

The day was to be cut short when Franz had to return to camp. He thanked the Green family for the most wonderful 'fest' of his life and, not wishing to look at Angela for too long in case he attracted suspicion, deliberately shared out his farewell glances between them all as he climbed into the truck that would return him to captivity.

Angela also tried to act nonchalantly but to no avail. Ethel noticed her continually waggling her head and brushing her fingers through her hair as she and Franz fixed their eyes on each other.

The truck trundled off and Franz leant back against the canvas canopy of the truck and again thought, *so that was an English Christmas.*

The feeling amongst the men back at camp was good as they swapped stories of their English Christmases. Otto had been lucky and had eaten goose cooked in exactly the same style as at home. A few of the men who had not had Christmas invitations were, at first, eager to hear what had happened but soon drifted away and lay on their bunks. The night guard patrol marched past their hut and the melancholy gradually descended over everyone.

Franz's thoughts were firmly on Angela, but he occasionally thought of Gerald. *What about when he returns? A fatal accident? That's disgusting, how can you wish something so bad on a man you've never met? No, you can't think like that. Nevertheless…,* **Franz.** *Simply continue to love every moment with Angela, and hope she'll choose you when he returns. If it comes to it, you'll just have to face him down.*

Angela eventually drifted off to sleep, but woke up in shock half an hour later. She had been dreaming of making love to Franz in the hay barn. She could even feel him inside her and was about to reach an orgasm when she woke herself up. She had had sexy dreams before, but never with the physical feelings as well. *How could I dream such a thing? God it felt nice.* The kiss, the dream, everything, her heart pounded. Was she actually having an affair?

25.

Try as he may, Franz was unable to engineer any time alone with Angela the next morning. They had to confine themselves to snatched glances, smiles and the occasional squeeze of the hand. Around lunchtime an army staff car from the prison camp appeared, Franz heard the officer say he wanted to speak about 'billeting' whatever that was. Franz got on with his work by the barn and cursed his luck that Angela had gone to the shop only five minutes before.

About twenty minutes later, he heard the car drive off and Dave's clumping footsteps approaching. He turned to find Dave grinning broadly. "No more camp for you, Franz." He almost knocked Franz to the ground with a hefty slap on his shoulder. "The captain says there's been a change of policy and because we've got a spare room, you can stay with us permanently, starting tonight. Ethel will give you some clean clothes, we've got plenty of Gerald's, and you can go back to the camp to pick up your things at the weekend."

Franz touched the peak of his cap and bowed his head humbly. "Thank you, thank you very much." He beamed and repeatedly pumped his fist. The hated camp would be in the past, and more to the point, it gave him more possibilities to see Angela. How his world had changed in such a short time. Although he had prayed to God in Normandy, he would not have described himself as being religious; nevertheless he looked up again and gave thanks.

Angela came out of the house, slowly walked over to the barn and leant against the door, flicking her gaze between her feet and Franz. She had her hands clasped behind her back and seemed quite bashful, but when their eyes did meet, their smiles said it all. Dave had gone, and they took the chance to embrace again. She pushed her breasts into him, she could feel his erection up against her. She squeezed his back and shoulders, but Dave's hobnail boots scraping on the yard outside warned them of his arrival.

Franz hastily whispered, "Come to the field with me when I get the cows for milking, we can be alone." Angela nodded as she straightened her hair and floated out of the small rear door back to the house.

Franz was working alone on the other side of the barn when he heard a vehicle drive off. A few minutes later the church bell struck twelve and he sauntered over to the kitchen for his lunch. He opened the door expecting to see his lunch on the table and Angela waiting with her parents. The first thing he saw was the army kit bag.

His eyes lifted and, Angela was sitting on Gerald's lap; they were passionately kissing. "Great news!" an ecstatic Ethel exclaimed, "Gerald is home. Kept it quiet he did. Thought he'd be home for Christmas but his ship broke down and marooned him in Gibraltar for three days." Franz looked at Angela, who beamed back a look of complete happiness. A look mirrored by her gyrating mother.

Act normally, give yourself time. As he shook the sun-tanned hand of the family hero, Franz even managed to give a slight nod of his head. Gerald greeted him with an equal lack of enthusiasm, almost irrelevance. Franz washed in a daze.

They sat down for lunch and Gerald held court as he recounted army life on the boring island of Crete. The Greens avidly listened to his memoirs, particularly Ethel who seemed especially enthusiastic as she refilled Gerald's plate. He spoke too fast for Franz to fully understand, even if he had wanted to.

Franz had hoped never to experience his bubble again but its descent was as fast as it was inevitable. He did of course remember to smile or laugh when everyone else did, but only pushed his food around his plate. He occasionally lifted his eyes towards Angela, who seemed completely absorbed by Gerald. The conversation slowed after about fifteen minutes at which point Franz, in a falsely jovial voice, said, "I'll go and see to the cows, Dave. You sit here and talk family talk. No problem."

"That's very good of you, Franz." Ethel said.

"OK. Bye, everyone."

Angela looked up and smiled a completely contented smile. Franz flicked a half-smile, lowered his expressionless eyes and flatly repeated his goodbye.

"Bye, Franz," Dave, Ethel and Angela chorused.

"Bye, Fritz," Gerald mumbled without looking.

Franz trudged away to the other side of barn and slumped down against the wall. He scanned the heavens and croaked, "Why?" It was still a clear, bright winter day. The weather had mirrored his mood so well until now, why did the weather lie to him? For the second time that day, he communicated with God.

"Why have you done this to me? Why do you show me the first real happiness I have ever had in my life; then take it away? What have I done so wrong that I deserve this? Why do you punish me? I know I am not perfect, but plenty of other people in this world are much worse, do bad things, and you let them have happiness. Why tease me... let me touch... let me feel... perfection, and then remove it so I may only know not happiness, but what I've missed?"

His outstretched hands implored an answer, but caught nothing until he pulled them to his face, where they only caught his tears. His grief went unheard, except by Katie the Labrador. She had followed Franz out of the kitchen and flopped down next to his crumpled form; she began to lick his bare ankle. This stopped Franz's sobs long enough for him to reach out a hand and gently stroke Katie's soft ears. She looked up at him with soulful eyes that matched his mood and nodded before she placed her head on her outstretched paws, closed her eyes, and went to sleep.

Franz knew he could not blame everything on God. He had known Angela was married. He was a fool to have let his emotions run away with him. "But Angela." Katie opened one eye and waited for more. Franz stroked her ear again and continued, "OK. She must have been happy to see him again, and to know he had returned safely. But how could she smile that last smile at me as she did? Was it only a game? A diversion? Sport? How can I be in the same room as them?"

He hauled himself onto his wobbly legs and started work. He constantly shook his head as tears rolled down his cheeks. He needed time to collect his thoughts. What if it had all been an illusion dreamt up in his frustrated mind?

His mind was always full of so many dreams and unanswered questions. Maybe he was the crazy one? They had only kissed a few times. He thought about what had, or rather had not, happened between them. Had he misinterpreted her friendliness?

After all, the English were not as formal as the Germans. In Germany, it was normal to go through your whole life calling colleagues Herr or Frau, never first names. If a person said to you "Call me Angela," that signified a close friendship, but here in England everyone called everyone else by their forenames. Yes. Probably he was the fool.

But why did Angela look at me as she did? Why did she allow me to touch her, to kiss her, and what about on the landing on Christmas night? If it wasn't for Ethel, I'm sure we would have kissed then, maybe even gone into the bedroom together. He kicked the ground. *Her bloody parents were always around.* He kicked a stone. It bounced three times before it smashed into the hedge with the crackle of breaking wood. *We never seemed to have more than one minute together since Christmas Eve and then we didn't do any talking.*

This will drive me crazy, we have to talk. Pull yourself together, act as if nothing has happened. Damn my luck. He pumped his fists. "I am German. I shall be strong." His expression hardened. "Fritz? You arrogant bastard! We'll see about you."

26.

The Green family listened to the wonders of Crete and the British Army until dusk. Gerald purred with satisfaction, he was the centre of attention and everyone must think he was wonderful, and brave, and intelligent, and perceptive and handsome. The more people listened to and looked at him, the more he pumped himself up and boasted of what he would achieve in the future. Nevertheless, he never forgot to show a little bit of false humility such as pouring the tea or handing the cat a small scrap of food so it would purr. Oh, wasn't he a wonderful husband and son-in-law. If she could have, Ethel would have purred too.

Dave, who had not said a lot for half an hour, yawned, and got up to help with the milking. Angela stopped him. "Dad! Today is a special day. Franz won't have a problem with the milking. After all, he did offer and I'm sure he wanted the family to have a little time together."

"How do you know that?" Gerald said.

"Well, he's a friendly, considerate sort."

Ethel coughed. "More tea, Gerald?"

"No thanks. I think I'll take my things upstairs and get out of this uniform. Come on, Angela, you can help unpack." Their eyes twinkled at each other as he squeezed her bottom. He became aroused; a fact that caused him some embarrassment as he got up from the table. He picked up his kit bag and casually held it in front of him as he and Angela moved towards the stairs.

"I'll clear up the dishes," Ethel said. Dave coughed and said he wanted to check on the cows after all. Wearing a lecherous smile, Dave pinched Ethel's bottom as he pushed past her; something he had not done for some time. She thrust his hand away, glared at her husband, and in hushed tones spluttered, "Not in front of the children." Dave sniggered, flicked his eyebrows up and down at his blushing wife and sauntered on his way.

By the time Angela and Gerald had reached the bedroom door, his jacket was off. One step inside, and her blouse was undone. The door closed and off came her blouse. His kit bag hit the floor at the same time as his trousers and she almost tripped over her skirt before they fell on the bed. Absolutely no foreplay, the whole passion lasted fifteen seconds at the most.

They rolled over with him still inside her; he was still stiff and she held on to him. He kissed her passionately on the nape of her neck, and slowly moved around to her earlobe, the feel and sound of his breath in her ear made her arch her head backwards in ecstasy. He moved slowly in and out of her again. Angela pushed back on him and inwardly gripped him as she wrapped her legs high around his back. "Yesss, yess, yes," she whispered quietly to herself, before sighing deeply.

Their lovemaking continued for another hour. The room became dark as Gerald displayed a repertoire of positions and expertise totally new, even slightly shocking to Angela. *How could anyone think to do such things?* She said nothing, her only sounds were when she whimpered each time she reached one of her three orgasms. As they lay exhausted on the bed, she stroked his perspiring brow. "It must have been so lonely for you in Crete."

"Yes, but the Minoan murals were inspiring," he chuckled. "You'd be surprised at what they show." Gerald wiggled his hips.

"So is that how you became so creative?"

"Certainly is." He gave her a very long, gentle kiss.

She rested her head on his chest and listened to his heart and smiled whilst she twiddled his nipple. Her mind wandered. *Thank God Gerald came home when he did. A baby. It would be so right now. The war's over. We would be a complete family.* She drifted off to sleep.

Angela's hair tickled Gerald's nose making it twitch. He wanted to brush it away, but did not want to break her bliss by moving his arm.

Three times in an hour. I haven't done that since my first afternoon with Krista. Seven times in a day was my best with her. Although, I am sure I could have beaten seven with that Arab beauty in Gibraltar, but she was too expensive. A pound an hour, whores must make a fortune. Christ she was good. He smiled. *I must look up Sue. I'll see if I can teach an old dog some new tricks.*

The smell of burnt toast awakened him from his dreams. One task Ethel had never managed to master was that of toast maker. It did not matter how hard she tried, how closely she watched or even how accurately she timed, the toast was always black. Neither Ethel nor anyone else had quite worked out how she did it with such consistency. Of course, theories abounded. They ranged from variations on absent-mindedness through sabotage to stupidity, a cruel last resort. Ethel said it was because of always being put-on by other members of the household, and consequently she had too much to do, which usually silenced the chorus. The smell of toast smoke and the sound of rhythmic scrapes coming from the sink always let the Green family know they were home. Gerald laughed. His laughs woke Angela from her pleasant dreams. "Sounds like the toast cremation."

"Certainly smells like it," Angela said. "Mother wants to remind us enough is enough and that we need to keep up our energy. "

Gerald smiled as he stroked her hair gently. "Have you had enough, Angela?"

"Oh no, I don't think I can ever have enough, I could do it again now. You were away a very long time, and it's made me very hungry."

"Talking of hunger, Marmite and burnt toast in front of the fire sounds great. Come on let's get up." Gerald looked out of the bedroom window and stared across the farmyard at the bright light filtering through cracks in the old wooden door of the milking shed. His eyes followed the knobbly fingers of light streaming across the uneven surface of the farmyard.

Shadows flicked back and forth under the milking shed doors. The door opened and he had a quick view of Franz industriously sweeping the slurry out of the door and into the drain. "Does Fritz always work that hard? Isn't it time he went back to his camp?"

"His name is Franz, and yes he does work hard," Angela answered earnestly. She joined her husband by the window, held his arm and rested her head on his shoulder as she gazed down on the light show. Her eyes cleared. Angela thought of the man behind the shadow and what had been. She stiffened slightly as she resolved that nothing had been. Just like the cavalry, her husband had returned just in time and her thoughts of Franz would remain her fond secret to treasure.

"He doesn't have to go back to the camp any more. He is living here now and sleeps in the room next door, here, next to us." She emitted a small sigh. An unthinking reaction; it just came out.

Gerald sounded surprised. "Who arranged that? He's a prisoner."

"He has worked here for some time. In fact, he arrived the day you left for Crete. He settled in quite quickly and his English gets better all the time. He has almost become one of the family. He stayed with us over Christmas. Anyway, it seems they want to close the camp and they knew Dad was the only man here. With you away and the fact that we had a spare bed, the commandant said that if we were agreeable, he could move in."

"You didn't tell me about him in your letters."

"It didn't seem important." Angela's stomach began to knot.

"Do you like him?"

"Yes. As I said, he's friendly. He's no problem."

"Yes, but do you *like* him? Do you think he's handsome?"

"What a strange question," she casually replied, grateful the darkness was hiding her blushes. "Yes he is quite good looking. Before you go any further, it's you I want. I waited for you. All I want is to have a happy, cosy family. Just you, me and our babies."

"What babies?"

"The three or four that will come, I hope." Gerald laughed as they turned from the window and dressed. Angela resolved to have more self-control when talking about, or near Franz. No emotion or blushing because after all, there was no emotion to show. Was there?

Franz joined the family around the large oak table for an evening meal of rabbit pie, mashed potatoes, carrots and Brussels sprouts, all covered with lashings of onion gravy. Candlelight softly lit the room and the crackling fire gave warmth to the winter kitchen. Talk ranged from the farm and hunting, to the army and the future.

Gerald put his knife and fork down, cleared his throat and sat up formally, "I know what I want to do in the future. I shall study electrical engineering!" He waited in vain for applause. Everyone stared at him. "I feel sure this is where the future lays. I will soon be out of the army and must look for work."

Dave looked slightly affronted. "What's wrong with the farm?"

Gerald moved his head to one side and pursed his lips, like a boxer riding a punch. "Franz is here, so this gives me the opportunity to learn a new trade. With this would come some extra money, which would relieve our reliance on the farm." Proclamation over, he continued to eat his pie.

Everyone thought about this for a few moments before Dave sat back in his chair and rubbed his chin. "If you're serious about this, Gerald, I could have a word with Stuart Bright down at the pub. You know him. He lives in the big house by the bridge and has an electrical company down in London. Maybe he'd have some work for you?"

"That's a great idea, Dave. Thank you. The army told us about some training courses to help us get work when we are back in Civvy Street. That's where I got the idea. If I get trained up and there is a job for me at Mr Bright's, that would be perfect."

"London's a long way away, Gerald," Ethel said.

Dave shook his head. "Stuart Bright manages it OK. We have the main line express to Kings Cross in Imton. So long as he gets paid enough, it should be OK."

Angela intervened. "You never know, it may not be too long before we have more mouths to feed. We'll need extra money then." Ethel sat bolt upright and grinned. Her eyes flicked between her daughter and Dave, who continued to eat his pie and pretended not to notice. Gerald looked uncomfortable and also pretended not to notice. Franz, who had understood, looked even sadder.

"Can we expect the patter of tiny feet soon?" Ethel asked to no one in particular before fixing her eyes on the bashful looking Angela, who looked nervously at her husband, who looked at the fire.

"Just an idea, Mum. Give us time."

"Mrs Evans has some nice patterns for baby clothes; I shall have to ask her. I..."

"Slow down, Mother."

Throughout the rest of the meal, Franz and Angela exchanged a number of glances and even the occasional smile. Franz's smile was unnatural. Angela's polite, but giving nothing away. She noticed Franz had not eaten. Later, there was a short moment when Dave was asleep, Gerald had gone to the toilet and Ethel was upstairs. Franz, who had been sitting at the table, got up to go to his room. Angela saw her chance and came to him.

She held both of his quivering hands as his pained eyes looked down at her. A door closed upstairs, her mother was coming.

"My husband is home. He is my husband and I love him. I know it's painful for you, but it would never have worked. I'm sorry, Franz, you will have to accept it, because that's the way it is. I very much hope we can still be friends." She kissed him on the cheek and gave him a kind smile. He nodded his understanding and smiled sadly. Their hands parted and he let out a long resigned sigh.

Ethel came into the room and Franz excused himself to go to bed. He quietly closed the door and flopped down on his bed. His tears welled up again. He did not blame Angela, she had no choice. That lucky bastard Gerald had her. Franz thought that even with the little of Gerald he knew, the man seemed arrogant and definitely did not deserve Angela. She needed love not arrogance. "The Swine. The lucky Swine." He punched his pillow.

About an hour later, Franz heard the top stair creak as the young couple came to bed. It was torture for him to know that when they were in bed they would be less than two feet from his head. He listened and heard some soft laughter, soon followed by the rhythmic squeaking of their bed, which went on and on, it seemed it would never stop. Then it did.

"Thank God for that," Franz spontaneously said out aloud. He was certain he heard some quiet chuckles. Maybe they had heard him. He did not know how he would put up with these noises night after night. Franz scrabbled at his scalp in frenzy before stuffing his fingers in his ears. He imagined Gerald on top of her, in her.

Control yourself or you'll go crazy because whether you like it or not you're here for some time to come. How quickly the world turns. I want to go home, home, home!

The activity in Angela's room continued well into the night, every night for about a week. It was difficult to decide who looked the most tired, Angela, Gerald or Franz.

Even Dave and Ethel seemed a little tired. Franz did not know if they had been disturbed or inspired.

Franz resolved that the less he saw of Angela the better, and whenever possible tried to work on his own out in the fields. Dave had taught him how to make a traditional English farm hedge and he was anxious to improve his skills. Although his German penchant for detail made his work a little slow, his hedges and ditches were indeed a work of art and took his mind off his other pressing problems. It also gave him a lot of pride to gaze down the finished line and know people would admire his achievement long after he had gone home.

Gerald had been home for eight days when he announced he had to return to Wisbeach barracks for two days for his demobbing, and whilst there, he would see about his electrical engineering idea. He would return on Friday evening, hopefully around six. Friday evening came and started to go, seven o'clock, eight, ten, no Gerald. "Not to worry," Ethel said.

"Typical army. Must be a delay with his papers, or they don't have a de-mob suit to fit him, or some other fine thing, I don't know. Let's go to bed."

"Or he's getting drunk with his mates," Dave said.

Four o'clock came and Franz awoke to hear someone climbing the stairs. He heard Angela get out of bed and rush to the bedroom door. When Gerald entered the bedroom, he heard Angela whine with pleasure as she flung her arms around him and kissed him.

It took Angela about two seconds to smell the aroma. She continued to kiss him as he fondled her breasts. She broke off the kiss, "I can smell someone else."

"What do you mean?" His eyes looked unsure, deceitful even.

"I can smell her on you, Gerald. Good demob party was it?"

He shrugged, screwed up his face and flippantly answered, "Well, it was just the mood of the moment. It was nothing. I'm home now. Your tits feel wonderful."

"As good as hers? But why? Why did you do it, Gerald?"

"I just called into the pub on the way home. To see the lads..."

"That tramp, Sue Moore? Was it her? She's been the pleasure stop for half of the U. S. Army Air Force. Why do you want her? Why not me?"

"It was just the mood, the moment. Look, I'm sorry. I didn't mean to hurt. It doesn't mean anything. Come on let's go to bed."

"It means a hell of a lot to me that you are only home for a little over a week and you are off having sex with that slut."

"Enough, Angela!" Gerald's face reddened and his veins started to bulge.

He clenched his teeth and his eyes widened, until suddenly, he deflated. He looked deep into her eyes, held her lightly by the shoulders, and then gently kissed her. She went to punch him off, but... A fight raged inside her, an ever depreciating fight. She mumbled, "Bastard," at him, and then he was her's again... or was she his?

27.

10 a.m, 4 February 1947, and Franz, third in a line of six men, waited nervously outside the major's door. It had been six months since his last 'attitude' interview. He had not known why he was there, but after forty men had subsequently gone home, he realised that somehow he had missed his chance. What were the criteria for return? Nobody knew, but this time all were determined to put on a good show. Everyone shuffled, coughed, scratched and looked everywhere except at each other. It was his turn.

The door opened to reveal a short staff sergeant who looked like a bald mouse as he peered over the top of his large round glasses. His nose twitched as he sniffed for cheese. Or Nazis! Although looking physically incapable of ever having fought anyone, he appeared sinister, a bit like a bald Himmler. Franz marched past him, stood to attention in front of the officer's desk and saluted with a military salute. Franz awaited events as the major read the file that lay open on his desk.

The ubiquitous portrait of the King and Queen hung on the wall behind the major. The steady tick of a clock on the mantelpiece over an unlit fire was the only sound in this bare, functional office. It must have been about two minutes before the officer looked up and stared at Franz with an unnerving intensity. The major sat upright and saluted, Franz saluted again. "What do you think about your officers in the war?"

"After training, I was only in Normandy for a few hours. I hardly saw an officer."

"What do you think about Adolf Hitler?"

"Originally he brought order and pride to Germany, but he did it through a lot of fear and racialism. Now Germany must pay the price."

"Were you a Nazi?"

"No."

The major leant forward, placed both elbows on his desk and clasped his hands together. His eyes narrowed and he nodded. "But you supported them?"

"No, I supported Germany. The Nazis were fundamentally bullies and thugs."

The major pointed a finger at Franz, "Why didn't you speak out?"

Franz remained unfazed. "To speak out was very dangerous. No one spoke out."

"But to support Germany was to support the Nazis, wasn't it?"

"No, the Nazis were just there, they were always there. There was a strong nationalistic feeling, it won over everyone. However, when I was in the hospital in Lancaster, I met many 'SS'-type Nazis, and I think it took that experience to show me just how fanatical and evil they all were. It was an evil empire when such people ran it. They have destroyed Germany and a lot of lives here in Britain too."

The major sat back in his chair, rested his hands on his lap and looked Franz up and down. His voice softened. "Have you enjoyed working for the Greens?"

"They're fine people and have been very friendly. But I want to go home."

"Do you?"

"Yes, I want to help rebuild Germany, and I want to see my home."

The officer leant forward again, his hands remained in his lap, he spoke firmly, "Many British servicemen will never return home, thanks to Germany."

"True. However, all I can do is play my part in building a land where that can never happen again. The Green family have shown me the power of forgiveness and compassion, and that normal people are the same the world over. If more people feel like that, there will never be another war."

The major's face relaxed as he rested one elbow on the arm of his chair. "Your home town is in the East of Germany. How do you feel about the Russians? They'll be the masters if you go back."

"I'll deal with that when I get there. I'll have to accept that others will tell us what to do for some time yet."

The major looked back down at the file and paused before he asked, "Are you and Mr Green the only men at the farm?"

"No, sir. Mr Clarke, the Green's son-in-law, has recently returned from Crete."

A further silence, during which the clock ticked, and the officer scratched at the file. Suddenly, and with a great deal of panache, he crashed a rubber stamp onto the paper and snapped the file shut. "You'll go home on Friday. Good luck."

Franz took the news without emotion. He saluted, turned and followed the sergeant out of a different door into another office where a corporal recorded his details. Franz stared straight ahead, his eyes glazed. *Home again!* Nearly three long years of imprisonment were about to end.

The Green family were delighted for him. Ethel baked a special cake in honour of the occasion and Dave opened several bottles of cider, most of which he drank personally. Angela had mixed emotions about the news.

She knew in spite of what she had said to Franz, that she still had strong feelings for him. No doubt, she would be very sad to see him go. However, on balance she decided that ultimately it was a good thing. After all, he was a prisoner, the war was over and it was only right he should go back to his home and family. Anyway, seeing him each day confused her emotions and stopped her from having a normal life with Gerald. Perhaps this was why Gerald went with that bitch Sue Moore. Yes, it was a shame, more than that, but better all round if Franz went.

They spent a last social evening around the fire reminiscing over the many laughs they had shared and speculating over how much Franz would find left of his shattered country when he returned. He had eventually received some censored letters from his parents, so he knew they were still alive, but he sadly added that he was unsure if his house still existed.

Gerald was absent. He had gone to Cambridge to attend an interview for an electronics-training course. He had said that due to its timing, he needed to stay overnight. The thought of that gave Angela indigestion. Franz and Angela frequently smiled at each other. It was easier to relax without Gerald around, but sometimes their smiles dimmed and they just looked; a last scene without actors or script, just an audience in a theatre of broken dreams.

Franz seriously thought about engineering a top of the stairs rendezvous. Angela wondered if he would too. Wondered, or hoped? They both lay awake in their rooms and thought of what might have been, and who for the last time, lay only inches away. That damn wall. They both cried.

The lorry arrived at eight-thirty next morning. The Greens and Franz hugged each other. Dave started to make a little speech to thank Franz for everything, but stopped and shook his head. "You're a great lad, look after yourself, son."

Ethel looked terribly sad. She flapped her hands against her side, shrugged, shook her head and then kissed Franz on his cheek. "I so wish you didn't have to go, but I know you must. Please keep in touch. Send us a card at Christmas." Even though she meant every word, she breathed a sigh of relief.

Angela was unable to stop herself, she did not want to. What did it matter what she said or did? She would probably never see him again. Her eyes overflowed as she embraced him, she kissed him on his neck and whispered, "I think you are the loveliest man I have ever met."

"Same for me, except you're not a man." They broke off the embrace, looked into each other's tearful eyes and laughed.

"Are you ever serious, Franz Schmidt?"

A last lingering look and the lorry revved its engine. Franz looked at the tearful ensemble for the last time, threw his kit bag into the back of the lorry and climbed in. The Greens stood where he had left them until the lorry had trundled out of sight down the bumpy lane. Franz did not look back, he had his last image. He must look forward. To what? He was about to find out.

28.

Franz's heart pounded as the train slowed down. He saw the sign 'OBERFELD' on the signal-box, sprang to the door and lowered the carriage window. A sudden rush of smoke, soot, steam and cold air entered the carriage and initiated a fit of coughing from an elderly man who sat nearby. As Franz stuck his head out of the window, the man elbowed Franz's rear-end as hard as possible. Franz was oblivious to anything but Oberfeld as he strained his neck to see his home. Three long years of waiting for this moment were over.

The train screeched and juddered to a halt and half a second later, Franz stepped onto the snow-covered platform. "Yes!" He punched the air. "Home!" He savoured two or three deep breaths of air and rocked back on his heels as he took in the scene. The station was OK, all in one piece. "Is it? Yes it is, Herr Baumann, the stationmaster collecting the tickets." Franz jauntily strolled up to him, beamed and with an outstretched hand said, "Guten Tag, Herr Baumann."

A limp handshake and a blank face returned the greeting. Franz looked into the old stationmaster's questioning eyes and imploringly nodded as if to say, "It's me. I'm home!" The tired man's eyes looked back as if to say, "Who the hell are you?"

"Don't you remember me, Herr Baumann? I'm Franz Schmidt. Irma Schmidt's son. Landstrasse Four."

At last, the stationmaster's eyes flickered. "Yes, now I remember you. I'd heard you were still alive. Don't expect a hero's welcome. Things are different now, our Russian..." he spat on the floor, "our Russian 'friends' don't always take kindly to old soldiers. Don't raise your hopes." He spat again and walked back to the warmth of his cabin to drink a large Nordhauser Doppelkorn Schnapps, his sixth today.

Franz looked around as he walked down Bahnhofstrasse towards the junction with Landstrasse. He saw no sign of any conflict, or indeed any people; a village untouched by the ravages of war. *Maybe they repaired everything? No. No sign of any rebuilding.*

The bus stop bench, where he used to talk to Freja, was still there. So was the bakery. He sighed deeply as he thanked God for this and for allowing him to see his home once more before abruptly halting outside the dilapidated house that was formerly the pristine residence of the Rabinowitz family. All the windows were broken. The door, daubed with a faded Star of David, hung off its hinges exposing a trashed hallway. Nature had reclaimed the once perfectly manicured garden. It all looked so sad and eerie. This was the only house in the street that looked unkempt; no one had touched it. Franz shivered as he remembered the ghastly 'football' game. He moved on, nearly home.

His mother was washing some potatoes in the sink when he opened the back door. She stared aghast at the phantom before her. The phantom stared back, shocked at how his mother had aged ten or fifteen years in the space of only three. She dropped her knife in the water and reached for a towel. Without averting her gaze, she slowly dried her hands, shook her head and quietly mumbled to herself, "Is this a dream, or are you really who I think you are?"

Franz gently closed the door behind him and grinned. "What's for dinner, Mum?"

His words stung her into consciousness. Towels and arms went everywhere followed by rivers of tears from them both. A quick look at each other, followed by more passionate hugging before she wailed, "I have dreamt of this day. Ooh, you're back. My son is back."

"Mum, you'll never know how much I've longed for this. Where's Dad?"

"Here," boomed a voice from the doorway. His tearful father stood with arms out-stretched towards his son. The three-man scrum hugged, kissed and cried. "Sit down, Franz," his father said. "Mum'll make you some coffee. We have a lot of news to catch up on. I'm sorry about the coffee. We can't get the real thing anymore, only this dreadful coffee substitute."

His father's eyes sparkled as he thumped his fist on the table. "No. The coffee will take time. Have a beer!" He bear-hugged his son again.

"I'll have both," Franz laughed.

They talked non-stop for the rest of the day whilst they had their malzkaffee, a plain 'rührkuchen' cake, several beers and a dinner of schweinebraten with klösschen. Franz recounted his army experiences, and a lot about the Greens. He did not mention the Schwanz incident; that would have re-opened a can of painful worms. After dinner Rudolf, Franz's father, drank a large swig of beer from his bottle, banged it down on the kitchen table, looked solemnly into his son's eyes and began.

Rudolf told how Oberfeld, which was a village of around six hundred people, had been lucky. When the Russians approached in spring 1945, the German forces had decided to make a stand in the Grunewald. They chose to defend a line along the ridge from the Zoll Haus to the Schwarzteich. Just before the battle began, the SS came to the village and took all the men they could find, Rudolf included, to the forest.

"They gave us guns, and about fifteen or twenty rounds of ammunition. And do you know what? My gun was Russian! Must have captured it... All they had. We had to defend The Fatherland with bloody Russian guns. I wonder how Göbbels would have explained that! They dumped six of us by a track in the forest and told us to defend the Fatherland at all costs, even if that meant death! **Should it** enter our head to return to Oberfeld, or run away anywhere else, they would hang us. The bastard stood there, swinging a noose and smashing it into his hand. Just so we'd get the message. The battle began at dawn and lasted all day."

Rudolf recounted how he had tried to conserve his ammunition and had killed at least two Russians before it had all gone. Unable to fight anymore, he had said his prayers. "And do you know what, Franz? God answered me. An officer jumped into our ditch and detailed me, and the other three men who were still alive, to become stretcher-bearers." Even greater luck followed when Rudolf replaced an injured ambulance driver.

Irma interjected to recall her terror when she saw the SS take Rudolf away, she was sure she had seen the last of her husband and told of how she cried every time the windows shook from the blasts, even though the battle was about eight kilometres away.

She put her head in her hands and thumped her elbows down on the table. "The village was full of lorries and all sorts of wagons. They took everyone to the school. It became a hospital. Arrived in hundreds. Old men and boys. Many died before they got proper medical help." Tears ran down her arm.

Another swig of beer and Rudolf continued. "It was getting dark. The Russians had virtually got the battle won. Someone, somewhere, must have given the order to retreat, or maybe everyone had just had enough? I don't know. Anyway, I was near Oberfeld, when I saw hundreds of our boys coming after me.

"At first, I thought they were Russians until they caught me up and told me to get the hell out of there, because it was all over. I managed to get my wounded men to the field hospital, but couldn't do more because the wagon ran out of fuel. I decided for better or worse, to find my way home.

"I didn't want to meet any SS, so I hopped over fences and scrambled through the neighbours' gardens to get back to your mother." He firmly tapped the bottle on the table. "The SS had already made some examples just as they had threatened to do. I saw two of them swinging from that oak near the sportplatz."

Irma gazed down at her hands, which were now fiddling with a bottle top. She said, "I was so relieved when he came in through the back door, I just fell at his feet and kissed his legs. I thought he was gone. Gone for good." Another tear dropped from her cheek onto the table.

Rudolf then went on to say how he hid in the attic and how he thought that every sound was the SS or the Russians. The next morning was calm, until about nine o'clock. Irma had just told him that the German soldiers had all gone in the night when all of a sudden they heard the rumble and squeaking of tanks, Russian tanks.

Rudolf opened another bottle of beer. "Fortunately they didn't stop in the village. Thousands of foot soldiers followed them but showed no interest in anyone or anything as they also just passed through. I felt safe enough to come down from the attic. After all, I was no combat soldier. It was weird. We all just waited. The village was silent." Franz and his mother stared at the table. The only sound in the Schmidt kitchen was Rudolf slurping as he drank half of his beer.

Rudolf blew his nose, cleared this throat, shook his head and continued, "Sure enough the peace was broken later that day." Franz noticed his father was now gripping his beer bottle tightly. "A group of Russian soldiers arrived in a lorry and searched some of the houses. They worked their way up the street. Your Mum and I didn't know whether to hide or run. Thank God, they didn't get as far as us. They found what they were looking for at number twenty, the Held family. Young Anna Held screamed for most of the afternoon, it was chilling."

Irma took a handkerchief and tried to stem her tears. Rudolf patted her on her arm, and looked at his son through sullen eyes. He leant forward. "The filthy bastards threw a mattress down outside her front door and gang raped her in the street for all to see. Until it got dark."

His sad, sad eyes were full of questions and empty of answers. "Different groups of Russians came to do the same thing next morning, but when another group arrived after lunch, they were to be disappointed, they found Anna hanging from a beam in her cellar. No one knew if the Russians had done it, or she had done it herself.

"Anna's mother, although we know she tried her best, had been powerless to stop any of it. The Russians also used her. Every other woman stayed indoors until the main body of the Russians had moved on.

"Frau Schunk hid her daughter, Heike, in a cellar cupboard for four days. Even to this day, some still don't like to come out."

Rudolf looked at Irma, who was shaking. Gently, he leant over and gave his wife a tender kiss on her cheek. She reached back and squeezed his hand.

Franz had heard enough. "What happened to all my friends?"

"Willi, Bernd, Jan and Dummer are all gone. Willi and Dummer in Warsaw, Jan on the western front at Arnhem. I don't know what happened to Bernd. Horst made it back OK. He married young Freja Jung two months ago. Nice girl."

Franz's head dropped. First, his friends, now the girl... the girl whose image had fed his fantasy, given him strength through those long, lonely hours in the camp had been stolen by that fat-arse, Horst Alm. He looked at the table and shook his head in disbelief.

"Things settled down a bit after that," Rudolf said. "Except that it's all change at the top now. The Nazis have gone and the Communists are in charge. At first, apart from the top people, the same people did the same jobs, Nazi one day, Communist the next." He shook his head and stared painfully at his son. "It takes your faith away sometimes, doesn't it?"

Franz stared blankly out of the window.

"Mind you, not everybody got away scot-free." His voice perked up. "Remember that yobbo Tomas Baumann? Well that young Nazi swine became a guard at Buchenwald concentration camp near Weimar. Do you know about Buchenwald?" Franz shook his head. "When people began to disappear, like the Rabinowitz family, they collected them all together in special camps where they worked them to death.

"My old mate Jens lives in Weimar. I saw him when he visited his mum last year. This place, Buchenwald, was one of those camps and Jens told me that when the Americans came and found Buchenwald, they marched most of the residents of Weimar up there and made them clean it all up.

"He said there were piles of bodies, well he actually said skeletons, three metres high. Anyway, when it was all over, the Herr Baumann managed to sneak back home and began work with his father at the station. He was responsible for booking-in all the returning soldiers and labourers," Rudolf sneered, "and arrogantly he did his job too.

"That reminds me, you will also have to register as having returned. Big brother Joe Stalin wants to know everything.

"So, one day the Russians turned up at the station, bundled him into a car and he hasn't been seen or heard of since." He smiled and nodded. "I heard there were a lot of German communists slaughtered in Buchenwald during the war." Then Rudolf's expression hardened and Franz could see the muscles of his jaw flexing as he clenched his teeth. A slight shake of his head, and he looked up at his son. His eyes appeared bewildered, but then they too hardened. "In fact, if he is still alive, he may even be getting some of his own medicine as we speak, because Buchenwald is still in use. It's where the Russians send all of the ex-Nazis and anti-communists." He shook his head again. "What goes around comes around."

Rudolf stared at his beer bottle as his finger stroked its neck. "Like I said, Franz, Nazi one day, Communist the next. You have to bend with the wind, Franz. We're all here to do as we are told, just like it has always been," he emptied his beer bottle, "just like it will always be."

Franz looked around at the familiar surroundings of his bedroom as he lay in his bed that night. His pictures, his books, his football, all exactly as he had left it. His mother had kept it spotlessly clean and fresh for his return. Throughout his captivity, he had longed for this moment. How happy he would be, how lucky he would be.

Wind and rain lashed the windows, Franz snuggled deeper under his quilt, only his eyes and the top of his head protruded. He rolled left and right to trap the quilt under his body. As a small boy, he had always done this and enjoyed the warmth and security of his bed on such a night. He felt lucky, and it made him think of those who were not so fortunate.

This night, it reminded him of the desolation of Drakesford; he shivered, wrapped himself even tighter in his quilt and gave a silent prayer of thanks.

As the candlelight flickered around his room, so the images of his fallen friends flickered through his mind; smiling faces sharing happy moments that would never come again. Happy eighteen-year-olds who would never age. "Goodbye, old friends." He cried for their loss.

He thought of Freja and Horst cuddled up together in the marital bed. Although more than disappointed at that piece of news, he was surprised at how quickly he accepted it. It was ridiculous to expect anything more. After all, he had never even kissed her or found out what she thought of him. She, like the pictures on the camp hut walls, had only been a fantasy. *I am a fool.* He was good at convincing himself of that. He needed comfort. He thought of Angela. She was real.

The next day, Franz registered with the authorities and had to attend an interrogation by some anonymous communist commissar. Franz had to exercise considerable self-control in order not to shake his head in exasperation too often.

His interrogator read the questions and accusations from a dog-eared question sheet provided by his masters. He was sure Franz was a spy, until he became equally as sure that he was not. Franz was now in the system, but what work could he do?

He had no formal educational qualifications, other than his very good class-ten certificate, and he did not have a trade. The authorities gave him work in a local mine, where he linked the ore-wagons together to form small underground trains. His initial optimism vanished after about two hours of this boring monotony. "There must be something more to work than this?"

His first day off saw him take the train to Leipzig and visit the university, where he felt sure his English proficiency might help him to get him onto a teacher-training course. He clung to the envelope containing his school report and asked to see the Professor of English.

The post-war chaos had also permeated the university entrance system and unusually for the German penchant for correctness, the university had relaxed many of the normal entry rules. The Professor, impressed by Franz's grasp of the language and desire to teach, said that subject to some written tests and 'one or two other searches,' he would consider Franz for entry that autumn.

Franz punched the air with delight when, after six weeks, a letter arrived confirming his university admission.

The Oberfeld girls had little interest in him. They had known him since he was small and throughout his spotty and scruffy period. They had all suffered his teasing or had their plaits tied together in the German lesson. University life was refreshing. Firstly, many young ladies; secondly, a lot of sport and thirdly many young ladies. Determined to make up for lost time, he attended every party possible. College girls had no Oberfeld prejudices and it was so refreshing to start with a clean slate and a clean skin.

He also joined the football club where he started well by getting into the first team and scoring four goals in the first two matches before his knee problems flared up again. At least it gave him a lot more time for girls, and a little bit of time to study.

He had been in college for about seven weeks and had stopped to read a notice board one morning when a voice to his left said, "Here we are again, Franz." He spun around and stared with disbelief into the eyes of Otto Stamm.

"Otto! When did you get back from Drakesford? What are you doing here?"

Franz clasped Otto's outstretched hand and they both laughed and vigorously shook hands. "Three months ago, and I study Russian. And you?"

"Intimate Feminine Anatomy and English."

"Sounds like a good course to me. 'Got to go, but let's meet for a beer tonight."

Sitting in the cheapest bar in town, they reminisced over past camp glories and sorrows, compared repatriation notes, discussed the women on their respective courses, and got drunk. Otto talked about a red-haired beauty from Worbis whom he had unsuccessfully tried to date. "Hey, Franz. Why don't you come to a party with me on Saturday? I know the 'Worbis Red Head' is going, why don't you try your luck?"

Franz and Otto walked past a former garden allotment area on their way to the party. It was a mass of large craters, weeds, concrete chunks, smashed gates and huts. They saw masses of tangled fruit trees that in their death pose illustrated how bombs had violently smashed them into each other and extinction. Even though it was now late 1947, the allotment had not been touched since the moment the bomb fell. "Your father works for the government doesn't he, Otto? Does he say why nothing has been done to places like this?"

"Ha, no money, no materials, no machines, no inspiration; the Russians have taken all the usable machines back to Russia. My father told me that they even dismantled a complete factory in Cottbus, everything went.

My father needed some cement recently. When it didn't arrive and he asked why, the boss, a Russian 'friend', said that it too had been sent to Russia."

"Why, when we need it here?" Franz asked.

"My father asked the same question, and the answer? 'Germany must pay for the war.' So he doesn't see the point anymore."

Many people in Leipzig lived in flats but kept allotments which, providing they still existed, they visited at weekends and at holiday time. Some of them built small weekend houses there, with a bedroom and a lounge. Perfect for a student party.

29.

After Franz had left the farm for Germany, Gerald 'worked' on the farm, but lacked in the motivation department. He continually moaned to Angela that farming was not for him. He often pledged his love to her and in their better weeks, he was indeed loving and considerate but would gradually degenerate into surly and aggressive moods. Particularly when he had difficulty explaining to his sceptical wife that electronics was the future.

"Why can't you just accept what I say is true? Why are you always challenging my will? I'm not so sure that you are as intelligent as you're supposed to be. Can't you see where the future is, 'Village Girl?' I want to be a 'somebody.' Someone that people will look up to and say, 'That's Gerald Clarke, a man with a vision!' They won't do that if I am an ordinary bloody farm labourer." Then the convincing argument landed. "A good wife should support her husband."

Whenever they went for a stroll or even out to the fields to get the cows, Angela often tried to give him a little cuddle, but he always broke off the contact by finding something to pick up, look at or run after or some other distraction. However, Angela's beauty made sure he was a willing partner in bed and she made sure she was always available. Lovemaking? Or was it only sex?

After they had finished, he would turn away. If she followed him, he rolled over and lay on his stomach. He once told her that she was 'too clinging.' Surely, wanting a cuddle wasn't 'clinging', was it? Wasn't this the normal wish of a partner in love?

Angela was prepared to put up with most things for love but that did not include sharing him. She did her best to ignore Gerald's propensity to ogle at other women for fear of him branding her as a 'nag' but there came times when it was impossible to ignore it any longer. She tried non-combative methods first.

"Do you like *Me* in this blouse, Gerald? Does it show off my bust nicely? You look very handsome tonight. I always feel so good when I am out with you."

Eventually, as if the strands of a spider's web had stuck to his face and were tickling his nose, Gerald would become irritated and look away, usually in the direction of another woman. Angela, unable to ignore his behaviour any more, would then resort to criticism of his targets, especially once at the village hall.

"She looks a bit rough. No style." This seemed to make him even more interested. "Enough! Why do you look at everyone else and not me, Gerald?"

"It helps me realise that you are the best."

"Why do you need help?"

"Don't start, Angela."

Firstly through clenched teeth but eventually after dragging her outside and at full volume, "All my friends can do what they want. Their girlfriends never challenge them and anyway, it's normal for a man to be a man sometimes."

"What does being a man mean? Who tells you what a man should do, Gerald?"

"No one tells you. You just know. Anyway, leave me alone. You know you turn me on. I won't go anywhere, I will not leave you and I'll still come back to you each night. That's what matters, isn't it?"

Angela boiled over. "Do you also 'just know' what it means to be a husband, Gerald? Do you?" She slapped her hands on her thighs. "Do you have any idea what it is like to be a wife to a husband who 'acts like a man' as you so certainly put it? Am I just an accessory to your world? It's not a good life, Gerald. What have I done that you should want to cause me such pain? Exactly why do you need another woman?"

Gerald exploded, "For the excitement!"

Angela stood in shock, not daring to retort for fear of the subsequent answer.

For him it was not a put-down. For once in his life, he had told her the truth.

Exasperated, she ran off and complained to herself all the way home.

"Why does he need someone else? What have I done wrong? I love him. Is that wrong? I have supported him in everything he wanted to do. I made him a good home. I make him laugh. I always oblige him in bed. He always tells me how proud he is of me. I don't cling. I've tried my best to give him as much space as I can but surely, there comes a time when I have to have my say. Surely, there also comes a time when he has to be a husband?"

She stopped by the barn and composed herself. There was always one theme that made her calm. "Franz would never have been like that. I could always talk to him about anything. Oh God, you're on about Franz again? Don't start harping back to something that never was. Yes, but if only Gerald would be a little... like Franz, then maybe we could both have a happy life."

The consequence of such an altercation inevitably meant Gerald would seek comfort 'with his friends at the pub,' a pseudonym for something else.

Gerald began a course in electrical engineering at a training centre in Cambridge and passed his exams with distinction. His pass grade, and a word from Dave to his drinking pal Stuart Bright, enabled him to get a good job as a technical sales representative for S. Bright and Sons Ltd., in Highgate, London.

Gerald enjoyed visiting Highgate, because it usually involved an overnight stay. The big city, West End lights, Soho, pubs, fun and excitement, London had it all and he wanted it all. Stuart Bright recognised this and used Gerald's thirst for life to the company's advantage. He instituted a prize and bonus scheme for his salesmen; a free weekend in London for the salesman who showed the greatest percentage improvement in his sales figures over the previous three months. Gerald won at his first attempt.

Angela and Gerald booked in at the Savoy. The grandeur of the chandeliers, luxurious carpets and the servants was the dream world of the movies.

The bed, wider than it was long, was inspirational. To Gerald's obvious delight, Angela had become quite creative in bed although occasionally, even they had to take a break from bed to come up for air and see the city.

Their continual stretching made walking a little awkward, and the reason for it made her smile. On the Underground, she whispered to him that she wanted more pain like this.

They revelled in the good life and Angela enjoyed the complete attention of her husband. She was happy for him that he was successful. He was happy for himself that he was successful. Now he was a 'somebody,' people looked up to him. "Gerald Clarke, number one in the company!" Angela loved the Oxford Street shops but understood that Gerald was unenthusiastic and maybe needed his own space. When it came to shopping, so did she. Mindful of this, she suggested he went and sat in a pub for an hour whilst she shopped. They would meet by Eros later.

Gerald picked his pub, the Queens Head in Haymarket, walked up to the bar and sat on a stool. The barmaid had her back to him, giving him a chance to admire her long black hair and the contours of her plump bottom as it stretched her crimson skirt. He rested his elbows on the bar to admire the view in comfort. Then she turned around, and he almost fell off his stool.

"Gerald!"

"Krista!"

30.

The thumping beat of western music told Franz that this must be the party hut. The door opened and he smiled as the stifling atmosphere enveloped him. His eyes took time to adjust to the flickering light provided by the five or six candles that glowed through the blue cigarette smoke; a smoke so thick that the candles had halos and when obscured by silhouettes, emitted a faint blue corona. About ten couples and five or six singles had sprawled out on the floor and all smoked in between swigs of beer and korn-schnapps. Some of the guests talked loudly, animatedly gesturing as they argued some great intellectual point.

Other couples knew what they were there for and writhed on the floor in a mass of legs and hands as they sought to entwine themselves deeply in each other's emotional and physical depths.

Through the haze, Otto saw the 'Worbis Redhead' talking to a tall blond-haired girl over by the window. He and Franz picked their way over the bodies and introduced themselves. Otto introduced the redhead as Brunhilde Ellmau who said she was indeed from Worbis, and a first-year student of Russian. Her dark blue eyes fixed him with a look of intelligent intensity, giving him her undivided attention. Franz wondered how Otto could have described her as a beauty, although she did have an attractive feminine voice and attractive eyes and a proportionate figure and ... *OK for a night.*

Small talk with her came easily and quickly turned into more intense discussion, although Franz had never been good at remaining serious in a social situation. Quick to answer his quips, she told a joke about an American, a Frenchman and a Russian in which, naturally, as she was a student of Russian, the two Westerners turned out to be the fools. She chuckled to herself at the punch line. Franz laughed enthusiastically and even more so when she said it was the only joke she knew.

Franz glanced in the direction of Otto and the blonde, and saw them indulging in their first kiss. Franz smiled at Brunhilde, shrugged and whispered, "When in Rome, do as the Romans do." He gently kissed her.

Otto and the blonde, now entwined as one, managed to slide down the wall and end up as a writhing knot along with the other writhing knots on the floor. On the other side of the room, the intellectuals were still in full sail although it seemed it was the schnapps doing the talking. They sounded boring and the room had become so smoky, that Franz started to cough. Brunhilde suggested they left and went for a walk.

This was not the walk of a pair of teenagers looking for a shadowy nook in which to have an intensive grope. Somehow, the 'OK for a night' plan had faded. They talked, walked and talked for hours and kilometres, past parks and bombsites, through tunnels and under bridges. Walking hand in hand, they swung their arms in accompaniment to their conversation. Brunhilde was interested in Franz's wartime experiences, in particular about life in the camps. He did not tell her about Schwanz. "What about you? You said you had been to Russia. How did you manage that so close to the war?"

Brunhilde sighed before explaining that she was born in the town of Worbis in 1927, near what was now the border between the new east and west zones of Germany. She had always been a good student in school but had never been a lover of the Nazis. She had seen their exhibitions of brutality and fear.

Franz heard how visitors sometimes came to her house at night and discussed things in hushed tones with her father. Although they never stayed long, Brunhilde had to leave the room whenever one came. Ever curious, she would sit on the stairs and try to eavesdrop. Her parents forbade her to speak to anyone about these people or their visits, under any circumstances. The terror of discovery was unthinkable.

She had often wondered exactly what her father did for a living because he was always so evasive about it. It was not until the war was over that it became clear he had been an engineer at Mittelbau-Dora near Nordhausen. "What was Mittlebau-Dora?" Franz asked.

"Dora was a concentration camp situated at the foot of the Kohnstein hills about five kilometres west of Nordhausen in the Sud-Harz. My father told me that Dora originally started as an offshoot of Buchenwald. The Nazis sited it near Nordhausen because the limestone caves offered protection against bombers. The Allies wanted to destroy the top-secret weapons produced there, the V1 and V2. The underground complex, called Mittlebau, grew until by the end of the war, the Nazis had bored a total of fifteen kilometres of tunnels into the hillside. At a human cost of well over twenty-five thousand slave prisoners, a lot of them French, ripped from their homes and beaten, frozen, crushed and starved to death in the pursuit of Fascist production. Six lives for every V2 produced."

Brunhilde kicked out at a stone on the pavement. It spun into the night and ricocheted off a wall. "My father worked in the rocket-motor part of the process. I remember that he had been a mild, homely person before he went to work at Dora. But after a short time, he became moody and aggressive. I did my best to keep out of his way." She squeezed Franz's hand.

"The Americans arrived in the last days of the war and took him and every other technician they could find, away for questioning about the technical side of his work." She frowned and then took a deep breath. "They returned him on condition that he remained under house arrest, 'just so we know where you are.'" Then Brunhilde's expression changed, she smiled wistfully. "Three months later, the Russians came.

"After only a day of questioning, he returned home accompanied by a Red Army officer." She laughed and tossed some strands of her red hair over her shoulder. "The Russian continually smiled through a Stalin-like moustache and a set of perfect teeth. He gave me a chocolate and my mother some real coffee. Real coffee, Franz. A gift from the gods." Brunhilde tossed her hair again and closed her eyes as she savoured the memory of the coffee. Then, just as quickly, her expression turned sad. "My father explained that he had to go to Russia to do some special work, and that we would join him soon, but neither he, nor the officer could say exactly where in Russia. He packed his bags and in half an hour, he was gone."

She turned her head away from Franz and her voice fell as she stared into the night. "As the door closed behind him, my mother fell on the floor in a fit of despair. Even though I was wary of him, he was my father and so I cried too. We were sure we had seen the last of him.

"After three terrible days, during which my mother lost at least three kilos, a knock came at the door. The Russian officer was back. He looked surprised, 'Oh! Are you ill, Frau Ellmau? Can I help?" Brunhilde stopped, turned to stare at Franz and spread her arms like a crucifix. "I mean, really, Franz. What did he expect? My mother wanted news." Brunhilde slapped her arms down to her thighs and continued walking.

"She asked him and we couldn't believe it when he said, 'You will soon be able to ask him how he is yourself.'" Brunhilde clapped her hands in pleasure, turned to Franz and her eyes widened; her excitement fizzed out of her as she relived the moment. "He said, 'You have one hour to pack your personal belongings. Only those you can carry. I'm afraid we don't have too much room. Anything you need that you can't carry will be provided for you when you get to Russia.'

"We shook our heads in disbelief. 'Russia?' my mother said. 'Yes,' he said. 'Your husband will be in Russia for a long time. Everyone will be happier if you are together as a family. As your husband said to you the other day, you will come and live in Russia. Don't worry, you will be very well cared for, you will have a good life. Lock everything up. We'll make sure no one interferes with your property.' Wow!

"Four days later, we were a family again in a high security compound somewhere southeast of Stalingrad, in a place called Kapustin Yar. We remained there for the next two years while my father, and some of his other comrades from Dora, helped our 'friends' start their own ballistic rocket programme. We and all the other Germans had excellent flats. Our friends gave us everything we needed. This was bad luck for the Russian scientists and workers. They had to live in tents. Cold in winter!"

Brunhilde told how she continued her badly interrupted education. As she was in Russia, her normal education also included learning about communism and the evil Americans, whom the Russian propaganda machine likened to the Nazis. They were having a good life under the Communists. They were not home, but her father said that when they did go back to Worbis, it was sure they would be able to help in the formation of a new Germany that would rise from the ashes of defeat. It would be a strong and fair Germany, a Germany for the people, a 'workers' and peasants' paradise.'

Her father eventually admitted that the secret wartime meetings he used to have at home were with fellow communist sympathisers, who would all soon have a good position in the new order. "This confirmed my suspicions formed by my eavesdropping at home in Worbis. I was happy about this."

Brunhilde returned from Russia a committed communist and reflected that overall, her two-year stay in Russia had been an inspiration. She was grateful of having the opportunity to learn Russian. Through this knowledge and an introduction from her Russian friends, she had been able to start her course in Leipzig at quite short notice.

Franz knowingly looked at her and laughed. "Ah ha. So, you have connections."

Brunhilde looked slightly affronted. "I don't know what you mean. This is an equal world." Before in the next breath, and with a look of wonder, she threw her head back and softly said, "Look at all the stars. It's a beautiful night." She squeezed his arm tightly and enthusiastically scanned the heavens.

As they walked on, she took every opportunity to gaze into his eyes in which she saw no arrogance, no chauvinism or no aggression, only trust and warmth. She gently stroked his arm.

It was now three o'clock in the morning, and they stood outside Brunhilde's flat. He did not ask to come in and he was not invited. They both fondly smiled before gently kissing. "See you soon?" Franz said.

"Tomorrow?" She hopefully enquired.

"You bet."

31.

"Gerald!" Krista clasped her face, and all in one breath said, "How lovely to see you. I am so lucky to bump into you in such a big city I was going to come and find you anyway but I didn't know where to start and have very little money so I decided to get a temporary job whilst I stayed with my Aunt Maria." She clapped her hands. "How are you, Gerald my dear?" Just time for a quick breath before.... "You have put on weight although you have lost your suntan. In fact, you look a little pale. You need a drink. What'll you have?"

Gerald failed to answer. White as a sheet, his head jutted forward his eyes blinked and, looking like a penniless drunk pleading for just one more drink, he clasped the brass rail around the bar to steady himself. Krista reached for a bottle of whisky but changed her mind and lunged across the bar, flung her arms around his neck and smothered him with kisses.

"Cor! If I fall off my stool can I have some of that too?" chipped in an old man at the end of the bar who had already started to wobble; much to the amusement of the other customers who were all agog at the show.

A belly laugh came from another old man in the corner, "I wouldn't be too confident about that, Bill. You've been falling off your stool every night for fifty years and no one's wanted to give you the kiss of life yet." The pub laughed as the old man shrank back into his jacket.

Krista's kisses nursed Gerald back to life. As soon as he could break away from her octopus embrace he croaked, "Why are you here?"

"I couldn't live without you, Gerald. All alone in that house, I only thought of you, here, alone, without me." A soft chorus of "Aaahs" murmured around the bar. "I missed the touch of your body, Gerald and..." Before she could continue, the gallery let out a chorus of catcalls and "Wha-heys!"

After the laughter died down and the pub got on with its business, a red-faced Krista quietly continued. "I missed you and couldn't get you out of my head. I knew I had to come and see you again. Maybe you have another girlfriend, but perhaps you could still find a little time for me?"

"Krista. This is crazy. You come all the way from your sunny island to wet and windy London on a dream. There is nothing here for you. I cannot guarantee you anything. You must go home."

"I can't. This, me, here in London, is all because of us. My husband was a patriot. He died for his country." Her expression fell. "So my neighbours expect me to remain an untouched widow for the rest of my life. You and I thought we were being discreet but my neighbours are not so stupid. They knew what was going on. They say I have dishonoured my husband's memory.

"When I go to get water from the well in the village, the other women spit at me before they turn their backs and stand in silence until I go. Then their tongues rasp with the venom of rattlesnakes." She shook her head before looking at Gerald with a burning intensity. "In daytime, especially when their wives are around, the men also look the other way. However, when night-time comes, and they have to go out to check their sheep 'because there might be a wolf,' they sneak to my house and knock on my door. They stand there dangling grimy money from their sweaty hands and make their filthy suggestions as they ogle at me. Even the children call me a whore."

Her eyes became tearful. "I loved my husband. However, since he has gone my world has been like a prison. You released me from that prison, Gerald. As I told you, an aunt of mine lives here in London. Therefore I wrote to her, I didn't know your address, and she said I could come and stay." She beamed at him and her eyes expectantly sparkled as she clapped her hands. "Here I am."

Shit, thought Gerald. Then he studied her whilst gently tapping the bar with his index finger. "Where are you living?"

"Camden Town."

He looked around at the full pub and checked the time. He had to meet Angela in fifteen minutes and so decided against a big scene in here. He put on his best sincere look. "Krista, I do have a girlfriend now." Her face dropped. "But it's not too serious." Her face lit up. "I don't live near here, but I come to work in London quite often and maybe we can still see each other when I do come."

She squeaked her delight and smothered him with kisses, "Oh, I am so happy."

Gerald beamed before glancing at his watch again. "I'm afraid I have to go now. I have a business appointment in ten minutes."

"On a Saturday afternoon?"

"I work very hard, Krista. After that, I have to travel straight home. I live up north and have to sing in the church choir in the morning. Give me your address or a telephone number and I will contact you next week. Then we can arrange to meet."

"Oh, what a shame you have to go, Gerald." She sighed and looked longingly at him with her head on one side as her long black hair flowed down to rest over her voluptuous bosom. "But I cannot believe our luck and that I will see you again very soon." She scribbled her contact details on a piece of paper, gave it a kiss and handed it to Gerald, who leant forward over the bar and kissed his long-lost Greek girlfriend. He turned to go but paused.

"See you next week, I'll be in touch." He smirked as he went out of the bar and strode up Haymarket towards Piccadilly Circus.

Gerald and Angela arrived at Eros simultaneously and greeted each other with a passionate kiss before Gerald broke it off and towed her back to the hotel. "Hey, what have you been drinking?" She said. "Looking into your eyes at the moment, I might even need some of that." She chuckled and tossed her hair as they entered the hotel foyer.

Gerald wasted no time in their room as he stripped Angela and laid her on the bed. Reminding her of his passion the day he returned from Crete, she beamed as he opened his trousers. However, this time he had only removed his jacket before he entered her, and did not bother with a condom. His vigour and passion as he pounded into her seemed strangely different from his Cretan return.

That time, through all the passion, she had felt love. This time she might as well have not been there; a total lack of his usual noises or comments. The thought actually entered her head that he was not thinking of her at all.

He climaxed with an almighty grunt, which lasted much longer than normal, before collapsing on top of her. She normally liked to feel his weight in this situation but not this time. He did not seem to care if she had had an orgasm or not. She twisted a bit which made him roll off.

Even his post-coital smile was different. Normally it was only just noticeable, but this time his face was clearly relaxed and contented; he had closed his eyes as if he had drifted off to sleep. She studied him. *He's not sleeping. Underneath those eyelids, his brain is working overtime.* "So tell me where you went when I was shopping."

"To a pub in Shaftesbury Avenue."

"Which one?"

"The George and Dragon. Why?" His eyes flashed open, the enemy was at the gate.

"Something or someone turned you on when you visited that pub," Angela said with a nervous giggle, "or did you maybe take a little detour to Soho first? Just to get an appetite so to speak." She silently cursed her lack of bravery.

Gerald looked thoughtful, then half smirked. "Well, I did have a little walk about first, but I didn't go in anywhere. Would you like to come and see?"

"Me? In Soho? Gerald, really!"

"Why not? It will increase your appetite like it did mine." His smirk became a grin as he twiddled her nipple. "I heard your little giggle."

Angela was speechless. "It will broaden your horizons; make you feel liberated, modern even. C'mon, let's go." He jumped off the bed and threw Angela her clothes.

She dressed slowly. *Soho? No. How could I have been so stupid? Look at him. He's so happy. He was so different, so*

*passionate just now. Well, if Soho gave him such enthusiasm...
'Make me modern?' Don't suppose it will hurt, simply to walk
about. He'll go crazy if I change my mind. I am his wife, I should
please him.*

It was chilly. The light drizzle dampened their faces as they
entered the smutty, hostile world of post-war Soho. Angela's
eyes widened at the scene; she had heard about this place but
had never dreamt of actually being here. Noting that Gerald was
already familiar with the area, she hid in his shadow as he
strode positively on and leered into the entrance of every clip
joint and bar.

He ogled at all the sallow, cold-eyed women with empty
smiles in every doorway. He even commented on the size of one
woman's tits to Angela who forced a smile without comment.
The women did not seem to mind the fact that Gerald already
had a partner, they invited Angela in too, "We've got whatever
you want, deary."

It did not take long. Two or three more bar entrances and
she felt like throwing up. "He's like a crazed dog," she muttered
before finally pulling her arm from his and tearfully whining, "I
want to go home."

"Home? Home?" He spun around to face her and raked his
fingers through his Brylcreemed hair before digging them into
his scalp so hard that his hand quivered. He hissed through his
clenched teeth, "Ten minutes ago you wanted to live London
and be modern."

She spread her arms as she looked in all directions. "This
isn't London, Gerald, and it's not me. OK, maybe I don't want to
go home but I certainly don't want to stay here amongst this.
I've seen it. It was an experience. Now let's go!"

She walked away pursued by a puce Gerald who tugged her
elbow and shouted into her face, "It was your idea. If you want
to make our life together happier, you ought to open your mind
to new ways."

"Don't I make you happy, Gerald?"

"No. Not all the time. No," he snarled. They looked into
each other's eyes for a few moments before Gerald let out an

exasperated sigh, tugged again at her elbow and dragged her back towards Beak Street.

Angela jerked her elbow free and tearfully pleaded with him, "I want to please you, Gerald, more than anything in the world, but not this way." They walked on. "Why do you want to hurt me? You are always so angry."

"And you are always so stupid. You have a village mentality." He gesticulated to the sky. "Open your eyes, look around you and open your mind. It is a new world now, with different ways and different attitudes. I love you, Angela, but you must understand that a modern man needs a modern wife who is both understanding and adventurous. Not a conservative stick-in-the-mud."

"Like me."

"Like you!"

They walked on in silence. Angela kicked out at a cigarette packet and caught the heel of her shoe. It occurred to her that maybe it was true that she was a 'village girl' and that because Gerald was so successful in his job, he would know of other worldly ways. He had said that he went with Sue Moore for the excitement, yet, *if I am not exciting, how am I able to turn him on so easily?* Angela broke out in a cold sweat when she remembered the hotel, *what, or who, does a man think of when he makes love to his wife? I had always assumed he thought of his wife. Maybe not.* She looked sideways at her fuming husband. *Maybe I am only a vehicle for his fantasies.* She glanced sadly at her scuffed shoes. *Is it so old-fashioned, or 'village,' to want a one-to-one relationship with your man? To want him to love only you?* She stared longingly at a poster of a happy couple smoking Woodbine cigarettes.

She had to find a solution, but could not discuss this with Gerald; he would get aggressive and tell her she was stupid. Not her mother, 'nice ladies do not discuss such things.' She would talk to Helen, and in the meantime, promised herself to be more 'open' and to listen to Gerald's suggestions. *I will show him how much I love him; I will learn from him.* She bit her fist. *Are you really so sure about that, Angela?*

32.

Franz and Brunhilde were seldom out of each other's company, except during lectures and when Franz was football training. Although his knee would never be strong enough to seriously play again, Franz was still fanatically interested in the game. His tactical knowledge and game analysis were first class, so much so that he became coach of the university second eleven. He took his job seriously and never missed a training session or game, which was more than could be said for the first-team coach, Doctor Schumann.

When this man failed to turn up, especially when it was cold, Franz took charge of the full University squad training sessions. Although he was about the same age as the training squad, they all enjoyed Franz's training because at least he made it interesting and they respected his obvious knowledge. However, the second team became more successful than the firsts.

Teams for the following Saturday were always announced at Tuesday's training. Doctor Schumann huffed and announced that there would be changes to the first team for the following Saturday. The opponents would be the league leaders from Dresden, who had beaten Leipzig by four goals only five weeks before. On hearing that they were to be promoted, two players refused to step up from the second team and announced they had a lack of confidence in the first-team coach. The doctor took umbrage and expelled the rebels. In the true spirit of communism, eight more players walked out in solidarity.

The good doctor had reached the rank of Lieutenant Colonel in the war and had survived by knowing when to retreat and making it look like someone else's idea. Here he showed his metal again when, before anyone else jumped ship he announced, "Before I was so rudely interrupted, I was about to announce that I have been called away to attend an academic conference this weekend and it therefore gives me great pleasure to announce that Herr Schmidt will act as first-team trainer on Saturday.

"With that regard and due to the number of self-enforced absences from the team I have just announced, I shall delegate the team re-shuffle to him." He nodded briefly at Franz, "Good luck, Herr Schmidt," clicked his heels, and departed to the sound of a raspberry blown by one of the remaining players.

Franz shrugged, straightened his posture and smiled at his merry group. "Well, let's hope that that's the back of him for a while. Only eleven of you left, so team selection is easy. Everyone, particularly the doctor, will expect us to lose. Let's turn that to our advantage and show we are strong. Let's train our arses off."

Brunhilde was slightly pensive when Franz relayed the news and none too pleased when she heard she was to come second to training on three nights as well as Saturday that week. Her affection for Franz meant she was prepared to put up with football, in moderation. However, she refused to socialise with the football club due to finding the players, "coarse and uncultured, especially when they sing those disgusting songs."

The crowd was larger than normal; a thousand spectators had shown up, many of them from Dresden. Even Brunhilde had come along. Although it occurred to her how stupid it was that so many people, including her, had turned up to see twenty-two grown men kick a piece of leather around a field for an hour and a half on a cold winter's day. "How much better it would be to sit around a warm fire and discuss Faust." she said.

The game kicked off and Dresden did not know what hit them. Leipzig, playing with a strong wind at their backs, refused to be intimidated and got stuck in from the first moment. They ran, tackled, pushed, shoved and kicked as far as the laws allowed, and often further than that.

To everyone's surprise, Leipzig's depleted warriors managed to draw the game, one goal apiece.

The players embraced their coach and the unbelievable became the believable. A draw was as good as a win in the circumstances and Franz's star had risen to its zenith. Of course, he paid tribute to his players but without him, this would never have happened and everyone knew it.

Even Brunhilde had to admit she had found the game exciting and had jumped and shouted with the rest, nicely of course. She even broke her socialising rule, clasped Franz's arm and smiled proudly every time the other girls told her how lucky she was to be his girlfriend.

Next Monday came the news that 'The Great Doctor,' "due to the call of the Academic Board, had reluctantly decided to hand over the management and direction of training of the University Football Club, with immediate effect, to Herr Franz Schmidt." Franz was now definitely a 'somebody' and Brunhilde wore a permanent smile.

Later outside her flat, Brunhilde invited Franz in. He accepted.

33.

Angela needed to see Helen.

"What do you mean Soho?

"He did not!

"Good God!

"Village Girl? This chap is unreal, Angela. Can't you find some way to talk to him about it?

"Oh, I see, yes of course, he is the master of the house, and what he says goes. You should stand up to him. The swine. You live in the same house as your parents, don't they ever say anything?

"Well they should. You have told me so many horrible things about him over the years, at least, since he came back from the army. Angela, why do you stay with him? How can you say you still love him? What is so special about him?

"Don't give me that wife thing anymore. A divorce is possible you know.

"OK, I know the scandal a divorce would bring, but at least then people would know what a bastard he is. No one would blame you.

"You think you can change him! Oh, Angela, get real? I don't understand you. Leopards don't change their spots.

"Something else, what?

"Second chance? You've given him too many second chances. He must be on his twentieth chance by now.

"What do you mean *you* are on your second chance? What are you trying to tell me? Come on, we have been best friends since infant school, you can tell me.

"You mean that German boy who was at the farm when Gerald was away. Did it get that serious?

"Oh, Angela. You know, I always wondered. Do you remember me joking with you about how you were sitting next to him at haymaking time? Well, I wasn't really joking. I know you too well, you were so happy. Not like your mum.

"Angela, I didn't push it then because I didn't really want to know the truth. How serious did it get?

"Well that's something. A few kisses are forgivable. You were young, you hardly knew Gerald. In fact, you had known the Jerry...

"OK, Franz, much longer than Gerald. Angela, it was one tiny blip that could have happened to anyone in the same situation. Nothing came of it, it's over and should be long forgotten.

"What d'you mean? You can't forget, because you feel guilty or ...

"You can't forget him! Oh, Angela. Here, have a handkerchief.

"Yes, OK, in your dreams, and when Gerald is bad to you. Yes, OK. The other man's grass is always greener, but...

"Oh dear, other times too? Oh dear. Really?

"Well, where is he now?

"East Germany. That's behind Mr Churchill's Iron Curtain. Angela, forget him. He's not coming to you. He can't come. Don't waste your life chasing an impossible dream or trying to make up for something that was really nothing. Forget it and forget Franz. What Gerald has done is Everest compared to a molehill. Here, have another handkerchief.

"So, if you are going to stay with him, why don't you have a family?

"Well if you want to be settled first, what about that tramp Moore? You're never going to have a settled life if she's always in the background.

"Yes. You should've sorted her out long ago. Promise me that you will do it soon.

"Good!"

34.

Ten days after Gerald had seen Krista in the pub, his body had attended a meeting at head office, but his mind had been on his planned extra marital activities later that evening. It would be convenient having a girlfriend so close to the office. Camden town was about ten minutes from his office by tube and he knew her road was only about two hundred yards from the tube station.

Full of anticipation, Gerald stopped at the flower shop by the station entrance. He selected a dozen red roses and exchanged cheerful pleasantries with the young lady owner. "Some lucky lady is going to have a nice evening I dare say," she sang as he gave her a ten-shilling note. She pressed the change back into his hand and wickedly batted her eyes at him.

He looked her up and down as he pocketed his change, gave her a smirk and quipped, "Well if she doesn't, what are you doing later?"

"Naughty, naughty." She turned and resumed her work.

Gerald knocked at the green door of Krista's house, which she opened. Krista reached out, gripped Gerald's red tie, silently towed him into the downstairs room at the left end of the short hall and closed its door.

Gerald placed the roses on a small table by the door, embraced her and edged her towards the bed two steps away. For the next two hours, the only unsatisfied sounds came from the bed as it rhythmically squeaked its protest.

During a brief pause, Krista raised herself up on her elbow and looked deep into Gerald's eyes. She gently kissed him on the forehead and stroked his hair. "There's nothing for me in Crete now. I have a job and a place to live, here in London." She shrugged, shook her head and looked up to the heavens. "This wonderful city. And now, I'm with you again. Oh, it's a wonderful life, Gerald. I want to make my new life here."

Gerald cleared this throat, twice. "Attitudes in Britain are a little different than in Crete, Krista. People often have more than one partner at a time. In fact..." he paused and put on his best sincere expression, "understand that things are very modern. The attitudes of the world have their roots here. Put simply, this means that you have to open your mind to anything and reject nothing. If you do, you will succeed here and have a wonderful life.

"In fact," he paused again, "I have a couple of friends who would like to meet you. You cannot live here and only know me. I will show you how to live a little."

"I'm not entirely sure what you mean, Gerald. Do you want me to go out with these people? I don't even know them."

"Precisely, Krista. I shall arrange a little party at my friend's house and you can get to know them a little. But remember, open your mind to everything and reject nothing."

Krista looked into Gerald's warm eyes and smiled hesitantly. She stroked his smooth skin and whispered, "OK, open your mind to everything and reject nothing. I am in London, it is a new life and I will make you happy." They embraced and continued their lovemaking.

As Gerald left for work the next morning, Krista clasped her arms around his neck and searched his eyes before playfully licking the end of his nose. "When will I see you again? I have waited such a long time. I can't bear to be without you."

"Are you working next Wednesday evening, Krista?"

"No."

"OK. Good. Then come to this address at seven o'clock." He scribbled an address on some paper and pushed it down her cleavage. "If you don't hear from me, assume it's all on and I'll see you there. Maybe you could wear that nice red skirt you were wearing in the pub last week."

He kissed her, and as an afterthought said over his shoulder, "My friends are going to love you."

As the door closed, Krista leant against it and twirled her long black hair around her fingers. She smiled wistfully. London was indeed going to be fun. "A London party with 'my' Gerald," she said. What sort of party it would be? "Open your mind to everything and reject nothing."

Gerald had a ravenous appetite upon his return to the farm and was delighted to see that Angela had roasted a pheasant for their evening meal. He laughed, joked and was the heart and soul of the party to the extent that even Ethel could not get a word in edgeways. Angela looked at him admiringly. Although she did note his eyes seemed a little bloodshot. Gerald blamed this on working hard and the London Underground, which was so dusty these days. "It makes everybody's eyes red. These are things one has to put up with when you work in the heart of such a vibrant city."

"I thought you worked in Highgate? That's not the heart of the city," Dave said as he slurped down his second cider.

"Principally speaking, Dave. Principally speaking." Dave was a bit confused about what 'principally speaking' meant, so he sagely nodded his agreement and decided to avoid further confusion by having some more cider.

Gerald continued to hold court. Ethel listened thoughtfully. *A little bit too full of himself..., quite the man about town. Or is 'Jack-the-lad' a better description? What's he trying to prove?* She glanced at her daughter. *Angela laps it up, almost as if she is trying too hard. Be very careful, my dear.*

Gerald excused himself to go to bed quite early that evening. Angela followed him close-at-heel up the stairs. She did her best with him and even managed to reach an orgasm, whereupon he promptly fell asleep on top of her without reaching one himself. He had never done that before.

Poor boy, they must work him so hard at work. At least he won't have so much energy to visit that cow Moore. I hope. Yes, Moore, I should've taken Helen's advice long ago.

Gerald stood preening himself at the bathroom mirror before he went to see Sue. What did a bit of deception matter to the women, when after all, they should be delighted to have him on any terms? He pursed his lips and shrugged at the mirror. *Anyway, what they don't know, they can't worry about. Just keep the plates spinning, Gerald.* He nodded sagely. *God! You're a handsome brute. Can't wait 'til next Wednesday.*

35.

'Football widow' was not a title Brunhilde would have chosen for her future. She told Franz she wanted to get on in life, and getting on in life in the new East Germany meant only one thing, she had to join the party. The Socialistische Einheitspartie Deutschlands or SED was the political party that had taken over the functions of state from the Russians and Brunhilde had all the right credentials. She was young, intelligent and a good communicator and came from a pro-Communist family that had worked for the Russians in Russia. Her views had already been positively noted and reported.

It came as a pleasant surprise to her when one of her lecturers, Frau Mittelmann, invited her to attend an SED meeting, which coincidentally took place on a Tuesday, football-training night.

Brunhilde made an immediate impact at her first meeting, when she vociferously joined in a debate about the loss, or 'haemorrhage' as she put it, of skilled workers from East to West Germany. She advocated stricter border controls, administered and overseen by Germans. She also mooted the point that maybe subversive American elements were the reason for such an exodus. Many influential heads nodded at the new recruit's views. Here was exactly the sort of 'child of the state' that would help build and secure the new East Germany.

Brunhilde became as fanatical about the SED as Franz was about football. He was also interested to hear about the latest plans for the state and naturally had many views of his own. They often argued their disagreements with great passion in a friendly, at least mostly friendly, manner into the early hours of the morning.

Brunhilde impressed Franz, most of the time, with the factual certainty of her arguments, "Franz. Do not talk such emotional rubbish. It is beneath you. You must always remember that matters of state are too important for anything else to block them.

"You have such an alert intellect you should not waste your time with football. There will always be someone else out there to kick a piece of leather around a field. You should join the party and serve the state. This is what matters."

In his less positive moments, it seemed to Franz that whatever Brunhilde liked was wonderful, stimulating and worthwhile, and whatever she did not like, was a waste of time. Consequently, he could never get over the cynical thought that politics was only important to Brunhilde because it was her idea. Unable to win the logical argument and with the emotional argument a loser, he often agreed with her for the sake of a quiet life. He did not want anything to spoil their relationship because he was now sure he loved her. Except football versus politics, they agreed to differ.

For the first time in her life, Brunhilde walked with a spring in her step and constantly smiled. She had found a man who had everything and who clearly loved her. And she loved him. There had not been a lot of choice in the German compound in Russia, and the Russian men were always a little arrogant with her. They often trumpeted that women were equal in Russia, that is, in the kitchen, or as long as they were not German.

She knew about the way the German and Russian peoples had slaughtered each other throughout history, particularly over the previous seven years. Therefore, she could understand the historical reasons for the Russians hatred of Germans. What she would not concede, was that any man was better than her just because he was a man, apart from on the physical side. Her potential Russian suitors always shied off when she proclaimed her feminist views. She had yet to learn that idealism always has a hard time against hormones.

About three months after Brunhilde had become a full member of the SED, she and Franz had arranged to have a few drinks with Otto at his flat. Otto had told Franz that he had a new girlfriend, the latest of many, and that he wanted to introduce her. What started as a light-hearted evening soon changed into an evening of political debate. Franz had never discussed politics with Otto, and it came as a great surprise to him that Otto was so vocally left wing about every subject.

Otto argued that the state must organise and 'retain' the people if a new communist Germany was to rise from the ruins of fascism and not bleed its best to the west. Subversive elements should be rooted out and destroyed. If not, then capitalist temptation would lead to personal greed, which had no place in the new Deutches Demokratische Republik. Fairness and equality for all was the only right path. Personalities were not important; policies were what mattered, state policies, the communist state. Nothing or no one was greater than this, and this should be everyone's first loyalty, bar none. Brunhilde beamed at him and clasped her hands together as she enthusiastically bounced in her seat.

Franz argued that although he agreed with the aims of communism, having been a prisoner for three years, he held personal freedom close to his heart and he could never equalise himself with the oppressive nature it needed to succeed. "I am not convinced about the need for too much state control over the migration of workers from east to west and vice-versa. My view is that if the state is good enough, then people will want to stay here of their own volition and the borders won't need controls."

By midnight, Otto's girlfriend had fallen asleep, and was snoring. Otto seemed a little shocked. He shook his head as he looked at his sniggering friends, "I'm not sure I can put up with that snoring all night." He tutted, shook his head again and returned to the discussion.

The passionate argument between the students continued until the small hours when finally Brunhilde asked, "Why don't you two come along and meet some people at the party?"

"Oh, I like a good party," Franz joked.

"SED, Idiot," Brunhilde said to Franz as she gave him an admonishing kiss on the cheek. "They have changed the Tuesday meeting to Mondays, as of next week." She smiled at him and brushed a hair from his brow. "So it doesn't interfere with your football, and we could be together. That would be wonderful." Franz agreed. Otto accepted with alacrity.

Franz and Otto subsequently became party members but not before Franz had heard another student give his views on personal freedom after the secretary had mooted the point of closing the border. "I think that the idea of closing our border with the west is a mistake. We should not have to control our people. We should inspire them. Then they will want to stay." Franz's eyes widened.

"Comrade Shultz," the chairperson interrupted, "I would remind you of the words of comrade Lenin, 'Trust is good, control is better!' Tell me, do you feel that you, at your tender age, know better than our inspirational mentor?" Commenting on the man's absence at the following meeting, the chairperson denounced him, "An example of a subversive element and fifth columnist." They never saw the man again.

Franz and Brunhilde became engaged on Christmas Eve, 1948 and were married in her hometown of Worbis, where they had both obtained teaching job offers, the following Easter. Otto was Franz's best man.

In the meantime, Franz's football team had gone from success to success; they had won the DDR Universities cup and were runners-up in the league. Early in May, Franz had just finished his daily training run when he noticed two men in suits get out of an official looking car that had drawn up by the training track.

Franz towelled himself down and nervously watched the men approach. *Stasi?* The bigger one, with a shaved head, one tooth missing and a twitching eye, coldly said, "Herr Schmidt, we want to talk to you about your future."

Half an hour later, Franz was in a daze, he even went two stops on from his normal bus stop before he realised where he was. No problem, he sprinted back to report to Brunhilde, whereupon he launched himself into her arms and covered her with kisses. Brunhilde disengaged herself and shook her head at her giggling man. "What's all this for? Have you won the Sachsen State Lotto?"

"Better than that! Dynamo Leipzig, that's "First Division National League Dynamo Leipzig, Brunhilde, want me to join their coaching staff." He threw back his head and laughed. "The big time. I'm into the big time!" He squeezed Brunhilde's cheeks together and gave her another big kiss before breaking off to receive his wife's congratulations, which did not come.

Brunhilde was no longer smiling. Her head tilted to one side. She then smiled condescendingly. "Franz, what about our plans? We have already accepted our jobs at Worbis. We would be separated. Do you want that?"

"Of course not. But this is my dream, Brunhilde. There must be a way we can work this out? You could get a job here. They'll understand and find someone else in Worbis."

Her blue eyes became cold, but she still had that smile. "Franz, we cannot break promises made to the party and my parents. You know they have already spent a lot of time and money renovating our flat in their house. I shall have to go." Franz's face fell, he let go of Brunhilde and his hands flopped to his sides.

Brunhilde closed her eyes and smiled as if she was about to have an orgasm. She continued, "When we move to Worbis, we could both make huge advances in the SED. Of course, it is your choice, but you have greater talents than football coaching. You should use these to build the new DDR. Isn't it your moral responsibility to do your best to help your fellow East German comrades?" Then the cold eyes flashed once more. "We have also talked of starting a family as soon as possible; a child should have a father, not a photograph."

Six weeks later, despite numerous attempts to change Brunhilde's mind, which always ended up with him feeling guilty for being so selfish, Franz left Leipzig with a glum face. "Bloody SED here I bloody-well come. I suppose."

36.

Krista was a little shaky as she undressed in her cramped bathroom. Her apprehension about the party had grown as the day neared. However, if this were to be her introduction to the London social scene, then she would look her best. Placing one hand on her hip and the other behind her head as if she was one of the Minoan temple women of Knossos, Krista posed in front of the full-length mirror. She closed her eyes and, just for a moment, her oleander-scented bath took her back to the sun kissed shores of Crete. She sensuously swayed to the sound of the waves, heat of the sun, scents of the flowers and her fallen husband. At which, her head dropped. Just for a moment.

She opened her eyes, sighed, and scanned the image looking back at her. For thirty-nine years old, Krista was in excellent shape. She slid her hands over her slim waist but tutted as she gripped what she considered was the excess fat around her bottom. There again, Gerald liked her bottom. Krista's long, curly black hair reached down to her dark brown nipples as she lifted her large breasts to their height of her youth. She sighed. Of course, they had dropped since then but were still firm and indeed larger than twenty years ago. It was a source of great regret to her that she had not had any children, but at least her breasts had not suffered the distortions and subsequent loss of shape of childbearing.

She lightly massaged her fine pointed nose and full lips, but her dark brown eyes looked concerned as this routine reminded her how difficult it was to maintain her skin amongst the grime and soot of post-war London. The skimpy white blouse complemented the crimson skirt that Gerald had requested. Black nylons and black shoes set off her outfit. With a flourish of her hair, Krista donned her coat, and was ready for London. Whatever that may bring.

Gerald waited outside his friend's terrace house in Highbury, his heart pounding with anticipation. Exactly on time, a magnificent sight approached him and his eyes widened. They greeted each other with a big smile and an even bigger kiss. "Let's go," Gerald said as he rapped the door knocker.

The door opened and John, a man in his mid-thirties with dark hair, blue eyes and shiny teeth that flashed out from under an RAF handlebar moustache, stood to attention in the doorway. His eyes widened as he scanned Krista from eyes to breasts, and legs to breasts. "I say! Welcome, Krista."

They entered the sparsely furnished lounge, which had an oriental-style rug on the floor as its centrepiece, around which were arranged a long sofa and two lounge chairs, plus a dining room table near the front window. The walls sported various pictures of RAF fighter aircraft and a portrait of a cigar smoking Sir Winston Churchill. John introduced Krista to two other men, whose eyes also duly widened as they peered downward at her cleavage.

Krista sat down on the sofa close to Gerald and smiled at everyone whilst John got his guests a drink; the men had whisky and Krista a large gin and tonic. Everyone took a sip and looked at everyone else. John sat next to Krista and broke the silence with some polite conversation about Crete. As they talked, he moved his leg so that it touched hers. Without any fuss, she politely apologised and moved her leg away.

As the relaxed conversation continued, Gerald wrapped his arm over Krista's shoulder and benignly smiled at her whilst he smoothed the nape of her neck. Krista thought how strange it was that the men seemed to nod so enthusiastically at each other every time they found agreement.

They all consumed three drinks during the first half hour. Not a big drinker, Krista was now a little merry, but the men encouraged her to keep up. John had manoeuvred himself down the sofa, close enough to touch her again.

She continued to politely move away until, with her other side pressed up against Gerald, she had nowhere else to move.

John now touched her with his leg and most of his body. Krista's face flushed, she could feel his body heat and smell a strange but not unpleasant, perfumed scent.

Scent on a man was new to her. She pleadingly looked at Gerald and slightly flicked her head in John's direction.

Gerald ignored her plea and whispered, "Nice friends, aren't they?" just before he gave her a little kiss on her neck. She nodded and gave him a strained half-smile.

John jumped to his feet. "OK, time for a game of cards and another drink."

Krista gazed into her empty glass and chuckled, "Oh, I think I've had enough."

One of John's friends, who had been quite quiet until now, moved to sit on the edge of his seat and dismissively gesticulated at her. "No, no. The evening is yet young. It's good to get a bit loose and relax." Another large gin and tonic arrived for Krista.

Gerald now wore an alcoholic smirk, indeed, everybody was now smiling. Krista was trying to think what John's friend meant by 'a bit loose and relax', when John suggested they played a few hands of whist. "What's whist? I've never played the game before." Gerald gave her a simple explanation after which, due to the gin, she was none the wiser and soon found herself playing her first losing hand.

"Oh dear, Krista hasn't won a trick," chortled John as Krista clasped her face and giggled.

"Forfeit!" John's other friend called out.

All eyes locked-on to Krista. She looked confused. "What's forfeit?"

"The loser in each round, that's you this time, has to take something off," John said. He swallowed loudly before positively adding, "An article of clothing, I mean." Krista seemed a little surprised and turned to question Gerald.

"Go on." He laughed uncompromisingly. "What's it going to be?"

"Oh. Well, if I have to. But it's got to be the same for all of you when you lose." As one, the men enthusiastically chorused their agreement. Krista giggled and removed a shoe to great applause.

Twelve hands of whist and two gins later Krista, who had lost the fight against the gin, had removed both shoes and her stockings whilst the male losers had removed jackets and shoes. Then Krista lost the thirteenth game.

Her audience looked on. No small things left. She had to remove a major item of clothing. What would it be, the blouse or the skirt? Hearts pounded. Krista pouted. "I don't know if I should," she said, "I don't know you all well enough."

Gerald interjected, "It's the same for us. Anyway, this is a 'London get-to-know-you party.' It's quite normal."

Krista shook a little as she began to unbutton her blouse. Her eyes flicked unsurely from one leering spectator to another. She had second thoughts at the second button, but reminded herself that she wanted to please her man. She tried to focus on him as she undid the third button. Gerald's expression confirmed that it did indeed please him. He smiled at her and gently nodded. The other men were transfixed; their eyes bulged like golf balls. Krista finally gave in to the alcohol, flipped the final button, and laughed.

First one shoulder then the other appeared to the delight of her onlookers. Then, with a final flourish, she whipped the garment off and twirled it over her head in triumph.

"More, more, more," the men chanted as they clapped their hands.

"Oh, no. I want to even this up. Not until all you men have removed your shirts as well." The words had not left her lips before there was a burst of frenzied male activity. Four bare-chested men looked expectantly at Krista and awaited developments.

"Krista, something is wrong here," Gerald said as he gestured at the other men. "We are all bare-chested and you aren't. Come on, make it fair."

Krista's head wobbled as she hiccupped before reaching behind her back to her bra clip, whereupon she stopped, looked every man in the eye, then chuckled and undid the clip.

The men sat on the edge of their seats like a wolf pack waiting to pounce as she allowed the bra to slip a little. Another chuckle and she let it fall onto her lap. The men gasped at her prodigious breasts as they flopped into freedom.

Gerald proudly sat on the sofa and enjoyed the looks of lust on the faces of the other three men. Krista lowered her hands to her hips and pushed out her breasts towards each of her besotted audience until quite abruptly, she covered them with her hands. "There we are then, you've had your fun, that's it," slurred Krista to the obvious disappointment of her three new 'friends'.

Gerald wasted no time. "OK. Dance with me, Krista." He stood up and dragged Krista to her feet. Somebody put some music on the radio, and the pair started a close, smooch dance. Gerald longingly looked at Krista and kissed her before he slowly moved one hand from her shoulder to her breast. They continued to smooch round and round until Krista became aware of touching other bodies that must have encircled her. A hand brushed against her bottom, then two. She continued to passionately kiss Gerald.

Suddenly, she broke off the dance, pushed through the ring of men and grabbed her clothes. "What on earth was I doing? I'm going."

"Hey, hey, come on we're just getting warmed up," Gerald pleaded as she dressed.

A tearful Krista pushed for the door. John half-heartedly blocked her way and looked at Gerald. "I thought you said she was a 'go-er'?" She pushed on out of the door.

Krista ran down the street to the tube, her black hair sticking to her tear-soaked face. Gerald chased after her. He caught her at the station. "What was all that about? I thought you were enjoying it. I would never have let it go on if I'd thought it would upset you, Krista."

"I feel cheap. I only went along with those stupid games for you, Gerald. You could have stopped it."

"So could you, but you didn't."

"You got me drunk." She clenched both fists and raised them to her mouth; her large, dark brown eyes flashed fire.

Then she screamed at him. "Don't you ever do that to me again! You did that for your own perverted satisfaction. I will not be abused!"

"Hark who's talking about perverted. This is the pot calling the kettle black, I think." She ran off to the train.

Gerald pursued her onto the platform where she crumpled up on a bench and sobbed. He sat down next to her and tried to cuddle her. She elbowed him away. Persistent, he softly whispered to her, "It must have been a misunderstanding between us about what you wanted."

"That's easy to say now, as you try to wriggle out of your part of the blame. There were no misunderstandings." The fire returned to her eyes. "Why did you get me drunk then?" she snapped at him.

"I didn't get you drunk. You drank the gin, not me. We all had a few drinks just to have a good time. It's normal here, and you said you wanted to live London."

"If that's living London, then you can stuff it! I came here for you, not to be a whore."

Gerald clenched his fists as if to explode, but then sighed and looked at his feet. "We'll just put it down to experience, shall we? You are not a whore, you are a lovely lady, who just wanted to please, and have a good time. Maybe it got a little bit out of hand, that's all.

"Krista, maybe you should understand that the long-term future with me is not good. What with the parties and all the travelling I do, and much as I think that you are lovely, you know I also have a girlfriend back in Drakesford. At least I'm honest with you."

The tube train rattled and banged into the station, and the sudden surge of noise pumped her up to her crescendo. She clawed at his face and screamed, "No. You are not honest. I came here for you. I was wrong. You are no better than the filthy old men knocking on my door back in Crete. If I ever get a chance to get even with you, I will."

Krista jumped on to the train, and screamed at Gerald as the doors closed, "You have shamed me. Get out of my life!"

37.

The more Angela had ignored the signs that Gerald had not given up on Sue Moore, the more blasé Gerald had become. She could not work out if his openness was because he thought she no longer cared and had acquiesced to his wishes; that he thought she had not noticed, and had become careless; or that he knew that she knew and therefore for some reason, he just wanted to hurt her.

It could not be the first because every time she hinted at some knowledge of what he was up to, he became aggressive and descended into a sulk for the next few days.

It could be the second. Her father had said that people often let their guard down if they think they are continually getting away with something.

The third possibility caused her the greatest torment.

Angela's eyes burned their way through the mirror. She ferociously combed her hair causing so much static electricity that her hair flew away from her head giving her the appearance of a ferocious Halloween witch. She swirled her coat around her shoulders and determinedly snapped her buttons into place. With a last look in the mirror and an adjustment of her beret, Angela strode out of the door. Full of confidence, she could not believe why she had not done this before.

White cumulo-nimbus clouds swirled in different directions overhead. Their edges looked wispy and jagged; the tops of one or two had pushed high into the blue stratosphere where Angela could see them flattening out to form the tell-tale 'anvil' shape, a warning of the thunderstorm to come. She threw back her head and defiantly shouted to the skies, "How prophetic! There's going to be a storm all right." She stomped on towards the thatched house that was the Moore family home.

She felt sure that Sue would be there because it was Wednesday and the baker's shop where Sue worked had a half-day closing every Wednesday afternoon. She would also be alone; Angela had seen Sue's parents boarding the Imton bus. The timing was right, and she judged she was in the right.

She rapped the brass doorknocker three times. Angela stared at her reflection in the doorknocker and waited. She heard movement from within and held her breath. The door half opened.

They stared expressionlessly at each other. "I want to speak to you," Angela said icily.

"I've been expecting you sooner or later." Sue beckoned her visitor in.

They stood in the hall and glared daggers at each other. Angela, with one hand in her coat pocket, faced Sue, who had folded her arms under her large bosom and was tapping the flagstone floor with one foot. Angela's eyes were on fire. There, in front of her at last, was her nemesis. All the pain, all the worry, all the problems all caused by this fat bitch. Angela's fingers spread and bent into hooks. Her nails were sharp talons ready to sink into their target. Sue's eyes widened as she unfolded her arms.

Angela had only raised her hands a fraction before something inside her applied the brake. The two women glared at each other for two or three seconds as Angela regained self-control and returned to plan 'A'. She humphed, and in cold and deliberate tones, began. "I want to know what kind of game you are playing with Gerald. He's married! Don't you have any scruples?" Sue stared blankly at her. "What kind of person do you think you are that you can meddle in other people's lives? Why don't you go and find another man? From what I've heard you found plenty when he was away in Crete!" Sue raised her eyebrows.

"Gerald and I want to build a happy home and raise a family. How can we do that if **you** are always in the background?"

Angela stood and shook with rage. She clenched her fists and stiffened her body. Her voice oozed desperate passion. "When will you go away and leave us alone?"

She had fired so many questions and now, wrapped up in a tent of her own frustration and anger, she waited for answers. Any order would do.

Sue tossed her head backwards and refolded her arms under her bosom before she calmly said, "Mrs Clarke. I love Gerald and ...."

"You have no right to be in love with another woman's husband," Angela slapped her thighs in frustration, "*my* husband."

"I know you don't like it, but there it is. It's a fact," Sue said.

Angela's voice started to wobble, "I lost a baby because of you. Where was my husband when I needed him? Cuddled up in your little spider's web, that's where he was." She burst into tears.

"Mrs Clarke. I admit that up until the time you got married, I was after Gerald too. But you won, you got married and I was prepared to let it die then, but he wasn't. Sometimes, he even knocked on my bedroom window and asked to come in. And I'm sorry, but I couldn't resist him."

"So it seems." Angela snivelled.

"I tried to get him out of my mind, but couldn't. All I could think of was Gerald. He kept coming to me, and yes, I enjoyed it."

"And you still enjoy it," Angela said, attempting to dry her tears.

Sue leaned forward, her brow furrowed and her eyes became pained, "Yes I do. I cannot wait for him to come. The days between our meetings are so long and he's all I think of."

"Oh you poor little thing," Angela's voice intensified, "he is my husband. Don't you get that? You have no right to him. Get out of our lives!" Angela lurched forward as if to strike Sue, but again managed to restrain herself about a foot from her adversary.

Sue held her ground and sneered as she continued. "What you have to ask yourself, Mrs Clarke, is why he still feels the need to come to me if you have made him such a lovely home, and are such a wonderful wife?" Angela moved back, folded her arms and hunched her shoulders. "But if you must know, it's not a happy relationship for me either.

"As I said, even though I didn't want to, I tried to walk away from this. But he came back to me and he told me how much he wanted me." Tears came to Sue's eyes. At first, she held them back, but then the dam burst and she fell against the wall, put her head in her hands and sobbed.

Angela shrugged and tutted dismissively before looking away. As she did so, her eyes fell upon a wall mirror and she could not help but see how wretched she looked. She cried to herself again. For two minutes, there was only the sound of sadness in the hallway as the adversaries wallowed in their own sorrow. Angela felt her legs growing weak, she looked at Sue and suggested, "Can we sit down and discuss this?"

"Come into the kitchen." Still sobbing, Sue turned and led the way.

"Sit down, please." Sue motioned Angela to sit at the large wooden table as she went to the iron stove in the fireplace, where a large copper kettle steamed on the hob. "I'll make a cup of tea." A dazed looking Angela sat down.

Sue made the tea in silence with her back to Angela before placing two cups gently on the table. Composure regained, the stony glare between them continued unabated as they simultaneously raised their cups to their lips. Sue was puffy around her red eyes. Angela's were bloodshot, but locked on to their target.

"Mrs Clarke, I think the problem is that we have the same problem. I love the man. I'm sorry, but I can't avoid saying that. I don't want to avoid saying that. Gerald says wonderful things to me. He makes me feel so good." She looked back into her cup and counted the tealeaves, then gazed at Angela. "And then he leaves, for you." Her voice dropped to a whisper, "And I feel empty. I tell him that I want him to stay. He says that I have to have him on his terms, or not at all."

"What wonderful things does he say to you?"

"That he needs me. That I make him feel like a man. That he loves my body."

Angela clattered her cup down and speared Sue with her cold blue eyes. "He tells me he doesn't feel anything for you, Miss Moore. That he only comes to you for the sex." She picked up her cup, humphed in satisfaction and sipped her tea whilst studying Sue's eyes.

Sue's head dropped. "Yes, I think..." she paused and drew breath, nodded and then sadly continued, "I know, that's true. I want more than sex, but I don't get it." Tears ran down her cheeks into the corners of her mouth. "He builds me up, and then he lets me down. Even though he knows I love him, he plays games with me."

Both women looked at the floor and wiped away their tears. "Mrs Clarke, you think you have a right to him because you are his wife, and I suppose that you indeed have, but I have told you how I feel too. I cannot hide that, and it's not possible to push it out of my mind, even if I wanted to, which I do not. However, I had resigned myself to sharing him with you because whether you like it or not, we have always shared him; from the first moment."

"Since when?" Angela looked perturbed as she slowly put her cup down.

"Since your first night with him."

"What do you mean?"

"Gerald told me once that his first time with me was on the same night as his first time with you. After the dance. After he took you home."

The colour drained from Angela's face and her eyes glazed as they looked into space. Sue continued, "To me, until now, there's only been one problem in all this. He tells me that he loves you but..." she paused whilst she buried her head in her hands and sobbed before she resumed control.

"He tells me that he loves you, not me. Yes, he has told me he only wants me just for the sex and fun. But I love him. I always hoped. But now..." She paused as she looked into her cup. "He also has a woman in London. Apparently she's called Krista."

"What?" Angela almost fell off her chair feeling as if she was about to faint.

"And now Krista."

"Who?"

"I told you." She looked at Angela imploringly. "Gerald has another girlfriend, in London, called Krista."

Angela clunked her elbows on the table and shook her head in disbelief. "How do you know about this?"

Sue took a sip of her tea. "We were together. You know. Together." Sue slightly nodded and shrugged in a 'you know what I mean' gesture.

Angela sighed. "Yes, I can guess what you mean."

"Well anyway, Gerald starts to get passionate and starts moaning and groaning. You know. Like he does."

"Please spare me those details, but go on."

"In fact, he was especially passionate. Then he starts to whisper about my long black hair. I thought, what long black hair? I don't have black hair, neither do you. So I stopped, and pushed him off. "What's this about long black hair?" I asked him directly. "Who do you know with long black hair?

"He looked quite surprised for a moment before trying to make some excuse about a slip of the tongue. I wasn't having any of it. I could tell by his eyes that he had lied. Like some kid caught stealing sweets. He looked at me, and knew I knew.

"Then he just rolled over, rested on one elbow, sniggered, and told me matter-of-factly that he had another girlfriend in London, and that her name was Krista. He told me she worked in a pub in Haymarket, but refused to tell me more. 'Like it or leave it,' he said.

"He added that he still liked me and still wanted to come to me. I told him to bugger off! Which he did. As he went, he said he would see me next Friday. The day after tomorrow."

Angela shook her head as she gazed into her cup. "Will you let him in?"

"I don't know. I don't want to, but there again I do. Mrs Clarke, this may sound a little strange to you, but I quite like it when he treats me rough. It makes him more attractive. It's like

I'm an alcoholic, I know it's no good for me, but I can't leave it alone."

"Miss Moore, I am not your friend. I will never be your friend. Nevertheless, I accept that we are both in the same boat." Angela drummed the table with her fist. "I am not prepared to put up with this any longer. I, we, both need some answers." Angela sat up and clasped her hands together on the table, her eyes had suddenly cleared. "However painful it may be, he must choose or go!" She bit her lip and quietly said, "Or something."

Angela's eyes sharpened, they flicked from one object to another, and then focussed intently on Sue. "Let's contact this Krista, and see if she knows about us. There cannot be too many pubs in Haymarket.

"There is a police station in Tottenham Court Road, I saw it when I was in London with Gerald, I'll phone them and ask them for the names of the pubs." She tapped the table in certainty. "I can then get their numbers from the operator, and then I will find her."

She thumped the table again and was now brimming with certainty. "He has told me he will be in London today and tomorrow, and that he will be home late on Friday. Presumably after he has been to you. I suggest we meet him together and get some answers."

Sue reluctantly nodded her agreement. Angela continued, "No. I think the three of us should meet. If this Krista already knows about us, and doesn't care, then stuff her. However, if she does care, which is the effect Gerald seems to have on his women, and if she has anything about her, she'll want some answers from Mister Gerald Clarke too. But, where?"

Angela looked surprised when Sue said, "Here will be OK. My parents go to the pub every Friday night and don't come back 'til midnight, we'll be alone."

"It fits," Angela said ruefully, "and Gerald usually comes at about eight o'clock and goes at around eleven?"

"Yes, that's right. How did you know?" Sue brightly asked before Angela raised her left eyebrow, tutted and looked away. Sue shrank back into her seat.

Angela stood up and turned for the door. "OK. I'll find her, and let you know what happens. I'll see you on Friday. We'll arrange a time and I'll work out a plan after I have spoken to this Krista woman. Thank you for the tea."

38.

Franz's first teaching job was at Alten Oberschule near Worbis. It was not exactly his dream occupation because he had to teach a mixture of subjects, Sport, German and Astronomy. Astronomy?

He mused over the fact that if he was the least experienced worker in a factory, he would be the tea boy. Now, as the least experienced schoolteacher, he was the Astronomy teacher. He knew absolutely nothing about this subject and his only teaching resource was a dog-eared map of the northern sky at night. The previous Astronomy teacher laughed as he informed Franz that the job would be his until the next trainee teacher joined the staff. English was not on the official daily curriculum but interested students were able to voluntarily attend his after-school classes twice per week.

Brunhilde was happy in her job of teaching Russian at Langenfeld Oberschule and immediately became a regular attendee at Worbis SED meetings, which despite her tender years, she began to dominate. Franz attended the first few of these but found his interest waned as his football commitments grew. He had jumped at the offer to take over the coaching job at Kickers Alten, a local-league team. Brunhilde confronted this dragon with precision.

She scanned the scratched door and window sill and flopped into an armchair with a frustrated sigh. She looked over at Franz who had arrived home from football training ten minutes before her and now dozed on the sofa, which she kicked hard enough for him to open one eye. "Wake up, Franz." He knew that tone, his other eye opened.

Brunhilde smiled condescendingly. "Now you have noticed that I am at home, when are you going to decorate our rooms? My parents did their best but they aren't young anymore. It needs doing properly."

He tried to look thoughtful. "I don't think there's any paint at the store. I'll do it as soon as I can."

"How would you possibly know they have no paint at the Konsum when, to my certain knowledge, you have not been there for two months?" She sat up. "Franz, it is I who queue for two hours to buy our groceries. It is I, who becomes chilled to the bone waiting for the next delivery. And what do you do? Spend all your time kicking a stupid ball around a muddy field, which gives me extra washing to do, which means I have to buy extra soap powder, which means I have to queue again at the Konsum, only to come home to find you asleep."

"I do the garden. I get the coal. I help with the cooking. I do many things here. I am not lazy. I also do a physical job, which means I need to recover. I will paint the room very soon. When I have some spare time."

Her eyes hardened. "Spare time! What's that? My day doesn't include spare time."

He sat up and cleared his throat. "Well, you go to a lot of political meetings." He knew instantly that he had crossed the red line.

She shook her long red hair and looked heavenwards before lightly touching her cheek with the fingertips of her right hand and saying wistfully, "I need them for my sanity. Would you deny me that?" After a short pause, her voice hardened, "I am not out as much as you are, and what I do is important. You have responsibilities, Franz."

He silently disagreed with her time assumption, but stayed quiet. He had lost. He wished he could have summoned up the courage to say he needed his football for his sanity.

Football dragons aside, they had a good love life and enjoyed socialising, which sometimes went on until quite late at night. On these occasions, Franz, due to his physical exertions, sometimes fought a lost battle against the onset of sleep. Such behaviour was grounds for stinging criticism upon their return home, the timing of which depended entirely on Brunhilde.

If Franz wanted to go home, but she was enjoying herself, a condescending smile and her back informed him they were staying late. If the conversation was not, in her view 'stimulating,' then they left early or certainly at a 'sensible' time.

On the journey home, she verbally dissected and annihilated the failed hosts, invariably the hostess rather than the host. His dragon had spoken and Franz would dutifully grunt his accord.

Brunhilde was not Franz's only lurking dragon. When he retired to bed after such a session, Franz was often unable to sleep, even though he may have been exhausted. He thought it strange, and sometimes it bothered him a great deal, that his thoughts often returned to Angela. He remembered the good times and what might have been. He had no doubt that they had been on the verge of something special. Try as he could, he found no fault in Angela, he had always been at ease in her company. She even appeared in his dreams. Dreams that were sometimes erotic.

Upon waking up from these, often sweating, he felt guilty and was angry that he should think of such things, rather than thinking of the woman lying by his side.

Life went on in a ninety percent happy mode until one day it unexpectedly jumped to ninety-five percent. It was almost a year after they had moved to Klein Worbis and Brunhilde came home from work wearing a huge smile. She flung her arms around Franz's neck and drowned him in kisses before she remembered she had something exciting to tell him and broke off the embrace with almost as much vigour as she had begun it.

She clamped his wet cheeks between her hands so he looked like a gurning champion, and with her face so close to his that he went cross-eyed, she blurted out that she had landed her dream job. She was to become a full-time worker for the party at their Worbis headquarters. Franz smiled broadly as he congratulated her but could not help thinking that this increase in her commitment would increase pressure on his own activities.

39.

November had come to Imton with its usual damp weather. Nevertheless, Gerald stepped off the London train satisfied with his week's work, and looking forward to his weekend. He intended to go directly to Sue's house, which effectively gave him a free evening as he had told Angela he would not return home until the last train. He had found this to be a better method of balancing his women, Angela asked fewer questions of him than when he came home and then went out again.

Buoyed by the thought that Sue's parents must already be enjoying their first drink in the saloon bar at the King Edward, he walked jauntily from Drakesford bus stop to Sue's house. His thoughts also returned to Krista, *Shame. John's mates were a bit pissed off. Could've been fun.*

Three positive knocks on the brass knocker, and as the door opened, Gerald smiled lustily. Sue waggled her head in a cocky fashion as she beckoned him in. She did not give him her usual vice-like hug, so Gerald took the initiative and bent forward to kiss her. As he did so, she leaned out of the way. Gerald's eyes questioned her.

Without waiting for comment, Sue beckoned him forward. "Come into the lounge, my darling, I have a little surprise for you."

His smile broadened as he followed her. An unenthusiastic log fire provided the only light for the dark lounge. Gerald paused as his eyes adjusted. The door closed behind him with a solid thud. It was now even darker. He could smell wood-smoke. Everything was silent.

Suddenly a familiar female voice hissed, "You bastard!"

Then another familiar voice, "So, Gerald. Your chickens have come home to roost." A switch clicked. The lights came on. His eyes focussed on the unbelievable.

To the left of the fire in a lounge chair sat Angela, her steely eyes fixed on his like two drill-bits boring through his head with cold precision. On her left, sitting on a sofa and with an equally venomous look, was none other than Krista.

Sue took her place on a chair to the right of the fire, her lips pursed. She waggled her head as her eyes, which looked black in the dim light, mockingly looked him up and down. "Sit down, Gerald," Angela ordered.

The women had placed a kitchen chair in the middle of the room, facing the fire. Gerald ignored this, as with a smirk, he went to sit on the sofa next to Krista. Like a lioness she lunged forward at him and growled, "You come any closer to me and I will tear you limb from limb." Her voice swelled, "Sit there!" She pointed to the kitchen chair.

Gerald drew breath to retaliate, but before he could do so Angela's voice firmly interrupted, "Sit in the middle, Gerald, then everyone has an equal view of everyone else." Gerald flicked a combative look at Krista and moved towards the chair, which he picked up and slammed back down one foot further back, in *his* chosen place.

He glared at each woman before sitting down with his legs crossed and arms tightly folded. Again, he scanned the three pairs of female eyes before he threw his head back and guffawed. The now statuesque women continued to stare. Then he leaned forward, uncrossed his legs, scanned his audience and casually asked, "Anyone for cards?" before glancing at Krista and chuckling to himself.

Silence reigned as a standoff began. The grandfather clock in the corner ticked and the fire finally died, at which point Gerald loudly sniffed and gave in. "So?"

Angela began in a cool and measured tone, "Gerald, I knew about Miss Moore, I didn't like it one bit. In fact, as you well know, I hated it, and you know how much pain it caused me. You know, and now these two other women know, that the stress of your little game probably caused me to lose our baby.

"You have consistently lied to me, and played with my emotions like a cat with a mouse. And now, this week, I found out about Mrs Theodorakis."

She cocked her head to one side, and looked thoughtfully up at the ceiling before she sarcastically questioned him.

"What was it you used to write to me? Oh yes, I remember, 'Beautiful island, bad food, bad sergeant, very boring, wish you were here, love Gerald.' We had only been married a few days and you were in this woman's bed!"

Gerald inspected his fingernails and flippantly answered, "No, it was a few months actually."

"A typical comment from you, Gerald. A few days, a few months, what does it matter to you? It's all a game to you, isn't it?" She sneered at him and turned to look at the smouldering remains of the fire.

Krista took over, "One of the first things I asked you in Crete, was if you had a girlfriend at home in England? You lied about your girlfriend, and, oh yes, you forgot to tell me about the small matter of your wife." She lurched towards Gerald who flinched backwards as she raised her arm before recovering her composure.

"And then when I came to London. Yes, OK, you said you had a girlfriend," she gestured towards Sue, "but it was 'nothing serious,' and of course, nothing about your marriage. Then you used me like a whore. You played with my emotions. You are in every way a bastard, Gerald Clarke."

"Would it have made any difference to you, back there in Crete, if you had known that I had a girlfriend and a wife? No, Krista. You were ready, and you got what you wanted."

"Yes, I wanted you, Gerald. In truth, it would have made little difference to me if I had known that you had a girlfriend, because then nothing is final. But a wife?"

Krista gestured towards Angela. "If a Greek woman sleeps with a man whom she knows to be married, then she is indeed damned. I would have never done it. The fact is that you have lied, lied and lied again." Krista shook her head. "It was only yesterday, when she rang me at work, I found out about your wife."

"Rang you at work?" Gerald's eyes widened and his jaw dropped. He glared at Angela, who, whilst continuing to stare contemptuously at her husband, allowed herself a slight smirk of her own.

"You are not as clever as you think, Gerald. You are so arrogant and cocky that you leave clues everywhere; like telling Miss Moore that Mrs Theodorakis worked in London." Angela sat upright and ran her fingers through her hair, "The rest was easy," and looked down her nose at him, "pure logic."

Krista sighed. "Anyway, I decided to come up here today. So here we are; the three of us." Gerald's eyes lost their focus.

Sue looked longingly at Gerald. "I gave you everything you wanted from me, Gerald, but you have given me nothing back, except when you are inside me." She flicked a nervous, apologetic glance at the other two women. "You said that I was your only girlfriend. You lied.

"Why couldn't you just give me some affection? You have kept me hanging on, like a fish on a line. I have feelings too."

She started to cry before she looked briefly at Krista and Angela, then, directly at Gerald, and with massive passion in her voice she accused him, "You have fun in a world of your own. It's just a game to you." She shook her head in disbelief and pumped her fists on her thighs before she screamed at him, "You just don't know what you do to people."

"OK, I'm a bastard," taunted the now fully composed Gerald, "What is this 'Witches Coven' going to do about it?" He haughtily glanced around the room, looked at his watch and sighed as he waited for the next onslaught prior to his summary dismissal. Krista and Sue composed themselves and looked at Angela.

"This cannot go on, Gerald. We have decided either we want you for ourselves or we do not want you at all. I think we should have a drink while we discuss our options, don't you, ladies?" Sue got up from her chair and went to the table behind Gerald, where two bottles of whisky stood. She poured three drinks from one bottle, and one slightly larger drink from the other.

Without a word, she handed a glass each to Angela and Krista, took one for herself and gave the larger one to Gerald. He nonchalantly shrugged, took a large swig from his glass, and then with a loud gulp, emptied it. "Good whisky that!" He licked his lips and scrutinised the empty glass. Sue refilled it.

Gerald uncrossed his legs, looked around the room as he leant back in his chair, took another large slug of whisky and started his defence. The women encouraged him and occasionally suggested he refill his glass. "We can't be too hostile if we are to get a solution to this." The women emptied their glasses, as did Gerald. Sue refilled them.

As his tongue loosened, Gerald told of how men were hunters and how he liked the chase, that a man needed sport and lots of variety in his life. How he liked them all, and how good in bed they all were; although they mustn't get complacent, they could always improve.

He held court and explained how he never meant to hurt anyone. "No. No. Never in a thousand years." The women listened in disbelief; they shook their heads and said little.

The copious amounts of whisky Gerald had consumed began to slur his speech. He had not eaten anything since his usual sandwich at lunch, but had now consumed three quarters of a bottle of whisky in about thirty minutes and had great difficulty in remaining upright.

"Gerald," interrupted the lusciously smiling Angela, "Do you remember that day when we walked around Soho, and you said that I must be more adventurous?" Gerald managed to look up.

Angela sat up and pushed her breasts forward, Gerald ogled at them as normal. "Well, I have an idea. We all know this cannot go on. Gerald, you will have to decide which one of us you want, and equally, we need to decide if we want you. I suggest we can do that here and now, tonight. What do you think, ladies?"

As the room circled around him, Gerald tried to focus his eyes on one of the two images of Angela that swam before his eyes. "Whashhhh? Here? Now? Rrrhow?"

"Yes. We can all go into the bedroom and you can test each one of us at the same time. What do you say, ladies?" Krista and Sue nodded enthusiastically.

Gerald forced himself into sobriety for a millisecond. "**Four** in a bed?"

"Yep! Just what you've always wanted, Gerald."

"I sshhay it is." He slumped back into his alcoholic stupor.

Angela stood up and turned sideways to her husband, accentuating her film-star figure, "You have always turned me on, Gerald," she purred.

Sue beckoned his eyes to her bottom. "You know you like this, Gerald."

Krista joined in. "You're sure to choose me, Gerald. I have some interesting things that we could do with ropes and belts."

Gerald smiled weakly. "Leshhh go then."

"I need another drink first," Sue said.

"Me too," the other women said in unison. Gerald chuckled and mumbled that he had better not, or he might fall asleep on the job.

Sue slapped her bottom and said, "Oh, Gerald, **come on**, you know how I like a man to be a man. Drink your whisky. Show us what you can do. Finish the bottle." She emptied it into Gerald's glass and poured three other equally large measures into the women's glasses to finish the other bottle. "Down the hatch," she cried, and all emptied their glass. Gerald slumped back into his chair. Not for long.

The woman bullied him to get on his wobbly, almost non-existent legs and the four of them stumbled and crashed into Sue's bedroom, whereupon Gerald collapsed onto the brass bed and closed his eyes. The women silently watched and waited.

He began to snore almost immediately; the women exchanged glances and knowing smiles. They would not have to tie him up now. Five more minutes of silence, and Gerald was comatose. Sue went and found her mother's bottle of indelible Indian marking ink.

Ten minutes later, their work done, the women pulled and punched Gerald until he grumbled a bit and sort of woke up. "You were wonderful, Gerald. What a man! We're taking you home."

They lugged him to his feet, dragged him out of the house into the cool air, spun him around, dumped him into the wheelbarrow they had placed by the entrance door and covered him with a blanket. The three women then pushed and shoved their paralytic cargo the one hundred yards down the foggy lane towards the King Edward pub.

Eventually, having narrowly avoided tipping him into the roadside ditch, they managed to get the wheelbarrow and its floppy occupant up to the main entrance. One last check, then they removed the blanket, ran back into the lane and hid behind the wall.

It seemed like an eternity before the pub door opened. No lesser person than Admiral Sonpat RN (retd.) stopped in amazement before he had time to close the door. "Bloody Hell!" he bellowed.

The pub emptied in a flash. Twenty-five assorted residents of the village, mostly men, stood open-mouthed. Then they laughed. The women amongst them gasped and hid their eyes.

There, in the wheelbarrow, with his feet hanging out either side, stark naked except for his boots, lay Gerald. Written, in large navy-blue writing across his chest was, SWINE FOR SALE! Two lines were written with the same marking ink across his forehead. Top line: I AM A, Bottom line: WOMANISING. On his left cheek, BAS. On the bridge of his nose, T. On his right cheek, ARD.

Gerald woke up at the commotion, but it took him a few seconds to be shocked into near sobriety whereupon he slammed his legs shut and covered his private parts with both hands. This sudden movement unbalanced the wheelbarrow enough for it to tip over and unceremoniously deposit him at the feet of his audience.

Shock grew into terror when he saw that among the throng were Police Constable Shilling, Mr and Mrs Moore, Stuart Bright and Dave Green.

Naturally, PC Shilling immediately took charge of events and called into the empty pub for a blanket. "What is all this indecent exposure, Gerald?" Gerald looked down at his shivering body, saw the writing and screamed. He turned to run, but was so unsteady on his legs that he fell over again. Most of his audience were beside themselves with laughter. "Not so fast, my boy." The firm hand of the law would to do its duty. "Thrown you out, has she?" Another man chortled.

Dave broke his silence. Laughter had given way to temper. "Explain yourself, Gerald. What have you been doing?"

"I hope you haven't been trying it on with my Sue," Mr Moore spluttered as he jabbed a finger at Gerald's face. "You're always sniffing around her."

"A bit more than sniffing by the look of it," a delirious onlooker croaked.

"Dave lunged forward. "Have you hurt Angela?" The policeman separated them.

"No. I - I - I'm not sure what happened. I was with her and the others..."

"Well you're not coming into my house tonight." Dave growled. "I'm going to find out what has happened before you set foot on my land again."

"I don't want any further trouble tonight, Gerald. I'm going to take you to your mother's to sober up, and I shall question you in the morning," PC Shilling said sternly.

Finally, a puce Stuart Bright stepped forward and hissed in Gerald's face, "And I shall require some answers from you on Monday morning, nine o'clock sharp, in my office," before storming back into the pub and emptying his gin and tonic.

Accompanied by much bellicose laughter, the firm hand of the law towed Gerald away to his mother's house. "God have mercy on his soul!"

"Do you have any more of that ginger ale, Sue?"

"Most definitely, Krista. Come on, let's go." Peering over the wall, the ladies nodded their agreement and walked off; outwardly triumphant.

Only the night witnessed their silent tears.

40.

"Bloody Hell! What have you been up to?" Gerald's father pulled his protesting son in through the door. Screams, swearing, growling and slapping. A small silence, then, crash! The sound of pan hitting bone. Lights flicked on in nearby houses.

"You'd better explain yourself yet again my boy. As if you haven't been a continual source of scandal, worry and disgrace to me all these years. Now the police." Innes threw her hands towards the heavens, looked up and implored, "God forgive me for my sins, for I must have sinned so badly in a previous life to deserve all this." Her eyes returned to her son's face. "So, what does all that writing mean?" Her voice lowered as she growled, "Explain that." Gerald peered down at his chest. "Go into the bathroom and look at your face," Innes bawled.

Gerald looked at the mirror, and clawed at his face. "Fucking bastards!"

These swear words had hardly left his lips before a right hand smash across the back of his head from his mother blurred his vision. "Don't you dare use such language in this house!"

Gerald scrubbed and rubbed until his skin was raw, but everyone knew that it would take two or three days for the writing to disappear. No one must see him like this. He would now have to stay put in his parents' house until it was gone. He sank to the floor, head in hands. "Oh my God, imprisoned here with Frankenstein's Monster for the weekend, the mother of all hangovers, the police tomorrow and, Mr Bright on Monday!"

Dave went straight home after the incident, arriving at about the same time as Angela. Whilst cuddling a mug of tea in front of the fire, Angela tearfully revealed all about her husband's womanising to her shocked parents. They were sympathetic to her, cuddled her, dried her tears and uttered many oaths against their son-in-law. Then Ethel returned to the point of the women's retribution.

"Why did you have to resort to that? Why didn't you come to us? You have hung out our dirty washing for all to see. How can I walk through the village again?"

Angela grabbed her mother's hand. "How do you think I have been walking through the village? Knowing Gerald, he has been boasting of his conquests to his friends for some time, they have all been laughing behind my back. The whole village will have known. That means they have already been laughing at you, Mother, if indeed they have been laughing.

"I could not come to you. Dad would have gone crazy, and you would have buried your head in the sand. At least it has come to a climax now. He is shamed. He has lost face. That's the only thing that can hurt him."

"I can think of a few other things that can hurt him," Dave said.

"**Precisely**, Dad, I know that's your reaction. It's always your reaction. Then what? You go to prison and it just gets worse. Gerald losing his face is much worse for him."

Ethel hid her face in her hands. "Well, maybe it will shake him out of it," she sobbed, "and then he can be a good husband and father."

"I don't want him back."

Ethel lifted her head. "Now just wait there, Angela." She hardened her tone, "We have had enough shame in this family, but a divorce is going too far. At the moment, people don't know exactly what he's done, but in a divorce court, it will all have to come out. I could not take that. Nor could you. I'm sorry, my love, but as I have told you before, 'Till death us do part.' Let him stew for the weekend."

In spite of hours of painful scrubbing, the writing on Gerald's face was still faintly legible on Monday morning when he had to run the gauntlet of the train. The ticket clerk at the station adjusted his glasses and sneered. Gerald bought a newspaper. As if he were a leper, the newsagent handed it to him rolled up, at arm's length.

He sat in a corner seat and hid behind the newspaper all the way to London before having to make an ignominious entry to the head office of S. Bright and Sons, where the secretaries relentlessly sniggered at him as he waited outside Mr Bright's office.

Stuart Bright had taken the whole pub incident personally, he said that it reflected on the company, and that if Gerald wanted to remain in a job then he was to change his ways and be a good husband. "You should think yourself lucky that the only reason you still have a job is because you have been the best salesman in the company." He put his hands on his desk, slowly leant forward and growled, "But no one is indispensable, Mr Clarke. This is your one and only warning. Get out!"

The secretaries had heard everything. There were no sniggers as they turned their backs to him on his way out. He cancelled his sales calls and spent the day on administrative tasks; the secretaries refused to help him, or even talk to him. One of the other salesmen saw Gerald scrubbing his scarlet face in the bathroom. Gerald had nowhere to hide and simply stood there with a dead-pan expression as his colleague collapsed in laughter.

Gerald bought some ladies' face powder on his way to the train at Kings Cross but cringed as he had to survive the wary looks of other passengers at this perfume-powdered man amongst their midst. In spite of the train being overcrowded, no one sat next to him.

Gerald stood in front of the farmhouse door. His stomach turned once more, just as it had done all day since his interview with Stuart Bright. Should he knock at the door, or walk in? He decided to knock. Ethel answered the door. "Please may I see Angela?"

Ethel stood stone-faced and folded her arms. Gerald folded his hands behind his back and tentatively nodded. "Please."

Ethel looked at him in disgust and hissed, "Swine!" before she slowly moved to one side and allowed him in.

Dave sat in his chair by the fire. He had anticipated this moment and had chosen it to clean his shotgun. His look was absolutely chilling. Even the muscles in his cheeks were visible as he bit his pipe extra hard. He remained unnervingly silent.

"Have you come to collect your things or do you have something to say to me?" Angela said as she appeared from the bathroom.

"I want to talk to you, Angela." His voice wobbled. Dave snapped the gun shut.

Angela's lips were pale but her blue eyes cold and strong. "We can talk upstairs," she said flatly before glancing at her father. Dave cocked the firing hammers of the gun, his eyes glued to his prey. Angela's voice became firm, "Stay calm, Father. I have this situation under control. Come on, Gerald."

They sat on the side of the bed. Gerald stiffened and rested his hands on his thighs. "Angela, what you did to me was outrageous. I have suffered total humiliation, may have to go to court on a charge of indecent exposure and have only been able to hang on to my job by the skin of my teeth." He folded his arms and looked at her enquiringly.

Angela looked flabbergasted. "**YOU** have suffered humiliation! **YOU** have been humiliating me and my family since our first night. **YOU** have the gall to sit there and tell **ME** what **I** have done wrong." Her eyes flashed fire. "All your women, all your lies, you know what you have done. You knew what you were doing. I tried, thousands of times, to talk about it but you ignored me. You got exactly what you deserved last Friday, Gerald.

"I have been the most patient wife that any man could wish for. Probably too patient. Definitely too patient." She cleared her throat. "I am not to be trifled with, Gerald, and now you know that. So, rather than sitting there like God Almighty, how about a bit of realism? There are your clothes," she gestured to his wardrobe, "start packing!"

"I don't want to start packing. I want to stay with you. I love you. I'm willing to forget last Friday if we can make a fresh start."

"If you want to make a fresh start, Gerald, the first thing that you have to do is **NEVER** forget last Friday.

Secondly, tell me honestly, why you womanise when you tell me that you love me and that I turn you on, and thirdly, sincerely apologise to my parents. We will take the first point as given and move to the second. I'm waiting."

Gerald looked sad, and bit his lip. He leaned towards Angela and looked deep into her eyes. "Angela, I know I am good at most things, but I must admit that I am a failure, I mean, I am weak when it comes to other women." Angela's jaw dropped. "Hear me out, Angela. Please hear me out.

"This weakness bothers me a great deal. It's almost like a sickness. However, I think I know the cause. I never had a youth."

"What the hell do you mean?"

He raised a hand and tried to press one finger to her lips. She moved out of range. "I mean that you were my first girlfriend, and you were pregnant after our first meeting, which meant that I was committed to you."

"Didn't you... don't you, want to be committed to me?"

"Yes. As I have told you, I love you. It was just that I never had a girlfriend before you. I wanted to live a little bit and have many girlfriends, but I had to get married. You had boyfriends before me. I didn't know what it was like. I am sure I would have chosen you anyway if we had met later and had a normal courtship."

He opened his hands imploringly. "Women find me attractive. They are always coming on to me, and I suppose it's that old feeling. I can't resist them and having done it once, it's easy to do again. Particularly when I was alone in Crete for two years. We had only been together for five months, and most of that was under stress. Then when I came back, it was normal for me to have a girlfriend, and I felt even more driven to it because you are so clinging."

Angela breathed deeply and blinked rapidly, she glanced at his picture on the wall. Her voice wavered a little.

"I am not clinging, Gerald. I loved you, and I wanted to be with you. You are often away, so we are not together all the time, you have your space. You think it's clinging because I interrupt your constant quest for extra-marital sex.

"I accept that our marriage has had enormous pressure from the very beginning. We did not have time to see how we felt, like in a normal relationship. Even if I accept your reasons, what about the lying, what about the future, do we even have a future?"

Gerald slightly tilted his head to one side, turned his palms upward and imploringly spread his fingers toward Angela. "The lying was only a symptom. It's important to look to the future. I am sorry for all the pain I have caused you. I have learnt my lesson. The girlfriends are finished now." He pursed his lips and nodded to himself in certainty.

"It took me this shock to see what I really wanted. You are what I want. I want to live happily with you and start a family." She started to sob. "Angela, you do love me, don't you. Can we start again?" He rested his hands on her shoulders, then wiped the tears away from her eyes.

"Even after all this, Gerald, I still want to make a go of our marriage but I just don't know if I can trust you."

"I understand that, Angela. I have a lot of ground to make up, and I will do just that. I will show you how much I love you and that you can trust me again. You'll see." They edged closer together, he stroked her cheek and they kissed.

I can't have a divorce. Nor am I perfect. He doesn't know about Franz. I have to give him another chance. "Gerald, you must go downstairs and apologise to my parents."

Accompanied by Angela, Gerald made a humbling apology to Dave and Ethel. Ethel grudgingly accepted it, and added that she hoped he had come to his senses and that time would be a healer. Dave sat in his chair, seethed throughout and could not look at Gerald until he made his one and only comment. "I shall expect you to apologise to everyone at the King Edward. Now go out of this room and start building a marriage."

As he followed Angela up the stairs, Gerald pumped his fist and smirked.

41.

Franz cycled to work as normal on the morning of 6 June 1952. Why were there so many army trucks on the road? He stopped at a newly erected army checkpoint as he entered Alten. "What is going on? Why are you checking identity cards?" he asked a stern looking guard.

"Nothing to do with you. Don't ask questions. Get to work!" The guard snapped.

When he arrived at school everyone was scuttling around with their head down, whispering and looking behind them. The Deputy Director stood sternly outside the staff room. "Herr Schmidt. Move yourself," he barked, "you're late for the Director's meeting." A giant DDR flag covered the entire rear wall of the assembly hall stage. This would be some meeting.

Franz took his place next to Frau Hahn. "What on earth is happening, Erika?" She shook her head, looked down and said nothing.

The director moved to the lectern, cleared his throat and began, "You will all have noticed the extra service activity in, and around Alten today. This is to facilitate the setting up of a special protective area, 'The Sperrgebiet,' needed to safeguard our border against Western imperialist forces and subversive influences.

"In order to secure this area, the authorities have removed subversive and unstable elements in the form of ideologically unsound families and individuals. This will in turn lead to a more secure and prosperous life for us all.

"This operation began at four o'clock this morning. I can report to you that it successfully concluded only two hours later. This is a testimony to the skill, courage and efficiency of the National People's Army, The Peoples Police and The Ministry for State Security. How superb it is that such principled comrades work tirelessly for the security of you, and every comrade in the great proletariat of the workers and peasants' society.

"The Sperrgebiet will extend along the entire border with the Bundesrepublik, and will be split into two zones; the first, demarcated from West Germany by a continuous fence, will be a five hundred metre forbidden strip. Only farmers and special workers will be allowed to enter this zone. The second zone, extending five kilometres from the demarcation line will have restricted access; residents and visitors will require passes. Details of the application procedure will be in your post box when you arrive home.

"These changes will also affect the organisation of this school. As of today, there will be one hundred and sixteen fewer pupils attending Alten Oberschule. This will mean a reorganisation of all classes, the details of which are available on printed sheets you will receive upon departure from here. Any questions?"

Without raising his head, he glared over the top of his glasses. "No? Very good, then let us sing our national anthem and it would, of course, be appropriate to follow it with a round of applause for our visionary government and brave protectors."

Everyone sang lustily and applauded for ten minutes; no one wanted to be the first to be seen to stop clapping. The first one would have to be the director. Nobody spoke until out of sight of the assembly hall, when Franz whispered to Erika, "You live in Teistungen. Tell me."

"This morning, at four o'clock, they hammered on the doors of some families and told them they were leaving. 'Now.' No discussion. They could only take what they could carry. That's it, gone! They took them east, permanently. They want to stop all this emigration over the 'Green Border.' We're in a big prison now, Franz."

After work, Franz rushed home and asked Brunhilde if she had heard the news. "Naturally, and quite right too. You know I've always advocated closing the border."

"What about the families? Some of those houses have been in the families for generations. People ripped out of their homes in the night without warning? Why?"

"Those people were subversive and untrustworthy, Franz. However, they now have a chance to better themselves, far away from those disgusting western influences."

Franz could feel his face reddening. "Is it fair that they should have to leave most of their possessions and memories behind forever? This will rip many families apart."

"They must suffer a little pain for their misdemeanours too. The same as you or I, if we should transgress."

Franz scratched at his scalp with both hands before he reached out to implore her, "What have they done wrong? In most cases probably only grumbled about the price of butter or something."

Brunhilde drilled him with her cold blue eyes. She answered her husband in a measured tone, "Such comments from these people, although I'm sure they were more serious than that, show a poisoned mind, Franz. They need re-educating. And that is exactly what they are going to get. Now, if you've nothing more to say, I'm going to help Mother with the dinner."

"Whew!" Brunhilde was his wife; he should be able to talk to her about everything, so why not this time? It was something about her tone. Franz sighed in disgust as he wondered how, after so much inhumanity of German against German under the Nazis, that this could happen again only seven years later.

Two weeks later, Franz was working in the garden when Brunhilde arrived home from work full of excitement. She skipped over and bounced up and down as she squeezed him.

"Guess what?" She sang. "We are soon going to have a house of our own! One has become available in Schwandorf."

"That's in the Sperrgebiet, isn't it?" Franz said as he disentangled himself.

"Yes, but that won't be a problem. Isn't it great? A house of our own, with a garden and trees." She kissed him on his nose.

"That's wonderful, but how did this come about? It can take years to get a house in a village. We only filled out an application form two weeks ago."

"There were some new vacancies after the recent removals, and they said, yes. Simple as that!" She kissed him again. "They want to reallocate the empty houses to trusted essential workers, like us. It will be closer to your work."

"But it's further away from yours."

"You're always so tired from your sport. Therefore, with less distance to travel, you will have more energy to dig the garden. I don't mind travelling, and anyway, I think I want to live a little way away from my work." There it was then.

Franz and Brunhilde moved into their new house in Schwandorf in October 1952. It seemed that the 'Big Brother' state controlled everything in this border area. Concrete bollards blocked many roads and checkpoints controlled entry and exit to the roads that remained open. It was quite normal for Franz to need to show his identity card and residential permit several times in one journey.

The Schmidt's found it easy to make friends in their new village but it was sometimes difficult to have too much of a social life because of the curfew. Guests like Otto, who now worked in Nordhausen, had to apply one month in advance for special visitor's passes. All visitors had to be gone by eight o'clock in the evening unless they had permission to stay overnight. Franz could never accept the reasons behind this, although he had no choice but to accept the reality as a part of daily life and like everyone else, keep quiet about his feelings.

He also had to accept the sudden erection of the frequently patrolled border fences, and the creation of a five-hundred-metre-wide protective belt of land directly adjacent to the fence on the DDR side.

A band of depressingly foreboding fortifications that was soon to extend along the entire border. He did indeed live behind an ever-strengthening 'Iron Curtain.'

42.

No unemployment, very little crime and a strong community feeling were successes for the DDR but its hypocrisy of 'equality' and the Stasi were always there and irked Franz like an incurable headache. The Stasi had virtually unlimited powers over the population, but unlike the Nazi Gestapo, it was much more careful how it used them. The Gestapo operated by the method of open terror, the Stasi more by 'firm coercion.' Franz and everyone else knew that if a person deviated from the state line, they applied sanctions of ever-greater severity until they regained compliancy.

The Stasi attempted to criminalise opposition and in extreme cases, even used the same heinous Gestapo torture methods in the same torture cells they had taken over from the Russians, who had taken them over from the Gestapo. New political arrestees were often taken to the Stasi Hauptuntersuchungslager, or main interrogation prison, in Hohenschönhausen, East Berlin in unmarked or disguised vans. Shoved into one of the van's pitch-black mini-cells approximately one metre square, one hand was manacled to the ceiling, the other to floor. Even if they were only being transported from somewhere in Berlin, the van would drive around for at least four hours. They had no idea where they had been taken. Unfortunates were always received at Hohenschönhausen in the middle of the night in a back yard under the glare of a dozen searchlights before being incarcerated, often naked, in cold cells.

Interrogation would begin in small, rubber lined, windowless cells. Non-cooperation resulted in sanctions that varied from beatings to incarceration in even smaller unlit cells.

Little more than cupboards, these cells were so small they were only just high enough for the average person to stand in. The length and breadth were so tiny that unfortunates would often need to be squeezed in and the door forced closed. These cells could then be filled with cold water up to whatever height the jailers determined, often to just under the nose. A favourite alternative was to use these cells to blast unending high frequency sound at the unfortunate prisoner.

Both methods usually elicited a confession upon opening the cell door. Having confessed, the unfortunate would probably be tried and transported to Bautzen, a special Stasi prison, where as a 'Staatsgefanger' they would be 're-educated' before returning home as little more than a 'neutered cabbage' or in the case of further non-compliance, being sold to West Germany for much needed west-marks or dollars.

The screw was turning in every form of life by 1959. Utta Langmann was a brilliant student at Alten Oberschule who had finished her studies in the tenth class with an outright note one, the highest possible grade. The morning she arrived at school to begin her abbitur, or higher education, the director summoned her and her class teacher, Franz, to his office. Franz inwardly gasped when the director coldly told her she was no longer welcome at the school for the reason that she, and her family, were catholic and attended church. Not only that, but, "It is known that your family regularly holds 'secret' prayer meetings in your flat. Your education is now at an end!"

Franz felt physically sick when heard this. He gnashed his teeth, *Stasi swine!* Someone, a full-time officer, 'IM' or unofficial worker, or one of the hundreds of thousands of occasional informants employed by the Stasi or to give it its full title, the Ministerium fur Staatssicherheit, must have informed. The Stasi had eyes and ears everywhere. Franz had no choice but to shut up and say nothing.

What made it worse was that Franz knew it was entirely possible the informant, probably a neighbour, was indeed very reluctant, but had been forced to inform. It may have been that the informant also had a child at the school who maybe wanted to go to a special university. Such an application would have to be approved by the Stasi. It was possible the Stasi had told the informant, "Yes, your child can go to this university, **but** the Staatssicherheit wants regular reports on the Langmann family; in particular, if they hold any meetings, and if they do, who attends? If such reports are not forthcoming, your child will no longer be able to continue its studies and will, hopefully, find career satisfaction as a cinema ticket clerk."

Franz told Brunhilde about Utta when he got home. She shrugged, and said, "Keep your head down, Franz. You must just accept that the state knows what is best. The church is a viper that wants to undermine us and bend the minds of true socialists. It is right that these meetings are not encouraged."

"Wiped out, you mean. So you condone this?"

"Yes. We have to make an example." Her eyes flashed. "If you are not careful, you may be the next one!"

Franz dithered, Dare he? *You're going to regret this, Franz. Yes, go on..., tell her...* "You know what, Brunhilde? You are a nasty piece of work sometimes. You have a very cold streak in you."

She turned her head slightly and cocked her ear in his direction. "Franz, tell me exactly what you mean by that comment."

He steeled himself. "It's always at these times. State business times. You are a different person. You don't seem to care about people."

"Oh, Franz." She looked dramatically pained. "It is precisely because I care about people that I work for the party. It is precisely because I care about the less fortunate that I battle to protect them from types like those subversive catholic swine."

"OK, Brunhilde, but that last comment, 'subversive catholic swine' and your sometime threats against me sum up exactly what I mean. You sound so vicious."

Her jaw dropped. "I am not vicious, Franz, simply passionate."

"It's true that you are passionate about your beliefs. I have always known that, Brunhilde, but I don't seem to know you sometimes. You do so much party work these days. Maybe your work for the party is too stressful for you."

"What!" She jumped to attention. "How dare you try to demean me? Neither you, nor any other man will ever demean me. I use my intellect for the good of mankind, you use your feet for the good of yourself. Do not try to kick me down, save it for your stupid bit of leather." She turned on her heal and stomped to the bedroom, slamming the door behind her.

Franz cursed his stupidity. He had always ignored this side of her. It had only rarely raised its head, although recently these incidents had become more common and he felt justified in raising his points. Now he must pay the price.

Over the following months, Brunhilde's power to upset Franz increased. Of course, in her defence, she turned the tables to attack him, and found reason to prove that it was he, who had upset her. Naturally. She knew exactly how to make him feel two centimetres tall.

After a row, she sulked for what seemed an endless amount of time; he could not wait to make up with her, but she refused all approaches. She did not seem to care if he spent days or weeks in stomach-knotting anguish, he must take his punishment. She was fortified by the fact that she was of course right, she was always right.

Even if Brunhilde committed the unthinkable and made a social mistake, she was incapable of admitting it, let alone apologising. Franz knew that if he pushed it, she would certainly have retraced her mistake and designated it a forgivable consequence of one of his own previous misdemeanours. Why challenge her? She was Frau Perfect, and he Herr Lazy-Dumb-Loud-Selfish-Chauvanist-Anythingelseyoucaretomentionist.

Although always energetic and outwardly optimistic, in his quieter moments, Franz could not stop shaking his head. What was going wrong?

Brunhilde's cold streak, her work and the fact that they were childless were, in his book, the major factors for the downturn. Her cold streak was now obvious. No one knew why the absence of children was so.

They had sex often enough, so it should have happened by now, but alas no. Franz often dreamt about playing football with his son. But hey, a daughter would be equally wonderful. They had often discussed this and hoped that it would come right one day. They would simply have to wait. However, maybe there was another reason for this downturn.

People liked them as a couple; always the life and soul of the party, they were an institution and no party was complete without them. Brunhilde was not a classic 'good-looker,' but she had style. She always made the best of herself and socially, he was always proud to be with her. It was clear to him that other men found her interesting and it worried him that she often flirted with them. What was unclear was whether she did this because she found them attractive or because she enjoyed her sexual power.

He watched these men as they exuded large amounts of come-on body language, and her, as she threw her head back and laughed at the secret whispered invitation. Was the laugh a charade, a delaying tactic, for the moment that Franz was not around and she could take the opportunity to whisper her acceptance?

He challenged her once after she had spent an evening sitting very close to a strange man at a party. "I see nothing wrong with a little harmless flirting, Franz. You talk to other women. Anyway, that was Hans Heidolf, Burgermeister of Hochwipper. We were discussing administrative details. He has such vision. Do you have a problem with that? No? Good." So, if she had denied it, then that must be the case. She only ever spoke the truth, didn't she?

When Brunhilde chose to speak of those she liked, her new acquaintances were always SO interesting, SO intelligent, SO witty and SO interesting and witty, not to mention how intelligent and witty they were and infinitely superior to the drunken village idiots at the football club. Those uncouth slobs; the drunks who used her as a coat hanger by draping their groping arms over her shoulders, whilst huffing their boozy breath down her cleavage.

Did she ever accept any of those SO interesting invitations he was sure she received?

This was the one reason for the downturn he had tried to avoid thinking about but it was starting to add up. She never talked about her work in any detail anymore. Franz had never met any of her work colleagues, and she always deflected his questions about them. She arrived home at irregular hours citing pressure of work and meetings 'for the good of the state.' Which state, he wondered but had not dared ask, the DDR or horizontal? Maybe Brunhilde had finally accepted one of those whispered invitations. He had to face it. She must have a lover!

43.

On the last Tuesday of September 1959, Franz decided to wait for Brunhilde down the road from her SED office after work. One by one her colleagues left until the last one switched off the lights and locked the door. "Gone. She must have left earlier, for a secret rendezvous. Who can it be? What am I going to do?"

Good heavens! He arrived home to find her already in the kitchen, cooking dinner. Where had she been? *Wait, Franz. You need more before you can accuse her. You'll only end up apologising again.* Opportunity presented itself next morning when she announced she would take the bus to Worbis, instead of the train. As it was a school holiday, he decided to follow the bus on his motorbike.

Franz parked his motorbike and discreetly followed her down the street towards the SED office. Then she unexpectedly turned left. Then right. And left again. Finally, twenty metres up the hill on the right, she confidently entered the villa with the yellow gate. He stood mortified. Everyone knew that house. No official sign existed outside, but everyone knew what it was, what it contained and who was in there. How could she?

Steady. Don't jump to conclusions, maybe she will come out in a moment. A mistake. Of course, it must be something she simply had to do. His brain crashed, his stomach cramped, he felt lightheaded and wanted to be sick. Two deep breaths and he regained some semblance of control. *I can't just stand here and look. Where can I go?*

He retreated down the hill to the café on the corner, where he could just see the yellow gate. Sitting near the window, he shivered and sweated his way through ten cups of coffee in four hours, whilst endlessly gazing at the yellow gate. The waiter frequently cast a suspicious eye at him. Was the waiter one of them?

Occasionally, he saw a car pull up to the yellow gate and deposit important-looking men and women. He shivered as they purposefully strode to the door. He watched as two women, holding hands, slowly crept up to the gate, stopped and embraced, before one reluctantly went through the gate and rang the doorbell whilst looking back at her partner. Her partner did not wait. She bowed her head and walked away towards Franz's café. She shuffled past the window. *My God! Look at her drawn face and hollow, bloodshot eyes. She is **shitting** herself with fear.* That face would remain with him for the rest of his life.

Brunhilde finally emerged at lunchtime. All smiles, she was with another woman and a man whom he recognised as being two of the important looking people who had arrived by car earlier. They jauntily walked up the hill, around the corner and out of sight. Franz quickly left his seat and followed. Hiding his face as he passed the yellow gate, he rounded the corner, and froze.

Having bought a bockwurst each from a kiosk, the group were already returning in his direction, forcing Franz to instantly about-turn and hide behind some bushes. As they passed, Brunhilde was chuckling without a care in the world. They re-entered the villa via the yellow gate and a side entrance. Franz shook and was full of indecision. He could do nothing except get away as soon as possible; it was too dangerous to hang around. "Oh my God! That explains it all. She works in the 'Stasi house.' She is no SED worker. Brunhilde is a Stasi officer!"

Franz screwed his fists up in anger as he wondered what her part in this odious organisation could be. What had the world come to? Franz shook his head in exasperation. Was it a state-sponsored corruption system; a boa constrictor squeezing the last breath of individualism out of every dissident, a chameleon with hidden eyes and ears everywhere? It was all of them and more. No one knew who was in the Stasi. It could even be your own father, mother, son, sister, or wife. *Oh God. Brunhilde is in the Stasi. Her cold side. It fits.*

On his way home he thought of how their snidey activities even extended to forcing kindergarten teachers to ask their four-year-old charges, "What shape is the clock on the television screens?" An answer of 'round' indicated that the house watched East German television; 'oval' convicted the parents of watching western ARD. Jobs and privileges could be lost, anything was possible. Was there no end to their devious filth?

Franz thought of Andreas Link, one of his former players at Kickers Alten, who after continually criticising the regime, had refused to be cowed by the threats and demotions until finally, he simply disappeared. When he unexpectedly returned two years later, his Stasi prison had bled him of personality and twenty-two kilos. Throughout the whole two years of his absence, without any trial, his parents had continually lobbied the authorities for information as to their son's whereabouts, only to meet blank stares and constant denials of any knowledge of his existence. *Brunhilde had known Andreas well. She often chatted to him, even danced with him. It must have been her! She would be quite capable of that. Poor, poor, Andreas.* How could Franz not have known?

OK, no one knew who was full-time Stasi or how many of them there were because no one dared talk about them and they usually lived away from their work, "I think I want to live a little way away from my work," returned to his head.

She came home as normal, but halted by the door as she saw his pale expression and the direct look in his eyes. "Are you feeling all right?"

"No." He drew a long breath. "I was in Worbis today, I had to go and see about some football fixtures." He paused slightly as he inwardly cursed himself for yet again feeling compelled to account for his movements. "It was a nice day so I stopped to have a coffee at Milchmann's, round about half-past eleven." Her back stiffened as her smile disappeared. He paused and stared at her questioningly.

"Go on." She removed her gloves and nonchalantly picked at a non-existent fleck of dirt on one of them.

"I saw you with your lunch partners. It looked like a working lunch to me." Her ice-blue eyes widened and her mouth narrowed as her jaw set. She stared at her gloves. His voice grew more determined and he gripped the arms of his chair. "Everyone knows what that house is, Brunhilde. Why didn't you tell me that you were Stasi? Is this why you've been so distant from me?"

She slapped her black leather gloves down on the table, ripped off her coat and roughly placed it on the coat stand before she faced him. Franz had a flash thought that took him back to when he stood his ground against Schwanz. *Don't let her off the hook.* He did not have much time to think before she attacked.

"Distant, am I?"

"Yes."

"OK, I probably have been. I can't feel warm towards you when I feel put on. You come home and you flop into that chair and go to sleep. You wait for me to do all the house jobs. Do you think that magic does them? I do them all...."

"That's not true. I do many things and I do the garden. Do you think that the garden does itself?"

"Every time you 'help' with the cleaning, you increase the mess rather than reducing it. I have to go around and clean up behind you. I have to do it all again. You just make more work. And the garden is a mess. You have no idea. You completely ignore my plans for an aesthetic haven of tranquillity."

He jumped to his feet. "I run around all day in my work, that burns up a lot of energy and I need to rest when I come home. The only gardening decisions of mine acceptable to you are the ones that you thought of first. What kind of sharing is that?"

"*You* need a rest?" She allowed her mouth to fall open, and give effect to an exasperated pause. "Don't you think that I need a rest too? I don't get any rest because of you. I have to do everything here. If you are in so much need of a rest, Franz, why do you have the energy to go out again to kick a silly ball around at the football club? I don't have time for such trivial things."

Franz was losing the argument again; he returned to his prime question. "Why didn't you tell me about the Stasi?"

The Chameleon changed again and she speared him with her gaze. Her posture became more erect, her cheekbones more pronounced; she looked sinisterly official.

"OK. I am a full-time officer in the Ministerium fur Staatssicherheit. I am proud to do this. It is my duty to the state, for everything that we are building here. And don't you forget something else, before you get on a high horse and criticise the Staatssicherheit. Please note that you are all too happy to accept its benefits.

"How do you think we got this house? How do you think we got enough money to buy your motorbike, and where do you think the telephone or the television came from? How many people do you know with a telephone? Why do you think that we're able to stay in a hotel on holiday, when most other people have to sleep in a tent?" Her eyes flashed with passion. "I am proud of my job and I am happy to accept its benefits.

"We are building a wonderful land and I intend to do my part to make sure that nothing, or no one, gets in the way. Nothing or no one includes you, Franz." She fixed him with her cold blue eyes.

He coolly returned the stare, but his stomach was in knots.

Brunhilde jutted her head towards him. "Don't you ever breathe a word of my identity to **anyone**. At any time. It would be a very bad move for you if you did."

He stiffened. "And a very bad move for you too. Your cover would be blown, and that is not tolerated, is it?" Franz got to his feet and moved towards the garden door.

Like a dog that wants the last bark she drew breath to retaliate, but as ever, when direct confrontation failed, she resorted to her favourite tactic of making a drama out of a crisis. She adopted her best dramatic pose and prepared to enter martyrdom.

"You be extremely careful, Franz. For yourself, and, if you have any shred of feeling, for me. Do not spoil what I have built here. I have tried *SO* hard to keep a good home. I have tried *SO* hard to do my best for us, in spite of the very little support I get from you. How you could show so little trust in me that you spied on me is unbelievable. Life is **SO** daunting." Then she hardened her tone. "But I will do anything within my power to see that it is not destroyed."

He went out into the garden to dig his carrot patch, yes, **HIS** carrot patch, which he dug furiously for two hours until it was dark. The comment about "How could you show so little trust in me that you spied on me?" ran around his head with deafening sarcasm. *How rich is that coming from a professional spy, who makes a living out of spying on everyone and trusting no one?*

The spade thrashed into the earth for the umpteenth time sending carrots in all directions. *Why didn't you tell her that? Coward. How is it that I can stand up to all the evil and terror of war, school bullies, Schwanz, anyone else, yet I can't stand up to Brunhilde? You know what, Franz? You're actually frightened of her!*

He remembered chatting to a group of his friends the previous week at a football match. They said that in their opinion, he was the most hen-pecked man they knew. He vehemently denied what he knew to be true, by using quotes from his wife that highlighted the correctness of her actions. *Brainwashed.* A tear rolled down his cheek. *Yes, you're frightened of your own wife. What is that for a marriage?*

He returned to the kitchen to find a cooked meal on the table. It was stone cold, but he had no appetite anyway. He gingerly entered the dark bedroom. She sat on the side of the bed staring into space, a picture of pathos. He sat next to her and promised to do more in the garden and the house. He began to apologise for just about everything. He meant it, all of it, he hated himself. She remained unmoved.

She was right of course, he could do much more in the house; he hated himself equally for this apparent laziness, and for the fact that he was apologising to her again. Just as he knew he would have to. Just as he always did.

In the sanctity of the bathroom, sitting on the side of the bath, head in hands, Franz again tried to analyse his situation. Socially, she always championed the fact of how well they communicated together; he would dutifully nod his agreement, which always made him sad because he knew that it was only half-true.

On a personal level, she certainly communicated with him. How was it that he was so unable to communicate his problems to her? Unless it was to agree with her. Whenever they had had these problem periods, it usually came to a crescendo with a deep heart-to-heart discussion. Provided the disagreement was not too severe, they would calmly talk about it for a while, and then agree that she was right.

It was only after she was satisfied and calm, that he realised she had always done most of the talking and twisted anything he had said back at him. He thought about how he rarely raised more than half of the points he wanted to discuss, and those were the less controversial ones.

Why didn't she ever see his side? Only a tiny bit of his side would do. One small victory was all he wanted. His only victory possibility was obstinacy in the garden, but eventually, that always got him into trouble too. He sighed and mumbled, "Why should it be, that a man should want a 'victory' against his wife?"

Later, they lay in bed; apart, stiff and unsleeping in the darkness before finally, she boomed, "Is there any point in going on?" All of her grudges came out, not in an emotional outburst, but matter-of-factly. She could present everything with perfect logic but with such pathos that it painted his worthlessness across his heart and mind. Feeling so responsible for everything, so worthless, his reaction was to hang on to the only thing he had. Her.

She was his only salvation. Instead of taking the realistic view that maybe a separation was the best thing, Franz did his best to be positive by finding other reasons not connected to him as to why she should feel like this. He loved her, and he did not want her to go. Eventually she allowed him to cuddle her and fell asleep.

Unable to sleep due to his stress and her snoring, Franz found his escape in his fantasy world. Now he could relax without fear of criticism and dream of what might have been and what could be. Everything was possible. Including Angela. She came to him then as she had done with increasing regularity of late. They talked and walked, swam by Ace Bridge and rode. After they had made love, she soothed his brow and whispered gently to him until she brought him sleep. How wonderful it would be to have a wife who didn't only kick, but who would, just sometimes, give him a complement and use the encouragement method.

Life returned to normal over the next few weeks, as the Stasi remained unmentioned and he did his best to remind himself to do more in the house. The ice finally thawed and they entered one of their better periods with each other, and with friends.

Otto occasionally visited or they went to Nordhausen; the mood always lightened when he was around. They laughed and drank a lot together, although Franz usually suffered criticism for some misdemeanour or another in the post-visit analysis. The fact that he never dared to say exactly what he wanted, angered and frustrated him more than anything he could imagine. This frustration was destined to ebb and flow. But he knew it must burst sometime.

44.

The second weekend of February 1962 had been good for Franz and Brunhilde, they were in one of their better periods. Franz had developed a psychological shield behind which he could hide and ignore everything to do with her Stasi. They had celebrated Otto's birthday with him in Nordhausen on the Tuesday and Brunhilde had been in high spirits on the Friday morning prior to her attendance at a weekend course in Potsdam. Although she was, of course, a fanatical party member, the thought of two nights in one of those cold Potsdam hotels, where the words customer and service were unknown, filled her with little enthusiasm.

She and Franz had a long and loving last kiss before she left for the railway station. As Franz watched her walk down the road carrying her briefcase and green overnight bag, he sighed with satisfaction that things were OK between them once again.

Brunhilde phoned on the Saturday evening and said that the conference was a bit of a bore and the hotel room dirty but she was just going out with some colleagues for a meal. He enthusiastically told her that his football team had won their sixth game in a row; for once, she actually seemed interested and happy to hear this. Brunhilde finished the conversation by telling Franz that she loved him very much, how she missed him, and how much she looked forward to coming home tomorrow.

Franz decided to meet her from the train. He had been counting down the minutes until her arrival. It was great to be excited about her again.

Brunhilde stepped out of the train into the bitterly cold night air well wrapped up in her sheepskin coat, but looking tired. He stepped forward and went to give her a big kiss but received no response as she allowed her arms to hang by her side.

He kissed her passionately. Her lips were cold, she hardly opened her mouth, nor moved towards him. He broke off the kiss. "Are you OK? That was like kissing a dead sheep." He awaited an answer with a half-smile on his face.

"Yes, just a bit tired." She glanced at her feet and nodded slightly. "The conference you know, and the journey." She turned and soulfully watched the red lights of the train disappearing into the night. Franz took her overnight bag and put his arm around her.

As they walked home through the dimly lit streets, they avoided the piles of freshly cleared snow that lay next to the uneven footpath. Franz did all the talking, Brunhilde mostly answered with monosyllable grunts whilst she gazed at the path, her expression blank.

Franz reached out for her hand, and held it in the warmth of his coat pocket. Her hand was limp, he was doing the holding. He became perplexed as after a few metres, Brunhilde removed her hand and put it in her own coat pocket.

Oh well, he thought, *she must be tired, and in need of a good night's sleep.* Indeed, almost as soon as they got home, and with very little ceremony, she went to bed. It was only eight o'clock in the evening when she turned off the light.

The light going off that Sunday night became more and more symbolic to Franz. She was different. She became more aloof, and excessively critical of everything he said, did, or did not do. Home seemed like a prison.

On the following Wednesday evening, he met Brunhilde after work at the station and as they trudged home through the snow, he counted twenty-three criticisms of him or something that he had done in the twenty minutes it took to get home. Brunhilde turned the other way in bed. She wanted no sex.

The following day, Brunhilde became hyperactive in the house, cleaning things she had only cleaned two hours before.

Franz could not see what was dirty about them. When he dared to ask why she was so furiously repeating this work, she curtly informed him that because he did so little in the house, nobody else would do it and she wanted to make sure.

Franz was beside himself with angst, and went into overdrive, doing everything possible to perform extra housework and not make a mess. Brunhilde treated this with lashings of sarcasm. He was being false; it was not his natural personality. Franz gazed out of the window. *I'm dammed if I do, and I'm dammed if I don't.*

Although Franz was used to these negative phases, he could usually work out its cause. However, he could not fathom this one; it had to be the Potsdam conference. She had been happy before then. One evening, after three false starts, he plucked up enough courage to ask, "What happened in Potsdam? You've been so different since then. It's like turning off a light."

Brunhilde bit back at him like a rattlesnake, "Nothing happened in Potsdam. Why do you look for distractions, Franz? Nothing happened. I'm just fed up with our situation, that's all."

"You were, we were, perfectly happy before you went away. I wasn't there to do or say anything wrong that could have given you the feeling that you returned with." She dismissively flapped her hand at him and stomped off to clean the toilet for the second time that day.

Life unrelentingly continued like this for the next few months. Sexual activity between them became almost non-existent. She was always too tired, not in the right mood, he did not do it properly or she had to get up early.

Franz became increasingly determined to try to please, but it was well-nigh impossible to get anything right, which was due as much to his stress as her demeanour.

Franz found it impossible to relax and be a normal husband who had normal male reactions to his wife when he always felt he was on his last chance. Whether or not it was his last chance was irrelevant, it was his perception. The more he feared, the more he failed.

He tried to speak to her about it. Her response was to listen with a bored expression and then enlighten him on how stupid he was. Then he felt stupid for having mentioned it because of course she was right. Another chance for atonement wasted. He felt that the sword of Damocles was poised above his head and could fall at any second. Such a feeling made its descent inevitable.

No sleep, stomach problems, forgetfulness and lack of concentration all became Franz's constant companions. So did the thought of escape to the west. How could he do it? It was so dangerous. If they caught him, the consequences were terrible, and what with a Stasi wife, he dreaded to think about what would happen to him, or her, for that matter. Maybe it would be easier to get a divorce. He asked a few general questions about divorce procedure with one of two friends at the football club whom he knew had been divorced. Never too many questions. He never knew if the person to whom he was talking had Stasi connections.

At school, he now took two lessons of geography per week, which he found interesting, although he became aware of how often he looked at the western half of the world map that hung on the classroom wall. It was a strange map, full of place names in Eastern Europe but showing only the capitals in Western Europe.

He knew he had to choose; escape, divorce or stay and make the best of it and try to turn things around. Although he had convinced himself that he still wanted her, he questioned himself as to his motives, was it love, or a fear of the unknown?

He convinced himself that it was a combination of the two and that his best course of action was to stick it out and try to reform himself yet again. Franz knew this was wrong. He knew he was a coward, and that he was stupid. She had told him so thousands of times and after all, if he were not stupid, then he must surely have been able to argue a case for his own redemption. Of course, in this he had failed miserably, so it must be true. He must try harder to improve himself and make Brunhilde content.

Through all the determination to reform, there came a longing that grew with each day, and refused repression. He so longed for an end to his pain.

Franz became increasingly frantic to break the deadlock. *Why is she like this? Why can't we return to normal, whatever that is? The only normality is when we spend some time with Otto, and then she becomes my Brunhilde once more.* On the last Saturday in June, four months after Potsdam, Otto came to visit.

He knew the moment his former best man came through the door. Otto embraced a beaming Brunhilde as if they had not seen each other for years. Her voice changed the moment they embraced. A voice full of such overwhelming endearment, that it told Franz everything.

Just for that moment, her guard had been down. Franz had heard that voice only twice before. The first time was when they were students and he slipped and hit his head on a kerbstone; her acute, caring concern gave her voice such a tone. The second time was the way she gently spoke to him after she had accepted his proposal of marriage. And now with Otto.

As he and Franz greeted each other with a handshake, and eyes full of questions, she stood close to Otto, wiggled her body and did everything but purr as she admired him.

Otto was polite and friendly throughout the ensuing barbecue as he chatted with Franz and kept his distance from Brunhilde. However, three times whilst Franz was cooking, Otto and Brunhilde disappeared to get something from the kitchen that took two minutes to find; when one person would have taken two seconds.

Due to the curfew, Otto would be staying the night, and anyway, he wanted to help with the haymaking the next day. The whole village would be out in the fields; giving further proof that the community spirit of the DDR was no fallacy. The weather on the day of the barbecue had been warm and tranquil and they had drunk plenty of wine and beer.

Late in the evening after much drinking, Otto excused himself and stumbled off to bed. Brunhilde was in a particularly jovial mood and somehow had plenty of energy. She and Franz had almost finished clearing up when Franz dropped a plate, which smashed on the floor at her feet. Franz immediately bent down to pick up the pieces and waited for the inevitable onslaught.

"Why don't you go to bed, Franz? You look tired, not to mention a little drunk and I want to see this set of plates last at least until my birthday next month."

Franz could not believe his luck in receiving only the mildest form of sarcasm. He jumped at the chance to follow orders, and quietly wobbled off to bed and waited for Brunhilde to join him. The alcohol had given him some courage, and he wanted some answers.

The sounds in the kitchen persisted for a few minutes, but then went quiet. As he lay on his bed, tossing and turning, sweating and thinking, trying to make sense of what had happened to his life, he realised he had been got rid of. An hour later, she still had not come to bed. The only sounds in the night were the barking dogs in the village, his thoughts and his pumping heart. And the squeaks of the bed in the guest room.

I should burst in on them, shouldn't I? I've seen the big confrontation in the movies often enough. Enough is enough. But he lay there, on a bed wet with perspiration. Just like Angela and Gerald all over again. Brunhilde would be the other side of that wall, three feet away from him at the most, screwing with another man as he listened. He hated himself for his cowardice; he had fought in the war, brazened it out against thugs, he could motivate men, everyone respected him, except his wife and he himself.

What should he do? He was not frightened of Otto, and he knew he was not so much frightened of Brunhilde as frightened of reality. He wished he were an ostrich. He simply could not face it. To face it, was to expose the consummate proof of his failure as a husband.

Just then, he heard her coming to bed. She crept in and took great care to close the bedroom door silently. Like the coward before her that he was; forget the answers to his questions, he feigned sleep. She began to lightly snore after only two or three minutes.

Round and round in illogical circles; confusion to logic and back to confusion, and guilt, and depression, and hate, and need and back to confusion.

45.

At breakfast, Franz watched the two lovers eating heartily and shyly glancing at each other. Throughout the whole meal, during which he merely went through the motions of buttering his bread roll, Franz had only one thought in his head. Each time he glanced at his one-time friend, the haunting thought blared ever louder until he thought his head must split open. *You're fucking my wife!*

Incessantly, it screamed at him, sang at him and haunted him. Franz smacked his knife down and got up from the table to go to the fields. To his surprise, Otto got up to come with him and Brunhilde cheerfully gave her royal assent to the departure, she would clear up and join them later. It occurred to Franz that her Stasi training had kicked in here; she knew how to maintain normality in the face of adversity. The bitch! Bitch. Bitch. **Bitch!**

Franz and Otto did not talk too much on their way to the field. Franz only had '*You're fucking my wife*' continually ringing in his head. Alone with Otto, he felt stronger, nervous, but strong as when leading his team out to play in the cup final or going into battle. He knew what he had to do. He stopped, turned to Otto and drew breath...

"Franz. Ahoy there! Where've you been?" Steffen Klein had seen them and was calling from his tractor. *Shit. Too late.*

About twenty minutes after they started work, a jolly Brunhilde joined them. Stefan asked Franz to work on the trailer and work began under the already hot summer sun. Otto and Brunhilde worked on the other side of the field not far from the copse.

It was only ten o'clock, but heat haze shimmered off the newly exposed earth. The children, who were supposed to be helping, had had a lack-of-enthusiasm attack. The work grew ever harder. Franz looked around. The lovers had gone.

Franz looked in all directions from his vantage point atop the hay wagon. "Gone! Definitely, gone." They could only be in one place. His eyes narrowed as he focussed on the copse at the bottom corner of the field. "Bastards!"

He realised it was too obvious to walk directly over to them, but he knew of a stream that bordered the field and ran down to the copse.

It was not possible to see the stream from the wagon because it meandered along a small sunken ditch. He told another helper that he needed the toilet and calmly walked towards the stream. A quick glance over his shoulder, *I'm clear*, and he jumped into the ditch.

Moving quickly now, he stooped as he ran along the stream's bank, he was certain no one could see him and he would not be missed. *Think clearly. What are you going to do when you get there?*

He knew what he wanted to do, he had rehearsed it fifty times in his sweat soaked bed last night. *Don't get sent to prison. Stay cool. Don't shut your eyes. Do it without temper.* His heart was pounding as he crept around the last bend before the copse. He was ready.

Franz dropped to his knees, listened, and slowly crept forward. He paused by the first bush. Nothing, only the distant sound of the haymaking. Utilising all of his military training, he crawled forward on his stomach. Then he saw them.

Lying in the grass, they had positioned themselves where they would just about see if anyone from the haymaking party approached. Brunhilde had removed her trousers, or more probably, he had removed them for her. Otto had merely pulled his trousers down as far as his knees, enough to expose his rhythmically heaving rump as it pounded between Brunhilde's wide-open thighs. *That's my wife, lying there like that, doing that, with* **him.**

He could not see their faces, he did not want to. He had planned that if he found them having sex, he would creep up unseen and kick Otto in the balls. But no, everything he had rehearsed left him. Instead of some imagined feeling of elation at catching them, a feeling of sadness and desolation overcame him.

He could watch no longer. He certainly did not want to hear them finish, Brunhilde was always a little noisy when she reached an orgasm and that would be too much to bear. He returned to the stream just in time to vomit into it, as quietly as he could. He glimpsed his timid reflection between the patches of floating vomit. He could not bear to look at himself. After all, how could nothing look at nothing?

He rejoined the other workers on the hay wagon, one of whom cheekily remarked, "You look rough, Franz. Too much sex. Brunhilde must've had a big appetite last night." The others laughed, Franz did his best to laugh as well. For the rest of the morning, he slipped in and out of a fog, mostly in. His only sanity was to simulate work and stop himself falling over and drowning in his own depression.

When he finally noticed that the happy couple had returned, he could not look at them. But they were only interested in each other. At lunch, Otto and Brunhilde sat together trying to appear normal, but failing miserably. Their body language broadcasted their closeness to all who cared to look. And some did indeed look.

Frau Engelmann never missed a trick and whispered to her friend of sixty years, Frau Weber, "Those two are together!" The two old women clucked and nodded in unison before turning as one towards Franz, who was blankly staring at his sandwich looking lost. "He knows," Frau Weber added sadly.

The day's work over, they were back at the house and just before Otto was due to leave for Nordhausen, he went to the toilet. Franz knew that Brunhilde was in the kitchen, *this is it! Now. Do it.* Franz marched confidently in and hands on hips, stood before his wife. "Is he your lover?"

Her eyes flashed fire as she rested one hand on the sink and the other on her hip. "What do you mean?"

"Tell me the truth. Just for once in your life tell me the truth."

She paused as the fire in her eyes went out before quietly murmuring, "Yes." Just then, Otto came out of the toilet. He was all smiles until he glanced at Brunhilde, and then Franz. His face fell.

"Explain yourself," Franz ordered of him. Otto moved over to stand next to Brunhilde, looking conciliatory. "I have never experienced such a feeling as when I'm with Brunhilde. We have incredibly strong feelings for each other." Otto's body straightened and he now stared arrogantly at his former friend.

Franz addressed his wife, "And you? What happened to all that trust that you used to trumpet so valiantly?"

"Trust has nothing to do with this..."

"Evidently."

Brunhilde ignored Franz's joust. She continued with theatrical sincerity, and a slight toss of her head. "This has everything to do with a bonding of souls."

Oh God, here she goes, even at a moment like this she tries to take the higher ground. "How long has this been going on?"

"Does it matter?" Otto said.

"Yes it matters. When did this start? In Potsdam?" He leant towards Otto. "Were you in Potsdam with her in February?"

"No. I was in Nordhausen all February." Brunhilde drew breath to speak, but changed her mind and stared at the floor.

"But you were with Brunhilde in February?"

"Yes."

"In Nordhausen?" Otto nodded. Franz looked at Brunhilde, "So no Potsdam?"

She sneered like a bored guard dog. "What does it matter?"

"It matters because you lied to me. You have continually lied to me. You, who have always reminded me of your honesty. You, who have always told me of my failings. You who have, according to yourself, never put a foot wrong. Do as I say, not as I do, huh?"

"Anything I may or may not have said to you was only a symptom, Franz, a symptom of an unhappy heart. A heart wanting love."

"I gave you love, you only gave me superiority. You treated me like a pet that suited your purpose, when it suited you."

"That's not true. You had plenty of chances to change, I told you often enough. You had a few rough edges when we met, but you were kind and funny. I always thought I could change you. I thought I could change what I didn't like. But I couldn't."

"If you were so happy you had got it together with dear Otto here, why were you so bad to me these last few months? You should've been happy, shouldn't you?"

"I wanted to make you hate me."

Franz's eyes narrowed, he ran his fingers through his hair and stared incredulously at his wife. "How cruel you are, Brunhilde." He shook his head. "You knew what you were doing all along. 'I wanted to make you hate me.' You callously decided to act out a cliché in real life."

Franz slapped his clenched fists against his side and with the the veins in his neck bulging, leant towards his wife. "You Swine. How could you deliberately set out to hurt me? You calculated it as if I was some laboratory test, in order to achieve your own end.

"But of course!" Franz threw up his arms in exasperation. "You are a professional! Part of one of your Stasi plans. You could see how I was suffering but you didn't let up, you turned the screw, you stuck the knife in, and waggled it about in my stomach.

"Brunhilde, you have always told me that you could read me like a book, that you communicated with me so well, but in fact you never knew me at all. If you had really known me like you say you do, you would have known that you could have come and talked to me, not at me, to me, with me, and told me that you had found someone." Franz jabbed aggressively at Otto and snarled, "Him!"

Otto stiffened and moved a fraction towards Franz who instantly squared up to him and barked, "One false move from you, boy, and I'll drop you." Franz's eyes burned. "And you won't get up!" Otto deflated and his eyes sank back into his head.

Franz returned to Brunhilde, "There was absolutely no need to act as you have done. I can accept that things go wrong between people. It is true that it has not been right between us, but to treat me as callously as you have, is unforgivable." Franz put his hands on his hips and stood feet astride, "To invite him here, and to have sex in the next room to me whilst you thought I was asleep, but without a care about my feelings even if I was awake, which I was, is just so arrogantly vicious. You have a hateful side to your nature. How I ever loved you as I did, I just don't know."

A long period of silence followed, as everyone looked everywhere else except at each other.

Then Franz glared at his former friend, "To think of how much you leant on me in the camp to keep you sane. How many times did I stop you from committing suicide? And that whatever has happened between you and Brunhilde, you paid me back by brazening out a lie. 'Fancy a drink, Franz? Come around for a meal, Franz?'

"In that way you are both well suited to each other. You even had the audacity," he glared at his wife, "both of you had the audacity, to screw each other when you sloped off to the copse this afternoon." He stabbed a finger at Otto.

"You, with your trousers down to your knees as you rode her. You are not as clever as you think. I have nothing but contempt for you..." He glanced again at his by now impassive wife and paused before loudly adding, "Both."

Brunhilde opened her mouth to speak but Franz beat her to it. "**Get stuffed!** I will not take any more shit from you, you have hurt me enough. You can't hurt me any more than you already have done and I'm not going to let you try." He glared at Otto, "Time for your train, lover-boy."

Brunhilde and Otto filed out of the room and as they left for the station, Brunhilde flashed Franz a contemptuous last glance.

From the window, Franz watched them walk down the road together, slowly and very closely together. His eyes filled. It was not the confrontation, Franz had handled that, and for the first time in a long while, possibly ever, he had said what he wanted. Seeing them walking so close together was what hurt him, terribly.

She had obtained new Western underwear two days ago, now it hit him that she did not intend her fashion show for his eyes. The sexy see-through style was to titillate someone else, who would devour her with his eyes and become incredibly aroused as she wiggled in front of him.

That someone else would be sliding his hands over the delicately woven lace between her legs, touching her in her private places, sliding into her, making her wet, making her throw her head back and gasp as only she could, and the realisation that she actually wanted that someone else, Otto, to do it. He slumped down in a chair and sobbed.

Eventually, a gibbering mess, he went to the bathroom and saw his red face and puffy, bloodshot eyes in the mirror. Twitches and further tears, he felt sorry for himself. Damn! Yes. He wanted to feel sorry for himself. He thought of how he had always helped other people when they had problems. He had always been a rock when other people needed one.

"Good old dependable Franz, always cheerful, always sensible, always knowing what to say. And inside, you are just a fool. Now it's **my** turn to be sorry for myself." He broke down again and slumped to the bathroom floor.

Through his clenched teeth in one final act of self-chastisement he snarled, "You could have done more to save this. You want her. Don't you?" Almost immediately, a voice inside his head calmly answered, "No. It's over."

He stopped crying. He felt slightly lighter. He felt relief. As quick as that, the pain had lifted with the realisation that his torture, particularly of the last five months, would soon be over.

"How can you feel relief in a situation like this?" he said. "You should be out there begging her to come back."

He hauled himself to his feet, supported himself on the washbasin and asked the dishevelled figure in the mirror, "But you don't want it, do you?" The reflection shook its head.

When she returned from the station, they said little to each other apart from arranging to sleep in separate rooms. In the following days, they did manage to discuss the situation rationally, although they both cried a lot. She seemed unable to recognise his pain as she inferred she had found a higher love; a higher love that would be difficult for anyone, particularly Franz, to understand let alone reach.

She smiled wistfully as she said Otto's name. Almost as if she were saying to Franz, 'You should be happy for me.'

"Are you going to move in with him?"

"I don't know at the moment. I want to be rational about it. I had originally hoped our new relationship would remain secret, until I had a chance to decide if it was real or not. Of course, Franz, you had to stick your nose in. **You** spoiled that!" Her cold expression returned. "You are not to mention a word of anything that has happened to anyone. That would be bad for both of us." She did not say how, and he did not bother asking.

After the confrontation, Franz often studied himself in the mirror. Although he did not rate the person who looked back at him, he had many questions for him about his future. Was there someone else out there for him? Was he worth having? Even Angela would not have wanted him like this. *Angela didn't want you anyway, Franz.*

In his present state, Franz could see no possibility of any happiness where he was and could not bear the thought of always seeing Brunhilde. Not only did he often look in the mirror, Franz often looked west and dreamt of life in the 'Promised Land'. At night, when he could see the border lights, he dreamt of being in a chic café in Munich, Paris or London.

Despite hinting at living with Otto in Nordhausen, Brunhilde had grumbled that Otto's flat was too small and 'not in the best area.' Franz knew what was coming. Her psychological war began when she proposed that 'for old times' sake' she might be able to get him a job near Leipzig, where he might possibly pick up where he almost left off with Dynamo Leipzig.

That suggestion made him stop and think for a while. However, he reasoned it was not certain that she had enough influence to get him back to Dynamo, even if she could get him a job in the locality. He decided to stall on it because he knew he could no longer trust her. How simple to have something happen to him when he was far away, which would then allow her to move back into the comfort of her own home and start her new life with her new man. He thought her quite capable of that.

"OK. If you are going to decline my Leipzig offer of help, Franz, it is time we discussed who should remain in this house." He stiffened for her thunderbolt. "Franz, I believe I should remain here, and you should move out." She sat on her cloud again, admired the room and wistfully smiled. "I'll find you a small flat somewhere nearby so you can keep your job. This house has so much of my style," she sighed and admired the room again.

"A woman's heart is in her house and I have done so much more than you to make it a home. Sadly, you were unable to provide me with children." She contemptuously sneered at him before looking out of the window and smiling her orgasmic smile. She said, "I am sure Otto will not fail me. We will need a place large enough for our children to grow and play. You will not need such a place."

Franz's stomach churned. He looked at her in disbelief. This was the first time either of them had ever apportioned 'blame' for their lack of children. She had to do it now, at this moment. And naturally, it had to be his fault.

She looked at her reflection in her wine glass and ran her fingers through her hair. "In this world we all get what we deserve." She looked down her nose at him. "The people deserve the freedom and equality of the 'workers and peasants society,' and those that maintain this equilibrium should have adequate rest and serenity in order to maintain the standard of their work."

Franz felt cut off at the knees again. He knew that to rise to this would surely result in the inevitable humiliation and apologies. But..., what the hell... "What ever happened to your communist ideals, Brunhilde? You're only communist when it suits you. What's wrong with a 'workers and peasants' flat in Nordhausen? I thought you were supposed to love him? Surely, it shouldn't matter where you live?" That was, of course, a wrong move. He was about to change from living in an atmosphere of icy tolerance whilst she wanted something, to re-entering the world of fire and brimstone.

So now, alone in his garden on a balmy September evening, one of those special man evenings, the type of evening where a man likes to think, Franz Schmidt leant on his spade and peered through the honeysuckle over the ploughed fields towards the border. He sneered as he scanned the new concrete watchtower, "Yes, Comrade. No, Comrade. Grey, roughshod and domineering, Comrade. All hail 'The Workers and Peasants Paradise'. Huh!"

He shrugged. "What am I talking about, the border, or my wife?" Franz strained his eyes to see if anyone was still working on the new second fence. He shook his head again. "Now we've got two razor-wire fences and separated by a minefield. What's it all coming to? It'll be like nineteen forty four all over again." He remembered what happened to Sergeant Nolte in Normandy and shuddered.

He smashed his spade into the earth as a Trabant, pride of the East German car industry, coughed and spluttered past, leaving him standing in a pungent blue fog. A fog that reminded him of his wife choking him, belittling him.

He flicked some mud away with his foot and looked west again. "Sod her," he muttered, "sod them all. The answer lies over there. A new life."

How long did he have in Schwandorf? The same reasons that had drawn Franz into becoming an escape candidate must also be obvious to a suspicious Stasi mind like Brunhilde's. He knew he must get a move on and go whilst he had the chance. But how?

Franz had seen the authorities embark on a programme of strengthening their border with the west during the last two or three years, but suddenly this process had gathered pace. On 13 August 1961, Walter Ulbricht, the DDR leader, gave the order to erect the Berlin Wall. That September, the National People's Army, or NVA, assumed total responsibility for all border controls. They had orders to 'shoot to kill.' Work had also begun on laying a strip of mines next to the DDR side of the fence along the whole border. Although, by the end of 1961, this work was not complete and escapes through and over the fence were still possible.

Indeed, in November 1961, a group of fifty-three people had escaped near Böseckendorf and in the following January, Franz heard of six families comprising twenty-two people, who had found a way out near Ecklingerode. Such successful escapes were officially secret; the news came from 'West Radio.' Conversely, the Eastern media vigorously publicised failed escapes, showing depressing 'mug shots' of the failed 'criminal' escapees.

He hunched over his spade, sighed and aimlessly prodded the earth before a softer image materialised, banished his nemesis and calmed him, as it always did. *If only,* he thought, *fifteen years of lost bliss.* At one with her memory, Franz looked towards the border once more, beyond the watchtower, west, at the setting sun. He saw her sensuous poise, felt her finger tips and remembered that English Christmas.

As the Trabant's fog cleared, the border floodlighting switched on, as did something inside Franz. "The net is closing fast, Franz."

He drummed his fingers on the spade handle, his eyes flicked over their new target, analysing it in greater detail than ever before; the watchtower, two guards strutting their stuff, a guard dog. He could feel his pulse pounding against his tight collar; the wire, another dog barking at an unseen foe, mesh, sirens on posts, floodlights, machine guns... "A man could die; or worse, spend his life in a Stasi prison..." He bit his lip and focussed on the gully, which ran under the fence. His drumming tempo matched his pulse as his eyes narrowed, "But maybe there..., I wonder..., if...?" Both of his parents were dead, he had no other close relatives to stay for or for the Stasi to victimise when he had gone. No one except for Brunhilde.

"She can have what is coming to her."

46.

It was about one kilometre from the stone bridge to the border. The river meandered through a small wood for the first five hundred metres before it opened out into a manmade gully, three metres deep and five metres wide for the final half kilometre to the wire. This completely straight gully was fully visible from the border as the authorities had been careful to remove all trees and bushes in a bid to curb the increasing number of escapes to the West. Upon reaching the border, the river passed under a temporary prefabricated concrete bridge, which carried a service road running parallel to the new second fence. It just so happened that throughout its straight section the river ran through land farmed by Franz's friend, Ralf Hamman.

As it was a Sunday, he had volunteered to help Ralf repair a broken down tractor in the field next to the river, about fifty metres from the bridge. Patrols were everywhere and were exceptionally jumpy about unknown civilians getting so close to the fence. It had taken the pair half an hour and four identification checks to get near this tractor and throughout the hour that it took to repair it, two gun-toting NVA soldiers stood barely two metres away and scrutinised the mechanics every move. Any escape through that border stronghold carried terrible risks; most failed. *Stay in East Germany and you're dead, Franz,* he thought. *You must try... but how?*

If he used a ladder to climb over the first fence, he could well land in the jaws of a waiting guard dog. If he was too quick for the dog he would then have to run the twenty-five metre gauntlet of the minefield, almost certainly terminal, before having to scale the second fence, definitely terminal. *Smash through with a truck? Wouldn't get past the Tank traps or the ditch.* He shook his head. *It has to be something different,* he thought. He glanced at the concrete bridge.

The bridge overhung its concrete supports and under the square-shaped arch, but out of sight of anyone on the bridge, the National Volks Armee had attempted to block any river route escapes by inserting a two-metre high, barbed wire capped, metal grille into the water fixed to the supports.

The river normally ran about half a metre deep along the length of the gully so that the grille showed about one and a half metres above the water level leaving a gap of about one metre between the wire and the underside of the bridge. "Naa, you idiot," he mumbled to himself as he resumed working. *Absolutely impossible to swim five hundred metres along a shallow river, through a heavily patrolled area, then climb a two-metre barbed-wire grille before finally swimming another twenty or thirty metres to the west without capture.* Then, he stopped working, stared intently at the grille. *But when it's in flood?*

The men who fortified the border were not local and their commanders frequently rotated their jobs so no one knew all its secrets. Whoever had built that grille had not used the normal fine-mesh fence panels probably because they would have created too much resistance in the water. Instead, they had used a grill that looked like wide mesh, two-metre concrete re-enforcing panels.

They had obviously not known or cared about the fact that the river, at least once per winter, rose so high that it filled the gully to its brim, sometimes even bursting its banks and flooding the field. Franz beamed. When the gully was brimful, the water flowed unimpeded in a westerly direction, one metre over the top of the grille. *Yesss...* He could feel his heart pumping, his hands started to sweat.

Franz got back to work but only bodily, he kept thinking about the gap, why a gap? Then he straightened up and spun around. *Maybe they did think about the river flooding and all the bits of wood and trees that will float down. That's why they must have left that gap.*

"You got a problem? What're you looking at?" barked one of the guards.

"Thought I saw a hare running towards the fence," Franz casually answered.

"Scheisse Hase," grumbled the guard, "always setting off the alarms. Get on with your work. I want my lunch."

However, flood or no flood, the border guards would still be there. They would see him swimming. He must swim submerged. He could enter the water at the boundary of the trees, but how could he swim five hundred metres to the bridge, and twenty, maybe thirty metres on the other side until he reached the west, all under water in a flooding river?

For the rest of the time it took to repair the tractor, Franz worked in silence, although not very efficiently. He kept dropping things, forgetting where he had put spanners, fiddling with his fingernails. Ralf humphed at him several times, he wanted his lunch too. When they had finished, Ralf thanked him and they went their separate ways. Franz did not go home.

"Plop." The stick hit the water and Franz ran to the other side of the stone bridge. "One thousand," he looked intently at his reflection below, "two thousand," *have you really got it in you?* "Three thousand," *C'mon stick.* "Four...," he let a spit bomb go at his reflection, "five thousand," *You can do this.* "Six thou..., Ha, the stick!" *That's about one metre per second. In flood, maybe two, maybe three times faster.*

Hands in his pockets, he sauntered back home oblivious to anything except the calculations screaming around his head. At an average of two and a half times faster, he calculated he would need about three-and-a-half minutes under water. In tests at sport university, he had often demonstrated his abnormally huge lung capacity, with this and excellent fitness, he knew he could hold his breath for that long. *Yeah..., sitting, in a warm room during a test.* What about when he was swimming?

His greater oxygen requirement would reduce his durability, but on the other hand, he would also be travelling faster than the water, therefore lessening his need for extended submergence. So, how far could he swim in underwater in say, two minutes? Could he even swim submerged for two minutes? Tomorrow was Wednesday and that meant his weekly staff fitness club swim, he would try then.

As the sports master, he normally lead a group of fifteen or sixteen other teachers in a quest to reduce their waistlines, although the numbers had dwindled somewhat of late due the ever cooler water in the outdoor pool. Only the hard-line 'Spartans' remained, convinced that cold-water swimming showed true German spirit and a love of the healthy life.

Shhiiiiiittt, it's cold! The cold water electrocuted his soul. *C'mon, if you can't take this then how'll you manage the real thing? Go for it.*

His body screamed surrender. Three times, felt his lungs were about to burst and thrust himself upwards only to dive again. His Spartan friends were shocked as the 'Blue U-boat' finally surfaced and gasped for air, veins bulging all over his blue body. In trying to conserve energy he had only covered about a hundred metres, but there was a bonus. He had swum for longer than he thought, two minutes and fifteen seconds. That would be his benchmark.

He lay in his bed that night, with his head full of calculations and empty of sleep. *If I swim for one hundred metres in two and a quarter minutes and if at the same time the river carries me along at two and a half metres per second, then I would travel for four hundred and thirty-seven metres towards freedom. No good. Do I really need to swim submerged?*

A company of forty soldiers guards each twenty-kilometre section of the border. One guard for every five hundred metres. Not many. I might have luck and no one would be there. Idiot. If the river is in flood, they'll be bound to have guards on the bridge or nearby He punched his mattress and heard the church clock strike one. *No. Can't cut corners and trust to luck, your life's at stake. You must be certain.*

Franz wrestled over these calculations for hours and came up with a different answer each time. Sometimes if the river was faster, the idea looked perfectly feasible. Sometimes, if it was slower, he was dead.

The problem is that I don't know the exact speed of the river, nor how long I can hold my breath in that situation. I have to be sure, I need an extra supply of air. The church bell chimed three times. He could not risk surfacing or making splashes by using some form of a snorkel, and he had no access to an aqualung. Where could he obtain an air supply?

Ha! A football bladder. I could get one from the school and inflate it with a football pump. That'll give me at least one breath of air. Yes of course, much safer. If I wear a T-shirt, I can stuff the bladder under it on my back and tie the T-shirt around my waist. That'll fix it in place, the bladder inflation pipe can stick out near my mouth. Good idea. I'll need a metal clip on the end of the pipe to retain the air. When I need to breathe, I can remove the clip as I breathe out, put the tube in my mouth, inhale the air and swim on. I might look like a Humpback Whale, but I reckon that'll work. He smiled. Two minutes later, he slept.

In school the next day, Franz found a bladder but the rubber inflation pipe was not long enough to reach from the bladder on his back to his mouth, *I can use some of that rubber piping from my wine making kit to extend it when I get home.*

The floppy rubber of the bladder-inflating pipe stretched nicely over the stronger wine pipe, which Franz then made permanent by using some rubber glue from his motorbike puncture repair kit.

Now his problem was finding a valve or clip that would keep the compressed air in the bladder for long enough, but was at the same time able to release the air when needed. No easy task in the dark and in cold turbulent water. Yes…, his old Simson motorbike!

He had often cannibalised it for spares to maintain his existing bike. It still had a petrol stop-tap, and that might be the answer. It fitted, and to his joy, he found he was able to turn the air on and off on demand. However, the bladder idea was a double-edged sword. *You will be buoyant. I can hear the machine gun now. 'Need some ballast. A weighted belt?*

It was going to be hard enough swimming submerged at night, in a cold, muddy river, in flood and flowing extra fast, let alone knowing how deep he was or indeed where he was. It could be that the weighted belt would keep him so deep he could occasionally touch the bottom.

If he touched rocks, then he would be in the middle, if he touched grass then he would be to one side of the gully. He would know which side because he would be able to feel the steep slope of the gully bank and could then swim back towards the middle; in theory. He had never swum in a river in flood.

C'mon. How much weight did he need? He could not test this in the swimming pool because all teachers, including him, were under orders to report all abnormal activity and someone might consider his special training abnormal and would therefore report it to the Stasi. That would certainly make Brunhilde close the net. A simple bit of practical physics solved the problem. He inflated the bladder at home when Brunhilde was out and tied weights to it in the bath until it sank. Now he knew exactly how much he needed to carry. Having solved this problem and even though he was training at superhuman levels, Franz was still concerned that his basic swimming efficiency needed improvement. How? He kicked himself for not thinking of it earlier, it was so obvious. The school swimming team used flippers for training. Flippers would surely increase his underwater speed and hence his distance before he had to come up for air. He would try them at training the next day.

"That's cheating!" Accused Bruno Emmerich.

Franz looked hurt. "No it's not. I'm doing some extra studies for my old college, comparative endurance graphs and all that. So this is all in order. You can observe, Bruno. I need exact time, distance, and naturally, your signature."

Having been elevated to a position of rank, Bruno stood to attention at the end of the pool stop watch in hand, chest puffed out and looked down his nose at the other "lesser" Spartans before doing what anyone of rank in East Germany should do; bark an order, which naturally, the others will follow.

"Do not enter the pool. Herr Schmidt is doing this test for science and I shall ensure that it is correctly effected." The others duly formed a respectful observation line, although Herr Bormann, Head of Science, looked as though he had inhaled snuff made from dogshit.

The test was spectacular; first, one hundred and twenty metres in two minutes. All applauded. The next day he changed his kicking motion to a dolphin style, meaning he kicked with both legs together and reached one hundred and thirty-five metres.

This exertion was also kinder to him than before, in that he did not use so much energy and surface in such distress, he felt he could have gone on longer. Now his calculations told him he could travel four hundred and thirty-five metres without distress, maybe more. How much more? Two and a quarter minutes and he might just be able to reach the bridge.

It was now the middle of October and despite the protests of Franz and the other nine 'Spartans', the Regional Sport Manager had decreed that all outdoor pools must be dry by the end of October. Franz hoped and prayed for rain but as the days passed, the weather remained dry. On the last day before pool draining, Franz managed to push his best performance to two minutes and twenty seconds and one hundred and fifty-five metres. *Enough to make it to the west on one breath. Maybe. With the extra help of the bladder? Yes.*

Some of his friends observed that Franz was looking a little tired of late and joked that he and Brunhilde must be very active at night. "She's active all the time," he laughed in reply as he thought, *many a true word...* His face fell.

Every night, no sleep only calculations. *That submerged grill is the problem. With the muddy water and the dark night, I'll be swimming blind, and deep. Won't see the grille. If I'm swimming in a normal position, I stand an excellent chance of hitting the fence head-on, certainly winding me, or even unconsciousness. End of escape. End of life.*

Wear your motorbike crash helmet, Franz. Na, don't be so daft. You can't swim with that on. Why not? It only weighs about a kilo. You can't take the risk of smashing your head on stones, or the grill. In the dark and in muddy water, you won't see a thing. Good idea, do it. Then he smirked. *If they catch you, you can always say you skidded into the river on your motorbike.*

Yeah, but how are you going to explain wearing flippers on a motorbike? The Stasi will have a field day with you.

Every night he sweated and fretted. *I'll have to estimate how many seconds it will take to get close to the bridge and count the seconds off as I swim.*

When I get to that point, I'll change to leg kick only and reach out with my hands. That way my head will be protected and help me control my impact on the fence.

No arm use means slowing down a little, Franz. Hmmm... you hadn't thought of that. Too bad. I'll muscle my way over the grille out of sight of any guards. Hope I don't cut up too much on the wire, although there wasn't much there when I saw it. What's a few cuts for freedom.

Under the bridge, and thirty metres to freedom. Having scaled the grille, you'll momentarily be on, or very near, the surface under the bridge. It should be possible to take another breath before diving again. You'll need every breath you can get by then.

Great plan in theory, Franz, in the safety and comfort of your bed, but it's one hell of a gamble. All this theory, it should work if you have control, but that's the bit you can't estimate. You've seen that river in flood, swim to the left, swim to the right, dive. Forget it, the river will push you where it wants to.

He clenched his fists. *Don't lose faith. You're always at your best when you are pushed into a corner. You know you can't stay here.*

Brunhilde'll find a reason to get you out sooner rather than later. Maybe even get you locked up. Flood or not, this is your only chance. He began to sweat. *Bitch!* He punched his bed. *She'll personally throw away the key. All I need is rain, lots of it.*

Every day he waited. Indeed it did rain, but barely enough to green up the grass and dampen the falling leaves. It was now the end of October, the pool was empty and the nearest indoor pool was thirty kilometres away; too far.

The only answer was to keep fit by playing football, running and joining in with all the activities of the children in his sport lessons with as much enthusiasm as possible and frequently practise his deep breathing exercises; he had to at least maintain, but preferably increase, his already prodigious lung capacity.

Alone in his bedroom he repeatedly practised the fixing of the tap on to the bladder tube with his eyes closed, simulating what he would have to do in the dark on the riverbank after he had inflated the bladder. However, with each day, his problems mounted.

Life in the house with his "Dear Wife" was now unbearable. He felt sure that she must be personally fabricating evidence in his Stasi file. She must close the net soon.

The weather was now colder and his plan would never work if he had to swim such a distance in ice-cold water. Why didn't it rain? "Why? Why? Why? Come on, damn you. Rain. Just for me. Please!"

Two nights later, on 6 November, the skies darkened. The weather forecast on the forbidden West television channel warned of heavy rain, East television said that there might be showers, Franz prayed.

It duly rained all of that night. Next day, he found it difficult to concentrate on his teaching as the torrential rain, as loud as a thousand drums, continued to hammer down on the metal roof of the sports hall. The drums pumped him up as they would soldiers before battle. They gave him courage; they concentrated his mind on the task to come.

After school, he went for his usual training run and, as he jogged over the stone bridge, his heart skipped a beat. The rain had now been falling heavily for about sixteen hours onto bone-dry land; most of it had run off into the river. *This wonderful river has risen two metres, and it is still raining. It's now or never. I shall go tonight!*

47.

Brunhilde was her usual caustic self when she came home; she wanted a "full and frank discussion" with Franz about the future. In her most official voice she said, "This situation must not go on one week longer. We must find a solution." She calmed down a little bit when Franz agreed with her and even looked slightly shocked when Franz suggested that he, Brunhilde and Otto met together at the weekend to iron out a logistic solution. Brunhilde put her hands on the kitchen table and leant forward. She looked like she was about to interrogate a dissident, "You won't kill him?"

"No. I accept what has happened. I can see you love him, and the two of you have the same interests and opinions. You see, Brunhilde, I am a reasonable man. I can accept it when things aren't right. Don't forget, I want a happy life too. However, I do not accept, I will never accept, the need for you to be as dreadful to me as you have been. Let's finish this in a civilised way and meet on Saturday evening."

Brunhilde became calm, and even cast a vaguely affectionate smile at Franz before she offered him his favourite evening meal of Schweinebraten and onions. During the meal, they made light conversation and spoke about the good times. Franz could not help wishing that this convivial atmosphere had always prevailed. It was a macabre situation; 'The condemned man ate a hearty meal.'

However, Franz did not eat much, and only drank water, but he made sure Brunhilde drank two good-sized glasses of red wine followed by a schnapps. As she got up to go to bed, she said she felt satisfied, full and tired. Franz, wanting her to sleep well that night, smiled warmly. He watched her slowly shuffle into her bedroom and close the door without looking back. He stared at the closed door. As it had closed, so had a chapter of his life. *Fifteen years. What had gone wrong? All the hopes and dreams, all the pain. Why couldn't it all have been different?* He hoped that her disappearing back was the last he would ever see or hear of her.

At three-fifteen in the morning he had climbed out of the window of his house and crept away. Now at three-thirty, the shock of entering a cold, colder than he had expected, river in flood dressed like a hunchback biker had not dimmed Franz's concentration. He had dived and was swimming for his life.

Nine, ten, eleven, where's the bottom? The swirling torrent buffeted and threw him in all directions. Oh God, had he made a terrible mistake, keep swimming. He felt a searing pain in his knee as it thudded against something hard, a rock.

Fifteen, sixteen, seventeen, a scrape of the arm, he was in the middle of the river all right. Whoof! An underwater wave caused by the current passing over a large object on the bottom pushed him up so fast that his stomach churned as though he were on a roller coaster. Higher, on his side, feet up, out of control. Would he break the surface?

He tumbled over in his pitch black, cold, heathen world for two or three seconds before, mercifully having not surfaced, he regained control and swam down again. A violent blow to his head on something solid abruptly halted his dive, probably another stone. A tug on his head, the helmet was coming off. *Shiit.* He tried to grab it. Too late, the helmet strap cut his nose as the current ripped the helmet off and away. *Stay cool.* He felt no pain anywhere on his body, such was his concentration on his task. *Kick your legs rhythmically. One beat a second. This isn't a sprint.*

His lungs were OK, *forty-five, forty-six, forty-seven, grass on my left, swim right and down, fifty-one, fifty-two;* thud, thank God again, rocks.

He had calculated it would take him between one hundred and twenty and one hundred and forty seconds to get to the grille under the concrete bridge.

He was sure he would be able to get that far on one breath, but decided against it because the pressure of the current would be likely to press him flat against the grille, making breathing too difficult.

That is, providing the speed of the current hadn't already smashed his brains out.

He planned to inflate at ninety seconds, and then swim on as far as he could with both hands free and one more breath in reserve in the bladder.

More scrapes, more bangs; at least he had enough weight in his belt. *Eighty-five, eighty-six.* His lungs were about to burst; this was much harder work than in the swimming pool. *Eighty-nine. Time to breathe.* He felt for the tap that had been comfortingly smacking against his face during the whole of his submersion and stuffed it into his mouth. With a great gush, he spurted out his old air and turned the tap on.

Tumbling as the current threw him this way and that, he gulped in the fresh air, refilling his lungs whilst trying to ignore the disgusting taste of rubber in the back of his throat. Wallop!

His buoyancy was lower and he hit the bottom again. His lungs full, he turned the tap off and spat it out. How long had that taken? He had stopped counting. *The grill. OK, swim with your arms out in front but first drop one of these weight bags.* He was now having difficulty keeping off the bottom.

Franz tugged at the weight-bag, nothing, and again, nothing. *Come o-o,n!*

Then the bag was in his hand. Franz gratefully let it go.

Where's the bottom? He could not feel the bottom any more. The second bag had fallen off at the same time. Suddenly, like a cork he surfaced.

Through his bleary eyes, he could see he was about fifteen metres from the bridge. Two guards were standing on it. The river swirled on, they must see him, but the guards were looking west. One second later, calamity struck.

The cir-clip joint between the pipe and the valve came off, the valve blew away and out gushed all of the remaining air in one giant fart.

The guards looked at each other. Assured that the other was not the source of the fart, they spun around to face the east. They strained their eyes to scan the distant darkness of the river and field. They saw nothing.

Had they looked down instead of into the distance they might have seen the black-clad Franz, floating virtually underneath them. In another two seconds, Franz floated silently out of sight under the bridge.

The river was brimming and he found only five or ten centimetres of space between the surface of the water and the concrete. The positive of this situation was that he had cleared the barbed wire at the top of the grille without even touching it and was able to take another breath.

The negative was that he smashed the side of his head against the underside of the bridge, lacerating his ear. Just before he emerged on the other side, he managed to use the bridge to push himself under the water again. About thirty metres from freedom.

The guards continued to peer east into the gloom, but shook their heads as they saw nothing. "That was a fart," one said to the other, "You sure it wasn't you?" The other, looking mortified and in a great show of innocence with arms outstretched protested, "It must have been a cow!"

Franz was now fifteen metres further on and fifteen metres from freedom when the guards shrugged and turned around to scan the western side of the gloom in case the sound had come from over there.

At the same moment Franz, who was now swimming on instinct due to the blow to his head and lack of oxygen, inadvertently broke the surface of the water by waving a flipper in the air only to smack it back down flat on the water with a loud slap. He had blown his cover.

As soon as they saw the flailing body on the surface, the guards sprang into action. They swung their Kalshnikovs off their shoulders and quickly took aim. The guns crackled in chorus, sending up waterspouts all around Franz, whom the current had carried another five metres.

He was now level with the second fence and only ten metres from the actual border demarcation line, at which point the firing would cease. *Push yourself. Push yourself. Swim. This is your life you're swimming for. Don't die, swim!*

His arms thrashed, his legs kicked, but his technique was gone as his muscles screamed. The guards fired again in one long burst, but their aim was not good. Franz tried to force himself under water again but did not have the energy; he could hear the cracks of the bullets and waited for a hit.

Then the firing stopped. He could still hear plenty of noise, but mercifully only sirens, distant cursing and the river slapping and gurgling in his ears. Franz had lost all his energy and was in pain; he had swallowed a lot of water and was coughing and retching. In his semi-consciousness, he felt that it was all over for him. *Come on...,* **one, last, push.**

Hoping, but not sure, that he was in the west, Franz struggled over to one bank and managed to hold on to a tree root to catch his breath before he hauled himself out. As he sat there on the grassy bank, bewildered, bleeding, cold and exhausted, he looked down at three bullet-sized holes in his flippers and shook his head in disbelief at how close he had come to death.

An approaching motor! Some shouting. Who was this going to be? Lights from the vehicle blinded him and he sat like a helpless rabbit in their beam and awaited his fate. He hung his head and mumbled, "What will be, will be. Done all I can. Nothing left."

The lights dimmed as a haloed silhouette of a soldier carrying a machine gun menacingly stood between him and the lights. Was this silhouette God or the Devil? He tensed himself for what was to come. "Where am I? Did I make it?"

"Thirty metres," answered the silhouette. "You are thirty metres into the Bundesrepublik Deutschland. You are a free man."

48.

As news of his escape broke, Franz attained celebrity status and the media flocked to his hospital bedside. He enjoyed this, and briefly congratulated himself as his description of his adventure improved with each telling. He had a visit from a representative of the BND, the West German security service, who wanted to know about his life in the East. "Just routine," the man said. Later that day the social services came and said they had a flat for him in Kassel. This was no dream. He had really arrived in the 'Promised Land.'

Then the press moved on, he received the keys to his flat and was now on his own. Smiling broadly, he stood outside a slightly dilapidated block of flats near Wilhelmshohe. "Oh well, it is winter. I'm sure it will look happier on a spring day." He managed to keep his smile as he climbed the stairs to the fifth floor and even when he pushed past a group of youths that did not smile or give him easy passage as they drank from beer bottles on the second floor landing. Key in the door. Heart beating fast. Click open. "Hello home."

The flat was warm, but it was so terribly bare. The brilliant white gloss paint that covered every wall and ceiling reflected the glare from the bare light bulbs so strongly that it hurt the eyes. His smile finally disappeared. Maybe he had swum the wrong way and ended up in Bautzen?

The bedroom sported a double bed, a chest of drawers and a bedside table. No carpet, no rug. The lounge had an old sofa, one beer-stained lounge chair, a small coffee table, a tiny rug and a small television. In the postage-stamp-sized kitchen, he found a mini hob/sink combination cupboard and a table with two old wooden chairs. The toilet could best be described as functional and a good subject for a creative decorator or estate agent.

Of course, no pictures anywhere and worst of all, no curtains. A home fit for a hero! Social services had given him a small amount of extra money, to buy himself 'something of what was missing,' but after that, he was on his own.

His hospital euphoria disappeared into an abyss of depression. He had found his longed-for 'Holy Grail'; he was now a resident of the 'Utopia of West Germany.' Where was the milk? Where was the honey? He bit his fist as he looked out of his fifth-floor window over concrete Kassel at the red autumn sunset and cried. He had never been alone like this. *Stop feeling sorry for yourself. You chose this, go out. Find some life.*

The wind blew from the north and first light snows of winter had arrived. Franz walked the two kilometres to the city centre and window-shopped for hours. Shuffling pedestrians pushed their chins down into the raised collars of their puffy winter coats and ignored him as they scurried for the warmth of their cars, houses and partners.

It seemed as if everyone had somewhere to go, and someone waiting for them. He tried not to look at his own reflection in the windows. To look at his sad reflection made everything worse, his reflection asked too many questions.

He noticed a large heap of rags and newspapers in one shop doorway. Suddenly it coughed. Franz jumped back in shock. Was it alive? Did it need help?

He bent over the heap and lifted up a newspaper to try to find the cough's source. The source replied with an explosion of guttural swearing in an East German accent and pulled the paper back over its head.

Franz stood and stared; he had never seen anyone sleeping rough before. How could this possibly be? Such things did not exist in the east, from where this heap had obviously come. Was it an escapee? Was this an apparition of his own future?

He prodded the heap with his foot. Maybe it could sleep in his flat?

The heap reacted even more aggressively than before, and warned Franz that this doorway was *its* place, and that Franz had better not try to touch again. The heap reinforced its point when it pulled out a flick-knife.

The stench of an unwashed body and dried urine reminded Franz of some of the new arrivals at Drakesford. He moved on, his body language almost dragging the ground.

However, he had enough money for a beer and took some comfort from nursing a large Löwenbrau in the bus station bar. Franz looked around, most of the other customers were loners like him and were well on their way to drunken oblivion or already there. He gazed soulfully into the remains of his beer and wondered if his reflection would soon mirror an empty, bloated face, just like the others. One of the drunks slurred some sort of question at him, then without waiting for an answer, broke into a drunken guffaw at his own pathetic wit before slapping his hand flat on the bar for more beer. Franz peered at his own reflection again. Of course, he should have asked the mirror, it always gave him the right answers.

His reflection told him that he had to help himself. He must not lie on the floor and capitulate into self-pity like the time he found out about Brunhilde. If he did not react positively, he would soon lie in his own drunken vomit. *Move your arse and do something. You have your future to look forward to, and your future is what you make it.* He left the drunks to their fate and purposefully strode out of the bar.

Outside, Franz adjusted his coat and puffed out his cheeks against the cold night air as he slapped his hands together in celebratory confirmation of his new confidence. The noise of his slap almost stopped him hearing a soft voice behind him. The voice asked a delicate question that pulled him up short. "You look like you need some warmth, honey."

He stopped, turned and looked into her big brown eyes. His eyes moved down to her cleavage. She opened her coat to his gaze. Even in sub-zero Kassel, she was scantily dressed in a red and black basque and thigh-length, black leather boots.

Franz had never actually seen a prostitute before, let alone near enough to touch one. He went to turn away, but paused for a moment as she parted her lips and pushed the tip of her tongue in his direction. He drew breath, "Not with you, love."

Franz walked on, but like hearing his conscience, he heard her jibe, "You'll be back."

Over the next two or three weeks his mood ebbed and flowed, but he finally struck lucky when he was offered a job teaching English in a local secondary school. He had left his qualification certificates back in East Germany, so his offer was subject to several competence interviews at Göttingen University, which he easily passed. At last, he thought he was going to make it in his new life, alone.

Franz only had his memories. He thought of his college girlfriends, also the time at Alten Oberschule when Erika Hahn came on to him after the swimming lesson. How he had turned her down, even though he fancied her, because of his loyalty to and his wish not to hurt, Brunhilde. *Not hurt her! My, my, my, when I think of what has happened since..... Erika was nice. I always liked her, but she had a husband.* And he thought of Angela. It would have been all so different if she had chosen him, not Gerald.

He repeatedly analysed what had gone wrong with Brunhilde. He replayed all the bad scenes. In his daydreams, he said all the things he had wanted to say, or should have said. *Yeah, great, Franz, it's easy to be brave now. You didn't do it. If you had, would it have made any difference?* In his night dreams she came to him too. In the night she was vicious, she belittled him, humiliated him, made him cry and destroyed him time and again. He would wake up soaking wet. Once, he beat the bed with his fist and exclaimed, "Bitch! You wanted to make me hate you. I congratulate you. You have succeeded."

He knew that nothing is ever completely one person's fault in a marriage break-up but what, apart from the political and social similarities, did she see in Otto? Franz had always had a good sex life with Brunhilde, until she slept with Otto. Self-doubt flooded into his mind and his smiles became rarer.

He had chatted to a few ladies in Göttingen, but they shied off when he asked if they would like a cup of coffee. Would he ever break out of this?

Christmas was coming and decked out in its sparkling festive decorations, Kassel town-centre looked pretty. In every shop, the luxuries that everyone in the East fantasised over were here, actually in his hands. So near, but without money, so far. He had lost everything; his home, his wife, his friends, his national identity, his history and his pride. With no one to share it with, he spent the loneliest Christmas and New Year of his life. Far worse than in the camps, at least there he had someone to talk to and the camaraderie in adversity kept everyone afloat. He thought of his 'English Christmas' at Green Farm. No Christmas cards this year.

What would Angela be doing now? What would she look like? Is she happy? "I hope so, she deserves happiness. She was lovely. I would have so much liked the chance to love her."

Night-time Kassel twinkled at him from his window. Lights everywhere. Some ribbons of streetlights, but mostly a mosaic of pastel-coloured rectangles and squares. "Each light, a happy family. I have swapped one Babylon for another."

Yes, he was rebuilding. It would take time. He looked forward to starting work; with that would come the money to refurbish his flat. **BUT!** He did not even know his neighbours. Everyone shut themselves into their flats and talked to no one. Here in the capitalist West, it was every man for himself.

In the New Year, Franz started his new teaching job. The other teachers were friendly to him and word had quickly spread about his daring escape, which made him the subject of continuous questioning from the pupils. He happily absorbed himself in his work and had little time to think of his future but he did find time to spend, what was to him, his newfound wealth.

As a child, Franz was used to not having many possessions and grew up to be non-materialistic. But now it was payday and he had buying power beyond his dreams and consumer goods without end to spend it on. However, even though he had great fun and his flat had now begun to look like a home, he only had his television and record player for company. And the mirror.

The mirror told him it was not so sure if he was attractive anymore. He had managed no success with western women. The mirror asked him if it was because he was from the east? Maybe 'Wessies' don't like 'Ossies?' "But we are all people," he answered in frustration, "It cannot be that." He had not even had a night-time erection since his escape. The mirror asked him why he had stopped greeting the women teachers at school, and indeed, was now avoiding their gaze?

"Because they think you're stupid and they must be laughing at you," it answered.

He continually shuffled around his flat, stared out of the window, failed to concentrate on his book and flicked from one television channel to another. It had now been nine months since he had last had a cuddle, let alone sex. Maybe Western women rejected him because they did not think that he was in every sense a man? He ached for the touch of almost every woman he saw.

The mirror knew how he was suffering. It could see his needs, his loneliness and his self-doubt, so eventually it advised, "Go on. Do it! You will find some warmth, remember what it feels like and most importantly, you will find out if you can still do it. No strings attached and no pressure, because *you* have control. If it doesn't work, so what! You will never see each other again. You must find out, Franz."

She stood on the corner by the bus station. He concealed his nervousness by warmly smiling at her as if she was an old friend. She looked at him without any hint of recognition. Her mouth changed into a thin smile but her eyes gave him a security check. She was open for business. He paid her thirty Deutschmarks and followed her into the darkness.

Her long curly blond hair bounced like a horse's mane and her high heels clopped like horse's hooves as she strutted along ahead of him. She did not speak, but her walk clearly said, "Come on, let's get on with it. I've got a living to make."

The unlit ally behind the bus station stank of piss, and he could only make out vague shapes in the half moonlight. These squalid surroundings brought back the vision of the drunk in the bar and the prostitute's departing words last time, "You'll be back." Just how low had he sunk?

She did not look at him as she unzipped her basque. This was not what he wanted at all, not here, like this. She unzipped his trousers and began massaging him. "I only want this," he whispered, "I don't want more."

"Please yourself," she answered matter-of-factly as her hands worked their magic on him before adding, "Nah. Here you are love, have a bonus. Don't just stand there, feel these, that's it, enjoy yourself a bit." He cupped her ample breasts as he stood there in the bitter cold for the thirty seconds it took her to finish her work. Then it was over.

She zipped everything up, and without even a goodbye, she wobbled off to look for her next trick. Franz walked home occasionally sighing deeply to himself. He felt as though he had been a pressure cooker and that someone had mercifully released his lid.

That night as he lay on his bed, Franz had no remorse about using the prostitute; he had needed to know if he was still a man. He never wanted to have full sex with her, but he was delighted she got him to react. He now knew he could still do it, and although it had been without affection, it was nice to touch the softness of a woman's breasts again. She had provided a service. No one had cried. Thank God, he was after all, normal.

Franz resolved not to use the prostitute's services again. He did not need to. He cursed himself. The west women must have seen him as a desperate idiot who could not see the wood for the trees. No wonder they had backed off. That night he had proved he had no need to worry, he must just relax, enjoy his work and let the world come to him just as it always had done. He was not looking for a new wife, he would just be Franz.

A week later, Frau Artern, Head of English at school, told him about the forthcoming school trip to Brighton in England that May. She had organised a party of twenty children and needed an extra teacher to accompany them. Would he be interested? This sounded fun and it would be nice to see England as a free man.

Marian Artern was a thirty-five-year-old widow whose young husband had died on his maiden U-boat voyage in 1945. She was only seventeen at the time, and her dead husband was her first, and only, boyfriend. Since then, she had been reclusive and lacked pride in her appearance. However, Franz could see that she had the potential to look quite smart, and her eyes noticeably twinkled when he accepted her offer.

Everyone at school was shocked when the next day her grey-streaked dark brown hair was now blonde; and again a week later, when she started wearing make-up. Franz, who had thought it terribly sad that a person could go through almost a whole lifetime in mourning, was pleased for her. It was clear that somewhere inside her, springtime had awakened. Franz could not help but notice how her eyes sparkled as she looked at him when they discussed the travel arrangements.

Brighton was good; it was the beginning of the swinging sixties and the British seemed to be enjoying their lives. The austere wartime days were now a distant memory and people were cheerful again. His party had been in Brighton for two days when late in the evening, Franz opened his door to find a demure Marian standing in the hall with her dressing gown clasped around her neck and an appealing look on her face. "Please excuse me, Franz, but I'm suffering from an invasion of spiders and I can't get at the ones on the ceiling. Please would you help me?"

As Franz left his room, the mirror warned, "Be careful, Franzy boy!"

Three fat back spiders with hairy legs glared down at him from the ceiling. Franz rolled up a magazine and positioned a chair underneath them, which he mounted and took aim, but the rickety state of the chair caused him to wobble. "Oh, do be careful, Franz. Let me steady the chair for you." In a flash, she was there. Franz felt Marian's hand on the back of his leg, just above the knee. Stability attained, he dispatched the spiders. Marian did not move as he dismounted, she was twenty centimetres from him and looking at him longingly.

She moved towards him, but Franz lifted his head so that there was no lip contact, although he kissed her lightly on the forehead. Marian looked up at Franz, first his eyes and then his lips, but he moved away and sat down on the bed.

Full of expectancy, she sat close to him, her thigh touched his. "No, Marian." Her face dropped. "This is not for me. I like you very much, you are a good friend, but I am not ready to have a relationship with you, and I am not sure if I ever will be." Her eyes filled and she looked like an abandoned puppy.

"When I first met you, I thought that you were a sad person who had grown old before her time. But not now, you have changed and for the better.

"You are attractive, and I saw today that men turn their heads to watch you as you walk by. I have suspected your feelings for some time and whilst this relationship may not be right for me, you can take something wonderful out of it. You must have thought that you could never love or maybe that you would never want to love again. If that was so, you would never have looked at me, but it did happen, you did look, and it can and will happen again. Spring has arrived and the ice block in which you have lived has been broken."

Marian looked questioningly at Franz. Tears rolled down both of her cheeks. He gently reached for her hand. "A whole world of 'Mr Rights' is waiting out there. One will love you as you desperately want to, and should be loved. You will never forget your husband. But your feelings for me must have shown you that you can love again." He wiped her tears away.

She clasped her hands on her lap, her wispy blond hair fell over her face as she bowed her head, "Why don't you want me, Franz?" she snivelled.

"It's not you, Marion. As it happens, I find you really attractive." She looked up and brushed the hair from her face to reveal eyes that sparkled once more. "You are intelligent, warm and friendly. It's me. I'm the problem, I don't feel right." Franz raised his hands and gently held her shoulders. She nodded and tutted.

"I could take advantage of you, we could lie here and have sex," she looked a little shocked, "but you would want more. I cannot give more. I will not play with your emotions for my own gratification." She bit her lip and half smiled.

"Your disappointment will pass. Remember how good you have been feeling over the last few weeks." She smiled warmly at him and nodded. "You have not made a fool of yourself here with me, I will not tell anyone else.

"Marian, you have been feeling good about yourself for the first time in eighteen years. Why stop?" She smiled and sighed.

"Franz, I don't want to, but I accept what you say about yourself." She cleared her throat. Franz..." she moved closer. He felt her breath on his lips. "Would you think me very stupid, if..., I asked you for just one kiss? I promise I will not ask for, or expect more." Her eyes pleaded with him. "It has been so long, I have forgotten how it feels."

Franz smiled. "You're not stupid, far from it." They tenderly embraced.

"Let's have a great week." Franz said as he stood up afterwards.

She returned his fond smile and rather unconvincingly murmured, "Yes. Let's."

Back in his own bed, Franz shook his head. He desperately needed a woman, but not that woman. He had enjoyed the kiss as much as she did. She was there on a plate for him and he had no one to answer to if he had made love to her, but Marian had geared her whole change of outlook to catching him as a permanent fixture. He had had one-night stands during his time at university before he met Brunhilde. Franz had no problem with them because the girls in question had not wanted anything more. Yes, Marian would have been different.

Franz went to the bathroom; the mirror gave him a sceptical look. He asked it, "OK, Dumbo, you know the question. What exactly do you want? What would make you happy? Has anyone ever made you happy?" No matter how often he had asked in the past, or today, the mirror always gave him the same answer.

On the last day in Brighton, Franz's excitement reached boiling point as he found time to enter a public phone box and call Long Distance Telephone Enquiries. He waited four long minutes before the answer came back, "Yes, sir. Got it.

Green, Green Farm, Drakesford, Cambridgeshire. Yes, that's Imton 357."

49.

The school party anxiously peered out of the waiting room windows at the darkening skies and churning sea as gale force winds whipped up the waves into 'white horses' across the stormy Dover straights. No one had been sick on the channel crossing from Calais, but Franz was not so sure that it would be the same on the return journey. The loudspeaker crackled into life and announced in a jolly voice, "Due to the inclement weather, the twelve-forty sailing to Calais is delayed for one hour." The phone box in the corner and Franz stared at each other. "No." He got up to walk around and caught sight of his reflection in the mirror at the back of the news kiosk. "Just do it!" the mirror demanded.

He told the operator the number and was slightly horrified when she told him to put two shillings into the coin box. The phone rang four times before a voice he knew so well answered, "Imton 357. Hello. Hello. Imton 357."

Without a word, Franz replaced the receiver.

During the hell of the subsequent ferry crossing, Franz, along with half of the ship's passengers, spent a lot of time in the toilets. Franz's stomach, and the mirror, severely punished him. The mirror screamed at his sallow, seasick face, "Serves you right. This is your punishment for being such a coward. You are a fool first-class. Fool. Fool. Fool. Why didn't you speak to her? You had no reason not to. You are a complete idiot! Your first chance to speak to Angela for sixteen years and you screw it up. You heard her. You actually heard her voice. Wasn't it wonderful?"

"It sounded better than wonderful." Franz managed a smile before he dived for the sink again. All the way to Kassel, he repeatedly heard "Imton 357," and continued to do so until the day six weeks later, when the engineers closed the door behind them, having installed a phone in his flat. Before the echo had disappeared down the stair well, Franz had the phone in his hand.

He felt more secure in his own home than in that cold, echoey phone box. At least, that is what he tried to believe. He had calculated that it would be lunchtime at Green Farm. "Here we go and don't be a coward this time."

He took a deep breath and asked the operator to connect him. His mouth was dry as he heard the tell-tale ring-ring of a British telephone. It rang eight times.

"Imton 357."

"Hello, Angela, this is Franz. Franz Schmidt. Do you remember me?"

"Franz!" she shouted. "How wonderful to hear from you. Where are you?"

"In Kassel, West Germany. I escaped from the east."

"You escaped? Are you OK? Did they shoot at you? Are you hurt? Oh, how wonderful after all this time."

Franz beamed. He asked Angela about Dave and Ethel but was saddened to hear that Angela's parents had both died. Ethel from cancer, and Dave in a hit-and-run car accident on his way home from the pub a year later. Franz commiserated with her, and told how he had also lost both his parents some years before. Angela said that she ran the farm now; Gerald was away a lot due to his job commitments. Franz noted a depressed sound to her voice when she spoke of her husband, but her voice returned to its happy tone as she quickly changed the subject.

She asked him about his life since they had last seen each other and she listened intently as he gave her a short version. Angela had many questions for him about his escape, but none about his failed marriage. They talked on for another ten minutes before the conversation changed to recollections of some of the happy times together at Green Farm. The only pauses came when they could not speak for laughter.

"Angela, I was so nervous about phoning you, but I don't know why. Sixteen years is a long time, but now it only seems like sixteen minutes. You're so easy to speak to. It makes me so happy simply to hear you laugh."

"I could not have said that better myself, Franz. It's exactly the same for me."

"Do you have any children, Angela?"

"Yes. I have a wonderful fourteen-year-old daughter called Sandra." There was a short pause before Angela's voice dropped its enthusiasm and sounded a little sad, "Sandra is a great comfort to me."

Franz raised an eyebrow, but tried to sound casual as he asked, "About your parents, or, Gerald?"

She paused again. Franz could almost hear her trying to decide where to start. "My parents, yes. But, Gerald and I haven't had the happiest of times since we last met, Franz. I know I looked happy when you were last here. And indeed, I was. I also feel very guilty about how terrible it must have made you feel, but anyone would be joyful to see her husband after such a long time. Nevertheless, as time went on, I realised he had changed. Or maybe he hadn't. Maybe he was like that all the time but I couldn't see it initially."

"Like what?"

"Gerald is happy when he is doing what he wants to do, so long as no one tries to question him or stop him. I don't know how it started. Maybe because we were apart for so long, I don't know, but it became clear to me fairly soon after his return that he was seeing other women. I didn't like it, I attempted to stop it, but that only made things worse."

Her voice weakened and trembled, "Finally, we had a big bust-up. Subsequently life returned to what I suppose you could call normal. This only lasted until just before Sandra was born." She paused and sighed. Franz fidgeted in his chair.

"Then he started womanising again. Anyway, we stayed together, I don't know why. Well, yes I do. Sandra. It was even more imperative that she had two parents after Mum and Dad died." Her voice began to tremble and she paused before continuing.

"Life isn't always bad with him, Franz. Sometimes we go through good patches and we begin to enjoy life again until he gets some sort of funny idea in his head, then the arguments start and he goes back to his other women."

"What funny ideas?"

"For example, he wanted to build a garage for his new car exactly where he knew I wanted to dig a slurry pit, at the back of the cow shed. A garage for his shining new Jaguar he so likes to show off to the neighbours.

"He is a terrible hypocrite, Franz, ever charming to the people in our social group and ever scathing about them when their backs are turned. Of course they are never as good as he is."

Sounds familiar, Franz thought as he sighed.

Angela continued, "He paid absolutely no regard to the practicalities of the garage idea. He ignored me and began excavating the foundations. When I managed to stop him, he went crazy and hit me. If I ever stand in his way, he gets violent," her voice dropped, "sometimes in front of Sandra."

Then her voice picked up as, almost too enthusiastically, she added, "He has been very successful at work. He now works as an export manager for an electronics company in London." Her voice dropped again, "This means that he goes abroad a lot, France mostly. I could go on and on, Franz, there is so much more to tell, but I don't want to spend such a wonderful moment as our first conversation in sixteen years, talking about him."

Franz changed the subject when he reminded her of the milking incident during his 'English Christmas,' which immediately lifted the mood. Like two teenagers, neither wanted to be the first to put the phone down but eventually parted by promising to speak again soon.

With a huge smile, Franz leaned back in his chair, clasped both hands behind his head, looked up at the ceiling and proclaimed, "Yesssss."

After gently replacing the receiver, Angela clapped her hands until they hurt.

Angela, Angela, a madness burned in Franz's mind and heart over the next two months. When he was walking, running, teaching or cooking, all he heard was her voice. He wanted to speak to her more than anything, but he knew that if things were not good at Green Farm and he kept calling her, the calls would only make matters worse.

Much as he had disliked Gerald from the moment he first saw him, Franz had no intention of breaking up a marriage. "Yeah. Franz 'Waiting' Schmidt. That's me." OK, that was the moralistic view, but on the other hand, he could not sleep for the thought that at that exact moment Gerald might be assaulting his beloved Angela. Beloved Angela? Had he fallen in love with her, or a memory?

No two ways about it, he wanted to see her again. He still remembered their few kisses as if it were yesterday. However, Franz had learnt from his previous experiences; if he pushed things too quickly, it could all turn sour. He had heard affection and despair in her voice during that telephone call, but maybe it was only affection for an old friend. No. If she was thinking the same about him as he was about her, then she should phone him. However, if she had not phoned him by the middle of September, then OK, he would take the initiative.

The days dragged until... Sunday lunch time, early September, the sudden ring, and hope, made him jump to the phone. She was terribly upset and sobbed for some seconds before she could put two words together. Eventually, "Hello, Franz, it's me."

"Angela. Tell me, what's happened? It will be OK. I am here for you. Calm down and tell me everything. Be strong. You must be strong."

"We had another row, yesterday when he got back from France. I could smell women's perfume on his clothes when I put them in the wash. I challenged him and of course he denied it, but I could tell from his reaction that it was true. He insisted the scent was his own aftershave, so I asked him if he had the bottle because it was a different smell from his usual. He went crazy and started smashing cups on the floor and walls.

"I'm used to that, but the problem was Sandra, she came into the kitchen just as he smashed the first cup. That poor little thing tried her best to defend me, but he was not going to listen.

"He said it was his right to react to persecution in any way that he saw fit. Persecution? He thinks that *I* persecute **him**!"

"Anyway, some flying pieces of china hit Sandra and she ran out screaming. I know it's hard for me, but my poor daughter..." Angela broke down again. Franz spoke softly to her until she regained control. "Gerald went after her and caught her by the garden gate. Of course, he then played the big, soft, caring father.

"She was ready for him, and let him know exactly what she thought of him and his bullying. She told him that over the years, she had seen and heard it all, and she knew exactly who was to blame for the family troubles and if he ever laid hands on me again, she would kill herself.

"He remonstrated that he did everything for us and 'you just don't appreciate me!' Franz, I have wanted him to be happy 'doing everything for us' but at what price? Is it worth putting up with the selfish arrogance of a king in his castle, and the retribution when things go wrong with his little plans, or when he is not the centre of attention? Is it also right that I should share him with other women?"

She broke into tears again. Franz heard her put the phone down and cry into her handkerchief. He could only wait and listen until she was calmer. He wanted to cuddle her; this distance between them was so frustrating. "Don't give up. Be strong, Angela. There will be a way out of this. There always is. Is he still there?"

"He's gone. I have phoned you only moments after he left to drive back to France. I had to speak to you. Last time when you called me it was so wonderful to hear your voice. You gave me such warmth, I smiled all day.... I just wanted to hear your voice."

"You can call me any time and as often as you want. I'm here for you. However, you must also help yourself, it is easy to fall over and give up. You must be strong. You are you. You are a lovely person, a good person and good people always come through in the end. Life is a wheel, it goes round, and the bad times always become good provided you remain strong and true to yourself. These may be the bad times, but the good times will come."

"How? What can I do?"

"Angela, I don't want to be provocative," he lied, "but why don't you leave him?"

"It is impossible with the farm. I cannot walk out and leave everything. Although I'm just a sitting duck for him to return to and take pot shots at me whenever he wants, he is also my husband. I have to respect that and live with it."

"No, you don't."

"Yes I do. I made a vow, 'til death us do part.'"

"Whose death? Or rather, whose murder?"

No answer. She blew her nose. Franz wondered if maybe he had gone too far. He softly continued, "If speaking to me helps, then do it. Actually, I would be very happy if I could hear your voice, you have a lovely voice. I always liked your farmer's accent." She even managed a laugh as she remembered how he used to tease her about it in the milking shed. It seemed to him that the weight disappeared from her shoulders as they spoke. It was not long before they laughed again, a fact Angela remarked upon by reminding Franz that he had always had the ability to make her laugh.

They called each other every three or four days, during which time Franz learned that Gerald sometimes stayed in France at weekends. "He has a lot of work to do, exhibitions and the like." Also that his boss was so delighted with the French side of the business that he had talked about setting up a French subsidiary company and that Gerald was optimistic of becoming 'Managing Director, France.' However, when he did return home, Angela told how he expected his family to greet him with open arms.

Three weeks after her first call to Franz, Gerald returned and whisked Angela off to bed almost as soon as he came through the door. Angela recognised this immense passion, as ever, she knew that he imagined he was making love to someone else. He was familiarly different. He even whispered a few words of French.

The following night, after they had had sex and Angela was trying to cuddle him, Gerald cleared his throat, and quite matter-of-factly as if he were discussing the price of milk said, "I have to tell you I have a girlfriend in France and, yes, I have known her for some time. I want to spend much more time with her than I do now.

"I shall move my things out in the morning, when I leave for Paris." Angela was unable to move or speak for the shock. "Angela, you have to understand that this is what I want in life. The French way of life is so much more my style, and my girlfriend is so elegant and intelligent. I feel compelled to live near her."

After a short silence, during which Angela spasmodically shook her head in disbelief at the situation, he pursed his lips as if considering some great matter of state and added, "I shall of course come back here from time to time to see how things are going, but don't expect me too often."

Angela was now coming to her senses. Pressure was building within her... "And does 'see how things are going' include your daughter? Have you considered her? Does it by chance also include having sex with me?"

"Yeh, well, that's not a bad idea if you want it. Sandra will be OK."

Angela drew breath, but stopped. *Why bother? It's all been said before. Let the arrogant, bastard, go.* Feeling empty and physically sick, she rolled out of bed, walked out of the bedroom and into the guest room where she locked the door, went to bed and cried for her marriage.

Gerald made his own breakfast early next morning. He was alone in the kitchen and just about to leave when Angela came in from milking the cows. They shook hands. No words. No kiss. Just a confident nod from Gerald and a blank stare from Angela. Sandra, who joined her mother just in time to see her father going out of the door asked, "What's the matter this time?"

"I think he's gone; maybe for good." Angela started to cry.

Sandra did not. "I have seen and heard enough of him. He is the one who has broken our home."

Sandra put her arms round her mother and whispered into her ear, "Do you know, Mum, when I was little, and heard you two arguing, I used to bury my head under my pillow or hide under the bed with my hands over my ears. Even when it had stopped, I still shook. Then it all seemed OK when he came to me and was nice to me, we would play games and he used to make me laugh. I used to like him, when I was little."

Sandra paused and shook her head as she looked out of the window into the distance. "You know, I took the shouting as being normal. What happened in every family. What I was used to, like Grandpa's cursing when the tractor wouldn't start." They stroked each other's hair.

"I have been a terrible mother to you."

"Mum, when I was a little bit older and understood what was going on, I didn't want to make things worse. I had this feeling that if I said anything or showed any fear you would tell him, and then he would have a go at me. You are a wonderful mum, the best." She kissed her mother on the cheek.

"Sometimes, when it was a bad time and I had to go to school; those were the days when I got into trouble for not doing my schoolwork."

Angela lifted her head and looked in anguish at her daughter. "What did Mrs Phillips say; did you tell her?"

"Of course not, 'Fatguts Phillips' would have humiliated me in front of everyone else. I didn't want other people to know. Anyway, what if I had, and she told him?

"We both know what that would have meant. I prayed for him to have an accident. Mum, I know, I heard, how it always started. How he always shouts over you," she paused... "And hits you."

Angela felt even weaker and broke off the embrace to sit down. Sandra sat next to her mother and resumed her hug. "Do you know that I feel sick every time I see his car in the yard? I put on a brave face and try to act normally when I come in.

That's only for you. I don't want him asking any questions, because I know a row will start.

"These days, if he ever knocks at my door, I pretend to be asleep so I won't have to talk to him." Sandra clenched her fists, her expression was hard. "I know if I let him in, it'll always end up with a lecture on something I have apparently done wrong. Boorish monologues, as he gives me the benefit of his vast worldly knowledge, playing the big father. I'm happy that he has gone. I hope he never comes back."

Sandra placed her hands firmly on Angela's shoulders and looked at her mother with gladiatorial determination. "Never, ever, will I forgive him for causing you so much pain."

Angela sobbed again. "I'm so sorry. So, so, sorry. You must have heard that you, and his treatment of you, were sometimes the reason for our arguments. I know about the monologues, I get them too. We both get them at meal times, sometimes. I had no idea of your real pain. I was so wrapped up in my own sorrow. Sandra, how can you ever forgive me? How could I ever have been so unfeeling?"

"There's nothing to forgive, Mum. I love you. I heard you defending me. I know how much you love me. I am good at hiding my emotions and the last thing I was going to do was trouble you. I want you to be happy, Mum. I pray that you can find some happiness now, and that he never comes back." They hugged each other and cried.

Angela waited until she was alone before calling Germany. She had to hear his voice.

50.

They now called once per day, and then twice, once before Franz went to work and again in the evening. Then it got silly. Three or four times a day and sometimes even in the middle of the night. Wasn't it only kids who were supposed to do stupid things like this? Sandra wanted to know why her mother crept around at night, almost every night. She also wanted to know who was the foreign man who so obviously made her mother so happy every time he phoned? Angela told her the truth, "Oooh, my mum, having secret phone calls from a man. It's the sort of thing you read about, but never actually happens. Oooh."

During one nocturnal call in October, Franz asked the question that had been on his mind since his first phone call. "The half-term holiday begins next week and… maybe we could meet? I know you can't leave the farm, so I could fly over to meet you."

Angela's heart thumped like never before.

"Maybe you could book me in at a local hotel? Hello? Angela? Are you still there?"

"I would like that very much," she said softly as her warm glow almost melted the phone, "but fly, that will cost a fortune."

"I have enough, I don't spend much money here. That's not the point, I would like to see you again."

"If you came late enough to allow me to leave here after milking, I could pick you up at London Airport. I think it is best if you stay at the George and Dragon in Imton. My friend Helen owns it. I don't want Sandra to get any more ideas than she's already got."

Franz shuffled on his seat and cleared his throat. "Yes of course. I wonder if we will recognise each other?"

"I'm sure. But, as I said, I do look a bit different to sixteen years ago, Franz."

"Me too. I'm not the oil painting I once was. I've got a few lines.

"Who ever said anything about you being that good looking?"

"Well, ah, yes. I was kind of wondering if you might have thought that once."

"Really? Well, that's for you to wonder then, isn't it? Franz 'Oil Painting' Schmidt. Na, doesn't really sound good. Franz 'Oily' Schmidt…, Yuck, even worse."

Franz bit his lip. Had he gone too far?

Suddenly Angela giggled. "It'll be fun if you come. How long can you stay?"

"Let's just make it three days. You'll be sure to have had enough of me by then."

"We'll see," Angela said calmly.

Franz was in high spirits when he stepped onto the escalator at Frankfurt Airport ten days later. Halfway up, the smile left his face as reality hit him.

He loudly scolded himself, "You have got to be crazy. Here you are, at your age, flying halfway across Europe on a blind date. You must be out of your tree!" Then he laughed loudly. Other travellers gave him a wide berth, he must be drunk. "Well, not a total blind date, simply a little visually impaired."

Franz knew he would enjoy his time with Angela. He resolved that although he would not force the issue, if anything developed, whatever was going to happen, so be it. His skin tingled as he entered the aeroplane. He had never flown before and he tried to assure himself that his stomach butterflies were only due to this. He laughed again.

Then his smile disappeared. *What if she changes her mind? What if she doesn't come? Should I change my mind? She is married.* "Ach." He hissed to himself, "Shut up and get on with it! Everything is going to be OK. Get a grip, Franz."

The palms of Angela's hands were wet as she tried to turn the pages of the map. She had never been much of a navigator, she had never needed to be, but a wrong turn near Watford had her waiting at a level crossing in Slough, wherever that was, when she should have been at the airport.

Normally, she only drove around the village or maybe to Cambridge, so London Airport was the furthest that she had ever driven in her Land Rover. At last! A sign for the A4 and London Airport.

Angela laughed. She had spent the whole day looking at her watch and trying to keep up an appearance of normality although she was not entirely sure if singing to the cows qualified as normal. She looked at her watch and then at her reflection in the mirror. "Two hours to landing, Angela. He must be in the air now. He's coming to me. Oh my God. I hope he hasn't changed his mind. No. He's coming. I hope. Don't jump at him when you see him." She squeezed the steering wheel. "Be formal. Take your time. You must be adult and not give in to passion." She frowned. "**Why?** Why on earth not? For the first time in your life, do what you want to do because you want to do it and don't think of others. It's your life, Angela. Tonight I am not mother, not a wife, I am me. Yesss!" She thumped the steering wheel in joy. "Ow!"

Franz sat next to an attractive young woman, and they exchanged pleasantries as the plane pushed back. Suddenly, Franz started to laugh again. The girl gave him a worried look. She shifted forward in her seat and strained her neck to look over the seats in front of her. She shook her head a little bit before flashing Franz a concerned glance.

Franz sensed her angst and decided he should tell all. Anyway, this girl was a total stranger, he would never see her again in his life so what did it matter if he told her everything? After all, he was not entirely sure he was doing the right thing, and if she also thought he was stupid, he could always turn around at London and return home.

She listened intently as Franz gave her a one-hour version of what had happened in his life and his relationship with Angela. Then he popped the question. "What would you do if you were me?"

Without hesitation the lady replied, "If she was in Australia, I would go to her!"

"Oh. Good. Thank you," answered Franz in a quietly gratified tone. "Thank you very much." They smiled warmly at each other and Franz settled back into his seat and anticipated a good three days.

In the arrivals hall, the mechanical flight information board ticked loudly as the letters fluttered around to change the status of the Lufthansa flight from Frankfurt from "Due" to "Landed". Angela's heart was jumping. For the third time that hour, she ran to the toilets to check that not a hair was out of place and her make-up was perfect.

Franz's travelling companion smiled and wished him good luck as she disappeared down the hall in the direction of passport control. Now he was on his own. He needed the toilet. As he washed his hands, the mirror smiled at him, just as it had been doing for some weeks now. "Go for it, Franz. Go for it." He combed his hair and made sure that everything looked spick and span before he wished the mirror good luck and strutted off to the Arrivals Hall. *Oh, you fool. What will she be like?*

He was now twenty metres from the exit. He saw three women facing him as they leaned against a barrier on the other side. *Which one is she?*

He kept walking purposefully towards the unknown, his own 'High Noon.' Fifteen metres away and he halted as he studied the image before him and thought, that one on the left looks vaguely like Angela should look, but much, much fatter. "Oh dear," he muttered. He continued walking, slower now.

Five metres away, Franz and the woman were staring intently at each other. *Is it?* Then Franz breathed a sigh of relief when he saw that the large woman was not Angela. *No turning back now. Here we go!* He stepped through the exit.

Statuesque, pushing his chest out, Franz slowly scanned the line of forty faces scanning him. No Angela. He looked further back, behind the first line, and around until his eyes fixed on a pair of familiar blue eyes. He gasped, "Oh my God, she's gorgeous!"

The blue eyes twinkled back at him.

She shook her head in disbelief as he approached. If they were dogs, they would have fallen over because their tails would have been wagging so much. Franz did the German thing and went to shake her hand. Angela ignored that and acted like a true Brit by flinging her arms around his neck and plonking a huge kiss on his cheek. Grinning broadly, each looked the other up and down, neither could speak. They laughed and hugged again. Arm in arm and with eyes glued to each other's they headed off to the car.

On the way back to Imton, Franz was embarrassed to stare at Angela; he resorted to leaning back in his seat as far as possible so he could see her without turning his head and only occasionally looked at her as he spoke. After a short time, he burst out laughing and told her what he was doing. "You silly fool, Franz Schmidt. My only problem with that is that I can't do the same or we'll crash." *Oh! Should I have said that?* She thought. *Yeah. Why not?*

Angela cleared her throat loudly as they walked up to the entrance of the George and Dragon. She pursed her lips and squeezed Franz's hand as she quickly glanced through the public bar window. It looked busy. "OK, we'll go into the lounge."

Angela raised her hand to cover her face and bowed her head as she towed Franz inside. The lady owner of the pub beamed when she saw them, Angela sheepishly smiled back at her lifetime friend as she paid for the drinks. "Thanks, Helen."

The log fire cracked and the smoke funnelled enthusiastically up the chimney as they sat close together, occasionally brushing arms. Helen had diplomatically found some work to do in the public bar. Even though the lounge was deserted, it felt warm and homely as they sipped their drinks and smiled until neither could hold back any longer and they began a long, tender and sensuous kiss. A kiss, as good as their first kiss those sixteen long years ago. Maybe even better.

They broke off and immediately looked around the empty bar to see if anyone had seen them, and chuckled at their audacity. "I must be careful," Angela warned, "I mean. I live close to this place. What would people think if they saw me?"

She flicked another nervous look round the bar and shivered as if a ghost had touched her.

"Then maybe we could go somewhere quieter," Franz said.

She looked into his eyes for a few seconds, finished her drink, and with a warm smile held his hand and stood up. She put her other hand in her pocket and pulled out a key, which she waggled in front of his face. "I didn't want to waste time," she chuckled, "I called in here before I went to London. Helen's given you the best room. She is my best friend. She knows all about us." They almost ran up the stairs.

The bedroom was warm and cosy, its centrepiece was a large four-poster bed, which did not have to wait long before it had two occupants. They looked into each other's eyes for some time before lightly touching each other's faces, only with their fingertips. Soft fingertips on gentle faces. Gentle kisses, and more gentle kisses.

They closed their eyes and felt each other's breath sensuously tickle their skin. Franz kissed the side of Angela's neck, goose-bumps tickled down her arms as his lips moved around to the nape of her neck. The tip of his tongue caressed her as she ran her fingertips through his hair and gripped his head.

She fondled his muscled shoulders, and ran her fingers down his back before she returned to those wonderful shoulders.

He moved his lips to her breasts, nuzzled them and enjoyed them. His tongue drew fine circles around her erect nipples before his lips enveloped and sucked them as her head arched backwards. All the time his hands gently smoothed her hips and back. *Soft skin, wonderfully firm body, she feels incredible. Oh, the bliss of this woman.*

They wrapped their arms around each other, intertwined their legs and enjoyed the fulfilment of a dream. They were not in bed to have sex. They were there to become one, and when that happened, floods of feeling washed through them both. It was very slow and gentle; they looked into each other's eyes the whole time. Except at the end, when their eyes closed and they shook and gasped in unison.

"Angela, I never experienced anything like that before. It was the strangest, most elevated feeling. I felt as though I was outside my body, floating weightlessly in a warm and gentle sea with light, rhythmic, waves washing from my head through the whole length of my body." He kissed her lightly on her forehead. "Incredible." She nuzzled closer to him, if that was possible. Both slept.

When they awoke a short while later, they did it again. Just to make sure that it was true. And again, a medium while later. During the third time, they both whispered, "I love you."

"Oh God, it's ten-past midnight. I have to go."

"Are you going to turn into a pumpkin?"

"It's Sandra. She's alone in the house. She will expect me back."

Angela dressed in double quick time, whilst Franz, who reclined naked on the bed like a Roman sculpture, admired the athletically feminine form of his lover. "You look magnificent, Angela. I so respect a woman who looks after herself. So many people let themselves go in their thirties and get fat. You're wonderful."

"That's what forced farm labour, roast beef and two veg does for you, Franz." They laughed. After a long last kiss by the door, Angela invited Franz to have breakfast at the farm in the morning. "I'll come and get you at eight-thirty."

"That's OK, I'll walk. I'll enjoy it and I know the way."

At the window, Franz sighed as he watched her car lights disappear into the night before whispering, "Brunhilde never gave me such a feeling of calm excitement. I'm so relaxed with Angela. Now I know what lovemaking really means. Until now, it's only been sex."

The lights had gone; he cleared his throat and lay on the bed. He picked up her pillow and gently held it to his face. Her scent lingered in his nostrils. He cuddled the pillow.

Angela arrived back at the farm to see lights still on in the house. "Oh."

Sandra sat next to what was left of the fire in the high-backed lounge chair that had been so beloved of her late grandfather. Her eyes locked on to Angela's as her mother casually walked over to the fireside and sat down opposite her daughter.

Sandra's face was noncommittal. She studied her mother, who politely smiled back as if awaiting a school report. Sandra was immediately aware that her mother was having great difficulty in returning to this world. *She's not with it at all.* Her full complexion, accentuated by her red, swollen lips, made her look as though she had just returned from holiday, and her eyes seemed as though she were still there.

Sandra watched her mother look down and gaze at the tips of her shoes as she rotated her foot aimlessly. This was a new experience for Sandra, who now, unable to contain herself any longer, broke into a big smile. "Did you have a wonderful evening, Mum?"

Angela smiled, ran her fingers through her hair and shook her head, unsure of where to start. She described her wait for him in the airport, how he looked after all this time and just what a handsome man he was. They talked for half an hour before Angela realised that it was one o'clock and she had to be up for milking in only four hours' time.

Angela was too excited to sleep. She even gave serious thought to creeping out of the house and returning to Franz. Sandra slept more peacefully than she had done in a long time.

Franz's sleepless night passed quicker than any he had known, he actually enjoyed it. The St Stephen church clock chimed four and he sprang out of bed like a child on Christmas morning. On with an old pair of jeans and a sweater before quietly creeping out of the pub and heading for Green Farm.

The high-tech wonder of the cowshed caused him to gasp. Gone were the milking stools, gone were the sounds of cows munching their feed. The place was a whirr of machines and the sucks of vacuum pumps. Then he saw her, dressed in overalls, wellington boots, rubber gloves, with outstretched arms and a big smile. After a long, passionate kiss, Franz simply rolled up his sleeves and had a wonderful time helping with the milking. No embarrassment. No looking over their shoulders. They kissed and touched at every opportunity. Anyone could have entered, they would not have noticed, which was precisely what occurred.

Just as they turned away from their twentieth clinch of the morning they both jumped, as there, sitting on a bag of feed, arms folded and with a shy smile was Sandra. "I got up to help you with the milking, Mum, but it seems as though you have everything in hand." She stood up and walked over to Franz, hand outstretched. "How do you do? My name is Sandra and you, I presume, must be Franz?"

Franz just about managed a stifled, "Hello. Yes. Pleased to meet you."

"So come on," Sandra said seriously, "Let's get on with the milking, and then we can get on with breakfast." She turned to prepare a cow before adding, "And then you two can get on with each other!"

Angela turned to Franz and murmured, "Caught with our hands in the sweetie jar there." Franz looked a little puzzled, but laughed anyway.

Much to Angela's pleasure, Sandra chatted her way through breakfast. Suddenly, Sandra's brow furrowed. "Why is Franz staying at the pub tonight, Mum? Why don't you sleep here, Franz? There's a spare room."

"Sandra! I'm a respectable married woman. What would other people think?"

"You sound just like Grandma used to, Mum. Franz, you can stay here!" She nodded in satisfaction, looked at her mortified mother and casually took another bite of toast. Then she giggled, stood up and skipped out to the farmyard leaving the sheepish couple sitting speechless at the table. So there it was, the Royal Seal of Approval.

Franz stayed at the farmhouse, in the guest room. Over the next two days, Sandra helpfully moved around the house accompanied by amazingly loud crashes, coughs and bangs. She even went to the extent of saying exactly for how long she would be out with her friends, and that she *definitely* would not return home before a particular time. Franz and Angela touched a lot, walked in the wet fields, cuddled in the hay barn, completed the milking in record time, talked and loved.

They talked about each other, trying their best to dodge the shadows of the past, which were nevertheless always there. In each other, they probably had the only person in the world that they could completely confide in. The relief of confession was within their reach.

However, they agreed not to waste time talking about sad things. This time they would get their relief from pure happiness and the knowledge that such a feeling was no longer a fantasy, only seen at the movies, alone in front of a log fire or in bed. Their happiness was theirs to enjoy for these few hours together.

Not wanting Angela to drive back alone from Heathrow along strange roads late at night in a Land Rover that he considered 'unreliable' at best, and 'dangerous' at worst, Franz took the train back to London.

Angela did not want to wait on the platform until the train disappeared, so they kissed and she returned to her car intending to drive home. No good, she simply sat in the driver's seat unable to move, shaking her head. "This is crazy. I don't want to go home. I don't want it to end."

51.

Angela had invited Franz over for Christmas and he was due to arrive tomorrow. As her venerable Land Rover chugged along between the bare hedgerows, Angela sang to herself. She turned into her drive, and her heart missed a beat as she stamped on the brake. "Shit!" There, parked outside the front door of the farmhouse, Gerald's Jaguar.

In the three months since he had departed for France, Gerald had only phoned his daughter three times and Angela had only spoken to him once. It had been a brief conversation; they had discussed health and work formalities. This would be more.

He was sitting in her father's old chair with his shoes off, warming his feet by the fire. He welcomed his wife as if he were the long-lost great adventurer, the hero of the nation. Angela greeted him with a face of stone. "What do you want? Has she thrown you out?"

"What's that for a greeting?" He leapt to his feet and wrapped her in his arms. She twisted herself free. He held on to her shoulders, tilted his head to one side and in his most practised appealing manner said, "Come on. Can't we be friends for a few days? Let's have a family Christmas."

Angela's eyes flashed as she hissed through clenched teeth. "Just who do you think you are? You breeze in here like you own the place, and let me remind you, you do not, three months after leaving me for another woman, or knowing you, women. You virtually abandon your daughter and you expect to find your loving wife ready to do all to your beck and call. Get stuffed!" She nodded in certainty. "It's over between us, Gerald. I want a divorce."

Gerald recoiled in shock. "Divorce? Is this all the thanks I get for working my arse off to provide for my family?"

"The only place your arse works, Gerald, is in bed!"

He pushed her back towards the door and pinned her against it with his body. His face close to hers, the big vein on his forehead bulged and he growled at her through a slit of a mouth.

"You are my wife. You will not divorce me. I don't want it. I will not allow it. I still want you. You only love once in your life and I'll not lose you."

"You *have* lost me, Gerald, long ago. I tried so hard to make you happy. All I wanted was a happy family; all you wanted was an in-house prostitute. You used me like one, as indeed you have used all your women. Go away from here. Go to your mother. If you want to arrange to see Sandra, you can do it from there. You can see her as much as she wants to."

"This is my house. I shall stay here."

"It's not your house, and anyway, there will be another man here this Christmas. I have someone else in my life now, Gerald."

"You? *You* have a boyfriend? And you dare to invite him here, into our family home?"

"Your family home is with your mother, or your concubine."

He grabbed her hand and dragged her towards the sofa. "Sit down. We must talk about this." He forced her to sit next to him. "Who is this man? When did this start?"

"Who? Is not important. When? Since you left. What matters is that I love him and he loves me in a way that you never have, or could do. I have invited him to share Christmas with me, in **my** house. You are not invited."

Gerald searched Angela's eyes; his manner softened. He affectionately looked at her as he raised his hand to her breast. She pushed it away. Gerald made sure it landed on her thigh as he leant forward to kiss her. She turned her face away. "No, Gerald, this is not what I want any more."

"You are my wife, Angela. You could never resist me, and I could never resist you. You know you want me. You've done so since our wonderful first night in the barn, I know you remember that."

In one movement, he slid his hand under her skirt and up her thigh. She closed her legs and tried to get up, but he pushed her back and rolled on top of her. "Come on now," he growled, "you are my wife. Let's take a little walk down memory lane."

"No!" she cried out, "Get off me, Gerald."

In three jerks, he had ripped her pants off. Angela struggled desperately under his weight, but he forced his knees between hers and prised her legs apart. He painfully pinned her arms backward behind her head and undid the front of his trousers. "You are my wife. You know you will enjoy it." Angela spat in his face. He only smirked and lowered himself down. "I like a bit of spirit."

Angela gave up the struggle. All she could do was to close her eyes, and turn her head away. He clenched his teeth and thrust his hips forward. She grimaced with pain and disgust as he penetrated her. Mercifully, it was quick.

Gerald rolled off her, stood up and with a swagger, swished his floppy penis around as though it were a rope and closed his trousers. Angela opened her eyes; they seared him with their anger.

She sprang off the sofa, picked up his shoes from the hearth and hurled them at him from point-blank range. "You are like a dog marking its territory," she hissed. He winced as the shoes thudded into his chest. Now she screamed at full volume, "Get out! I never want to see you again! You are filth, filth, filth!" Gerald's mouth hung open and he cowered slightly before edging towards the door, whereupon he blankly looked at Angela and shrugged. The house shook as he slammed the door behind him.

Angela sank to the floor and looked blankly into the fire for a short time before a pained expression came over her face. She struggled to her feet, staggered to the bathroom and washed and washed, and even though it hurt, scrubbed. She could not look in the mirror. The scent of the Camay soap did its best, but she could still smell him. She shook her head and shuddered continually.

Sandra had been out riding her horse throughout and returned about an hour later. She found her mother aimlessly dusting the mantelpiece. Then she saw Angela's puffed eyes. "What's the matter? You look like a zombie."

"Your father was here. He has gone now. He knows exactly how I feel about him. He will probably contact you over Christmas." Angela started to shake again. "I expect that he will be staying at Granny Innes' house." Sandra walked over to her mother and hugged her. Tears rolled down Sandra's cheeks and blended with the flood that was coming from her mother's eyes as she wailed her despair onto her daughter's shoulder.

They stood there for some minutes until Angela's sobbing ceased. "Sit down, Mum. I'll make us a cup of tea, OK?" They sat close together on the sofa and drank their tea. Then the phone rang. "Oh my God, it's him," uttered Angela as she started to shake.

Sandra jumped to her feet and strode to the phone. "Don't worry, Mum. I won't leave you alone. Never again!"

"Imton 357. Yes. Hello. I'll get her for you now. Telephone, Mother," she sang, as full of smiles, she beckoned Angela to the phone.

"Who is it?"

"Not saying. But it's someone nice."

The relief in Angela's voice told Franz something was wrong. She responded to his question with a brief explanation of Gerald's return and departure. Nothing was mentioned about the attack.

Sandra and Angela decided to sleep in the same bed that night, but neither slept well. Every sound, every creak in the timbers of the house, every noise outside in the yard, made them hug each other tighter. In the time that she had to think logically, Angela resolved that if she wanted peace, she would have to try to treat what Gerald had done to her as the last act of their marriage, not the rape that it was.

Yet again, she went over her married life with him as she had done so many times before. What had gone wrong? How much was she to blame? Could she have done better for him?

Of course she could, but he could have done a hell of a lot better for her too. There had always been a mystic feeling between them, but mysticism alone did not make a marriage, the chemistry simply was not there. They wanted different things from life. The mysticism was dead. She hoped, she prayed, she knew, it would be different with Franz.

Angela's spirits soared when Franz arrived, but later, as they lay together, she perspired as the memories of her ordeal returned. Franz sensed that she was trying too hard to be normal, but was unsure how to approach the matter with her until she insisted that Franz put on a condom before the first touch. "No babies." Angela said.

"Of course. Is that why you seem a little nervous tonight? You don't have to be nervous with me. Don't be nervous about him. I'm here, I will protect you. You've told him what you want, he'll soon be out of your life."

She smiled and flexed her hands, rested her head on the pillow and said, "You always know what to say to make me feel good, Franz. I always feel so safe with you." Afterwards, she blamed the condom for her soreness.

On Christmas Eve, Gerald phoned to say he wanted to deliver his Christmas presents for Angela and Sandra at three o'clock that afternoon. Everyone kept looking at the clock and the farmhouse fell quiet as three o'clock approached.

The car engine stopped. A car door slammed, then another. Footsteps on the gravel. Angela swallowed hard and straightened her back. Franz flexed his fingers and toes. Sandra clenched her fists and flexed her jaw muscles as her eyes locked on to the outside door.

Gerald walked straight into the house bedecked with parcels, a bunch of red roses and a huge smile, which vanished as soon as he fixed eyes on Franz. A moment of puzzlement as Gerald racked his memory. "Who are you?"

Avoiding Franz's gaze, Gerald slowly put everything down, tapped his finger lightly on a parcel and bit his bottom lip before turning, slowly raising an accusing finger and pointing it at a cool looking Franz. "I know you! The Kraut who was here after the war. You're not that Jerry? Are you?"

"My name is Franz Schmidt and yes, I worked here from nineteen forty-five to nineteen forty-seven." Franz suppressed his immediate instinct to offer his hand, but then his culture took over and he did so. Gerald refused to oblige.

Gerald glared at Angela, "You were a busy little bee then, weren't you?"

"I was busy running the farm, Gerald and only that. As I recall, you were busy doing other things with other people."

Gerald turned and resumed glaring at Franz. "I want to speak to my wife, alone."

Angela motioned to Franz and Sandra that it was OK. She fixed her husband with a glare and warned, "He'll only be upstairs. You too, Sandra." Like twins, Franz and Sandra humphed and gave Gerald a threatening look before clumping up the stairs to their rooms.

Franz paced up and down his small room, fists clenched in anguish. *I should never have left her alone.* Every time he was near the door, he stopped and strained to hear the events downstairs. The tone of this discussion ebbed and flowed. Angela sounded pained, but firm. He could not make out what Gerald was saying. Quiet whispers preceded staccato grumbles, followed by a mild explosion, then silence. *Prepare yourself, Franz.*

Prepare yourself for what? Don't get carried away, Franz. Angela can handle him. He shook his head. *Yeah, verbally, what if he hits her? He's done it before. The first time is the hardest. He can do it again. If you have to step in, Franz, what are you going to do?*

He could hear movement in Sandra's room. What was she up to? *She obviously can't sit still either. C'mon get warmed up, prepare for the worst.*

He flexed his fingers, rotated his head, and did ten press-ups. *If he gets violent, go for him. Make it quick, make it hard and make it positive. Keep your eyes open, don't let temper take over, hit through your target.*

With his hands on his hips, he made large circles with his upper body. *You have surprise on your side, don't let him settle.*

Five more press-ups against the door post. *Which? Which method? Use your strongest muscles. Legs, back. Feet or head? You can win this in one if you use all your power. Can win? You must win.*

A shout from Angela. Franz froze. Mumbling from Gerald. Franz strained to hear. Silence. Movement from Sandra's room. Bi-directional conversation downstairs again.

Ten more press-ups for Franz. *He's wearing a jacket, use your head. If he's still standing, pull back and kick to the knee. Hard as you can. That'll hurt like hell and immobilise. Then strike with your fists. Move him around, get him off balance. Speed, speed, speed, Franz.* The staccato 'discussion' downstairs persisted. "*I **wish** I could hear everything they are saying.*

His wish was momentarily answered as the 'discussion' reached full volume this time. "I want out, Gerald. The magic is gone. You disgust me now. I don't want to be your wife. I will **not** be your wife anymore. You can't stop me. End!"

"For the twentieth time, you are my wife and you **will** remain so. End!"

What if Sandra steps in? Stop her if you hear her come out. She must not get in the way. Franz's mouth went dry. *Everything will go wrong.*

No it won't. Not if you're quick. C'mon, concentrate. He turned to the mirror, it would give him the verdict. "OK. Are you up for this?"

He clenched his fists in front of his face and glared into his own eyes. "Oh yes. You're up for it. It's chips down time, Franz. Like the bullies; Schwanz, your escape, you have to. You will. If you concentrate; follow your plan, you will." *Stay in your room, Sandra.* He turned, fixed his gaze on the door latch and flexed his fingers. "OK, you bastard," he hissed, "touch her, and you're dead meat."

After a quiet phase below, Franz heard the noise level rise yet again before he clearly heard Gerald proclaim "Court? What do you know about court? Slut!" immediately followed by the unmistakable slap of skin striking skin followed by a muffled cry from Angela.

"Here we go!" Franz exclaimed as he flung open the bedroom door and descended the stairs in two leaps, hotly pursued by Sandra.

They burst into the lounge to see Angela slumped in her father's chair holding the side of her face and Gerald towering over her like a lion hunter dominantly posing over his kill. Franz fixed his gaze on his adversary's eyes and strode towards him. *Concentraaaaate...*

Gerald's face broke into a dismissive smirk as he turned to face Franz's approach. Immediately he was within range, Franz reached out and grabbed both lapels of Gerald's jacket, arched his body backward then drove forward to smash his forehead into Gerald's face. The 'crack' was like a whip. Gerald's face opened up from the bridge of his nose to the top of his right eye, his legs buckled and his eyes glazed as he fell to the floor.

Angela shrieked and clasped her face, but Sandra stood emotionless as she folded her arms and looked impassively at the slowly writhing body as it groaned and held its face. Sandra raised her arm and pointed to the door, then commanded, "Get up and get out. That's the last time you ever touch her. Get out!" She stamped her foot and glared at her father.

"Hold your tongue, girl. This is my house," Gerald groaned. His wound looked like a split tomato, blood poured down his face and dripped over his white shirt.

"It is Angela's house and you are leaving for good," Franz shouted as he grabbed hold of Gerald's collar, dragged him to his feet and threw him outside. Franz's force was such that Gerald stumbled and thudded down onto the stone path; he gasped out in pain as his left knee took most of the impact.

Like a bouncing ball, he got up almost as quickly as he had fallen and painfully hobbled towards the safety of his car.

"I'll get even with you. Fucking bastard, Kraut. You didn't win the war, so you think you can come back and take our women. Fuck you!" Gerald slammed the car door shut and the Jaguar's engine screamed as the car's wheels spun in a cloud of dust and spitting gravel. Franz, who looked impressively massive, stood in the doorway, erect, feet apart, arms folded.

He glared in Gerald's direction until the car had disappeared out of the drive.

Franz found Sandra comforting her mother on the sofa. Angela reached out to him and smiled painfully. He knelt down and cuddled her. "He's gone," Franz said calmly.

He looked at her and drew breath before Angela raised a finger, pressed it to his lips and smiled. "I'm OK, I'm safe now. I always feel safe when you are around. Come on," she said softly, "let's get on with Christmas." That night, they officially slept together.

Christmas blew hot and cold on Green Farm. Hot, from the shared love between Franz and Angela and the warmth in Sandra's smile at her mother's happiness. Hot, because Franz and Angela talked seriously about their future and decided they wanted to be together. "Nothing would delight me more than to work on the farm with you, Angela. If you have enough work?"

"Yes, I do have work for you. Old John is getting on a bit, and said to me only last month that he wanted to go part-time or even retire. As ever, Franz Schmidt, your timing is perfect. But farm work or not, I would be so joyful if you were here."

Franz squeezed her. "We would be joyful," he added. "A life at last."

Cold, because every strange sound, every vehicle they heard, every time the telephone rang, maybe it was him? Total calm, total warmth, even with Franz in residence was impossible to find, especially after Ines rang on Christmas Day.

"You filthy, Slut! You have dragged my son's name through the dirt. It was you who corrupted him. You trapped him on your first night. Your quality was clear to all then. You're more suited to night working on your back in the docks. "

He has tried so hard to be a good husband and provide everything a woman could want. I'm going to report that Nazi to the police. The brutal swine. You dare to sleep with him? That really shows your quality, you Tramp. You don't deserve my son." Without waiting for any reply, Ines terminated the 'conversation' by slamming down the phone.

52.

Gerald made one attempt to contact Sandra before he returned to France. She hung up. *I am her father. She must listen to my side. After all I have done for her. She can't want to forget me. Angela will soon get over that Kraut. He's a new boyfriend. Just like me with a new girlfriend. Let her have her fling. She'll come running.*

When the divorce papers arrived at Gerald's Paris flat, he stared at them in disbelief and shook uncontrollably. How could she do this to him? Constantly, over the next two days, he picked up the papers, slowly read them and shook his head. Disbelief turned into resentment, which turned into anger. Eventually, he screwed up the papers and flung them against the wall before running after them and screaming insults at them where they lay. "Bloody Kraut. Imagine him slipping into my wife's bed when my back was turned. Don't care what she says, I'll bet the swine was at it even whilst I was in Crete. I don't mind if she does it with someone else, so long as she is there for me when I return. Just as I have always been there for her." Anger turned into helplessness as he sank to his knees, clasped his head and sobbed as he beat it on the floor.

Gerald embarked on a campaign of phoning Angela to 'talk some sense' into her, and explain how he had meant no harm. "Anyway, Angela, Fritz won't find work in England. I can provide you with everything you need. You know you still want me, just as you always have. It's OK," he chuckled, "enjoy yourself for a bit. You'll soon want me back."

"Gerald, you can provide me with everything I don't need and nothing of what I do. I now realise I should have made this decision years ago, but the thought that Sandra needed a father and the forlorn idea that I always thought I could change you and make a 'happy family' stopped me. No turning back now, Gerald. You've had your nine lives."

Gerald wrote to the court rebuffing the divorce. He was sure that this was all a big mistake and he still loved his wife. Despite his protests, Cambridge Divorce Court summoned them to appear in late April. The court was at first unwilling to grant a divorce; the judge wanted them to reconcile their differences. Angela steadfastly refused to do this. Whilst she had hoped not to have to reveal all details of her abuse to the court, in the face of defeat, she felt obliged to do so. The judge looked increasingly disgusted as Angela gave the details, and even more so when Gerald stared at the floor and refused to either confirm or deny them. The judge immediately granted Angela her wish, arbitrated the settlement and closed the proceedings.

Angela tried to leave as fast as possible but Gerald pursued her. He stood on the top step of the courthouse, his unfastened coat theatrically blowing in the wind and shouted after her, "*You* will be responsible for what happens to me now. Look at me." Passers-by stopped and stared.

"Look at me now and remember this moment. Look at my face and see the pain that you have caused me. Fix it in your head for when you have to go to the mortuary to identify me! You can have as many pounds of flesh as you want, you Vampire, you. My blood will be on your hands." He lunged towards her and attempted to grab her arm, but she was too quick and ran towards her car. He stopped on the lower step of the courthouse, raised his fists above his head and bellowed, "Your regret will surely drive you to your grave and my ghost will be there to dance on it. Look at me! Remember, *you* caused this."

Angela got into her Land Rover as quickly as possible and left him standing in a cloud of blue smoke. Tears streamed down her face for the passing of a marriage that had ended so squalidly.

On his way back to his mother's, and even more so when Innes' anger pumped him up, Gerald became mercenary. How could the judge not accept his side?

He prowled up and down his mother's bathroom smashing his fists into his thighs. "That bitch has taken what was mine. I have been wronged, but I'm not finished yet," he vowed. He glowered into the mirror and snarled, "No one wins against Gerald Clarke!"

Angela was on the phone to Franz when she saw the glow through the curtains. "There must be a wonderful sunset today, Franz. It seems that the sky is all orange." She pushed the net curtain back and glanced in the direction of the flickering glow then screamed, "Franz, it's not the sun. It's the barn. The field barn is on fire!"

She slammed down the phone and ran out to see flames licking up the walls and over the roof of the barn. By the time the fire brigade arrived, it was too late to save the structure and the hay within. Angela staggered around the outside, hands clasped to her face in disbelief. "Charred timbers and ash. How?" Maybe the power socket? That was all it could be. Then she stumbled into the empty creosote can. "That's not my can. Arson!"

From the wood, two satisfied eyes surveyed the scene through a pair of binoculars and were able to make out Angela standing silhouetted against the glow, hands raised in despair, talking to Sergeant Shilling. Gerald smirked. His job done, he quickly moved to where he had parked his car on the other side of the wood and with a great deal of satisfaction sped away south, to Dover.

The depression washed over him when he first saw the sea. His plan had gone pear-shaped. All he ever wanted was a girlfriend or two where he worked and a pretty wife at home. What was wrong with that? Now he had lost everything. He had lost his wife; he hung his head as he thought of her in bed with *that fucking German.* Gerald's face crumpled and he blurted out, "This is not right. **Just not right!**" He stamped his foot on the floor of the car. "Have I been so stupid that I have finally lost her? You fucking idiot. You pushed it too far, once too often." He stopped the car to compose himself.

The unthinkable had happened. He had lost Sandra. That other bastard would take over from him as her father. "My daughter calling another man 'Dad'?"

It was now impossible for him to see her when or as often as he wanted, even though the court had said he could have access. When he had managed to speak to her, the venom and hate she had spat in his direction had cut him to the quick.

"After all I have done for her, and she wants to forget me." He smashed at the steering wheel and shook his head repeatedly, so that in his frenzy his tears splashed onto the windscreen. "I just can't believe that my own daughter doesn't want me, at all. Ever. Never." He threw back his head, opened his mouth wide and screamed and stamped his feet.

He had lost his home, his oasis. He had absolutely nowhere to go he could call his own. His mother's house was no good because he could not stand to be in her company for more than two minutes and anyway, Gerald Clarke was not a mother's boy. All his possessions, both in his rented flat in Paris and in his car, probably only filled three suitcases. "My whole world in three suitcases, all I have left." With tears still pouring down his cheeks, he realised that he must move on in order to catch the ferry.

On board ship, he stared at the waves. He turned to look at the white cliffs of Dover diminishing behind the churning froth of the ship's wake. The waves washed away below his tearful gaze. It all hurt. Only then, did it dawn upon him that if he returned, the police would surely question him and maybe send him to prison as an arsonist. That moment of retribution, even if she deserved it, and oh yes, she deserved it all right, meant he could not go back for a long, long, time, if ever.

Even if he could go back, how could he face people? He had always been the success story of the village, the man who had it all, beautiful wife, family, farm, successful international businessman, money, Jaguar and, and, and...

Now he was a loser, and everyone would know it. People would laugh behind his back, exactly as he had enjoyed doing to other community unfortunates. "Humiliated," Gerald thumped the railings, "I can never recover." He sobbed as the ship's wash pummelled beneath him.

You're a bad man, Gerald. The game has gone sour. How could I have been so blind? Angela told me often enough. It's so easy to get carried away. I suppose Angela had every right to

326

*find another man. But **why** did it have to be that fucking Kraut? He must love her to defend her like that.* He painfully smacked his hand on the railing. *To hell with her!* Gerald turned and glanced at a man and woman happily promenading with their two children. How he wished it could be him.

"Oh, Sandra!" He clamped his hands on the railings and turned once again to gaze down at the deep. "What have I done to you? I'm **so** sorry." *It's too late, Gerald. She doesn't want to hear it anymore. Krista was right that day, 'You are in every way a bastard, Gerald Clarke.' So was Sue, 'You just don't know what you do to people.'* He kicked out at the railing. *But, was it all really just my fault? Everybody blames me.* He shook his head and shrugged. *Maybe it is me.* His nose overflowed and the wind whipped away a long trail of his snot. He watched it spiral away towards the waves. "It is, just, me."

Then he stiffened and said sternly, "You don't deserve this life, Gerald." His grip tightened and his leg even twitched to climb the railings, but no, the thought of choking in the water stopped him. Maybe some tablets?

Condemned. His current girlfriend would only be that. There would be others, but for how long? One day he would just be an old, crinkley swinger. No one would want him. Whichever way he looked at it, he was a nothing who had nothing.

Epilogue

June came, the semester ended and Franz packed his possessions into six large boxes and three suitcases. The problem had been how to move all this to England, but Franz had solved that when he had visited the farm the previous weekend and picked up the Land Rover. Angela was unsure. The Land Rover was very old and was 'a farm vehicle, not a motorway racer.' Franz chugged up the driveway of Green Farm twenty-five hours after he had said goodbye to Kassel. Angela waited at the door with open arms to hug him. Franz looked at her, flapped his arms against his sides, shrugged and with a shy smile said, "I did it. I said I would come, and here I am. I did it!"

Franz was often able go to sleep in Angela's arms. He had never shared this experience with anyone before. No sarcasm, no refusal to apologise, no always right. Franz often told her that one of the reasons why he loved her so much was because she was not perfect, which in his eyes, made her perfect.

Angela accepted him for what he was. She did not try to change him. She had found someone whom she knew genuinely loved her and wanted to show it. It made her so delighted to see how much pleasure he got from simply giving. He was a man to whom she could open her heart, give her love, and know he would gladly receive it. She knew the chemistry was right.

With no tension they often felt the need to kiss and cuddle, not because they had to, or they thought they should, but because they wanted to. Because they must have one.

They often talked about their past partners. Neither could shut theirs out of their mind, they would never be entirely able to do that, but it helped to talk about it. They realised that to have peace, they would have to talk about everything in their past. They had to let it all come out; had to bleed themselves of their pain, even if they did not want to depress themselves, which they often did.

Unusually, this depression was not immediately obvious. It came at night, when their ex-partners, always at their worst, returned in their nightmares. Franz and Angela agreed they would have to accept their past as a chapter in the book of their life that would always remain in their memory. But a closed chapter. As time went on, the nightmares became fewer, and finally disappeared. Franz and Angela wished they could have come together earlier, but circumstances decreed that it was not their time.

Angela and Franz married at Cambridge Registry Office in June 1964. They celebrated a quiet, private ceremony, just as they wanted it with only the Registrar, Franz, Angela and Sandra. Eighteen months later Ralf David was born, the fulfilment of a destiny.

Brunhilde was viciously interrogated in Hohenschönhausen for two weeks following Franz's escape until following the obligatory official denunciation and subsequent signing of divorce papers against her husband, the Stasi were sure she was non-complicit in Franz's escape and could be trusted again. Her interrogation seemed to serve as an added inspiration to her single minded pursuit of excellence for the state. Strangely, she did allow herself one hobby, she began to learn English and was indeed very successful. This was of course noted in higher places.

The "Workers and Peasants Paradise" recognised talent when they saw it and to her great delight, she was later seconded to General Wolf's HVA or Foreign Espionage staff at Potsdam. Part one of her plan, hatched as she shivered in that dank cell in Hohenschönhausen, had been achieved.

Coincidently, an informal celebration took place in Potsdam on the same weekend as Franz and Angela's wedding. General Markus Wolf raised his glass of Rotkäppchen Sekt to toast the success of 'Georg,' a Stasi spy with the real name of Günter Guillaume, who would ultimately become a mole in the office of Bundeskanzeller Willi Brandt.

Those attending the toast could not have guessed that this man would go on to become the most important and successful Stasi spy in history who would pass, amongst a host of other things, secret documents detailing the entire NATO nuclear battle plan in the event of a Warsaw pact invasion.

General Wolf toasted, "To an absent friend." As Brunhilde raised her glass, she gazed out of the window at the setting sun in the direction of a different 'absent friend.'

She lustily responded, "To an absent friend," before her expression hardened and she muttered, "Coming soon to a town near you."

ABOUT THE AUTHOR

CHRIS WOOLGROVE

I was born in London, where my father was a policeman, but lived most of my youth in a small village, Dinton, near Salisbury. I remember Dinton fondly as a village that still had a two room village school, a smithy under a chesnut tree and a village lake where we young boys spent hours fishing for tiny roach and wild carp.

I went to Gillingham school in North Dorset, a happy time, where I became a nationally ranked long jumper, before studying Physical Education at the then Cardiff College of Education, now part of Cardiff University. I taught Physical Education in three different South Wales schools during which time my first daughter, Amy, was born.

Sport has always been a part of my life and whilst teaching, I was privileged to become coach to Llanharan RFC, a very enjoyable and successful four years. I got bored with teaching and left after seven years to open a sports shop with my wife and later, an import export business during which time my second daughter, Lucy, was born.

I continued to work in the sports business with a major sporting goods manufacturer and later as a management and marketing consultant to many firms throughout the UK. Nevertheless, I still found time to stand as a European Parliamentary Candidate in the 1994 election in South East Wales. This was a challenging experience and although I didn't win (I was up against Glennys Kinnock, wife of the former labour leader who was defending the safest seat in the whole of the European Parliament), I had some great experiences.

Towards the end of this time my first marriage dissolved and I met my present partner, Siegrun, who lives in East Germany and the rest is history. I now teach English to companies, organise tours to the UK and indulge myself with golf and by writing.

Printed in Great Britain
by Amazon.co.uk, Ltd.,
Marston Gate.